THE VIKING PRIEST

A SAGA OF FATE, FAITH, ADVENTURE AND LOVE

THE VIKING PRIEST

A SAGA OF FATE, FAITH, ADVENTURE AND LOVE

LINDA KAY DAHLÉN

BEAVER'S POND PRESS
MINNEAPOLIS, MN

Edited by Angela Wiechmann
Maps by Echo Martin

ISBN: 978-1-59298-775-7
Library of Congress Catalog Number: 2018900769
Printed in the United States of America
First Printing: 2018
22 21 20 19 18   5 4 3 2 1

Book design by Athena Currier

 Beaver's Pond Press, Inc.
7108 Ohms Lane
Edina, MN 55439–2129

(952) 829-8818
www.BeaversPondPress.com

To order, visit www.ItascaBooks.com or call 1-800-901-3480 ext. 118.
Reseller discounts available.

For my parents and all who have gone before

PREFACE

THIS IS A NOVEL. Its principal characters and many scenes are imaginary. On the other hand, certain historical incidents and people are woven into the story. In addition, many plot elements are based on the legends and lore of the Norse people and of the indigenous people living in what is now Mexico and Central America.

Around AD 1000, the Norse people—those who would someday become the Norwegians, Swedes, and Danes—were in the process of dramatic change. The era of the Vikings, the feared and fierce Norse marauders, was coming to an end.

Although the people of the European continent had been Christianized many centuries earlier, the Norse had retained their belief in their own gods and goddesses. Human sacrifice was still occurring, though rarely, in Europe and had not yet reached its zenith among the people living in the great land mass to the west.

In addition to their conquests, the Norse had established trade routes and colonies, connecting people by blood and culture. Norse explorers reached as far as present-day Canada. No one knows how much farther they may have traveled along the North American continent, south, into the unknown.

BOOK ONE

Good and Evil

GREENLAND

Brattahlid

Vinland

SEA O
DARKNE

AROUND A.D. 1000
THE NORTH ATLANTIC

CHAPTER ONE

Old Uppsala—an ancient town in what is now Sweden

I T HAD BEEN NINE DAYS since the *blót* had begun. The heads and skins of sacrificial stallions, rams, boars, and bulls hung in the sacred grove outside the temple at Uppsala. All that remained to be added to the ceremonies was the *manblót*, a human sacrifice.

The Norse people generally met with their gods alone, and in solitude they spoke with and worshipped Thor, Odinn, Freyja, and many lesser gods. But in Uppsala, they gathered every nine years for a very special religious festival. King Erik Segersäll required all in the region to attend. And more, he required all to offer sacrifices, which greatly upset the Christian folk, the followers of the White Kristr.

For weeks, great crowds had overflowed the town and populated the surrounding woods and fields. By day, smoke and dust filled the air, and by night, hundreds of campfires glowed—tiny points of light in the darkness.

There was no lack of entertainment. Contests of strength and speed, horse fighting and bearbaiting—with the associated thrill of gambling—occurred daily. There was feasting on the meat of the sacrificed beasts. For the common folk, there was extravagant drinking of ale. And for the elite, honey mead drunk from upended horns.

There were many pleasant distractions. But if one looked closely into the eyes of the men and women assembled there, a shadow of anxiety could be found. In the previous three years, the summer skies had withheld life-giving water from the land. Crops had sprouted exuberantly in the spring, only to dry to nothing in the summer sun. Streams grew dry, and lake levels fell. Animals, both domestic and wild, looked lean and hungry. In some places, strange illnesses had appeared.

Three years of drought had taken a toll on commerce as well. Many trade tents had been erected on the grounds just outside the temple area, and the sound of barter talk and the clank of silver pieces could be heard from early day into the long twilight. But normal trade was considerably diminished, for lack of goods.

Despite the impact of the drought and the apprehension it created, it was a time of considerable excitement for the young people of the region. Especially for Brand.

At nearly seventeen, Brand already was one of the tallest of all his kinsmen, and one of the most handsome. He had a broad brow and large eyes that shone green in some light, blue in others. His straight hair fell to his shoulders, indicating he was a free man, not a thrall. A faint beard—of the not-quite-fully-a-man-but-no-longer-a-child kind—covered his jaw. Everything he wore indicated he was highborn: a gold arm ring glittered on his bicep and silver clasp held a deep-blue mantle across one shoulder. His tunic was of the whitest linen, and his pants were of fine brown wool. His feet, shod with ankle boots of soft cowhide, carried his long legs confidently over the whole of Uppsala.

But as often as possible, he roamed the grounds on his black horse, Sleipnir, named for Odinn's magnificent eight-legged steed. Brand knew he made an unforgettable impression when mounted on Sleipnir, sitting tall in the saddle—with both youth and horse holding heads high.

He had been a child of seven winters at the last festival nine years before. That was the last summer he spent in Uppsala. When the festival had ended, he was sent away to Hedeby to be educated and trained by a foster father. Brand had done nothing to merit banishment. It was not uncommon among the Norse for a young boy to be raised as a foster child away from the place of his birth. Indeed, it was thought that the mentorship would increase the child's skills and experience. Many fathers would have it no other way, for they feared that if the boys stayed, they would be weak men, spoiled from much doting and petting from their mothers. Sören, Brand's father, settled the matter with Brand's mother. "Solveig," he said, "it will be better so."

Brand returned to Uppsala after nine years. It was then he learned his mother had died and his father remarried.

As a distraction, he threw himself fully into life at the festival, indulging in the myriad of enticements the blót offered. He was of an age when women of all sorts excited him, and he discovered the delights of their caresses. They found him irresistible, it seemed to him, and he was accommodating in all ways to every maid who invited him to bed. On one matter, though, he was most careful—that was to avoid the wives and concubines of the assembled lords of the region. To intrude on these relationships would result in unwanted consequences—banishment or even possible death in holmgang combat.

Despite his efforts to avoid such entanglements, there was one woman of high rank whom he could not avoid. Vigdis. It was no surprise that his father chose her after the death of Brand's mother. At twenty-five, she was nearly twenty years younger than Brand's father. In addition to her fair face and graceful body, she brought with her a full dowry of lands and goods. No one doubted the propriety of the match. But after the marriage, there was no peace. And even though Brand had so recently returned to Uppsala, he was aware of harsh words and angry looks between his father and stepmother.

Vigdis summoned Brand one evening, and as soon as he received the message, he immediately felt a small dark kernel of fear in his heart. He had been carousing with his friends most of the day and evening and had thoroughly enjoyed sharing mead with them. He tried immediately to clear his head, but as he entered the longhouse and walked toward her, he noted his steps were not steady.

Several people were gathered around a smoky central hearth, and some were lounging on the benches along each side of the immense room. With a wave of her hand, Vigdis dismissed them all, and in moments she and Brand were alone.

"Brand, your father has left me by myself all these days and nights as he tends to other matters."

Her voice was as smooth and soft as a kitten's purr—a kitten with sharp claws. She pulled a curtain across the area she and Brand's father used as a sleeping place. Soapstone lamps filled with whale oil hung from the rafters and flickered in the private space, making the shadows dance across her face.

Brand knew his father had indeed been spending many hours in the company of the chief priest and other assembled nobility, including Vigdis's brothers. Serious matters needed to be decided as part of the rituals and ceremonies, both religious and political. But knowing this did not ease his anxiety.

Vigdis motioned to an eiderdown coverlet flung across the wooden bed frame. "Come here and sit with me."

Reluctantly, he sat next to her on the soft bed. She slowly removed her kerchief from her head, and her hair flowed softly in brown waves down past her shoulders. Her skin was milky white, as white as that of any woman in Uppsala. A necklace made of small domes of rock crystal set in silver gleamed like tiny moons around her delicate neck.

She had already taken off her overdress and was wearing only her inner linen shift. She took his hand and placed his palm upon her bosom, all the while her eyes staring into his own. He immediately felt the warmth of her skin. The flickering light should have softened her gaze, but her eyes glittered cold and detached, like moonlight on hardened snow.

"Why," he asked, delicately removing his hand from her bosom, "why have you summoned me?"

"Only to talk with you, Brand," she said with feigned innocence. "Your father has left me to entertain myself, and I have grown bored."

"But what of the musicians, dancers, and mirth men? Can they not amuse you?"

"I desire only one person to amuse me, Brand. And that is you." She moved her body closer to his. Suddenly he could smell her woman's perfume, her natural scent so enticing and mysterious.

He was acutely aware that he was being treated in the manner of a pet and that it was a dangerous place to be. He quickly rose and moved to the farther side of the sleeping space.

"I can recite stories and poems to entertain you, or I can have the court skald summoned to amuse you with his poetry."

"No," she said with a sigh. An odd kind of sigh.

He needed to extricate himself from the situation—and do it skillfully, for he could ill afford his stepmother as an enemy. He was unsure of what to say. The day's alcohol had dulled his reserve, so he blurted what first came to his mind.

"If you are unhappy with my father, why do you not divorce him? Other women have done it when marriage is intolerable. You have only to say the word, and the divorce will be done and all lands and dowry goods returned as they were before the marriage."

Indeed, as a woman in heathen Uppsala, Vigdis had the right to divorce—upon her own demand.

She looked at him with an intensity that made him want to flee. "Brand, you are so young. There are many complexities to be considered."

"I must go now," he said as he moved toward the curtain and began to open it.

"Go then, if you must," she said matter-of-factly. Then her voice changed. "But it will not be long until we speak again. And maybe then you will not be so anxious to leave my presence."

She picked up her comb, pulled it through her dark locks, and said nothing more to him.

CHAPTER TWO

BRAND LEFT VIGDIS AND WALKED quickly out into the warm spring night. He had no wish for bed play with any of the women he passed, though several looked at him enticingly. One woman called out, "Does your sword need a new sheath?" in a voice that was low but not sweet. There was raucous laughter, for all who heard it knew she was not offering up fine leather goods.

As he walked out among the assembled people of the region, he passed near the tents of the White Kristr folk from a nearby town. A small group was quietly gathered around a campfire.

His thoughts must have been revealed in his face, for as he passed, he heard a small unfamiliar voice.

"What has caused such worry, my lord?"

He stopped and turned to see who had guessed his inward turmoil.

Again the voice said, "What has caused such worry, my lord?"

The question had come from one of the young women. In the flickering firelight, he could see she was neither comely nor plain, but when she smiled her eyes were kind and welcoming. Another young woman and an older woman sat next to her. All three had hair the color of a sunset the night before a storm.

The young woman moved a space apart and with her hand offered him a seat around the fire. "I am Ardis," she said.

He had no idea why, especially so soon after the disturbing scene with Vigdis, but he felt himself drawn to the warmth of her invitation. In spite of himself, he sat down.

He began by introducing himself. "I am Brand, son of Sören and Solveig. I have recently returned from Hedeby, where I lived with Rolf the Wise, my foster father."

"We know. Your reputation precedes you. The camp girls have made sure of that!"

Simultaneously, Brand felt pride and a little embarrassment at her remark. He was unsure of what to say next. "How do you find the days in the camp?" he asked awkwardly.

"Well, we follow the White Kristr, so we are not here by choice. We are required to attend unless we pay a fine, and are too poor to pay it." She paused, then continued almost in a whisper. "There is talk of human sacrifice."

The fire crackled, and a heavy piece of alderwood fell down into the heart of the flames, creating a small cloud of sparks.

When he lived in Hedeby, Brand had learned the language of the English priests but little of their White Kristr religion. Once he asked his foster father, Rolf, about the Hvíta Kristr, the White Christ. Rolf had sternly forbidden any discussion for fear the new philosophy would weaken his ward.

Brand was not even sure why the Christian god was called the White Christ. He knew it was not a description of the appearance of the god or the followers. Some thought it was because the new converts were often given white robes on the day of their baptism.

Others thought it was related to the meekness—some thought cowardice—of the converts. The heathen Norse were instantly suspicious of the Christian priests' preaching of peace. And even more, there were rumors that at least some of the priests were *argr*, men who took the feminine role in a sexual act. And that led to disgust. Rolf had warned Brand, "Have as little as possible to do with them!"

So now, as a young adult, Brand knew almost nothing of their beliefs. He asked the first question that came to his mind, and even as he asked it, he was not sure why.

"Tell me, does your god require the sacrifice of men?"

"Well, yes and no," responded the red-haired maiden. "We believe we are sinful creatures, and because of this, we anger God. God would rightly judge and reject us, but instead, he sent his Son into the world to bear the punishment for us. Through his sacrifice and resurrection, we are purified and made clean."

"So," said Brand, "the White Kristr god is not so different from Thor and Odinn, who also demand sacrifice."

"No, Brand, they are not the same!" She smiled. "But I can see that what I am saying is hard for you to understand. We can talk more of this another time. Come and see us tomorrow, and we will tell you more of our faith."

Brand rose to leave, then turned back. "If you are so upset at being here, why are your faces so calm? Why are you not filled with anger?"

"It is because we know that the True God loves us and will never abandon us, no matter what. This gives us the power to endure anything."

Endure, thought Brand as he walked into the darkness. Maybe their god should have been powerful enough to protect them from sufferings, so that they did not have to endure. But still, the faces were so tranquil.

Brand intended to revisit the little group of Christian women and ask more questions. But early the next day, his father approached on his own steed, holding the reins for Sleipnir, who followed after.

"Ride with me, Brand," was all he said, extending Sleipnir's reins to his son.

Brand struggled to hide his surprise, for time spent with his father was exceedingly rare. Since his return, Brand had proudly demonstrated all the skills he had learned from his foster father, but the acceptance and approval he so longed for never came. His father had changed and become a different person. He was distracted and spent almost no time with his son.

So when Brand heard these words from his father, he instantly jumped onto Sleipnir's back, and they were off.

Their first stop was the mound where his mother had been buried two years before. Brand had heard rumors about her death. His mother's dreams had turned ominous, it was said, and she became fearful. Then suddenly, she died. Some said she had been cursed by witchcraft or that she had been poisoned.

Brand lamented greatly that he had not been there when she had been carefully laid to rest, wearing her best dress and jewelry and placed in the position of a sleeping babe. Now as they gazed at the mound, Brand longed to hear words of sorrow, or comfort, or anger, or *anything* from his father. But there were none. Each man stood before the grave mound in silence.

They continued on their journey for another hour. Sören scanned the trees and meadows often, to ensure no one was following them. They stopped briefly at a hut, where they ate their cheese and bread and allowed the horses to graze leisurely on the sweet spring grass. Leaving the horses, they set off for a short walk on foot.

Sören pointed out landmarks—a large stone, an ancient oak, the place where a brook took a sharp turn—and told Brand to memorize them. Finally they stopped. Sören stood close to his son so his whispered instructions could be heard.

"There, see the three large rocks?"

Brand nodded.

"At the foot of the large rock in the center I have hidden a hoard of silver."

He pointed but did not approach any closer to the buried treasure, in case someone somewhere in the forest was watching them.

"This silver is for you to use whenever you need it. It is not mine to give. It is from your mother to you. When I remarried, I did not tell Vigdis's family of this silver, for it was meant as an inheritance to you from your mother. Tell no one of this place. No one."

It was afternoon by the time they started their return journey. The sunlight dappled their faces as they passed in the shadows of tall pines and green birches. Again, they traveled along in silence, with only an occasional snort from one of the horses and the rhythmic sounds of hooves striking the earth.

As they rode, Brand's mind could not stop recalling the memories of his gentle mother. And more than anything, how he longed to have her with him, instead of the cold metal coins.

CHAPTER THREE

THE HIGH POINT OF THE FESTIVAL was approaching. The king and many chieftains were in serious discussion with the high priest. Brand and his friend Olof, the son of King Segersäll, had tried to be present at these discussions but were forced away like young hounds.

"Away with you!" shouted Vigdis's brothers. "Only landed men are allowed in this place!"

The young men were stung by the rebuke, their faces red with adolescent indignation. But they complied without retort and quickly joined a group of friends busy gambling with dice.

As a small child, Brand had spent time roaming with Olof and other boys, moving like a flock of ravens flying in and out of the temple grounds, calling to one another in excitement. The boys ran foot races, held wrestling matches, and challenged one another to mock holmgang combat with child-size shields and wooden swords. Now reunited after Brand's long absence, they had taken up their friendship anew.

Björn, the most talkative of the group, began to share the latest news around the encampment.

"We have heard rumors," said Björn, looking directly at Olof.

"What kind of rumors?" asked Olof.

"Rumors that there has been insufficient sacrifice to Freyja and Odinn," explained Björn. "And that there must be human sacrifice. Not of a thrall or criminal, but sacrifice of a noble—a sacrifice of sufficient value to appease the insult."

A silence fell over the group. Everyone knew the story of ancient King Aun of Uppsala, who was said to have sacrificed his nine sons, one after another, in an effort to prolong the day when the gods would take his own life. The young men all looked at Olof, whose face showed real concern that the rumored sacrifice might be him.

Brand held the dice and rolled them gently in his hand. "I know what you are all thinking, that princes have been sacrificed in ancient times." He paused. "But the Norns have not fashioned this end for Olof."

Everyone also knew of the Norns, the trio of shadowy female spirits who wove the threads of destiny for human life and death. The spirits decided when the time for ultimate fate, good or bad, had come.

Olof laughed a little self-consciously. "How can you be so sure?"

"Because last night I had a dream," said Brand. "And in my dream, there *was* a human sacrifice."

Now everyone was listening intently, leaning in toward Brand. They knew his mother had the gift of dreams that foretold the future; perhaps he had this gift as well.

"Everything was in thick mist," continued Brand, "and I could not make out the features of the man. But his eyes—his eyes were *blue*."

All heads spun in unison toward Olof.

There was a brief moment of quiet. Then Björn slapped Olof on his shoulder and exclaimed, "Well, see? There is nothing to worry about! Your eyes are brown!"

Olof smiled, and though he tried to hide it, his eyes still reflected worry. Too much was being kept from the younger men.

CHAPTER FOUR

LL TIME PASSES WITH THE PERPETUAL CHANGING of night into dawn, and soon the vernal equinox had arrived and the final day of the festival had begun.

The crowd was large, for everyone was required to participate in this important gathering. Brand had not yet seen his father, but many of the highborn were still inside the temple, assisting in the ancient rites.

The temple was a large rectangular building hung with tapestries of amazing color and detail and divided into two parts by a partial wall. In the larger room, the priests and leaders assembled for their ceremonies. It had benches and a high seat for the ruler to preside over the temple activities.

Beyond the low wall was the smaller room, where the animal blood sacrifices were made. In it, images of the major gods were arranged on pedestals in a half circle: Odinn in the center, and Thor and Freyja on each side. There, in the dark recesses of the temple, inside the most sacred area, the priests venerated the wooden images. In the center of the arc was an altar built of heaped stones, with a consecrated bowl to collect the blood of sacrificial animals, whose flesh would later form part of a ceremonial banquet. Upon the altar, a fire burned day and night, never permitted to go out.

Ceremonial horns filled with grape wine or honey mead were passed over the fire to purify the liquids. The first horn would be drunk to Odinn for victory in battle, then to Freyja for abundant harvest. Thor would be remembered as well for his power and strength. On some festival days, two-handled loving cups would be filled and the contents drunk in memory of beloved kindred, long dead but not forgotten.

It was nearly midday, and horns and great drums called the people to assembly on the temple grounds, under a cloudless sky. The temple was adorned with large disks of copper and bronze, which shone brilliantly in the sun. Everyone gathered, crowded shoulder to shoulder, in the temple area. The women stood to one side and the men to the other.

"Brand!" called one of the elder chieftains. "Take your place here, next to your stepmother."

Reluctantly, Brand took his place on the large platform outside of the temple, where the rest of the chieftains, their sons, and some of their wives had gathered. The sounds of drums pulsed throughout the young man's body and distracted his thoughts. He stood uneasily next to Vigdis. She glanced at him briefly, and he felt a sudden chill in his heart.

The crowd began to shout "Odinn! Odinn! Odinn!" in time with the cadence of the ceremonial drums. Odinn was the only god who demanded human sacrifice at the blóts. The shouting of Odinn's name became even louder and more insistent. The pulsations of the drumbeats overpowered Brand's heart.

Suddenly, the high priest emerged from the sacred area of the temple. His long robe and cape were gleaming white, pale as snow, as were his hair and beard. His steps were swift, and as he strode onto the raised stone veranda at the temple entrance, his robes flared like the wings of a winter bird of prey. Elevated above the crowd, he held the eyes of all the spectators.

Brand watched as the high priest raised up his arms, holding Mjölnir, the silver hammer of Thor, between his palms. Instantly, the blaring horns, drumming, and shouting ceased.

"Behold, our most precious sacrifice!" the priest intoned, looking to his left.

The people strained to see. From the far edge of the crowd came a small group of the king's retinue, dressed in their finest capes, shirts, and leather boots. In their left arms, they carried their decorated shields, and their right hands held their spears.

Following the warriors, two thralls slowly drew a small oak cart— every inch covered with ornamental carving—toward the altar. The slaves' rag-clad bodies hunched over like the heavy boughs of a willow in an ice storm, and their eyes were downcast. They dared not look at any of the crowd. Some dreadful day they might be the sacrifice to Odinn.

From the other side of the gathering, the women stood nearly immobile, frozen on tiptoe with their necks straining to see what would happen next. Ardis and her family stood out, their fiery hair unmistakable in the small crowd of Christian women at the edge of the assembly.

The men in the crowd pushed and stumbled to make way for the doomed passenger. A bearded man around forty years old stood tall and calm in the cart. A long red silk cape covered his entire body. At last the cart stopped.

The crowd remained silent and stilled. The man untied the silver fastener at his neck, and the cape fell to his feet in a crimson swirl. He wore nothing but two gold arm bands on his left biceps. He was well muscled, and his bearing indicated he was no mere thrall; this was a man of high rank. He was also a man of combat—several battle scars, long healed, were apparent on his arms, legs, and back.

Brand stared into the bright-blue eyes of his father.

"No!" shouted Brand as he sprinted toward the cart, his warrior heart aflame. Brand reached his father in an instant.

Sören took Brand by the shoulders and spoke in a slow and deliberate voice, all the while looking directly into his son's eyes.

"Brand," he said, "I have sworn to Thor on the holy ring of gold on his altar that I would accept this fate, and I will keep that oath."

Brand began to plead with him, but Sören continued. "My son, no man—no matter how rich, how strong, how wise, or how powerful—can escape his own death. Death comes to every person at a time and place already chosen. And once the Norns decide to cut the threads of life, all we can do is meet it with courage. That is the true measure of a man's honor and character."

Brand stood shaking but silent as his father ascended the platform.

As lord of the festival, the high priest took a *hlaut-teinn*, a bundle of fir twigs, and made the hammer-sign over Brand's father—a short downward movement followed by a swift movement from left to right.

More prayers were said to Odinn's glory. Someone passed the sacrificial knife to Brand, who held it in his hand, staring in horror at the twelve-inch blade. He wanted to plunge it into the priest.

But he heard the voice of his father, saying, "Brand, you must have courage."

Brand dropped the blade to the ground in revulsion, and the priestly assistants quickly picked it up.

Sören moved to the center of the platform. White Kristr men and women—those who were too poor to buy their way out of attending the spectacle began to quietly pray. Ardis and her family fell to their knees. Even the spring insects were still.

Then the high priest plunged the blade into Sören's chest. Blood gushed from the mortal wound. Sören crumpled to the ground, looked up to the skies, and took his last breath.

Brand stared, eyes wide with incomprehension.

The priests collected Sören's blood into a bowl, then wiped the hlaut-teinn onto the smeared blood. The crowd roared with excitement as the priests flung the sticky liquid over them, staining everything and everyone with the sacrificial fluid.

Brand did not flinch as the droplets of blood reddened his face. He stared at his stepmother.

Vigdis. She had coveted him, she had desired him. He looked hard into her face and saw a flicker in her eyes, a trace of something. And in that instant he knew. *He knew.* She had planned it all.

Sören's body was carried away for immediate burial in a sacred mound near the center of the groves. Brand wanted nothing more than to flee, to get away from this place of death and deceit as fast as possible. He immediately ran to the stable. Sleipnir whinnied a surprised greeting. Brand saddled him quickly and rode out of Uppsala, saying good-bye to no one.

He stopped to collect the silver hoard his father had shown him. Then he rode Sleipnir long and hard. He wanted to ride far enough so the blue-gray smoke of the festival grounds could no longer be detected in his clothing, lungs, or possessions. But as long as he would live, the smoke from the burning campfires of Uppsala would never leave his heart.

CHAPTER FIVE

AT FIRST, BRAND'S THOUGHTS WERE wildly erratic, and he could do nothing but listen to the rhythm of Sleipnir's hoof beats. But as he rode along, he began to realize he must formulate a plan. It was now clear to him that he had powerful enemies in Uppsala and that he would need to find another place to make his home.

He was uncertain if anyone would come after him. Travel by water would be the quickest means of escape. He considered going to the port town of Birka. Once the premier trading town in the area, its harbor had fallen into disuse for most traders, and there would be fewer people to ask questions there. But there was also a possibility that he could wait a long time for a ship. He decided instead to head to the busy port of Sigtuna.

He reached Sigtuna in early morning and went straight down to the docks. He tied Sleipnir to a willow tree to rest and graze on the dewy green grass.

Over a dozen ships bobbed in the water, the wooden hulks shrouded in heavy mist. A single *knarr* showed signs that she would be sailing soon. Men were rolling barrels of fresh water and other provisions onto the trading ship's deck.

Brand called out to them, "Who is your master?"

The answer quickly came. "None! We are equals!" shouted the crew raucously

At that moment, a tall man emerged from behind a cluster of water barrels. It was easy to see he was the captain of the trading ship. He stood on the wharf, supervising each activity with his eyes and occasionally consulting with one or another of the men on some detail. His blue cloak revealed his travels had been wide spread and profitable. Brand noted that several of the men wore billowing pants and other clothing that showed they had traded with the Rus in the east.

"Good day," said Brand, approaching the tall figure.

The trader did not immediately answer. He had borne many perils—sometimes at sea, sometimes on land, but always in the presence of alien people. He had escaped danger many times by taking his time before deciding how much information to share. He would not, however, be so rude as to refuse the obligatory shaking of hands.

"I am Arn," he said, extending his hand.

It was strong but not work hardened like those of the ship's crew. He had a broad forehead, which seemed as if it would overtake his entire countenance, but it was equally balanced by a substantial square chin. Altogether, his features made him look intent and determined, even when relaxed. He had the weather-worn skin of an experienced mariner, but his eyes were young and alert, and only a few gray hairs were visible in his dark blond hair.

"And I am Brand."

Brand left off the usual inclusion of his father-name and his home. This was duly noted by Arn.

Brand continued, "It appears you will set sail soon. I seek passage."

"I am taking no passengers," Arn replied bluntly. "I am a trader, not a ferry service."

"If the matter is payment . . ."

Brand opened a silk folder and displayed a glittering handful of silver coins. The amount was handsome; more than enough for passage to the farthest port.

Arn turned his head slightly aside as he inspected the man more closely. He noted Brand's clothing, posture—all signs of health. The would-be passenger was obviously a man of rank and wealth.

Still, he demurred. "I have no need of your money."

"Sir, what can I do to persuade you? I desire only to be away from this place, as soon as possible."

"My crew and I only take men we can trust." Arn glanced at the sword half hidden beneath Brand's cloak. "You carry a weapon." He looked directly into Brand's eyes. "Can you use it?"

Brand's hand unconsciously moved and rested on the pommel of his sword. But before Brand could answer, Arn pulled his own sword from its scabbard and held it with anticipation. Instinctively, Brand's eyes flashed, and he drew his own sword, ready to block the blade.

In an instant, every member of the crew stopped their collective labor and reached for his own weapon. Then Arn yelled, "For sport, not combat!" and they all relaxed.

For the next few minutes, there was impromptu dance between Brand and Arn. Each combatant elegantly executed each maneuver—not to kill but to overpower the opponent. The crew loudly shouted encouragement as every brilliant move was made and then countered.

The combat play moved off the wharf onto the land, yet no one man dominated. As the minutes passed, the sheer exuberance of the moment engulfed the men. Mutual admiration replaced all other feelings.

This was no brutish combat of slow and hulking opponents. They leapt up and to the side in quick bounds, their athleticism displayed as each man avoided the blade of the other. Arn, the older, made up with experience to counter the speed and agility of his younger opponent. The blades played about them like lightning. Even the lookouts with their sharp eyes could scarcely follow the motions.

Growing tired and gasping for breath, they fought on until of a sudden, Arn dropped his sword, bent low on one knee, and stated for all to hear, "I yield!" He breathed hard, then laughed most heartily.

Cheers and jeers erupted from the crew.

Brand did not laugh but sheathed his sword. "I take it now you will accept me as a passenger?"

"A mere passenger? No! I regard you now as part of our crew—an able defense in time of attack. In my travels, I have learned well when to trust and when to distrust a stranger."

Arn paused to fully catch his breath, then continued.

"You must have heard the wisdom of Odinn, the High One: 'He is truly wise who has traveled far and knows the ways of the world. He who has traveled can tell what spirit governs the men he meets.' You see, I trade in exotic, expensive goods, tempting for pirates and thieves of all kinds."

Arn paused again, then began to breathe more normally.

"You do not seem to be a thief or a criminal intent on thwarting capture. And you clearly are not a runaway thrall. Tell me, what is the purpose of your travels?"

Brand had anticipated this question but knew he could not answer. He merely stated, "I wish to leave as soon as possible."

Arn pondered this reply for a moment. "And what is your destination?"

"Any destination."

"*Any* destination?" A quizzical look flashed across Arn's face.

"Well, anyplace . . . anyplace . . ." Brand knew he had to say something more definite, so he responded with his first thought. "Anyplace in Christendom."

Anyplace in Christendom? thought Arn. Was this man one of the Norse who followed the White Kristr? And anyplace in Christendom could mean anything from the land of the Irish folk to the city of Rome and beyond. Brand's answers puzzled Arn.

"What has caused such urgency?" asked the captain, hoping for a better understanding.

"It is . . . it is difficult to explain," said Brand. "I assure you, I have committed no crime. Grant me the respect to press no more for details of my journey."

Arn eyed him closely for a full three seconds, slowly stroking his chin, then he nodded a silent consent. Brand felt himself exhale with relief.

"How long before we sail?" Brand asked.

"The wind will be adequate soon, and the mist is clearing. I expect we will sail no later than midday." Arn glanced toward Sleipnir. "But I have no room for your steed."

"I know," Brand said with no hint of the sadness he deeply felt. "I must find a buyer for my horse. I will return shortly. But crew member or not, accept this as down payment on my fare."

With that, he swiftly deposited an ample amount of silver coins into Arn's hand, then walked to where Sleipnir waited.

Before mounting to the saddle, Brand stood for a moment, stroking the black hair of Sleipnir's mane and deeply inhaling the sweetness of his muzzle.

"Sleipnir, Sleipnir—I will not forget you. Do not forget me."

Sleipnir shook his head as if he understood, and his bridle clanked. Then the two began to ride off together, heads held high, for the last time.

"Wait! Wait!" shouted Arn. "Do you not want to know where we are going?"

But there was no reply.

CHAPTER SIX

I F THE PEOPLE OF THE NORTHERN LANDS were strong and hearty, it was because the land, seas, and skies gave them no choice. They occupied lands that left little room for indolence or error in judgment. Either could result in deadly consequences.

The Norse lived on peninsulas, so water was a constant companion. One peninsula began in the Arctic and ran southward. A smaller peninsula jutted north from the continent of Europe.

On the western edge of the large peninsula, the steep mountainsides slipped unobstructed into deep frigid waters. Spectacular waterfalls came crashing down, like veils of white cascading down the back of a beautiful dusky woman. Misty crowns of clouds lingered midway up the mountaintops, both summer and winter. Rugged fjords made up the coastline; there were very few peaceful beaches. When there was shoreline, it was starkly spread with black rocks sprinkled with green and gold lichens. In such places, the land spirits dwelled.

Arn was on the last legs of his journey back home—back to his ancestral home in Bergen, on the wild western coast, where his wife and child awaited him.

The seas were mostly calm and the route familiar, so Arn and Brand had time together with nothing to distract them from their thoughts. Like many Norse, Arn was normally not talkative, but something about Brand kept the words flowing, especially when mead was involved. Arn talked and Brand listened, and it was acceptable to both.

"A more beautiful woman you have never met, Brand. My wife, my Ragnhild. Although, to be sure, she is as mysterious to me as the northern lights that shine down on us. And my little daughter, Kathleen, she is as bright as the sun at noon."

Arn told Brand of his many travels, the people he had met, and his tactics for success. When Arn learned Brand had been trained by Rolf the Wise in Hedeby, he had his own observations to share.

"Ah yes," said Arn. "I know Hedeby. I have been there."

Hedeby was a great trading center at the southern end of the Danish peninsula. It bordered the lands of Rolf's people—the Germanic tribes—and was near the Saxons as well. As Hedeby was a crossroad for trade from all the great routes, it was not unusual to see travelers dressed in the curious clothing of their own lands. Brand had delighted in watching and interacting with the Slavs, the Germanic tribesmen, the Rus, and white-robed men from the hot lands far to the south.

Arn was familiar with the singular reputation of the men of Hedeby. "They have the habit of combing their hair every day, bathing every Saturday, and regularly laundering and changing their clothing. Thus the men are able to entice even the most virtuous of maidens to be their mistresses, and sometimes even the wives of visiting nobles!"

With this observation, Arn laughed, Brand nodded in affirmation, and both men took another drink of mead.

Brand learned that the ship's chests were filled with only the very finest of trade goods—Chinese silk, Byzantine embroidery with delicate gold thread, boxes of ivory, hand-carved combs, amber, honey, wine from the Germanic regions, and coins of gold and silver. And possibly the most valuable of all, ingots of crucible steel, to be made into the finest of swords.

Sometimes they talked of religion. Brand learned that Arn himself was no convert. Yes, he had gone as far as the *prima signatio*, being signed with a cross by a priest, so he could trade with the White Kristr folk. A full conversion was not really demanded. He had done what was necessary—a halfway step—but stopped short of baptism.

Arn explained his philosophy: "When you wander into foreign lands as I have done, then you must do what is needed to trade with as many as possible. The Kristr men are much more willing to mingle with the prima signatio men than with those who have not taken the step. So I had myself signed with the cross. But make no mistake—I have not forsaken the gods of my fathers. There was no water, only the words and the sign over me."

Brand studied Arn's face and silently reflected on his captain's pragmatism.

Normally Arn asked few questions of other men, out of a kind of respect. But he found himself curious and fascinated by his young passenger.

"Tell me, Brand—why do you seek a port in Christendom?"

Brand took a moment. "I do not know exactly. It was just something that came into my mind. I do not know why."

And that was the simple truth.

"Well, I hope you find what you are seeking," replied the sea-tested captain. "The stories of the White Kristr god are interesting, but I believe the gods of my ancestors are the true gods. But what is more important than any god is luck. *Luck.*"

Arn took a long drink of mead, smacked his lips, and continued. "Now, you know there is woman luck, which every member of this crew wishes for. And there is weapon luck, where you are able to face a battle and win. Then there is victory luck, when no one and nothing can defeat you, and you are invincible. Without luck, nothing you do will help you. No man lives till eve whom the Norns doom at morning."

Brand listened to Arn and could not help but recall the words of his father in Uppsala—words of resignation, not words of hope.

Brand sailed with Arn as far as Aggersborg on the north of the Jutland peninsula, where they parted ways. Brand liked and respected Arn. He felt some sadness that he would leave behind this new friend. Another loss.

They stood facing one another, the right hand of each resting on the left shoulder of the other.

"May the gods be with you, Brand. May you find the answers to whatever it is you seek."

"Good-bye, Arn," said the younger man. "May you have victory luck."

Arn laughed and replied, "And you, Brand, may you have woman luck!"

CHAPTER SEVEN

Bergen, an ancient town in what is now Norway

ARN AND HIS CREW SAILED ON FROM AGGERSBORG and began the last segment of their long journey home to Bergen.

Arn had no need of victory luck himself; he was a merchant, not a warrior. And he had an abundance of trading luck. And as far as woman luck, he had already found his.

Ragnhild. She was the daughter of a thrall who had been made free and had married into a prominent farming family. They owned some of the best and most fertile meadows in the entire area.

Ragnhild was not the most beautiful of the women Arn and his family had considered as possible marriage partners. But she was the one he could never get out of his mind.

Her delicate features were surrounded by light-brown hair, and her eyes were a soft gray, like the breast of a dove. She was gentle, like a songbird, and her voice was rich and warm, like the caress of a fine fur on a winter night. Her figure was not tall, but she was formed very pleasingly, with curves around her tiny waist and graceful carriage.

Yes, she was delicate and gentle, but her mind was more than enough to best any two women of the town. Many women in her extended family had tutored her. She knew everything about running a household: how to dry and preserve food, how to keep the hearth fires from going out at night, how to make soap, when to replace the bed straw, where to hide silver, when to punish a thrall, and when to praise.

Three years was generally needed for trading to the east, and Arn's journey, far into the land of the Rus, had been no different. After a journey so long, Arn and his crew could hardly contain their excitement as familiar landmarks came into view. When they saw *de syv fjell*—the seven mountains—a collective shout rose up. The far travelers were returning in triumph as rich men to their beautiful meadow town. They quickly removed the wooden dragon's head from the prow of the ship, so as not to offend the land spirits.

Word of their coming had already spread, so as they sailed up into the harbor, a crowd of men, women, and children ran headlong to meet them. Not soon enough, the ship was in shallow water, and the crew threw a gangplank onto the shore and raced down it.

Breathless, Ragnhild rushed to meet her husband. There were tears of happiness and cries of relief all around.

He kissed her face and mouth, over and over, in enthusiastic joy. Then he stood back a few feet and took in every detail of her. In the three years he had been away, some changes had occurred. Faint lines had appeared around her eyes and mouth, and her skin seemed a little pale. But to Arn, Ragnhild had grown even more beautiful.

When he wrapped his arms around her, he could feel she had become somewhat thin. The pewter cross she always wore pressed against his chest. He was very familiar with the pendant, the cross of horizontal and vertical bars of equal length, set onto a medallion covered with intertwining vines and small dots in geometric patterns. Since her conversion, it never left her throat.

A girl of eight years appeared from behind Ragnhild's overdress, her face shining bright with happiness.

"Kathleen!" cried Arn.

In the three years of his absence, Kathleen had grown healthy and strong. Arn swept her up in his arms. He pivoted in a circle, and she giggled in delight as her braids swung outward. She remembered him well and, like her mother, had longed for his return.

The little family settled into a new routine. But it was not an easy homecoming. Arn struggled to adjust to being on land and tending to the day-to-day issues of household and farm. And Ragnhild struggled to let go of many things she had learned to do on her own, without Arn's involvement. Now the decision-making was much more complicated.

And always, a perennial chill of anxiety weighed on Ragnhild's heart. She was more than enough woman to please any man. She knew Arn loved her, loved her with all his heart. And yet . . . and yet . . . already she waited in dread for the next time he would leave her.

When spring would come at last to Bergen, and the sap would begin to rise in each tree and blade of grass, all the ships would be refitted with new repairs and the smell of pitch would be strong in the breeze. Ragnhild knew Arn could not stop yearning for yet another voyage, another chance to see new horizons.

At least for now, he had returned, and they were together. She would make the best of it. Even as misunderstandings and arguments ensued, they struggled together, each one to find his or her place with the other.

On one thing, though, they were in agreement.

They wanted another baby.

CHAPTER EIGHT

Winchester, England

AFTER ARN AND BRAND PARTED AT AGGERSBORG, Brand made passage on a ship sailing to York. From there he made his way to Wessex in the south of the English isle. Immediately he began using and improving his understanding of the language of the English. As always, it came quickly and easily to him.

As much as he tried, he could not prevent himself from recalling the events that had transpired in Uppsala. Sights, sounds, and even smells were still vivid in his mind, including the chance encounter with the White Kristr folk. They had sparked a curiosity within him that he felt compelled to explore.

Along his journey, he inquired of the Christian people and priests he met: "Who are you?" And they answered, "We are children of God."

To Brand, the Norse gods were powerful and mighty, sources of creation and wisdom. But they were also somewhat human—sometimes jealous, spiteful, and capricious. He had never heard of a Norse god who wanted worshippers to see him or her as a father or a mother. Brand knew of no god who said, "You are my child."

Sometimes the people Brand met, including converts, shared stories—stories of signs and miracles that had occurred because of faith. They told him, "We saw something unexplainable, and we had to know more."

All this made Brand hungry for more information but also confused. Did the Christians worship one god or three? Then there were words

Brand found hard to understand, such as *sin* and *grace*. And another word, which they said had to be the response to evil: *forgiveness*.

Brand asked where to go to learn more of these mysteries. The people had a common reply: "If you seek a good and respected teacher, you must go to the bishop of Winchester."

"What can you tell me of him?"

"Bishop Ælfheah," they said with conviction, "is a very pious man."

Ælfheah had been born to wealth, they explained. At an early age, and over the objections of his widowed mother, he entered a monastery. He attempted to live a life in seclusion, but he was appointed abbot at Glastonbury, contrary to his true desire. Eventually, he received permission to move from Glastonbury to a secluded place near the hot springs of Bath.

"Did he find the peace he was looking for?" asked Brand.

No, they would answer, it was only temporary. His students continued to seek his counsel, so he never found the solitude he so yearned for. Then when the bishop of Winchester died, Ælfheah became the new bishop.

"He did not seek this for himself," they emphasized. "But it is what God led him to be."

Brand decided that this man was special and that he would strive to learn from him. He made his way on foot toward Winchester.

He had been walking for weeks and nearing Winchester when a huge thunderstorm broke out. He sheltered under a towering oak. At times, the thundershower was so strong the air was white with rain. Finally, in late afternoon, it let up. He wiped the water from his face and eyes. The clouds broke, and sunshine revealed his destination. Before him was the mighty cathedral and the busy priory monastery, which provided clergy for the church.

He knocked at the gate of the priory, and almost immediately the reedy voice of an old crone answered: "A blessing upon you!" She lived in a small room near the entrance to the priory, a home in recompense for her duties as greeter and sentry. She scuttled out and opened a small opening in the wooden gate.

"What is your business here?"

"I come as a visitor."

She was an intelligent and wise soul who had lived much in the world. She thought she recognized something in his voice.

"You are Norse?"

"Yes."

Her mouth shot open, and her hand moved unconsciously to protect her throat. Brand's reply carried the fearsome reputation of a marauding and plundering people. For over two hundred years, monks had repeated a singular prayer: *A furore Normannorum libera nos, Domine!* Or, "From the fury of the Norsemen save us, Lord!" The seafaring Norse came in stealth in their longships, killed whom they wished, enslaved women and children, and destroyed and desecrated holy places throughout the region. The priory itself had been attacked twice more than a hundred years before but had survived and recovered.

Despite her trepidation, the old woman knew what she had to do. "I will take you to Simeon, our prior."

Simeon was no less anxious than the old woman, but he showed none of it. Some thirty-odd years before, Benedictine monks had been installed in the priory, and the Rule of Saint Benedict was expected to be honored. The rule of hospitality could not be ignored.

First, the prior said a prayer with Brand, thanking God for bringing Brand safely to the place of pilgrimage and refuge. Then he gave Brand the kiss of peace and bowed his head in homage to the soaked traveler. In Simeon's mind, what he did for the stranger, he did for Christ.

Two monks—one tall, one short—brought bowls of water and towels. They helped Brand remove his sodden outer garments. All was done in silence, for they were forbidden to speak to guests unless explicit permission had been granted. Their somber-hued brown robes and hoods gave them the same outward appearance as all members of the community; as alike as a flock of sparrows.

And so, with no more inquiry, Simeon said to Brand, "You are welcome here." He glanced at Brand's side. "But your weapon is not."

Slowly, Brand loosened the sword from his waist and handed it to the tall monk. As required by the rule, Simeon sat with him while Brand ate the bread and cheese they offered.

After the meal, Brand was brought to the guest house, where he spent the night. He awoke partially refreshed and somewhat less damp. Simeon sat with Brand, and they shared a breakfast of cooked gruel of rye and wheat, which lay somewhat heavily on Brand's stomach.

Simeon then took Brand to meet Ælfheah, the bishop of Winchester. Again Brand received the formal greeting and welcome.

Although Brand had heard much about the bishop, Ælfheah's appearance was still a shock. Ælfheah was much renowned for his extended fasts and austerity, so much so that he seemed more an animated skeleton than a man of flesh and muscle. His long, thin face was made even narrower by the gaunt hollows of his cheeks. The monks themselves declared they could see through his hands when he uplifted them at Mass.

For every day he went without food, Ælfheah provided a powerful example. If Ælfheah fasted for two days, then surely others could fast for one. And why not use the food saved from the fasting for the general good of the community? Indeed, for years it was well known that no one in the area around Winchester—not even the poorest of the poor—went without a filled bowl once a day.

Having dispensed with the formalities, Ælfheah was blunt with Brand. "I want no one here who intends to make vows without fundamentally changing his way of life."

As a stranger, Brand did not know the whole story behind Ælfheah's directness. But he had heard rumors—Ælfheah had been in significant conflict with the monks at Bath when he was appointed abbot. It seemed the monks had become quite lax about adhering to the Rule of Saint Benedict, and Ælfheah would have not of it. Immediately, he set about reforming the backsliders and imposing his own expectations for an austere monastic life at Bath. And Ælfheah was not about to allow any such issues to emerge at Winchester.

Brand's answer was equally direct. "I do not know if I will make any vows. I am here to learn more about the way of the White Kristr. I know only that I have a desire to learn, not where this will lead. I can assure you: I will adhere to any rules of the community. I was trained by my foster father, who taught that discipline is needed to achieve any purpose."

"Yes, even the Norsemen who have come here to plunder and to terrorize have been bound by the rules of their own society," Simeon observed—not knowing the understatement of his comment.

"You are right, Brother Simeon," agreed Ælfheah, adding, "but the discipline of the Norsemen is created apart from the instruction of God and so is of no real value."

And with these understandings, Brand was permitted to stay on at the priory. Of course, he was under constant observation, lest this visitor turn out to be a spy or intend to harm anyone inside the walls of the priory. He slept and ate in the guest house. He was read the Rule of Saint Benedict each day. He was told, "Here is the law under which you wish to live. If you can observe it, enter; if you cannot, you are free to depart."

Although Brand knew he could leave, something—he did not know what—something compelled him to stay. It did not even seem to be a hard decision, rather something that just evolved.

At first, it was the draw of community, of family, that called to him. The idea of an adopted family was not foreign to Brand. Through all of his early years in Hedeby, he had lived with people not of his own blood.

Then Brand began to feel a deeper draw. As if it had its own gravity, there was something about this community that pulled and held each member. Brand learned that some of the monks had joined the priory because they felt a special call from God. Others had been encouraged by figures in the church or their own families. And others seemed to have become monks due to special circumstances even they could not fully know or explain.

The longer he stayed in Winchester, the more Brand felt a stirring toward Christ, a desire to be with others who took the scriptures as truth, living the Gospel without compromise.

For many of the ancients, coming to baptism and entering a monastery went hand in hand. Once he made the decision to be baptized and to stay, Brand's novitiate began. And with it, the need for observation began to recede, until at last, Brand was no different from any other novitiate, on his own spiritual journey.

Brand's bits of silver, left from his mother's hoard, were used to provide food for the poor and care for the sick. Ælfheah presented Brand's sword to Ethelward, a somewhat pompous yet effective alderman who had provided protection for the priory and cathedral. Ethelward received the fine sword with extreme pleasure.

All novitiates would face the same questions six times before their year as novitiates would end. After that, they would enter the community of the priory for the rest of their lives.

"Are you ready to humble yourself?" Simeon asked.

Of all the questions, this was the most troublesome for Brand. He had never been encouraged to be humble in his life.

Rolf, his foster father, had taught him all manner of *idrottir*, those specific skills that would make him a man of high esteem and value in the eyes of the community. Brand was a quick learner and excelled at everything from archery to falconry, the casting of silver to astronomy, horsemanship to chess. He was trained as a warrior—but a warrior with a mind. And now he would use his mind, and his will, to transform himself into a true follower of the White Kristr.

Brand no longer had a foster father like Rolf, and his own father lay in a mound in Uppsala. But now he had brothers, many brothers. And there were men he would call Father, and they would respond, "Yes, my son."

The year passed, and Brand had made his decision. When the ultimate question was put to him, he had but one answer.

"Yes, Bishop, I am ready."

Brand was prepared for the ceremony. With scissors, Ælfheah cut Brand's hair into the sign of the cross—a cut for the Father, for the Son, and for the Holy Spirit. Then Simeon took over, to remove the rest of the hair on the crown of Brand's head.

Brand did not move from his knees or speak. He was at peace with his decision.

But he felt a twinge of something—when long tufts of his hair, once a source of pride and virility—were removed from his head. They fell softly to the stone floor, like autumn leaves on a very still and windless afternoon.

CHAPTER NINE

To visitors, the priory at Winchester was a farm, an inn, a hospital, a school, and a library. But to the community who lived there, it was home. Every necessary aspect of their lives could be met from the labor of the brothers. There were over two dozen buildings in the compound, made at different times and with different materials—some wood and some stone.

In addition to the guest house and guest kitchen, there was a kitchen for preparation of food for the monks. Gardens, a cornmill, fish ponds, a piggery, and brewery provided a variety of nourishment. There were stables and workshops, a bakehouse, and even a small prison cell for people in the area who had committed major transgressions.

When not at work, at meals, or asleep, the monks worshiped in the chapels or the cathedral as appropriate. There was an infirmary for the care of the sick or aged, and a cemetery for final rest. For the outside community, there was an almonry, where alms in the form of food or money were distributed to the needy.

Every aspect of life was regulated. Some were regulated by the church calendar. Some were regulated by the seasons, as there was a summer schedule and a winter schedule. And much was regulated by the hours. Matins began at two in the morning, and the rest of the day was organized into segments until the final period of prayer in the evening.

At first, Brand found it difficult to accustom himself to the unyielding routine dictated by the book of hours. There had been discipline in Brand's life before, of course. But it had always been balanced by liberal periods of relaxation and the drinking of substantial quantities of mead or wine.

For his orientation to the life of the abbey, Brand was assigned to the tutelage of Oswald. Oswald was nearly as austere as Ælfheah in body, and in belief, he was even more so. He was painfully thin yet thought his waist too fat. Not accepting that aging changes the distribution of fat on the body, he tightened his belt until it pressed harshly into his flesh. He refused food until his stomach had shriveled, and his arms and legs became ever more weak and puny. His hair fell out, and his skin was dry. Without realizing, he scratched himself often. The healthy monks were not permitted to eat of the flesh of four-footed animals, but even when fish or fowl was offered, Oswald declined to eat it. Secretly, Prior Simeon observed that Oswald seemed to relish the limitations of the monastic life more than he should.

Oswald's specialty was tending the abbey herb garden. Silence was required on most of the abbey grounds, but was acceptable if needed for instruction. Brand started by working an hour a day alongside Oswald in the garden, learning the names of the various herbs and their uses. Oswald was obsessed with the plants and often tried various plant cures on himself. Sometimes Oswald would eschew even the minimal fare—a pound of bread and two cups of wine per day, plus modest servings of seasonal fruits or vegetables at the two daily meals—in favor of fasting with only water and herbs. He claimed the herbs cured everything from back pain to headache to dandruff. But to most observers, he seemed to move stiffly, and the color of his skin was never healthy, despite his protestations that the many herbal potions had cured him of all ailments.

To the monks, silence was of the utmost importance. Passing one another, they did not speak, although some silent signs were made to indicate thoughts or feelings. There was a special gesture, done with a flourish, which meant "thank you."

Brand found it hard to adhere to the rules of silence because he loved language. But he accepted the holy silence and used the daily Mass as his way to connect to the sound of the human voice. The beautiful words of the service kept him from feeling the loneliness that sometimes gripped his heart, even though he was surrounded by community. The Kyrie, the Agnus Dei, and the Eucharistic prayers moved him as nothing he had ever felt before. The Mass was a remembrance of sacrifice, yes. But unlike the sacrifice of his father, there was resurrection.

There were two rules Brand found exceptionally difficult to understand. The first was the prohibition against laughter. He was not a jokester nor prone to levity, but he remembered fondly the times spent with friends in Hedeby and Uppsala. His foster father was renowned for his hilarious stories, and Brand had learned many a poem meant to amuse during the long winter nights. Contests were held to see who could contrive the funniest way to insult an enemy. In Uppsala, he and his friends could pass hours together, with or without mead, and it was not uncommon for the young men to roll on the ground and laugh until tears came.

The second rule that perplexed him was the requirement that no one was to come to the defense of another. He had been tending the garden one day when a young child working on another plot lost his balance and stepped into and then fell fully onto Oswald's precious herbs. Seeing the crushed plants, Oswald immediately upbraided the unfortunate boy. Brand saw the child tremble and mumble requests for pardon, and his heart was moved.

"But it was an accident!" Brand exclaimed. "Leave him alone!"

"You have no place in this. Go back to tending the herbs!" Oswald barked.

Brand returned to his weeding, his blood hot with outrage. Oswald immediately left to find the prior.

The next day, Brand was summoned to meet with Simeon.

"You must obey the rule, Brand. You may never come to the defense of another. If you do so, there can be severe punishment."

"But why? I do not understand."

"We have discovered over many centuries that disputes must be settled by bringing them before the prior for resolution. If brothers come to the defense of brothers, factions can be formed, which are detrimental to the health of the community. Since you are new to the community, and this is your first offense, I will be lenient. You are admonished. You shall eat alone for the next three days. Speak to no one about this incident."

Brand did as he was instructed and spoke to no one about the matter. But alone at night in his cell, he thought of it. He finally concluded that within the monastery, perhaps such a rule was required to keep harmony, in the context of all the other rules. But in the outside world, it seemed totally unworkable. How could a man *not* come to the defense of family or friend being attacked? How indeed.

There was another matter that occupied Brand's mind and that he chose to keep to himself. It was his dreams. He had already learned from his study that some Bible figures had dreams that foretold the future— especially Joseph, the interpreter of dreams in Egypt. And there were many others. Samuel had such dreams as well as the magi who visited the infant Jesus and even the wife of Pontius Pilate.

Brand had dreams of chaos and impossibility—the stuff of most dreams. But he knew some of his dreams meant more. One night he dreamed the kitchen was empty and the hearth fire had gone out, an event that never happened in reality. He knew what it meant; the chief cook would die, and soon. He tried to tell this to Simeon, but was rebuffed.

"Your faith is too new to be mystical, so anything from the dream world must be of the devil."

Within a week, the cook was dead.

Brand tried to stop the dreams, but they continued. He never told anyone in the community about them again.

It was immediately clear to everyone that Brand was no ordinary student. He had the gift of a finely tuned ear, and his English improved exponentially. Simeon noted his intelligence and earnestness, so Brand was included with the students learning to read and write scriptures and made exempt from most manual labor. The runes Brand had learned in Hedeby helped him with the Latin alphabet. Soon he could read and write Latin words with ease. Even more quickly, he had committed to memory the daily recitation of the Credo and the Pater Noster and the words and songs of the Mass.

As summer turned to fall, Simeon summoned Brand to the calefactory, the only room in the monastery (other than the infirmary and the kitchen) where a fire was permitted. Brand relished the warmth and the discussions, for Simeon was an excellent teacher and an excellent listener as well.

Simeon and Brand sat close to the fire, and soon the smell of drying wool permeated the room.

"Why do you request we meet here?" asked Brand.

"Because I know the warmth of the fire helps illuminate this place and will benefit the flow of our communication."

Simeon poked the fire that smoldered in the hearth. With the oxygen, it flickered, then burned bright.

"I have something important to discuss with you, Brother Brand."

He moved closer to the flames and rubbed his hands in the warming air.

"I know you have traveled far to come here. I have often wondered what brought you here, what has kept you here. It is not an easy life. You must follow our rules of poverty and humility. And there is the requirement for obedience."

Simeon stopped rubbing his hands for a moment.

"Why did you come here, and why have you stayed?"

Brand stared at Simeon. He, the man who knew words in multiple languages, struggled to answer.

"Sometimes I do not understand myself. It all started one night in Uppsala, with a simple question from a young woman seated by a campfire, and it has never stopped. The more I learn of the White Kristr, the more I want to know."

Simeon nodded. "God has been beckoning you, and you have answered. Your faith is growing. And you have done exceptionally well in your studies."

Brand felt a surge of pride at these words, which he immediately struggled to repress.

"Brand, I have a specific reason to speak with you today. Ælfheah has asked me to select from among the community one who is suited for priesthood and who will therefore leave the monastery for a life in the world. I have thought deeply on this. I have selected you."

As if he had read Brand's thoughts, Simeon continued. "But the man who is chosen must be on his guard against arrogance and pride. That man will move about in the world outside the priory. He must not attempt to do anything except that which he is commanded to do. Even though he is a priest and can engage in priestly functions, he is still bound by the discipline of the rule. Perhaps, by being in the world, more so."

Simeon leaned forward to emphasize the seriousness of his next words.

"Brother Brand, you know you must accept any command I give you. If I ask of you an impossible thing, you are to trust in God to help you. But I want to know if you can accept this responsibility of your own free will."

Simeon's gaze was fixed on Brand with intensity.

"Can you?"

Brand did not take long to reply. "Prior Simeon, I know I have never truly felt more at home, more my true self, than during the Mass. It is where my heart, my soul, is truly at peace. I believe I could—with my free will—accept what you ask of me."

"But are you truly at peace? There is something about you that is restless. You came to us as a traveler, but are you running *away from* something or *to* something? Until you are certain, I will not require a final answer from you. You must go apart as did Christ when he went into the wilderness. You alone can decide if God is calling you to be a priest."

Brand stared at the fire, now dying down a little but still warm. He looked deeply into it, as if in the light all things would be made clear.

CHAPTER TEN

FOR FORTY DAYS, BRAND STAYED APART from the community, in a deep wood northwest of Winchester. A small hut provided him with partial shelter from wind and rain. The silence, stillness, and solitude were intended to lead him to openness and obedience.

Every other day, he found at the door of the hut a small bundle of bread, some butter or cheese, and a jug of buttermilk left by a silent messenger. Brand placed the bread and butter in an earthenware bowl and covered it with a plate and a clean stone atop to keep the curious and hungry mice at bay. Water was readily available, as a well had been dug nearby. He was permitted to eat any plants or fruits he found for himself in the woods.

Although he was alone and could only guess at the time by reckoning with the sun, he kept the book of hours, the priory's rigorous prayer schedule, as best he could. Brand had also been permitted to take with him a small book with the four Gospels and selected Psalms. This was a great favor; so precious were these books that in many cases they were chained to the monasteries in which they were kept. He had sat in the scriptorium of the priory and copied some of these same verses in his own hand.

During his solitude, Brand recalled words of Bishop Ælfheah: "Holy obedience requires holy listening. Holy obedience is saying yes to God before you know what God is asking of you." Brand spent hours at prayer, beseeching God to allow his will to be known.

When he was not at prayer, Brand thought deeply on his life in Uppsala. It seemed a long time ago, even though it was not. He recalled his friends and his days filled with sport of all kinds: athletic, sexual, and intellectual. One image he tried hardest of all to keep from his consciousness—the eyes of his father.

Sometimes the image of his mother and her soft voice and gentleness came to him. More than once, the memories were so powerful that his eyes became moist with tears. He recalled the day he had left Uppsala for Hedeby. It was a beautiful spring day, with an incomprehensibly blue sky, when he stood before his mother and waited for her blessing. Solveig bent down and whispered to him.

"I have dreamt of great things for you. You will be a traveler, beyond the world we know. You will be known as a great and wise man, and your influence will be great and last for untold generations."

Still bending close, she caressed Brand's blond hair with her soft hands, and Brand kissed her cheek. He watched as she straightened and waited, her face fixed in resignation as her only child prepared to sail away from her.

As the days of his voluntary solitude continued, Brand's thoughts turned more and more to life in the priory: the other novitiates, Simeon and his other teachers, the children who lived there, the pervasive silence. Even the somewhat-prickly Oswald.

Brand's dream life accompanied him on the retreat as an uncontrollable presence. Sometimes he dreamt of women, often the comely maidens he had known in Hedeby and Uppsala. On those nights, he awoke with signs of nocturnal emissions.

One particular dream was the most intense. It was of a woman, quite young. In this dream, she appeared in silence before him, her face hidden. He yearned to touch her. But each time he reached for her, invisible bonds constrained his arms. He could not caress her or even move, though he struggled and struggled. He would awake breathless. This dream troubled him more than the others. He could not make out if it was a dream that foretold the future or merely an ordinary dream to be forgotten.

Toward the end of his isolation, he dreamt repeatedly of travel, of sailing to a foreign land and suffering many trials. This dream also confused him. He sensed it foretold what was to come, yet he knew that as a priest, his travel would be no farther than a day's walk from Winchester, where he would live out his life, tending to the spiritual needs of the brothers in the priory and the people of the nearby villages.

At the end of his retreat, Brand returned to Simeon.

"What have you learned?" said Simeon, his eyes kind but alert.

"I feel sure that a life in the church is the correct life for me. Nowhere else do I feel so much at peace. And I want to share this with others in the world. I want to become a priest."

"Yes, I am glad to hear this decision" said Simeon, trying hard not to smile as broadly as he wished. "Our Saint Augustine wrote in his confessions: 'My heart is restless until it rests in thee.' Remember, you are not going to God; you are *returning* to God. It was always within you."

"I am ready. I will accept whatever destiny God has chosen for me. I am ready to live to God's purpose."

Simeon had to probe further. "Even if that purpose is one which you find physically or mentally repellant, or one which you do not understand?"

"Yes, on my honor," replied the Norseman with complete solemnity.

There was one further matter Brand and Bishop Ælfheah needed to discuss. It was a matter of no small controversy in the church. But not to Bishop Ælfheah. To him, the issue was as clear as the expectation of obedience and poverty required of all the monks and priests.

Brand was summoned to meet with Simeon and the bishop. As always, Bishop Ælfheah was direct. Brand responded equally directly.

"But why celibacy?" Brand demanded, close to impertinence. "Many priests are married. Why do you ask this of me? Was not Saint Peter himself a married man?"

"We do not like to think or speak of it, but abortions and infanticide have taken place in convents and monasteries after the activities of noncelibate clerics," countered Ælfheah.

Simeon attempted to add another perspective to the conversation. "Would it not be better to follow the teachings of Saint Ulrich? In his letter to the Holy Father in Rome, he argued from scripture and common sense that the only way to purify the church from these excesses is to permit priests to marry. And the worst sin is not lust." He paused. "The worst sin is pride."

"Some have said that letter is a forgery," retorted Ælfheah, giving Simeon a sharp look.

Ælfheah continued with his explanation. "Brand, you know you are more than unusually handsome. Saint Augustine wrote that nothing is so powerful in drawing the spirit of a man downward as the caresses of a woman. If you can avoid temptation, it will serve as a lesson to the people that they too can resist evil."

"I understand what you are saying, my bishop," said Brand. "I too have heard of the problems caused when priests are married, of how the property of the church has become entangled in competing claims from wives and children of deceased priests. But still, what you are asking of me is a great commitment."

Ælfheah decided to change tactics a bit. "Brand, it is more than property disputes."

The bishop looked directly at Brand. "Has there never been a time in your life when the desire of a man for a woman or a woman for a man has led to destruction and loss?"

In a flash, Brand recalled the encounter with Vigdis. And more than rationality, more than humility, it was guilt that formed his decision.

And so, on the first Sunday in the church season of Epiphany, Brand—who had never felt the deep joy of true love for a woman—knelt before Ælfheah. In the presence of his brothers in the faith, he swore he would forevermore be celibate, in obedience to his bishop. And for his whole life, he intended to keep this promise.

CHAPTER ELEVEN

Southhampton, England

I T WAS ANNO DOMINI 994. For years, the English lands had been subjected to an increasing number of raids by marauding Vikings. The newest threat was Olaf Tryggvason, the handsome and charismatic Norse chieftain. Olaf had *gone a-viking*, as was said of the plunderers, and attacked London. Twice before he had invaded and obtained ransom in danegeld coin. This time, though, Olaf was repulsed by brave Londoners, who were tired of being the continual prey of the violent Norse. Though Olaf threatened them greatly and even torched London Bridge, the English forced him into retreat as far as Southampton, where he wintered with his longships.

King Ethelred, ruler of the English countryside, believed that negotiating with the Vikings was his only tactic. But the coffers of his treasure-house were low; he had only ten thousand pieces of silver and no more. He had already angered the populace by extracting wealth from them to pay the extortionist Vikings during a previous raid. This time, he would do whatever it took to ensure that the payment would bring safety from the violent men from the north. King Ethelred was in a precarious position, and he knew he needed help.

He sent notice requesting that Bishop Ælfheah come to him. Upon the king's summons, Ælfheah set off immediately.

When they met, Ælfheah noted that Ethelred's face was haggard from lack of sleep. Gray hair was sprinkled like threads of spider's silk in his dark beard and hair. Ælfheah knew that gossips and political enemies blamed Ethelred for the relentless and successful Viking raids. Behind his back they called him Ethelred the Unready.

In turn, the king noted Ælfheah's fragile appearance. Like everyone, he was stunned. But Ethelred detected something else, something immovable in the frail bishop—a fierce stubbornness.

Ethelred offered Ælfheah a cup of wine, which was promptly refused. He then set to the business at hand.

"Bishop Ælfheah, you know we have been greatly bruised by Olaf Tryggvason. I have need of someone to meet with Olaf in Southampton and persuade him to stop his men from looting and killing the people."

"Why do you believe I can obtain his cooperation?"

"You are a man of God, a Christian presence in an evil world. I have heard that Olaf had a mystical experience with a hermit on the Isles of Scilly. Perhaps he will listen to you."

"Yet even after this encounter, the raids have continued against our Christian kingdom?"

"Yes," answered the king with weariness.

"Perhaps this mystical experience has not truly changed Olaf's hardened heart," said Ælfheah quietly. Then he said with boldness, "My king, I will do anything you command that does not harm my relationship with Christ. I will attempt negotiation with this sea wolf. But I will require help to deal with this Olaf of the north."

"Yes, of course. I will instruct Ethelward, the chief earl of the southwest counties, to accompany you."

Ælfheah nodded. "I know him. I understand that three years ago he worked with Archbishop Sigeric in negotiating a peace with the Danes."

"That is true. Ethelward is the best negotiator I know. But this Norseman will sorely test you and him. Olaf Trygvasson is a dangerous and ruthless man."

"Then we shall pray and fast to ensure he will not be victorious. But I will need other earthly help. In addition to Ethelward, I would like to bring with me a newly ordained priest. His name is Brand, and he is Norse."

"Are you sure he can be trusted?" asked King Ethelred.

"Yes, I believe so. No one can ever know the true heart of another, but this man has pledged himself in obedience, humility, and chastity. And I trust his pledge. He is most intelligent. And he is familiar with the ways of the Norse people, which may help create an advantage for us."

Ælfheah immediately returned to Winchester, then he and Brand began their journey to join Ethelward in Southhampton. When they met, Brand's precious sword was hanging by Ethelward's side.

Olaf agreed to meet with them, but only after kidnapping several prominent Englishmen and keeping them captive aboard his warships, to ensure his own safety. Finally, Olaf came to the appointed meeting place where Ælfheah, Brand, and Ethelward were waiting.

When the three saw Olaf, they all thought, *The tales are true.*

Olaf was a handsome man—a head taller than other tall men, with shoulders broader than most men's by a hand's width. Dark-auburn hair framed a bright face with ever-alert eyes. But his smile was most striking. When he smiled, his upper lip curved. It was difficult to determine if it was a smile of genuine warmth or a sneer. This was especially intriguing for the females he met. Olaf had been married several times, and it was widely believed he had been married to more than one wife at the same time.

Olaf had dealt with some Christian priests before. He had heard that the holy Ælfheah was a gaunt man who continuously pushed the limits of physical privations. And he was not surprised when he met Ethelward, whose bearing was imposing, whose clothing was sumptuous, and whose face was prone to fat.

Olaf was expecting to see men like Ethelward and Ælfheah. He was not expecting to see a man like Brand. Olaf was an athletic man; some said that in every physical way he exceeded every Norseman who had ever been known. Yet here before him, in humble tonsure and monk's robe, stood a man who rivaled Olaf's own physical presence.

After the greetings and preliminaries, the four began to talk in earnest. Brand acted as interpreter between the fierce Norse marauder; the emaciated and gentle bishop of Winchester; and Ethelward, the pragmatic and patient negotiator.

Ælfheah began with a question for Olaf. "We have heard you have had a mystical experience. Will you tell us of this?"

Olaf visibly brightened at the chance to tell his story. "I was a heathen, plundering many monasteries and churches of the White Kristr faith. But that all changed when I came to the Isles of Scilly."

"Isles of Scilly?" asked Brand, not understanding the term.

"Yes," explained Ethelward. "Father Brand, you are new to this area, and so you would not know. The Isles of Scilly form an archipelago on the far southwestern coast of England."

Olaf continued. "A man lived there alone on one of the islands. He was famed for his excellent learning and knowledge. It was said that he knew many things hidden to others and that he could foretell the future. I was eager to test the hermit."

Olaf lifted his mantle to allow the negotiators to see his finely tailored and costly clothing. Gold threads were woven into fine designs at the edges of his tunic, and the colors were brilliant, not the muted greys and tans of ordinary men.

"I dressed one of my bondsmen like a king, so that under this guise he might seek the hermit's counsel. But the holy man saw through the deceit at once. When I heard this, of course, I was even more eager to see him, for I knew he had the gift of special knowledge. When I met him, he told me this:

You have been a slave, Olaf. In Estonia, you were sold for the price of a good ram and sold again for the price of a fine cloak. But you are not a slave to the White Kristr. This god loves his children. And the sacrifice has already been made, so it is no longer necessary to fill the groves with the hanging corpses of beasts and men.

This is your future: You will be a king of renown and do celebrated deeds. You will bring many people to faith and baptism, both to your own good and the good of others.

You will be betrayed. A battle will take place, and many of your men will fall. You will receive a wound and will be at the point of death. Yet within seven days, you will be healed from this wound, and you will let yourself be baptized.

"And as I returned to my ships, it was exactly as foretold. I was attacked by a group of traitors. Then after seven days, I was well from my wound. I went back to the hermit and asked carefully how he had this wisdom to foretell the future. He said the god of the White Kristr followers let him know all he wished. I spoke much with him, and he told me of many great works of God. And this is how I agreed to be baptized."

They all listened to Olaf intently and then listened as Brand interpreted the Viking leader's words.

Ælfheah spoke first. "But you continue to harass and extort us here in England—we are followers of the White Kristr."

"Well, yes, I continue to do what is necessary to gain the wealth I need. But I no longer sack churches, destroy relics, or kill monks."

Brand, Ælfheah, and Ethelward exchanged glances.

Ethelward spoke next, with a sigh. "We are tired, Olaf. Let us meet again in the morning, when we are more refreshed."

No sooner had they finished the shared evening meal than the three men began to discuss the strategy for the next day.

"Did you hear what he said?" whispered Ethelred. "'The wealth I *need*'? It seems he is more than just accumulating wealth in order to be rich. We must know what is really behind this relentless need for silver."

"Yes, I sensed that too," said Brand. "I will see if any of his men are willing to talk with me."

Brand went into the night and approached Olaf's bondsmen. They were guarding the English hostages and had gathered around a camp fire that strategically lit the area. A collection of tree trunks and stumps formed an impromptu seating area.

Brand gestured to an open stump in the circle around the fire. They knew he was one of the English negotiators, but out of curiosity, they did not dismiss him. No words were said, but with the nod of a head, Brand was given permission to join the guards. Before long, Brand entertained them with the skills he had learned so effectively in Uppsala and Hedeby.

It amused them greatly when the English priest spoke their language, told them ribald jokes, and sang outrageous drinking songs. Yet they were still cautious and would reveal little.

Brand continued to gently probe. "And what is Olaf like, this man whom you follow and obey?"

"He is a true leader, and we will follow him anywhere!" declared one of the bondsmen.

Another followed, with equal enthusiasm, "And we will stay loyal until he is the king of all the lands of the north!"

That's it, thought Brand. Olaf's real goal was to be the great chieftain of all the chieftains of the north and for all the leaders to be subservient to him. He wanted to be an earthly king over all the land, not just the region of his ancestral home.

Brand bade them all good-night, then hurried away to confer with Ælfheah and Ethelward. This information might help them persuade Olaf to change his violent ways with the English people. Ælfheah spent the night praying that Olaf's heart would be softened.

The next day, Ethelward began the negotiation with a question and an observation. "What does it merit us to fight, like two scorpions in a bottle? One will be left dead, and the other nearly so."

Olaf replied, "My men are willing to do all that I ask them, including fighting to the death." Then his tone softened. "But you may be right that all may be left weak or dead. What do you have in mind to avoid this outcome?"

"An alliance."

"What kind of an alliance?"

Ælfheah answered, "You will agree to receive instruction in the White Kristr faith, and King Ethelred will adopt you as a son and act as your sponsor. You will receive a gift at the christening."

Olaf was intrigued. "What kind of gift?"

"A gift of ten thousand pieces of danegeld," answered Ethelward.

"And what do I give in return?"

Ethelward said simply, "The promise to never invade England again."

"And," said Ælfheah, "to bring the true religion back with you to your home country, and to bring with you teachers and others who will support you in your faith. A country united in one faith is a united country."

Their offer fit in neatly, almost too neatly, with Olaf's goal to consolidate his power. The danegeld would finance his future campaigns of conquest.

Olaf did not hesitate too long before he answered, "This I will do."

They all immediately traveled from Southampton to Andover to share this arrangement with King Ethelred. As agreed, Olaf received faith instruction from Ælfheah and Brand.

Brand observed how eagerly Olaf learned the stories of mighty warriors from the sacred texts: David and Saul. But with the gentler side of faith—the White Kristr's requirements to love one's enemies—Olaf quickly grew bored and disinterested.

This frustrated Brand, yet it seemed to him that it was progress. He knew from his own experience and that of others that conversion is never a simple decision. It often comes from multiple conscious and unconscious motivations. He decided to let the Holy Spirit move Olaf as it would and not take onto himself the personal responsibility for Olaf's life as a Christian man.

On the day of his confirmation, Olaf knelt before a font with King Ethelred of England as his sponsor. Bishop Ælfheah presided, and Ethelward, Brand, and Olaf's men solemnly looked on.

Olaf swore his oath: "On my honor, I will never again come to England with warlike intent. When I leave, I will take with me the priests and the learned men of King Ethelred. And I make another solemn vow, to bring my new religion back to my country and all who live in it."

Later that day, Olaf, Ethelred, and Ælfheah met to discuss the details of Olaf's vow, as Brand interpreted. Olaf stated that he wanted no less than twelve White Kristr priests to accompany him back north.

"Why twelve?" asked Ælfheah.

"The White Kristr had twelve disciples who surrounded him in the land where he lived. That is my requirement as well."

"Yes, of course, Olaf. We will send such men with you," answered Ælfheah. "Among them will be Grimkell, a priest of Danish blood, who will attend to you personally."

"And I want this priest too," Olaf interjected, turning to Brand. "I want him to sail back with me. He will be a good addition to my court."

There was a brief silence before Ælfheah answered, "I have already prayed on this matter, Olaf. Father Brand must return with me to Winchester."

And the thin, little iron-willed bishop said it in such a way that Olaf did not even try to argue.

CHAPTER TWELVE

Winchester, England

BRAND AND ÆLFHEAH WALKED MOST OF THE WAY back to Winchester, as Ælfheah used the money King Ethelred gave them for transport on food for beggars instead.

Back in the community of the priory, Brand quickly and quietly settled into a priestly routine. He spent much time singing Mass for the monks and hearing their confessions. He performed last rites for them and for the people of the villages surrounding Winchester. He baptized infants and the occasional adult.

He was content with his life, yet he was still haunted by dreams. He kept having dreams of future events, but he had long since refrained from sharing them with anyone—not even in confession. And the one special dream, of the unattainable young woman, came to him more than he wanted, and he always awoke with a sense of confusion.

A year passed, and Ælfheah summoned Brand to meet with him. Brand knelt, kissed his bishop's hand, then stood and waited for instruction.

"Father Brand, you have been a faithful and attentive priest, and you have tended to the people with care. Simeon and I have taught you all we can, but it has become increasingly obvious that you have more to give. And that you have more to learn. Would you agree that you have more to learn?"

"Yes. Yes, my lord bishop. Of course."

"To learn more, you must travel. It will instruct you more than anything else. I am sending you on a journey."

Brand's mouth opened slightly in surprise, as he had never imagined that he would leave Winchester. Still, he replied without hesitation. "Yes, my lord bishop, if this is what you desire of me." Brand slowly lowered, then raised his head as a sign of submission. "Where are you sending me?"

"The archbishop of Canterbury has asked for our assistance. The journey will be to Rome. You will have letters to deliver to the Holy Father of Rome on behalf of the archbishop. I trust no one more than you to deliver them."

Brand took these words in, and his heart soared. He had heard how pilgrims sailed south, to Normandy and on to the Kingdom of León, round the south of the Iberian Peninsula to Sicily, Rome, and finally to the holy city of Jerusalem. To be able to make a pilgrimage as far as Rome was more than he could have dreamed.

But his reverie was cut short with the bishop's next pronouncement.

"You will not go alone. Brother Oswald will accompany you."

Brand tried hard not to show his disappointment—he had promised to be obedient to his bishop in all things.

"Brother Oswald knows more about herbs than anyone else. I have received a request that he visit Rome and spend time there as an instructor, then bring back with him curative herbs to see if such plants can be grown here."

Brand understood the importance of Oswald's work, but the presence of the unpleasant herbalist would undoubtedly make the journey more difficult. He decided instead to focus on the excitement the journey would entail. Once again, Brand would sail the deep and mysterious seas. And this time, each new harbor would bring him closer to the seat of his Christian faith. Rome. He was going to Rome.

Preparation for the journey began immediately. Oswald gathered the seeds of many medicinal plants and herbs, then dried and carefully labeled them in tiny sacks or jars. He made provision that a quantity of dried bilberry be included for him and Brand to eat. He also insisted, in his high, squeaky voice, that rose hips be included to fortify him and Brand against the disease "that makes sailors sick and their teeth to fall out."

The entire Winchester community gathered to pray for and bless Brand and Oswald as they began their journey.

Bishop Ælfheah intoned: "O God, you have called us all to be your servants and the servants of others. Bless Father Brand and Brother Oswald as they begin their journey, and be with them at each step. Save them from every peril. Give them faith to go with good courage and to know that your hand is leading them and that your love is supporting them as they travel through dangerous and unknown lands."

The bishop moved his hands in the sign of the cross over them, ending with the familiar honor to the Triune God. Thus prayed for and blessed, Brand and Oswald were ready to begin the journey that would take years to complete and would tax every ounce of courage and endurance within them.

CHAPTER THIRTEEN

Near Trondheim, in what is now Norway

AFTER THE NEGOTIATED PEACE AT ANDOVER had been settled, the baptized and newly confirmed Olaf Tryggvason sailed out with his fleet of *drakkar,* his mighty ships of war. Only twenty-seven years old, he felt the nobility and possibility of his mission. He was Odysseus returning home from exile; he was Saint Michael on a holy mission.

True to his word, he converted people as he made his way home to the Norse of the western seas, the shorelines of the fjords. Everywhere he went, he ordered a tent to be assembled and High Mass sung there, and afterward for a church to be constructed on the same spot. He converted first the people of the Orkney Islands, then the Shetland Islands, and the Faeroe Islands. He effectuated many of these conversions by threatening trade sanctions and through the persuasive use of hostage-holding. Yes, Olaf was in his heart still a Viking warrior, cruel and bold. And now his passion was to convert his heathen homeland.

He set his sights on being named king at the next general Thing, the assembly of free men of the area. The timing was right. The people who lived in the land of Olaf's ancestors were getting restless. A spirit and urgency for change increased throughout the wild and beautiful land. Everything was ready for Olaf Tryggvason to return to the land of fjords and assert his birthright as the people's leader. He was excited to sail to the land of his people, even though it was a land in which he had almost never lived.

Olaf's fleet reached his homeland in early summer. Olaf had planned to pursue his chief rival, Hákon Jarl, who had ruled over the western shores of the land, where it meets the sea. But Olaf never had to use his force against him.

In his arrogance, Hákon often abducted beautiful young women, some of low status but also some daughters of highborn men. He used them for sexual diversion, then sent them home, broken in spirit, after a week or two. Hákon could scarce have committed an insult more powerful than this behavior. And so, before Olaf could even engage his adversary, Hákon was pursued by outraged fathers and brothers, and he lost his head to a thrall. After this bizarre murder, it was easy for Olaf to take over leadership of the area.

A general Thing for the Trøndelag district was convened, and Olaf was selected to be king. He lost no time in announcing his plan to spread Christianity across his entire kingdom. He would, he declared, "either bring it to this—that all should be Christian, or die!"

He began by converting the chieftains of all the districts, one by one—even the most resistant. He gathered his bondsmen and relatives from the eastern part of the countryside and with this force proceeded to the mouth of the Nidelva.

Next, Olaf sent out messengers to landowning men from eight districts to come to an assembly. From time immemorial, the area had been the home of the Trønder folk. It was an attractive place to settle. In winter, snow-covered highlands and lakes frozen to ice offered the possibility of overland travel to inland routes not accessible in the summer. Yet the southern ocean currents ensured that the fjord did not freeze over, even in the bitterest chill of winter air.

Everyone was full aware that the Trønder people balked when they felt a leader was unjust in any way. So when the chieftains traveled to the assembly, they armed themselves and brought both free men and thralls, swelling their numbers. By the time Olaf arrived, there was a host of people—most with weapons.

Undaunted, he addressed them: "I ask you to accept the god of the White Kristr and to put away your worship of idols and heathen gods."

He hardly got the words out of his mouth when the loud voice of a landowner rang out. "Olaf, son of Tryggve! We know you are the foster son of Ethelred the English king."

There was a rumble of derisive laughter from the crowd, but Olaf ignored it.

The landowner continued. "Keep silent, or you will be set upon and driven away from this place. This is how we treated Hákon the Good, also the foster child of an English king, when he demanded that we convert. And we do not value you higher than we did him!"

All together, they displayed their weapons. Olaf knew he had to make a decision. He quickly altered the tone of his voice, and he flashed his distinctive smile.

"Yes, of course, you are right. You are correct to honor the gods of your ancestors and follow their rituals and laws in every way. I wish to be in good relationship with you all. I will come to your midsummer meeting and observe your customs."

The group decided that the midsummer meeting would take place inside the fjord at Mærin and that all the chieftains and influential landowners should attend, as was their custom. Olaf was to come too.

And so as midsummer approached, Olaf's ships came to lay anchor at Mærin. There were thirty vessels in all.

Plus one.

Arn of Bergen had unwittingly sailed into the middle of this massive struggle of wills. He was not on a long trade. He had come merely to discuss possible trade relations and to inquire about the best men to do some delicate refurbishing of his knarr. But as soon as he entered the area where the Nidelva emptied into the sea, Olaf's men set upon his trading ship.

"Look here!" protested Arn. "I have come to this place on a trading venture. I am not from this area—I am from Bergen."

"We have orders from Olaf, our king, to confiscate any vessels that enter here."

"Confiscate? You have no right—"

"We are in particular need of traders, for our need for supplies is great." This reply was made offhand. And it was all the explanation Arn would get as men boarded his ship as if he did not exist.

Arn had no desire to become part of Olaf's entourage, but he had no choice. He had only a few men on his crew, and Olaf's bondsmen were many and strong and exceedingly well armed.

The king's fleet needed provisioning ships, and Arn's vessel served that purpose very well. The sturdy trader was emptied and then filled to the gunnels with a singular cargo—nothing but casks of mead. As instructed, Arn expertly sailed his knarr up to Mærin, along with the rest of Olaf's fleet.

Once they arrived, King Olaf himself supervised the unloading of the mead and its distribution to the landowners of the district. Olaf took note of Arn's bearing and Arn's ability to assert silent ownership of the vessel, even as Olaf's men swarmed over it. He liked what he saw and pulled Arn to one side.

"Can you hold your mead?"

"What?"

"I repeat, can you hold your mead?" said Olaf, growing a little impatient.

Arn ran his fingers back through his hair and considered how to respond. This would be tremendous fun, or it would end very badly for him. He decided there was only one way to answer.

"Of course! Why do you ask?"

"I am in need of someone to match me in a drinking contest."

"And what do I receive for staying with you, swallow by swallow?"

"What do you wish?"

Arn placed his nose directly in front of Olaf's handsome face. "Only this—that wherever I or my family go, we will have your protection."

"Done!"

The promise was sealed with a vigorous hand shake.

That night, everyone gathered in the great meeting house. The contest began, with Arn matching Olaf, horn for horn. But each time one of them took a drink, all men at the assembly took also. By the end, Olaf and

Arn were still standing, but the others had drunk twice as much as they. They all had passed out or were on their way to doing so.

King Olaf was usually very generous in providing mead for his own men, and therefore he was very popular. But none of the landowners noticed that his men had stayed on their ships. And no mead was shared on board that night.

The next morning, the chieftains were very hungover. The sound of sodden snoring filled the air. Sleeping bodies were scattered carelessly wherever the landowners had fallen in their drunkenness.

Olaf had Mass sung before him. After, he ordered the horns blown to summon the men for the Thing. The chieftains slowly stumbled into the assembly hall. On a signal, all of Olaf's crew quietly left their ships and positioned themselves around the perimeter of the great wooden building.

The assembly opened with the recitation of prayers to Odinn, Freyja, and Thor.

Then Olaf spoke to the people: "When we met before, I asked you to become baptized. But you refused. So I agreed that we should meet here and return again to ways of the old gods. That I am prepared to do."

There was much agreement among the chieftains that Olaf had quite rightly made the proper decision: they would be allowed to live with their ancient beliefs and defy the ways of the converted king.

Olaf continued. "But if I am to remain true to the old gods, then I must sacrifice with you. And there shall be a sacrifice that is the greatest of all—the sacrifice of men."

The general agreement in the crowd now changed to murmurings of concern.

"And I will not select for this sacrifice ordinary thralls or criminals—I shall select prominent men." Olaf then called out the names, one by one, of the six most notable chieftains of the entire region.

Olaf's men, who had surrounded the hall, now stepped into the building and blocked the two entrances. Olaf ordered them to seize and bind the chieftains immediately.

"I shall sacrifice these men to ensure peace and a fruitful season."

It was clear to the landowners that Olaf's men were stronger and more numerous than their forces. There was only one choice to be made. The chieftains agreed to be baptized—they and all their households. They took an oath to Olaf and renounced sacrifice to their fathers' gods. Olaf did not release the chieftains until they provided him their sons, brothers, or other close relations. The cunning Olaf held them as hostages, to ensure the chieftains' pledges would not be broken.

But some men did escape baptism.

Arn watched carefully for his opportunity. In the chaos of the day, Arn and his small crew sailed quietly away on his empty knarr, without the White Kristr priests sprinkling the waters of baptism over them.

CHAPTER FOURTEEN

The journey to Rome via the Sea of Darkness

Brand and Oswald eagerly set sail with other pilgrims journeying to Rome. Their captain was familiar with the risks of travel to such places. He had successfully survived sudden storms and attacks from multiple enemies. His manner reminded Brand of Arn of Bergen, except that this captain was a devout and disciplined follower of the Jesu the Christ, as was every member of the crew.

Brand found the voyage exciting, and he relished every day of the journey.

"Oswald, come here—you must see this!" Brand would call enthusiastically to his companion.

But Oswald was deathly ill from the very beginning. Even his most potent herbs did little to combat his seasickness.

They sailed south to Rouen, then on to Nantes and Bordeaux, down to the isthmus of España, to A Coruña, Santiago de Compostela, and Lisbon. They continued on to the Caliphate of Córdoba, ruled by a man the Christians called Almanzor; his power within all of Al-Andalous was absolute.

For a fee paid to Almanzor's representatives, the sea travelers were granted permission to pass through the narrow straights, past the land known as the Rock of Ṭāriq, into the large, warm inland sea. They were two days on their way to the isle of Sicily when their lookout spotted another vessel, very close by and racing ever closer.

It was a ship as the pilgrims had never seen before: long and low and very light in the water, with a great white expanse of sail. They strained their eyes for some sign of the origin of the ship. They saw no flags, banners, or markings. And certainly, no crosses.

There were rowers, two for each oar, their backs strained against the water. Two dozen men with black beards and white wrappings around their heads held knives and swords at the ready.

The inland sea had long been a home for raiders—the Egyptians, the Phoenicians, and the Greeks. The Romans had initiated a furious and successful effort to rid the waters of all them. But as their empire declined, plundering increased. And with the conquests of the followers of Mohamet, the sea was once more a very dangerous place.

"Pirates!" shouted the captain of the pilgrims' ship. "Prepare for battle!"

Within minutes, the pirate ship was alongside. The leader of the pirates called out in his Arabic tongue, "Are you traveling under protection? If so, show me your documentation!"

The captain of the pilgrim ship understood the pirate's question. Had the captain held up papers with the seals and ribbons in the colors of Almanzor, the pirate ship would have sailed quietly away. Such was the power of ruler of the caliphate. But the pilgrims had no such papers.

The captain called back, "We are traveling under the protection of the Lord God Almighty and his Son, Christ the Redeemer, who preserves us from all evil!"

No more words were exchanged. The attackers grappled the two ships together with chains and iron hooks. They began to board by jumping across the narrow gap between the vessels, all the while filling the air with murderous shouts.

Brand and Oswald had traveled with no weapons to defend themselves. They had put all their fate into the hands of God. But when the fighting began and a wounded pilgrim breathed his last and dropped his sword, Brand immediately picked it up. He began to slash and stab as many attackers as he could reach. Oswald watched on in double horror at the carnage around him as well as Brand's violent efforts.

The fighting was brief and, for the pirates, hugely effective. The crew of the pilgrims' ship fell first, followed by the first mate and captain. Before long, the pirates took all the passengers prisoner, including Brand and Oswald. They stripped the corpses of their clothing, then indifferently threw them over the side. Then the victors began to rummage through the ship's stores. Brand worried what would become of the precious letters to the Holy Father, while Oswald worried over his books of remedies and his pouches of herbs and seeds.

The prisoners sat grouped together, waiting for death and silently staring toward the horizon. At length, a man came and offered them food and water. Brand bowed his head in silent prayer and gratitude that he still lived. As he looked at the food before him, he suddenly realized they would not be executed. But as he gazed at everything and everyone on the ship, he was not sure his fate would be less troubling.

The pirates added the prisoners to the group of oarsmen who had rowed with speed to overtake their ship. The speed had not come without extreme effort. The oarsmen's backs gave mute testament to the use of the lash.

Some of the prisoners had ebony black skin and hair as tightly curled as wool. They were the exotic Blue Men the Norsemen described in stories when they returned from plunder in the south. Other rowers had straight black hair. There was no gray, for no man could endure the rigor of such a life for long.

Brand was placed next to a brown-eyed man whose dark skin had been made even darker by days in the sun. Oswald was placed in a section behind Brand, so they had few opportunities to see or communicate with each other.

Almost immediately, Brand was expected to row in sync with the stranger beside him. For the first few hours, Brand and the other man had to focus all their combined efforts on keeping up with the cadence of the drum. They soon fell into rhythm, exchanging glances and nods to silently coordinate their movements. Brand knew he was struggling and worried about how Oswald was doing.

As the sun fell beneath the waves, the rowing ceased and a period of rest began. Brand was exhausted—mentally, physically, and emotionally. But he was desperate to speak to the man beside him.

Brand tried words in all the languages he could think of—his native Norse, the language of the English and the Germanic peoples. Nothing provoked a positive response. His oar mate too tried different languages: Arabic and the languages of León and Castile. Brand concentrated mightily on each sound coming from the mouth of the dark man.

Finally, both grew silent. They were each saddened by the thought that the man whose body was so close it seemed very nearly part of his own would be a stranger. If it were true, as the heathen Norse believed, that luck above all determined a man's fate in life, then Brand had found little luck with his oar mate.

CHAPTER FIFTEEN

THE NIGHT PASSED. BRAND DESIRED SLEEP but was unable to ignore the other prisoners' pitiful moans and groans. The next day brought bright sunlight and a meager portion of bread and brackish water.

Brand started his morning with prayers, as he always did. He began to repeat the words of the Pater Noster quietly to himself.

Suddenly, his oar mate fairly leaped up against the ankle chains that bound him. The dark-skinned man smiled. Then he laughed—his mouth open and his white teeth flashing.

"Pater Noster! Pater Noster!" he repeated.

For a brief moment, Brand could not believe what he heard. Then it was Brand who smiled. It was Latin. Latin would be the bridge between the two prisoners.

Brand immediately interrogated his oar mate, whose name was Ibn Beshir. "Are you alone here?" he asked in a low voice.

"Yes," came the reply. "Most of my shipmates were killed immediately. Those who were left survived only a few days."

"How long ago were you taken?"

"A few weeks. I saw you and the other man when you were captured. You are like all the Norsemen, tall as date palms, blond and ruddy. Your friend is not as tall and is slender like a marsh reed. His hair—what there is of it—is dark. Is he a man of the north?"

"He is an Englishmen, not Norse. But we are brothers because we serve the same god."

The oar mate nodded, having already deduced that the new prisoners followed the prophet Jesu.

Brand continued with his questions. "Do you know what they mean to do with us?"

"I do not know. Some, such as me, are meant to be held for ransom. Others are meant to be kept or sold as slaves. Will anyone try to ransom you?"

"No. We are not men of wealth. No one will pay for our liberty. And you—will someone ransom you?"

"I do not know. I pray to Allah that it will be so. These cursed men have asked me many questions regarding my family and the reason for my journey. I am sure they intend to make it known that I can be freed for a price."

"How long do you think it will be until you are ransomed?"

"When, I do not know. I may well be dead before that time."

Seeing the concern on Brand's face, Ibn Beshir decided to change the subject. "You handle a sword well."

Brand's use of the sword was already weighing heavily on his heart. He knew the words of Jesu, that if you were struck on the cheek, you should offer the other to the attacker. But he also knew of the writings of Saint Paul, who indicated that taking up the sword for self-defense was permissible. He also knew his teachers back in Winchester would have wanted him to refrain from violence. And as a priest, they would hold him to a higher standard.

"I was wrong to do it. It was a sin. I have confessed to God for forgiveness."

"This I do not understand. It is a sin to kill your enemy so he does not kill you?"

"I must resist evil. I have sworn to be a follower of Jesu, a man of peace. I failed in my promise."

This confession of failure was the first of many things about Brand that puzzled the brown-skinned man.

During the days that followed, the two filled their time with the utmost exchange of information possible. At night, when navigation was too dangerous, they could rest, each one lying exhausted in his own space on the ship's damp and fetid floor. Conversation did not extend beyond a few fleeting words until they heard the snoring of their guards. Then they could explore any and all topics, limited only by the search for the right Latin word or phrase.

The two captives felt a reciprocal need to share as much as possible about themselves, their knowledge, and their beliefs. Each one knew instinctively that a man with a free mind is never really a captive. Their conversations could not remove their chains, but made them lighter.

Ibn Beshir had been trained in medicine by one of the most famous doctors in the world, Abū al-Qāsim, who lived in the Caliphate of Córdoba. Ibn Beshir was traveling from the city of Córdoba to Granada, then on to Valencia by sea.

Like Brand, he was carrying important documents. And also like Brand, he had been sent away from his home during childhood. At the age of seven, Ibn Beshir was sent to Córdoba for education.

"It was there that I learned to read and write in Arabic and in Latin," he said. "There I met Abū al-Qāsim. At first, I was in awe of him. But then, as time went on, he became like a father to me. Well, not only to me—he called all his students his children. His students followed him each morning as he met with the sick, diagnosed their problems, and instructed on therapies. Each afternoon, we retired to the library, and each advanced student worked under his direction on a segment of his medical treatise. When I was captured, I was carrying two copies of the treatise, thirty chapters in all."

Brand was fascinated. "Tell me more about your teacher."

"He taught me many things. First was the importance of a positive doctor-patient relationship. I observed how he unfailingly spoke of healing and curing, even when such a possibility was remote for a patient. He knew it would help to give the patient hope, and it did. He spent time with each patient as an individual—asking questions, inspecting the body—in order to make the best diagnosis."

Brand also asked Ibn Beshir about the use of plants and other materials to make medicine. The physician knew about several plants, including cumin, dill, thyme, sage, and oregano. But sharing knowledge was difficult as Brand did not recognize the names of the plants, and they had no way of touching, seeing, or tasting the herbs to clarify the information.

Brand hoped he could somehow share what he learned with Oswald. He yearned to be able to converse freely with Oswald, but the arrangements on the ship made it difficult. The belly of the ship was filled with rowers on each side, facing front, with a narrow aisle between.

Oswald was not doing well. In the dark, he would shriek and wake everyone with his night terrors. Oswald's place was several rows behind Ibn Beshir and Brand. He could see the two having lengthy conversations. Sometimes he could hear and understand the Latin phrases. He was becoming filled with jealousy. Oswald and his own oar mate could communicate only with crude gestures and grunts.

Not all the talk between Ibn Beshir and Brand was of medicine. Ibn Beshir often spoke of the beautiful women he had known. With detailed and vivid recall, he described their beautiful skin, flowing hair, soft lips, and the touch of their delicate hands.

"Do you not think of women?" asked a curious Ibn Beshir. He had expected Brand to share his own stories of the joys of women.

"Yes," answered Brand truthfully. "But I have made a vow of celibacy."

"What? You will not ever take a woman as wife or even as a concubine? I do not understand."

And even after Brand tried his best to explain, Ibn Beshir still shook his head. He was amazed that the Christian men and women believed that their god would create in them such strong and powerful feelings, then expect them to refrain from expressing them.

CHAPTER SIXTEEN

I T DID NOT TAKE BRAND LONG to understand the Arabic orders the captors shouted to the prisoners. One phrase he heard many times, but he knew it was not an order. That phrase was *Allah u akbar*.

"Ibn Beshsir, what does this mean, Allah u akbar?"

"*Allah* is the word for our god. The words together mean 'Allah is greater.'"

"Greater than what?"

"Greater than anything or anyone. Greater than any other god. Greater than *your* god."

Brand did not agree that any god was greater than his own, but he decided to wait until another time to discuss that with Ibn Beshir. Then another question occurred to him.

"How do you say 'God is great'?"

"That is easy, but not so often used: *Allahu kebir.*"

Allahu kebir, Brand repeated to himself. Yes, this was a phrase he could say and believe, the words from his own mouth.

One religious ritual affected nearly everyone on the vessel: salah, the obligatory prayers. Five times a day, the captors would line up in an easterly direction, prostrate themselves foreheads down, and recite prayers. The prisoners were also required to face east and bow down while the prayers were recited. Brand tried as hard as he could to ignore the prayers of the men around him. He did not understand many of the words or what the ritual meant. He worried he would disrespect his own faith, so instead he recited his Pater Noster in silence with all his concentration and intensity.

One time, after the final prayers of the day, Brand decided to ask about something that particularly confounded him.

"Ibn Beshir, how can these men pray when they are criminals, pirates who have killed and kidnapped so many and are holding us now?"

"These men are evildoers, to be sure. But they see themselves merely engaged in commerce. They pray because they consider themselves believers. The prophet Mohamet said the difference between the believers and the disbelievers is prayer. Prayer is the second of the five pillars of my religion. Consider the five pillars like a contract, or agreement, between the believer and Allah. The believer must fulfill his part of the bargain, or he is in violation of the contract."

"And what happens if a follower of Mohamet does not perform the prayers?"

"If a follower deliberately neglects prayer, and never makes it up, and never asks for forgiveness before he dies, he may very well go to hell." Then Ibn Beshir added, "But Allah knows best and can forgive whomever he wills for any reason he chooses."

The galley ship did not spend every day on the great inland sea, looking for ships to prey upon. The pirates would sometimes make port to put out the news of the high-value captives they hoped would be ransomed. Docking also allowed them to make minor repairs and resupply.

One day when they made port, an incident occurred that would change many lives forever.

The captors herded the captives from the docks into a small building. The prisoners would remain there until the ship was again ready to sail. The strangeness of walking on stable footing made the captives' legs tremble. They struggled to keep their balance on the wharf. Oswald's oar mate suddenly lurched and fell into the water with a tremendous splash.

Despite his captivity, he was still a strong man and worth saving, so the pirates struggled to fish him out of the water and onto the wharf. But by then, the man's lips were purplish blue and he was not breathing.

"He is dead!" Oswald cried out.

The pirates immediately began calculating the cost of the loss of this slave.

Suddenly, Ibn Beshir was kneeling next to the man. Brand helped roll the lifeless body onto its back. The doctor placed his ear over the man's chest.

"There are no breath sounds," he pronounced. "Help me, Brand! Hold his head so the windpipe is not bent."

Brand knelt down at the man's head. He tipped the man's chin up and gently pulled his neck straight.

Ibn Beshir clasped his fingers tight over the man's nose. He placed his mouth over the man's mouth and began to blow short puffs of air into it. He made a series of quick pushes directly over the man's still heart. Then he repeated the cycle of actions.

Oswald watched as the scene unfolded. He became agitated and began to shout.

"Father Brand, what you are doing? This is forbidden. Only God can alter the boundary between life and death. This is blasphemy!"

Brand ignored him, as did Ibn Beshir, who continued the exhalations and compressions.

Oswald had now worked himself into frenzy. Brand had to use a free arm to push the outraged Oswald away from the drowned man.

"Would you have us let him die?" Brand asked in exasperation.

At first, there was no response from the man, only stillness. Then a mouthful of greenish water gushed from the side of his mouth. His chest began to move. The man had revived and was breathing on his own.

All around them, the observers stood in silent awe, their jaws slack and mouths open. Even Oswald was quiet.

Ibn Beshir put his ear to the man's chest again and listened. "Cough!" he said to man.

The bewildered man coughed.

"Cough again. If there is still water inside your lungs, it will become stale, and you will yet die."

As instructed, the man coughed again.

Oswald turned on Brand and hissed in English, "This is blasphemy!"

"The prophet Elisha revived a child by breathing life into its mouth," countered Brand.

But Oswald was unmovable. "No. That was an example of divine power, not for humans to emulate. To intervene between life and death, that is the exclusive realm of God!"

Ibn Beshir, who understood none of the words said between Brand and Oswald, pulled the drowned man up to his feet. He said quietly, "Allahu akbar."

Yes, said Brand to himself. *Allahu kebir. God is great.*

CHAPTER SEVENTEEN

A FTER THE REVIVAL OF THE DROWNED MAN, the pirates realized they had a hostage of even greater worth. Ibn Beshir could fetch a larger ransom. The pirates intensified their efforts to let it be known that they had a high-value prisoner. They waited for rescuers to appear.

In the meantime, the captors made use of this newly discovered healer. Whenever anyone on the ship needed care, Ibn Beshir was summoned away from his oarsman duties. He would listen to the heart, the belly, touch the skin, tap on the body, and smell breath and urine. He recommended rest or water cures, and sometimes he performed minor surgeries. He asked for more food and more rest for all the captives, but the pirates were unmoved by his pleadings.

Brand watched Ibn Beshir as closely as possible.

"You take as much care with the lowliest of captives as you do with the leader of the pirates. You care for us, even though we are dirty, stinking, and sometimes dying."

"I do so because I am a student of my teacher, and he emphasized the importance of treating all patients equally."

"This teacher," said Brand, "it seems to me that in some ways, he lived the life Jesu requires, to love all without exception."

The physician nodded. "Yes. In that way, they are the same."

It was not long after this that Oswald's health worsened. Oswald's self-imposed privations back in Winchester had left a legacy of physical weakness. He had little stamina, and eventually his body just gave out.

Nothing, not even Ibn Beshir's attentions, could help him. He fell into a coma and simply stopped breathing.

Brand deeply lamented that he had not been able to offer Oswald confession nor anoint him with oil as a final sacrament. Ibn Beshir and Brand were tasked with moving Oswald's body from the belly of the ship to the deck. Oswald's body was so light, a girl could have done it.

The herbalist's rags were deemed worthless; they were not even taken from his lifeless body. The pirates casually flung it overboard into the deep. Brand watched as the body—nothing but bones and skin—plummeted down into the depths until he could see it no more. He remembered what he could of the ritual prayers and prayed for Oswald's soul. And his own.

Brand did not realize how much he would miss Oswald, even the scoldings and screams in the night. Brand yearned for the sacred texts to help him in his struggle to survive. He recalled the feel of the paper, the dark ink at the tip of a feather quill as he would sit copying precious texts back in Winchester.

Sometimes he despaired. He thought of the teachings of Ælfheah— that our own suffering helps us move closer to Christ and understand the suffering he experienced on the cross. "This suffering gives us immense spiritual knowledge and power. Never flee from it, Brand," Ælfheah had taught him.

Brand and Ibn Beshir continued to discuss their beliefs about God. Sometimes they found common ground. Other times, a rift as wide as the sky is high separated them.

There was one spiritual figure who provided some surprises. It was Mary.

"Yes," explained Ibn Beshir, "Mary is the only woman mentioned by name in the Qu'ran. And she was a virgin when she gave birth to Jesu."

The virgin birth? Brand was astonished to learn of Ibn Beshir's casual acceptance of this essential tenet of his own belief.

Ibn further explained: "It was a miracle. Allah breathed his spirit into her while she was yet chaste. In our teachings, she is one of the most revered of all women, and we honor her in many ways."

Brand was still trying to absorb what this follower of Mohamet had just told him, when Ibn Beshir added, "But we do not believe that she or her son were divine."

"Who do you think Jesu was?" asked Brand.

"We are taught that he was a prophet, like Moses or Abraham," he replied in a matter-of-fact tone.

Brand responded with his own tenets. "We are taught that God desires all to be saved and come to the knowledge of the truth: that there is one god; and that there is also one mediator between God and humankind, Jesu the Christ, himself human and divine, who gave himself as a ransom for all."

"Hmm. A ransom." Ibn Beshir smiled wryly at the irony. "These pirates know that process very well."

For a few moments, Ibn Beshir stared out over the blue waters that surrounded them, his brown eyes squinting in the sun. He continued, "The followers of Mohamet are taught that the Torah and Gospels are from God, but these writings have become corrupted."

Everything inside Brand urged him to confront what he believed was a grievous error. But he decided against it. With enough time, Ibn Beshir would see things differently, just as Brand himself had. Brand decided to make an observation instead.

"In your religion, the focus is on the obedience, that the love of Allah is conditional. We are taught that we have God's grace unconditionally."

"Obedience is important. Our obedience is how we show Allah our respect."

"I understand respect," Brand replied. "I was taught about respect from an early age, as I knew many gods, the gods of the people of the north. But when I learned about the life and teachings of Jesu, I changed how I believed."

Brand continued, this time with a question for Ibn Beshir.

"Is it true that the punishment for those who follow Allah but change in their hearts and decide to follow the Jesu, is death?"

Ibn Beshir nodded.

"Does that not trouble you?"

"There is no god but Allah, and Mohamet is his messenger. To reject the teachings of Mohamet is the ultimate insult to Allah, and death is an appropriate punishment," Ibn replied without an ounce of uncertainty.

Ibn Beshir was sure of his beliefs and unmoved, as was Brand. This conversation ended. But each man was still naturally inquisitive. They continued to try to learn from each other on many other occasions.

"Brand," Ibn Beshir once said, "there is something that confuses me about the concept of three gods in one. You say there is but one god. But this god is in three parts—a father god, a son god, and a spirit god."

"Not gods, but *persons*."

"Still, I do not understand. You say that your god sent his son to earth to live as a man yet still be a god."

"Yes."

To Ibn Beshir, such a concept seemed to confirm that Brand was slightly insane. Or most certainly, that he was a confused infidel. He glanced at Brand—his face revealing all of his thoughts.

Brand understood the look and sighed. Oh, how he wished he had better command of Latin, or that he had books to aid him, or that Prior Simeon could be with him to guide him with his wisdom. In the end, all he could do was speak his own truth.

"It is a mystery, Ibn Beshir. A mystery."

CHAPTER EIGHTEEN

WEEKS PASSED, THEN MONTHS. IF the reality of God was in the power to answer prayer and rescue petitioners, then surely Brand's White Kristr and Ibn Beshir's Allah had abandoned them both.

The prisoners had become friends, with a genuine affection for one another. They each silently noted that the other was becoming slightly weaker as their captivity wore on.

"Brand, what do you know about dreams?" asked Ibn Beshir one day.

This question startled Brand. He had not told Ibn Beshir of his ability to sometimes foretell future events by the information in his own dreams.

"Why do you ask?"

"I had a strange dream," said Ibn Beshir, "and it was about you."

Brand's interest was piqued, and he leaned closer to hear what his oar mate had to say.

"Here is what I remember," Ibn Beshir said. "You are sailing in a ship. But it is not a ship of the Christian pilgrims. Nor is it a galley. The other people on the ship are not of your kind, nor of mine. But they see you as their leader. I think, perhaps, that the dream means you will someday sail to the east, to the Indies, and be with the people who live there."

"I do not think that will be, Ibn Beshir. I may die on these waters, as did Brother Oswald. And even if I do not, I must return to my home in Winchester and be a priest to the people there."

Just as Brand was about to ask what the ship looked like, a shout rang out from a lookout. An Arab ship approached. It was clear that the crews of the new ship and the pirate ship were equally matched in strength.

The captain of the approaching vessel called out, "We have heard you have the physician Ibn Beshir among you. Is this so?"

The pirates replied by immediately bringing Ibn Beshir up from below so he could be seen.

A man aboard the Arab ship took one look at Ibn Beshir, then whispered to the captain. It only took one look for Ibn Beshir, in turn, to recognize the man. It was his brother.

"We have heard you will trade him for ransom," shouted the rescuers.

"Yes, that is true."

"We have come to take him. We have the money."

Ibn Beshir immediately began to shout with joy. "Allah be praised! Allah be praised!"

Brand heard this exchange and understood all of it. His heart sank. He wanted to feel only happiness that his friend would be released. But the moment he had dreaded had come: now he would be alone on this vessel with no human friend. The only person he could speak with, the only person who had kept him sane, was leaving.

The rescuers pulled closer alongside the pirate ship. The exchange of money was a delicate matter. All hands on both ships were at the ready for any treachery. The captain of the pirate ship climbed aboard the rescue ship. Ibn Beshir would be allowed to go aboard to his waiting brother only when the pirate captain had his chest of coins.

The pirate inspected the contents of the box handed to him, then shouted to his comrades, "I am ready to reboard. The prisoner may be released!"

Ibn Beshir was supposed to step onto his ship of freedom just as the pirate returned to the floating prison ship. But the newly freed man did not move.

"What is wrong with you, my brother? Come aboard!" his brother shouted. Though the two ships were close, it was sometimes difficult to understand words over the winds and waves and incessant creaking of the planks and rigging.

Ibn Beshir shouted back, "You must ransom my oar mate too."

"Who?"

"My oar mate, the Norseman."

At this point, the pirates understood that they had yet another prize, so they brought Brand out into the sunshine of the deck. Everyone stared at the tall man with blond hair.

"What? Why? Is he your slave?" Ibn Beshir's brother shouted back.

"No, he is not my slave."

"Tell me he is a follower of Mohamet."

"No, he is not a follower of Mohamet."

Ibn Beshir's brother struck his own forehead in frustration. "He is in infidel? Then, why?"

"What?" Ibn Beshir strained to hear.

"Then, *why?*" shouted his exasperated brother.

The boats were nearly touching now, and the wind had briefly calmed, so Ibn Beshir could speak to his brother without shouting.

"Because Allah has shown me that he is a holy man of peace. And someday all the north lands will be under the rule of the followers of Mohamet. London, Paris, even the cold lands to the north. And all who live there will say, 'There is no god but Allah, and Mohamet is his messenger.' It will be better if there is someone among them who knows our language and the teachings of our Prophet."

Ibn Beshir stood still, waiting.

Finally, his brother turned to the pirate captain. "I will pay only one-twentieth of what we paid for my brother—the cost of an ordinary slave."

The pirate captain knew this was but a pittance, but one Norseman was already dead, and this one was growing weaker. And it was unlikely anyone else would offer more in a slave market.

"Agreed," said the pirate leader. "You can have them both."

And so, the exchange was done. As Ibn Beshir stepped onto his brother's rescue ship, right behind him stepped the Norseman, tall as a date palm.

"Do not worry," said Ibn Beshir, his face filled with a smile. "You and I have been prisoners long enough. I will do everything in my power to see that you have your freedom and never be a slave again."

"Yes, God is great," said Brand. Then he fell to his knees in utter gratitude to his god.

CHAPTER NINETEEN

BRAND NEVER MADE HIS WAY TO JERUSALEM—or even to Rome. The letters he was to deliver had long been lost.

Ibn Beshir was true to his word, helping Brand journey to the relative safety of Sicily, where they parted ways. They stood facing each other, a hand on the other's shoulder, for a final farewell.

"May we meet again in peace, Ibn Beshir," said Brand.

"Allah u akbar," replied his oar mate and friend.

From Sicily, Brand joined a group of pilgrims returning to the lands of the north. He delighted in hearing of the places they had seen and the sacred sights they had visited. He longed to have seen them as well—to have walked the roads Saint Peter walked and to have prayed in the holy places.

But these dreams were not to be fulfilled, at least not then. First, he needed to return to England. It took him almost a year from the day he said farewell to Ibn Beshir. Along the way, he had to depend upon the hospitality of strangers and endure uncertain food and shelter and endless walking. Though nourishment was always limited, it was in better quality and variety than what he had received in captivity. Slowly he regained health.

It was raining the day he saw Winchester again, just as it had been raining that day years before, when he first found his new home, his new community, and his new god.

He was greeted with shouts of joy and everyone calling out his name in the excitement. Ælfheah opened his thin arms to give Brand a huge embrace, and Brand held his bishop close, in friendship and relief.

"You have returned—thanks be to our merciful Lord! I could scarcely believe it when I heard the news," said Ælfheah. "We never ceased to pray for your safe return, even when the months passed and we had no news of you. What of your companion, Brother Oswald?"

Brand shook his head. "Our ship was attacked. He was enslaved, as was I. But he was not physically strong." Then he added, "Oswald never wavered in his faith."

"We will pray for his soul. Come now—refresh yourself. We will talk later."

After a few days had passed, and Brand had eaten and washed and regained some strength, he and Ælfheah settled in for a real discussion.

"I had hoped, Father Brand, that your travels would teach you about life. Tell me, what have you learned in your travels?"

"Many things, many things," said Brand, his eyes searching the space around him, as if to recall unseen memories. "I observed great heroism. And great cruelty. And great mercy. I have learned that participation in forced religious ritual is no conversion. While I was a slave, the circumstances required that I do as the followers of Mohamet and prostrate myself for prayers. Many times a day, my body was bowed toward Mecca. Each moment I touched my head to the ground, I thought only of the Triune God."

"Your faith has been tested. Has your faith been strengthened?"

"Yes, my bishop."

"And you still remember your promises of faith, obedience, and chastity?"

"Yes, and I will honor them all my days here in Winchester."

"You shall not stay here for long."

The shock of this announcement made Brand stop breathing in surprise. "What do you mean?"

"Bishop Grimkell has asked that I send someone to assist him in Trondheim. You understand the language of the Norse, so you will be a great help to him. Olaf Tryggvason is there, and he is in need of instruction. Do you remember him?"

"Yes, of course," answered Brand, recalling the charismatic Olaf and the efforts to negotiate with and instruct him in the faith. "How could anyone forget him?"

Ælfheah continued, "You will soon hear much of his activities to convert all the people of the north. He is a bold leader, a skilled warrior, and as cruel as any heathen in his zeal. He has no real understanding of the teachings of the Christ. At times, he has used his athletic skills as a tool of persuasion. He has used trickery as well, threatening to sacrifice chieftains, not slaves—they were his most powerful opponents."

Brand felt the sting of memories of his father in Uppsala. He easily imagined the chieftains' fearful reaction to King Olaf's threats.

"Olaf's ways do not follow the ways of Jesu," Ælfheah observed with some sadness. "Heathens are rational humans who will convert to Christianity if Christianity is preached peacefully and with love. Bishop Grimkell is with Olaf, but he cannot control him. Grimkell needs help so that Olaf will have a real understanding of Christianity, which will lead to true conversions."

Brand had not anticipated this new assignment, nor was he sure he was ready for it—in body or spirit. But he replied as his vow of obedience required.

"Yes, my bishop. I will go where you send me. May the Holy Spirit guide me."

Once again, Brand was being sent away from Westminster, which he had believed would be his home forever.

Ælfheah blessed and prayed over and for Brand as he began his journey to the court of the great King Olaf Tryggvason. Ælfheah was certain that the priest knew that real conversion would never occur through force or violent means. And that if anyone could influence the reckless Olaf, it would be Brand.

CHAPTER TWENTY

Bergen

SEVERAL YEARS HAD PASSED SINCE ARN, the intrepid trader, and Brand had bid each other good-bye. While Brand had spent the years in study and in captivity, Arn had settled, awkwardly, into the life of a farmer with his little family—Ragnhild and Kathleen. Despite their trying, Ragnhild had not conceived.

Kathleen had grown from a child into a new creature. She was beautiful—it must be said. She was *auga-fagr*, having light eyes as blue as the sky on the brightest and coldest day of winter. Straight hair the color of ripe wheat spilled down to the middle of her back.

And at fourteen years, Kathleen was a fully formed woman. She could be married at such an age. Some of her friends had already become brides and quickly became pregnant. Arranged marriages were the best way to ensure a family's continued economic strength—and in some cases, to prevent or ease friction and feuds. But Arn had no intention of approving of marriage for his daughter until he was certain it was what she wanted.

Kathleen's beauty was not the usual kind. It was true that her features were regular and her mouth as soft and pink as rose petals. But she was not sweet and yielding, as was so often true among other girls her age. There was a determination in the tilt of her chin, an alertness in her eyes, and strength in her carriage and movement. She had something of the beauty of a falcon when it swoops and soars above dappled forest and shimmering water.

Another spring—long awaited and welcomed—had come again to Bergen. As the warmth stirred the trees and plants to a new season, so the sun's rays stirred old longings in Arn. He had been planning in secret until at last, Arn could no longer wait to announce his intentions.

It was midmorning on an early spring day. The strengthening sun had warmed the stones of the family courtyard. Kathleen was nearby, playing a solitary game of knucklebones while Ragnhild washed and cut Arn's hair. Kathleen knew her father and mother both especially enjoyed this little intimacy. She was vaguely aware of their murmuring voices and laughter.

Arn smiled as his wife used a clay pitcher to scoop warm water from a basin and pour it gently over his head. When she finished, she handed her husband a linen towel. Arn decided now would be a good time to tell of his plans. But he was wrong.

Kathleen's chin jerked with a jolt at the sound of the water pitcher on the flat courtyard stones. She watched as the water spread slowly among the scattered clay shards at her mother's feet. Ragnhild stood oddly still, motionless.

Then Ragnhild awoke from her shock.

"Husband, why must you go and forsake your home?" she demanded. "The sea can so easily take you into her cold embrace. And does the sea have arms to hold you as I do?"

"Ragnhild. Ragnhild, I . . ." Arn struggled to find words.

Kathleen's body tightened with apprehension as she watched the emotional scene between her parents unfold.

Her mother continued with her pleadings. "I know how many men die at sea. And if you are lucky—*if* you are lucky, Arn—your body will be found on the rocks, with green sea plants for your shroud, and on the land you will be buried!" Her eyes were dark with emotion.

"But I do have luck!" Arn exclaimed. He was desperate. "I must go. I must. If I do not, my mind will become sickened. I will be no good to you or to myself if I stay."

Ragnhild was fighting back tears. "Why? *Why?*"

"I know I can never make you understand." His arms quickly encircled Ragnhild's waist, and he pulled her tenderly close to him. "I will return within a year," he said, stroking her cheek. "And until I do, no other shall touch my hair. Do you understand? No other."

She said nothing, just stared at him, unable to fully take in his promise of fidelity.

"No other," he repeated, then kissed her soft and precious mouth with his own.

Ragnhild decided to waste no effort on further protest. No doubt Arn had already collected the crew and obtained their oaths of loyalty. She surrendered to his kisses and the strength of his arms around her—which would become memories to warm her when he was gone.

"This time, I will be away only for a year," Arn reassured her. "No more three-year absences for us. I promise: next summer, I will see you again. No more than that."

Arn had one more thought to help aid him in persuasion.

"And you and Kathleen will be entertained while I am gone. You will stay with King Olaf Tryggvason at court in Trondheim. The town is filled with converts, and you will not be lonely."

It was more than companionship that Arn wished for his family— it was security. Three years before, Olaf Trygvasson had established his court and founded his new town. Olaf's sharpest-eyed bondsmen stood as sentinels at all times. The presence of the bondsmen would ensure that his wife and daughter would be protected from unwanted male advances, another concern that weighed heavy on Arn's mind.

"Yes, Ragnhild. Only a year, and we will be all together—safe, again."

Kathleen watched in silence as her mother bowed her head in acceptance of Arn's intention.

Within a week, Arn's well-provisioned ship left Bergen with his loyal crew. He knew his route, he knew the trading towns he would visit, and he knew how long the trip should take.

What he did not know was that he left a tiny bit of himself behind, deep inside Ragnhild's womb.

CHAPTER TWENTY-ONE

Trondheim

I N THE LATE SPRING OF THE nine hundred ninety-ninth year since the birth of Christ, the northbound ship carrying Ragnhild and Kathleen sailed into the safe harbor at the mouth of the Nidelva. They had arrived at the royal compound of King Olaf Trygvasson.

In the beginning, Olaf's stronghold had simply been called Kaupangen, or "trading place," for it was but a hamlet without streets. Then it was called Nidaros, for the swirling Nidelva that framed its banks. And eventually, it became known as Trondheim. It had an excellent and sheltered harbor. The river made a hairpin turn and nearly circled around itself just before emptying into the embrace of the sea. This river-made peninsula, with its narrow end, was easily defended against land attacks.

As their ship sailed toward land, Ragnhild and Kathleen gazed in awe at the banks of the Nidelva, fringed with bobbing ships—Olaf's magnificent drakkar, crafted for war, as well as the traders' wide-bellied knarr. New vessels were being built in the ship sheds, and finished ships sat waiting on rollers, ready for launching.

Tents for the visiting chieftains had been erected on the blossoming hillsides and riverbank, and streaming flags fluttered energetically in the breeze. The entire area thronged with horsemen and hunters, noble chieftains and their women, and thralls for work and thralls for trade.

Birch willows sported their spring yellow-green colors along the riverbank. In the distance, flocks of sheep dotted the verdant hillsides. And men could be seen plowing the damp earth, its wondrous smell invigorating the spirits of everyone who had survived the long cold winter.

Despite the newness of the town, many buildings had already been built. Lumber was plentiful, and Olaf had made certain there were ample carpenters and wood-carvers to establish his royal compound.

Several longhouses had been built to shelter Olaf's royal court as well as the populace rapidly settling into the new town. The wooden rectangular buildings were all the same in functional design. If you stood inside and looked up, you saw exposed rafters; there was no ceiling. Fire pits were placed directly beneath holes in the roof so smoke and other vapors could rise upward and escape into the skies. The living areas had small window openings for light and air. Some windows had oiled cloth or the afterbirth membrane of newborn calves stretched over a frame. Others had wooden shutters.

The nostrils of all who entered a longhouse were assaulted with pungent smells: the smoky air, the smell of bits of uneaten food, the damp hair of the hounds. And menstrual blood. Unlike women in other cultures, women of the north did not separate themselves when it came time for their periodic flow. All of these odors were not repulsive but rather welcomed in the unconscious mind, for each one represented security and life.

King Olaf's longhouse was the largest. Wide benches lined the inside perimeter of the building, and there the courtiers would relax and sleep. The high seat dominated the room. Massive wooden support pillars, covered with exquisite carvings of fantastical animals and geometric designs, delighted all who visited the hall.

The main entrance to the longhouse had a small porch supported by square pillars to protect from rain and snow. Intricate carving made it appear that the posts were covered with elegant twisted braids. Here visitors would wait until they were permitted entrance into the interior of the longhouse. Inside, the most important speeches would be heard, stories would be told, and promises would be made—and of course, feasting, drinking, and occasional fighting.

There were many other buildings of utilitarian value in the compound—the kitchen and storehouse, and the bathhouse for bathing in water or with steam. The bondsmen had their own sleeping house, and there was a *gesta hus* for travelers and guests. The free women had their own special building where they met nearly every day for weaving and other tasks done more pleasantly in the presence of other females.

Sometimes in the quiet of night, some drunken rivalry would ensue among the tents of the visiting chieftains. Loud voices would grow louder. The sound of a flying object would be heard, followed by a groan.

Ragnhild and Kathleen had never before visited any town except Bergen and the tiny shore hamlets at which they had stopped on their journey to Trondheim. Ragnhild was somewhat overcome and subdued by all the activity, but Kathleen was delighted. She was fascinated by the sheer number of people living at Olaf's court. The volume of interesting and illustrious visitors kept her endlessly entertained.

Olaf Tryggvason honored his promise to Arn, welcoming the two women of Bergen and protecting them as family. He was, of course, the most powerful among all the men. His personal bondsmen were never far from sight. He held court in the high seat, with Thyre, his new wife of less than a year, at his side. She was his fourth wife.

Another who never was far from Olaf was Hallfredr, the skald of the court. Hallfredr was an unusually perceptive and sensitive poet, and his intelligence shown in his face. He knew how to read people, to discern their secrets. The Icelander knew how to use the power of words to persuade. He used words most cunningly, to bring honor to kings and to destroy the reputations of their enemies. For this skill, he was as much, or more, valued than a mighty warrior.

Olaf's large house dog, Vige, was there. No dog was ever smarter. Vige was so intelligent that when he was told to divide cattle among different owners, he proceeded to do so, without mistake or error, herding them into different paddocks. Vige was never forced to stay outside in the cold or rain like the other hounds. And when Olaf was in Trondheim, Vige always slept no more than a few feet from his master.

But sometimes Olaf would leave without Vige. On his return, Vige would race out to greet him, run deliriously in a large circle—first clockwise, then counterclockwise—before stopping breathlessly. Olaf would laugh and tell him, "Vige, you are the very best of dogs!" giving the canine's furry back a vigorous rub.

Olaf's bondsmen, when not traveling with the king, busied themselves with the maintenance of their weapons. No sword would be allowed to rust or deteriorate. To enhance the connection between weapon and owner, most swords were given a name. For what person would have a reliable friend with no name? Considerable thought went into the matter. Some of the favorite names were Leg Biter, Striker, and Serpent's Fang.

Bishop Grimkell—the Englishman of Danish blood—was there as well. He was a flighty and somewhat silly man with a puffy and perpetually pinkish face, but he attended selflessly to the ecclesiastical needs of the court and the visitors.

Kathleen quickly became a court favorite with her curiosity and intelligence. She demanded to remain with the adults while they played their *tafl* board games and discussed news from the traders.

She loved to sing—alone or with others—and her sweet voice was a constant presence during morning Mass. Her voice was as clear as an icicle formed during a winter thaw. Yet it was not cold; it was as warm as a May meadow, full of the hum of bees, with the larks providing the high notes. Her voice was musical honey for the ear.

Although the settlement was well positioned for defense, Olaf was always alert, keeping his bondsmen as sentries. The ever-present tension energized some people. But for others, the anxiety gnawed at them. At times, these types were irritable and mean, even with loved ones, without knowing why.

And for some—especially the elderly and some of the young women—there was something more: the persistent melancholy of the people of the north. The black companion ate at their hearts, magnified every sadness, and blunted every feeling of pleasure.

CHAPTER TWENTY-TWO

ONE EVENING JUST BEFORE THE SUMMER SOLSTICE, a ship sailed in from the sea, its anchor splashing noisily in the river just across from the busy town of Trondheim. Impatient travelers made ready to clamber into the ferry boats that would take them ashore. The long twilight gave sufficient light to guide them.

Grimkell ran down to the riverside to greet the newcomers. As soon as he saw the man in priestly robes, he waded right into the water, excited as a puppy. He shouted, "You are here! You have come!"

Grimkell embraced Brand enthusiastically. "Yes, Bishop Grimkell," said the obedient priest. "I have come in response to your message to the bishop at Winchester."

"I thank God for your safe journey! Please, please—come with me, and I will introduce you to the court."

Brand and the other travelers had a light meal and washed their bodies and hair clean of sea salt. Then they were taken to the great hall to meet Olaf and his queen.

"King Olaf, Father Brand has arrived!" shouted Grimkell, as excited as if Brand had just flown in on the wings of a giant raven.

Olaf, sitting on the high seat, lifted his hand, palm outward, in a gesture of official welcome. "I have not seen you since the days we spent with Ælfheah and Ethelward in the English court of King Ethelred. You are now a priest?"

"Yes, King Olaf. Bishop Grimkell sent a letter to Bishop Ælfheah saying he needed help with all the visitors here and the town's growing population. I am here to assist him and to attend to you and your court."

The king eyed the priest. "Father Brand, the years seem to have changed you. There is something different about you."

Brand knew Olaf was right, of course. So much had happened on his ill-fated journey to Rome. So much, that Brand himself had not had sufficient time to work it all out.

"Yes, it is true. I have encountered trials. But they have made my faith stronger."

"And strong it needs to be, for the heathens of this area are in need of immediate conversion," came the quick reply.

Olaf introduced his wife and other highborn members of his court. "My queen will introduce you to the other guests who are staying with me. Tomorrow we shall have a great feast in your honor."

Brand retired that evening to the gesta hus. Early the next morning, Queen Thyre took Brand through the compound. He asked first to see the chapel. They were on their way when a woman came out from a trail near the edge of the hamlet.

She was dressed in somber tones, her hair braided and modestly hidden under a pleated head covering. Brand noted that she carried herself with dignity, and though not a great beauty, she exuded compelling warmth.

"Father Brand, this is Ragnhild of Bergen," said Queen Thrye.

"Bergen? I once knew a trader from Bergen. His name was Arn," said Brand. "I sailed with him from Sigtuna to Aggersborg."

Ragnhild gave a broad smile. "You know my husband? Father Brand, I am so very glad to meet you!"

"And I as well. I heard much about you. Is Arn here?" asked Brand, looking around as if he could soon see his old acquaintance.

"No. He is on a trade journey but will return here next summer."

It made Ragnhild feel better to say aloud the promise her husband had made.

Brand searched his mind for other memories of his voyage with Arn. "And your daughter—her name was . . ."

"Kathleen."

"Yes, I remember now. Is she here with you?"

"Yes. She spends time everywhere and with everyone, so I never know where she is from dawn to dusk. I am sure you will meet her soon."

The queen brought Brand to the chapel, where Grimkell and Hallfredr waited. The king had ordered the skald to keep a sharp eye on Brand.

The group held a brief prayer service of thanksgiving. Afterward, Brand began settling in to the small area at the rear of the chapel. A sleeping space had been created there for him. Grimkell and Hallfredr helped with Brand's chests, bags, and other bundles. Nothing was his own; all were gifts sent with him by others. Brand carefully unwrapped a chalice to be used for the ceremony of Holy Mass—a gift from the priory at Winchester.

"Haloo!" cried a young woman's voice from the doorway. "My mother sent me. I have sweet grass and dried mountain flowers for the traveler's bed."

"Ah, yes. Come meet our new priest," said Grimkell with his usual enthusiasm. "Father Brand, this is Kathleen, daughter of Arn and Ragnhild of Bergen."

Brand turned and faced the doorway, his hands still holding the chalice as he saw Kathleen for the first time. Something inside of him stirred, something he had never felt before. Somehow, he knew this young woman. She was not a stranger.

Hallfredr noticed Brand's hands trembling and the chalice moving almost imperceptibly. Brand did not put it down but held it close.

Brand bowed his head toward Kathleen in greeting. "I once sailed with your father, Kathleen. May God see him home safely to you and your mother."

Grimkell continued his happy sputtering. "How wonderful it is to have new visitors, especially visitors who are really old friends!"

But Grimkell was impatient to continue the inspection of the items Brand brought from Winchester. "Kathleen," he continued, "we are grateful for your help. You can go now."

"Of course, Bishop Grimkell." She placed her bundle down in front of Brand. "I hope to spend more time with you, Father Brand." She smiled eagerly. "There is so much I want to learn, and I am in need of a teacher."

"Yes, that one wants to know everything," said Grimkell once Kathleen departed.

The men resumed sorting the bundles and discovering what surprise would be revealed from each. Brand was unusually quiet, which Bishop Grimkell took for the fatigue of his journey. But Hallfredr sensed it was something else.

Mass was sung a little later in the morning, with nearly all the members of court in attendance, including Kathleen and her mother. Again, Hallfredr noticed the look on Brand's face whenever he glanced at the young woman.

That night, evening torches were lit in the great hall. Thralls and servants sweated and groaned as they carried plate after plate from the cooking house to the assembled guests. The tables were covered with the most esteemed of dishes: herring, roasted veal, poultry, pork, crusty loaves of rye bread, summer vegetables, honey, and mounds of butter and cheese. And to slake the thirst, imported wine and endless casks of mead. As befitting the newly Christian court, no horsemeat—a remnant of heathen sacrifice—would be found.

Toasts and compliments flew back and forth like swallows on the wing. It was customary to drink the *minni*, a toast of remembrance. Olaf drank to his father's memory. Then he drank to the death of Hákon Jarl, his father's murderer.

Olaf settled into his high seat, thick with robes of fur. He described to all how he became a Christian. Then the singers and skalds came before Olaf and sang the songs and poems they had composed, celebrating his victories and deeds of valor in combat. Eventually the dancing and singing settled down, and quieter voices could be heard.

Most Norse skalds, like Hallfredr, were male. But there was a special visitor to the court that summer, Jórunn the Poet Maiden. She could recite poems and sing bawdy drinking songs with the best of the men.

But she could also change the mood with a softer song. Her full-throated voice would effortlessly sail up and down from one beautiful note to another, like a nightingale. When Jórunn sang, no listener could turn away from the sound, and they loved her.

Jórunn began to sing a lullaby, a song everyone knew from childhood. Voices—young and old, high and low—spontaneously joined with hers. Some people even wept.

After this quiet and moving moment, Queen Thyre posed a question to the new visitor.

"Father Brand, we are told by the White Kristr priests that Christ will come a second time to the earth. Will now be the time of a final battle between the forces of evil and good?"

The people gathered in Olaf's great hall had an awareness of calendar. The world was approaching the thousandth year after the birth of Christ. There was talk of end times.

But conjecture about end times was not limited to the newly converted Christians. In the villages and temples, there was talk of Ragnarök, the age of the wolf, the terrible end time. The heathen priests taught that Odinn would become an agent of destruction, and punishment would be meted out to all. In the time of Ragnarök, the spirit of the wolf would swallow first the sun and then the moon. The bright stars would fall and disappear. The sky would go black. The earth and mountains would tremble and crash down into the sea. Then silence, darkness. Out of this chaos and destruction, only one god would triumph: *inn ríki*, the Mighty One. And the world would be renewed and made pure.

Brand answered, "Queen Thyre, the Holy Books say we do not know the day nor the hour, but we are to be prepared at all times."

As he spoke, he made an intention to talk with her privately as soon as he could, as it was clear she had been attentive to the teachings of other priests. Perhaps through the queen, Brand could influence the king.

Olaf was growing bored with the serious talk that was not about him, so the subject was changed.

"Father Brand," said Olaf, "I am told you know the trader Arn from Bergen."

"That is true. I sailed with him once years ago. Before I became a priest."

"And now you are here with his wife and daughter," observed the king. Olaf scanned the room until he saw the two women from Bergen. "Come closer, Kathleen," he said, bidding her with his hand.

Kathleen stood up and approached the high seat.

"Ragnhild, your daughter grows prettier every day—she is as beautiful as her mother."

Ragnhild smiled, somewhat awkwardly.

"Someday she may be the most beautiful woman in my kingdom," Olaf said. "Except of course, for my queen."

It was common knowledge that Olaf was addicted to women, so such talk was not unusual.

From the corner, Hallfredr strummed his harp and sang:

A ship is made for sailing,
A shield for sheltering,
A sword for striking,
A maiden for kissing.

Everyone in the hall chuckled at Hallfredr's verse. Everyone except Brand, who found himself quite unable to stop staring at the young woman who stood, straight and proud, in front of the king.

CHAPTER TWENTY-THREE

A S THE DAYLIGHT HOURS WORE ON and the sun warmed the air and earth, everyone busied themselves with the tasks of summer: planting and gathering, airing clothing and linens, fishing in shallow and deep waters, hunting small game, and gathering herbs and grains. Everyone relished lying in the warmth of the sun during the day—and lying in the arms of a lover at night.

Every day began the same, with Brand or one of the other priests singing the Mass. Olaf attended whenever he was present at the compound, as did his bondsmen and virtually all the women and children.

It was common knowledge that tension was growing between Brand and the king. It started with looks between them: Father Brand refusing to bow his head when it was expected, and the king glaring back. Everyone waited until the day when the two would come to words. What would happen to the priest if he challenged the king?

Brand taught the young people and the newly converted adults the basics of the church's requirements of faith. Ragnhild and Kathleen attended Brand's little classes. With Kathleen there, he found he could get through the lessons only by focusing on the content for the day and ignoring the distraction the young woman created for him.

Sometimes in the middle of a sentence, he would catch sight of her from the corner of his eye, and everything in his mind would fly away like a flock of startled doves. When this happened, he would abruptly refocus, explaining to the group that his mind was dull because he "did not sleep well the night before."

Try as he might, Brand could not come to a rational understanding of why she affected him so. It was a puzzle, and the pieces never seemed to fit. He knew she was the mysterious young woman of his dreams over so many years. But why? He also knew she was forbidden to him, no matter how much he was drawn to her.

Brand was certain he could keep this secret hidden from her and everyone else. He had to—there was no other option.

For her part, Kathleen was supremely oblivious that she had any effect at all on the priest. He was her teacher, of course, and she admired and respected him. But that was all.

Hallfredr and Brand frequently went on long walks together. Hallfredr would pepper the conversation with question after question about the White Kristr faith. Though it was not really a confession, Hallfredr frequently shared his difficulty with the new faith.

"I know the power of words," said the poet. "Words, since the beginning of time, have been used to invoke the power of Odinn, Thor, and Freyja. I remember the exquisite words my forebears spoke. But now those gods and those words are no more. Now I serve the White Kristr. I miss the words. I am lonely for the words I can no longer recite."

Brand looked on Hallfredr with compassion.

"Hallfredr, I know that you struggle with your conversion. But we all face the same struggle of faith. I myself am a convert. I know something of what you feel. That is why the holy words teach us to pray: 'I believe; help my unbelief.' I entreat you to continue your struggle."

Hallfredr stopped his steps and turned to Brand. "And you have another struggle as well, do you not?" he asked, although he knew the answer.

"What?" Brand's eyes opened wide.

"You know what I am talking about. I have seen what you are trying so hard to conceal." Hallfredr did not need to say anything more.

Brand's shoulders slumped. He turned his face to the sky in resignation.

Hallfredr, who knew something of secrets, said with all earnestness, "Your secret is safe with me." He continued his advice to his friend.

"But perhaps, Father Brand, you should discuss this with Bishop Grimkell. Maybe he can provide you counsel."

Brand was certain of Hallfredr's word. But Grimkell was excitable and flighty. Brand questioned whether Grimkell could keep Brand's confession known only to the two of them and to God. Yet Grimkell had studied the scriptures and was quite sincere. And he was Brand's superior. Brand decided he would go to Grimkell, but be wary.

The next evening, the young priest sat facing Grimkell and began the rite of confession.

After the preliminary words, Brand began to share the details of his burden.

"There is a person here, whom I do not wish to name, with whom I am constantly distracted."

Grimkell nodded, and Brand continued. "I would like to avoid this person, but my duties do not allow that to happen. When I see this person, I try not to let my thoughts be affected, but they always are."

Immediately, Grimkell assumed Brand was discussing his relationship with the headstrong Olaf.

"What have you done to avoid this distraction?" asked the bishop.

"I have fasted and prayed, but it continues. Every day."

"You must do whatever is necessary to keep your relationship with this person true to God's purpose in your life. We know from the Holy Scriptures that even Saint Paul endured struggles. He wrote in his letter to the Corinthians that he was given a thorn in the flesh. We do not know what this thorn was. Some say it was the continuous persecutions he endured from unbelievers, or it was a physical infirmity. Or the thorn may have been within his own heart, the temptation of unbelief. Or a tendency to lust or other sinful desires. Or a person in his life who annoyed him to the point of anger."

Grimkell waited for Brand to confirm his suspicions about the distraction being the king. But Brand said nothing, so Grimkell continued.

"I believe the struggle was Saint Paul's own pride. He wrote in his letter that he asked God three times to remove this thorn from him, that it might depart his life. But God denied his petition. Rather, he gave him the message that 'my grace is sufficient for you, my strength is made perfect in weakness.'"

Still, Brand was silent, so Grimkell forged ahead.

"The Lord may not remove this thorn from your side, Father Brand. But trust that it is part of a greater purpose, and do not cease your struggle to overcome it. You, like Saint Paul, may be made strong through your weakness. Continue to pray until God, in God's time, removes this thorn from you."

CHAPTER TWENTY-FOUR

KATHLEEN AND RAGNHILD WERE ENTERTAINED and delighted by the many activities at Olaf's compound. But their favorite place of all was the women's building. There they assembled for respite from the raucous men and a chance to tend to their weaving and sewing. There they wept and laughed and sang. There they found a community of women to support them through life's challenges.

Except for her hair, Kathleen was largely indifferent about her appearance. Many of her friends were not. They often gathered in the women's building to experiment with the juice of lingonberries, staining their lips and cheeks a darker hue. All the women experimented with hairstyles— even the married women, whose hair was normally covered. Sometimes they tied their hair in casual knots or twisted it into ordinary braids at each ear.

Women also used kohl to accentuate their eyes. Men did as well. Among the vain people in Trondheim—and there were many—the vainest was Olaf himself. He rarely appeared without the dark substance applied carefully to the outline of his eyes.

One rainy afternoon, Kathleen and Ragnhild sat in the women's building with other girls and women of the court. Beautiful and modest Princess Ingeborg, Olaf's sister, was there. She was beloved by all and admired for her honest and direct manner. She was very fond of the Icelanders who had come to visit the king. Everyone knew her favorite was Kjartan Olafsson, and she did not blush or protest when they teased her about it.

And Queen Thrye, who was prone to tears, was also there. She sat and cried for her baby, who had died before it reached its first year.

Jórunn the Poet Maiden sat to the side, strumming a small harp and quietly singing. Her unruly brown hair was loosely tied in a knot at the base of her neck. Her eyes needed no kohl; they already made her seem both familiar and exotic to the Norse people. Some ages before, one of Jórunn's ancestors had traveled east, beyond the land of the Rus, and found there an almond-eyed beauty. He bought her as his thrall but treated her as his wife, taking her back with him to the land of the Norse. He loved her face and long straight black hair, but he loved her voice more. Generations passed, and the almond eyes and beautiful voice had never really disappeared, still present in Jórunn.

Ragnhild sat quietly, sewing delicate embroideries. She planned to decorate the edges of a special cloak she was making for Arn's return. Kathleen struggled to complete a small piece of embroidery to add to her father's cloak. It was not going well; her stiches were uneven and crude. No matter how hard she tried, she could not make the small, even stiches her mother made. In frustration, she decided she would have to rip them out and start over. She reached over to her mother's sewing basket and began to pull out a scissors.

"No, Kathleen! Not that one!" Ragnhild cried out.

Kathleen dropped the scissors as if they were a glowing ember.

Ragnhild softened her voice. "I am sorry to startle you, daughter," she said, picking up the special scissors. "But I am saving these for when your father returns." She placed her hand tenderly on her daughter's shoulder. "The first day when he sails back, I will cut his hair with these scissors."

Kathleen wanted to quickly forget her mother's uncharacteristic outburst. She decided to change the topic of conversation. She glanced around the room. A group of girls were fussing and playing with their hair, one combing the other's long tresses, like sisters before bed.

"Mother, what was your mother's hair like?"

"It was beautiful—the color of the last oak leaf to fall in autumn." Ragnhild paused, remembering. "And it was curly like a newborn lamb."

"Curly!" exclaimed Kathleen. "How I would love to have curly hair," she said wistfully, imagining her grandmother.

Sometimes after washing and then rinsing their hair with diluted vinegar, women tied it up with strips of linen and let it dry. For some of them, this resulted in undulating waves. But not for Kathleen. No matter how long she let it dry, as soon as the linens were removed, her thin and straight hair fell flat. She grew so disappointed that she had given up trying.

"Jórunn, tell us about love poetry," said Kathleen, putting down her frustrating piecework and wanting to forget about her flat hair. "I have heard about the *mansǫngr*, the love poetry that men write to women, when they are smitten with desire."

"The men do not want us women to know about this poetry," Jórunn said definitively.

"Why not?" said Kathleen, a little surprise in her voice.

"Because they already think we cast spells on them."

Most of the women smiled or laughed softly, but some in the gathering believed this was possible.

"I love to sing and tell these stories of mighty passion too. But there is one thing I may not do." Jórunn put down her harp to emphasize the seriousness of what she was to say. "That is to create or write mansǫngr."

"Why is that?" asked Ingeborg.

"Well, mansǫngr are inspired by the goddess Freyja. Men fear that love poems recited to them will ensnare them in women's power, like moths lured to flames. And it is equally dangerous for a man to recite a love poem to a woman, even if he is utterly sincere. It carries the implication that the man knows the woman intimately. And you all know that if there is any scandal, all the males of her family—father, brothers, uncles, and even cousins—would respond with violence to correct the implication."

Heads nodded in silent agreement.

"Because of this, mansǫngr are dangerous. And any skald who dares compose them might be met with banishment or even death."

"Jórunn, have you ever heard a mansǫngr?" asked Kathleen.

"Yes," replied Jórunn. "When I was in Iceland—"

"You have been to Iceland?" interrupted Ingeborg.

"Yes," said Jórunn again. "I asked the skald Kormákr Ögmundarson to teach me a mansǫngr, and he became greatly alarmed. But I begged and begged. We went away to a quiet, lonely place. He made me promise to never repeat the poem—and that if I did, Freyja would remove from me the ability to ever make a poem again. Only then would he recite it."

One woman, not caring about poetry, exclaimed, "You have met Kormákr? Tell us! I have heard he is very handsome, with dark skin and hair."

"Yes. He is very handsome. And I cannot repeat his poem. But in his poem, he told how he fell hopelessly in love with a maiden named Steingerdr, when all he had seen of his beloved was her ankle! Can you imagine! Her ankle!"

They all laughed.

"He swore that all the rivers in Iceland would run uphill before he would abandon his desire to have her."

"How did it all turn out?" asked Kathleen.

"That is the odd thing. For all his profession of love, he never did marry Steingerdr. She grew weary of waiting for him and married a man named Bersi instead!"

At such strange male behavior they all laughed again. Soon the giggles quieted down. For a few moments, all that could be heard was the wind in the trees and the sound of cattle ambling through the courtyard.

Ingeborg asked absentmindedly, "Does anyone believe in love at first sight?"

"I do not know," said Kathleen. "Maybe."

An unmarried young woman of fifteen years sat at the weaving bench. She was pale and freckled, with eyelashes so light they seemed to disappear. All this talk of love had her thinking of another man at court.

"Have you seen the new priest?" she asked in almost a whisper. "He is most excellent to look at. As excellent as Olaf himself," she said, smiling at Queen Thyre.

Although Brand sported the usual shorn head of the Christian priests, all agreed he was more handsome, by far, than nearly any other man in Trondheim.

One homely girl, whose face had all the charm of a shovel, put her needlework down in indignation. "Yes," she said, "it is most difficult when a priest is more comely than even many of the women here!"

"Is the new priest married?" another young woman asked.

The freckled weaver answered, "I heard that in England he took a vow to his bishop never to marry."

"Why?" said Kathleen, somewhat surprised. "Other priests are married."

"Yes, but in so many places, that turned out badly," replied the weaver with a shrug.

The homely girl joined in—a tinge of hope in her voice. "But everyone says it is almost impossible for men to leave women alone."

Ragnhild quickly responded, "Well, it is true enough that some men are addicted to women, but there are many others who love their wives and are faithful, even when they are separated."

She said the words she wanted to hear, that her heart longed to be true. It was during this conversation that Ragnhild felt the movement for the first time. And with it came joy. Nearly every woman she knew had borne six or more children, even if many of the children did not live beyond their seventh year. She touched her abdomen, and she realized with certainty that her suspicions were confirmed.

New life grew inside her belly.

CHAPTER TWENTY-FIVE

ALL SUMMER LONG, BRAND AND KING OLAF alternated between avoiding one another and arguing. Neither tactic was very satisfactory. The arguments always ensued whenever Brand brought up Olaf's violent conversion tactics.

One morning, Brand asked to speak with Olaf after Mass. Olaf sat in his high seat, and Brand stood before him. The longhouse was nearly empty, and Grimkell was nowhere near.

Brand went straight to the point. "King Olaf, you are a great chieftain. You must stop killing those who refuse baptism and stop torturing the heathen sorcerers."

Olaf had fallen into the habit of having sorcerers rounded up, bound with rope, and thrown into shallow water at ebb tide. All the sorcerers could do was wait until the salty waters rose. In the end, a long-awaited drowning gave them peace.

Brand continued with arguments he hoped would influence the king. "The White Kristr wants his Gospel to be preached with enticements, gentleness, and all meekness. He wants heathens to be led to the truth not by force but by holy examples and the word of God. Olaf, when you use violence, you give the unbelievers opportunity to hate the sacred name of Jesu and to hate the true religion. If the truth of the Gospel is hated before it is either understood or heard, if human beings are slaughtered in a war waged on the pretext of preaching the Gospel and spreading religion, then you make a mockery of the coming and passion of the White Kristr. Olaf, you are wrong to force conversion. Do you not understand that the White Kristr—"

Olaf could no longer contain himself.

"No, Father Brand! You are the one who does not understand! It is my duty as king to turn the people from the false gods. If I know the truth, I must do whatever I can to proclaim it. If I as king do not do this, what am I? The White Kristr god must be more powerful than all the others, and the only way to protect my people is to require them to bow before that power. You were there when I made this promise in the cathedral, in front of King Ethelred and your bishop."

"Yes, I was there. Sometimes I wonder if you made this promise for God or for your own ambitions." Brand continued as Olaf stared at him with mounting rage. "Haakon the Good—king before you—*he* did not force his subjects to accept the White Kristr or die."

"It is true," Olaf conceded, "that he had no interest in it. Maybe he was weak. In any case, *I* am not *him*."

Brand pressed on. "Why did you have the heathen priest Raud killed? Why was it necessary to do it with such cruelty—with the adder?"

"He would not renounce his service to the heathen gods. And he cursed and blasphemed against the White Kristr. Like Hymir's maidens, I piss in the mouth of anyone who insults my god."

"But what have you accomplished, other than creating a heathen martyr?"

"He is dead. His name will be forgotten. One thousand years from now, my name and that of the god I serve will live on. And it is well known that once your name is forgotten, your life on this earth is no more."

"Even your own skald, Hallfredr—"

"What about him? I was there as sponsor at his baptism, as he himself requested."

"He suffers."

"What do you mean, he suffers? Are you insinuating that he is disloyal to me?"

"No. I mean he suffers in his heart for having left his old gods and their words in the past. He loves Jesu, but it is difficult for him to forget his old gods and how he served them in the past."

"It is good that he is forgetting the old gods. The old gods required sacrifice. Sometimes even humans have been put to death to appease them. But it did no good, for the old gods are weak."

Brand did not need to be reminded about human sacrifice to the old gods. "Nevertheless," he said, pushing memories of his father aside, "waging war against heathens is likely to implant a hatred for the White Kristr in their hearts."

"War can and should be waged against them in order to prepare the way for the preaching of the White Kristr faith. Did not Jesu command his servants to go out and force people to come to a wedding feast?"

"No, King Olaf. You are wrong in your understanding. There is no passage in the Gospel—which is good and joyful news—such as that. There is no passage saying the salvation should be proclaimed with weapons and threats and by subjecting people to death and torture. What do joyful tidings have to do with death and destruction? Many of your people will go to hell rather than learn the advantages of the Gospel."

Olaf knew he was being severely challenged, and he did not like it. "Are you saying that what I am doing is sinful?"

"It is unlawful to kill."

"I am king. Whatever the king does is lawful. Therefore I am not breaking any law!" Olaf was nearly shouting now, and the sound of his own booming voice startled him. He swallowed, then said to Brand, "Why are you a priest when you were born to be a warrior?"

"I have consecrated myself to God," was all the explanation Brand could offer. "King Olaf, I know all the terrors you use to keep the people under your control—"

"You may know these things," barked Olaf, "but you do not understand them. I was a slave, and now I am king. As king, I must do what I believe is best."

Brand fell quiet as Olaf stared up and to the right, remembering his own life.

"Did you know I was a slave?" he asked the priest. "I was sold for the price of a ram, then sold again for the price of a fancy cape. When I was captured and enslaved, my foster father was killed because they thought he was too old to serve any purpose. Years later, I saw the man who killed him. Do you know what I did? I thrust a cleaver into his brain." Olaf seemed to relish the memory. "All these things happened to me to make me a strong leader. Someone who is strong enough to change the heathen ways to the ways of the new god."

"I too have lost a father," said Brand. "I too have been a slave. But—"

Olaf suddenly stood up. "Why do you keep opposing my will?" Olaf's face was mottled with red temper spots. "I will not stop doing what I must do for my people, for my kingdom!"

"And I cannot stop reminding you of the Kristr I have learned to know!"

There was no more to be said. Brand bowed, then turned and walked away.

Olaf sat in his high chair, fuming with pursed lips. He did not know how, but he would find a way to be rid of this priest with the annoying conscience.

CHAPTER TWENTY-SIX

I T WAS NEARLY FALL; ALREADY THE NIGHTS were crisp with cold. Many field crops had been gathered, and mounds of hay had been stored in lofts to sustain the milk cows through the coming winter. After the first frost, the slaughtering of animals fattened through the summer would commence.

Most court visitors had arrived, then moved on. But some planned to stay the entire winter in Trondheim. The court had begun to settle into a semblance of routine when a new ship appeared in the harbor.

First the lookouts spotted the vessel, then some children. Within half an hour, a whole throng of people had assembled. The ship was not entirely unexpected, as some rumors had been heard about its long-awaited arrival. The *Sea Deer*, a sturdy ocean-going vessel, had finally made its way to Trondheim. Everyone was filled with curiosity. These visitors had come from far away—farther than Iceland. They had come from Greenland, the most westerly settlement of Norse people.

Leif, a young man of twenty-four years, strong and of pleasant appearance, stood at the helm of his ship. His father was Erik the Red, previously of Norway and Iceland. Having been banished from both places for murderous anger, Erik founded the new settlement of Greenland. Leif had inherited his father's restless spirit, if not his violent temper.

The young captain led a crew of fourteen and his foster father, Thryker. Hairy and barrel-chested, Thryker had been a member of the Germanic tribes. The Norse took him into slavery but did not keep him as a thrall. He was homely in the extreme, with bulging brows and protruding eyes. For all his coarse appearance, however, Thryker possessed a keen and learned mind. He was a mentor to Leif, teaching him the reading and writing of runes, ways of trade, and the use of weapons.

Leif had set sail from Greenland with gifts—pelts of the great white bear, tusks of the narwhal—for the court of the new Norwegian king. The trip was to promote good relations between Olaf's court and the far-flung outpost.

But the crew of the *Sea Deer* had sailed far south of their destination of Trondheim. The sailors spent nearly a year in the Hebrides. It was not an unpleasant delay, for it was there that Leif fell in love with Thorgunna, the daughter of the local chieftain. Some said she had the gift of prophecy. When Leif left to continue his journey, she told him she would bear his child and it would be a son.

After departing from the Hebrides, unfavorable winds and seas delayed them repeatedly on their journey. It was harvest time when Leif and his men finally splashed ship's anchor into the Nidelva.

Once ashore, Leif set out immediately to visit Olaf the king. The initial meeting could not have gone better.

"Leif, welcome!" exclaimed Olaf as he warmly greeted the newly arrived mariner.

The king noted that Leif did not have the red hair and beard of his father. Olaf also noted that Leif had a certain set to his jaw, a certain stubbornness that pleased him. And he had sailed from Greenland. That alone showed him to be a young man of courage and strength.

On that day, a new friendship was formed.

Introductions followed, and soon Leif was no longer a stranger to Olaf's court or to the chieftains of the surrounding area. Everyone pressed him for stories of his journey, news of Iceland, and details about life in Greenland. He was well spoken, charming all who heard him speak. The only ones annoyed with him were those he beat so badly at the chess board.

After the initial flurry of introductions and exchange of gifts had died down, Olaf summoned Leif. It was a conversation Leif had anticipated.

First, they sat together for a game of chess. The contest was brief, with a decisive win for Leif.

Olaf called for wine.

"Leif, ever since you arrived here, you have impressed us with your tales of travel. You have come from the farthest western seas our people have ever sailed upon. You are a survivor. You are a man I would like to call upon, a man whose loyalty I desire."

Leif knew what was coming.

"Will you become a bondsman to me?"

And Leif was ready with his response.

"King Olaf," said the explorer with a slight bow of his head, "I am honored with your words."

"It is true," replied the king. "What I offer you is a great honor. I demand loyalty from everyone, but few are offered the chance to become bonded to me by solemn oath."

Olaf took a quick swallow of the dark-red wine and continued. "Of course, you must accept the White Kristr faith."

"My father is a strong adherent to the old ways. I know almost nothing about this new faith," said Leif in an equally matter-of-fact tone.

"The new god is the most powerful god," said Olaf. "That is all you need to know from me. Bishop Grimkell or Father Brand can teach you anything else you need or desire to know about the White Kristr."

Leif knew Olaf expected an answer to his offer, and expected it immediately.

"King Olaf, I cannot make such a decision now. I request that you give me time to consider my reply."

"What?" said Olaf, his voice tinged with surprise and disbelief.

"I am saying, you cannot crowd an honest and true Norseman, such as I am."

Olaf grudgingly granted the request, while admiring Leif's small display of pride.

After this conversation, Leif turned over his options in his mind. Because it was so late in the year, it was not possible to make the return trip back across the icy and storm-filled north seas. He knew he had no recourse but to remain in Trondheim until spring. Olaf was an excellent host, by whom Leif was well entertained. And besides, what could it hurt to learn more of the White Kristr god? The world was already filled with many gods.

Leif made his decision quite soon but intentionally took as long as he dared to respond to Olaf. Again, he met with Olaf at the chess table. Vige lay quietly near Olaf's feet.

"Have you considered the matter of the bondsman oath?"

"Yes, King Olaf, I will accept the White Kristr. I will no longer be a heathen."

Olaf smiled at hearing Leif's decision. He turned to his hound and said, "Did you hear that, Vige? We shall have a new bondsman!"

Vige gave an excited yip.

"Leif, you have chosen wisely. You will start your instruction today."

CHAPTER TWENTY-SEVEN

L EIF, ALONG WITH ALL HIS MEN, accepted the new faith as instructed by Father Brand. They were clothed in white gowns and baptized by Grimkell as followers of the White Kristr—heathens no more.

The day after the baptism, everyone gathered in the great hall for a special ceremony. Many people had washed and taken steam in the bathhouse and carefully arranged their hair.

Kathleen and Ragnhild, like everyone else, had put on their very finest clothes. Ragnhild wore her best linen underdress and her favorite overdress. All women wore loose, unstructured garments, and Ragnhild appreciated how this custom accommodated her growing pregnancy. She covered her hair with a finely pleated linen veil and wrapped a silken shawl around her shoulders. Kathleen wore her newest underdress and an overdress dyed the color of yellow-green willow leaves. Her hair was twisted in tiny braids all around her face, pulled back, and held with a silver clasp.

Grimkell was dressed in his ceremonial robes. He stood beside the king, a large metal cross in his hands. Brand, in his customary black, stood next to him.

Olaf was seated on his throne with Thyre beside him. She wore a dress of royal blue with an embroidered headband across her brow. A silken veil spilled from the headband down to her shoulders. Embroidered lambskin gloves matched her embroidered slippers. A shawl decorated with ermine graced her shoulders.

Olaf's royal sword rested lightly across his knees. His ringed hand held the gorgeous weapon in a relaxed caress.

Grimkell called out, "The oath-giver shall come forward!"

Leif was surrounded by Thryker and the other Greenlanders at the rear of the hall. He left them and walked slowly forward toward the high seat. He knelt before the king. He placed his right hand on the golden ring on the hilt of the sword, then kissed Olaf's fingers.

From his knees, Leif began his recitation, loudly enough for all in the hall to hear.

"I am Leif, son of Erik the Red and Thjodhild. I come from a line of courageous warriors and explorers who have endured danger and survived the mighty seas and unknown lands."

Unconsciously, eyebrows raised. Many in the crowd, especially the Icelanders, were aware that Erik had murdered more than one man and had set course for new lands only as consequence of his banishment. Still, he had gone farther west than any others. And Greenland was opening up for settlement because of his sins. So, grudging respect was due. The eyebrows returned to their normal places.

Grimkell offered the cross to Leif. Leif took it and held it aloft. Then his lips briefly touched the cold metal of the cross.

Turning to address the others crowding the hall, Leif made his declaration: "I take you as my solemn witnesses to this vow. I swear to be eternally loyal to King Olaf, son of Tryggve and Astrid. I promise to do whatever he asks, even to battle unto the death. May I be cursed if I fail to fulfill this oath. I swear by the Lord Jesu Kristr."

Leif then returned the cross to Grimkell. Olaf rose to complete the covenant with his retainer.

"I, Olaf Tryggvason, swear to you, Leif, son of Erik and Thjodhild, that I will be your leader in battle against all things evil in this world and the next. I will protect you and all of your family from theft or destruction of your lands and holdings. You will be rewarded for your loyalty. I give you this sword, a sword of worthy lineage, to seal this oath."

As Olaf placed the sword into Leif's hands, Grimkell proclaimed: "May this bond be unbroken, as long as the sun shines and the world endures henceforth forevermore."

Leif had joined the ninety or so men who made up the warrior elite bonded to Olaf.

Instantly the musicians began to beat their drums, and a joyous shout came up from all in the hall. Brand moved to the side, as he usually did, to observe the proceedings from a place apart.

Jórunn and Hallfredr took turns reciting poems, to the delight of everyone. They alternated ribald poems with poems that insulted Olaf's enemies.

Leif wished fervently that Thorgunna could be with him, sitting at his side and smiling.

Later, after the feasting and dancing and music were but pleasant memories, Brand and Hallfredr gathered around Leif to admire the ornate sword. It was exquisite—graceful and strong, larger than the traditional Norse sword. Everyone noted that it was not squat or plain, as most men liked their swords. This sword had a sense of nobility and character. The entire sword was well balanced, with edges that ran nearly parallel for most of the blade. They began their taper nearly at the end of the tip. It was inscribed INNOMINEDOMINI, or "in the name of the Lord," and decorated with a cross and orb inlay. It was refined, with a savage glint to it, much like Olaf himself.

Brand could not keep from inspecting the sword up close. It had been made in the German region of Solingen, by the Ulfberht family. He noted that it easily rivaled the southern blade-makers of Toledo or Damascus, whose craft he had seen on his ill-fated travel to Rome. He longed to hold the black leather grip in his hand. But as a man of peace, he knew he could not.

Leif repeatedly turned over his new sword, pleased at how well balanced it was. But his reverie was caught short. Hallfredr moved close to his side and spoke into his ear.

"We shall see. We shall see what King Olaf will command you to do," whispered Hallfredr to Leif. "Do not forget the old proverb, 'A gift always looks for a return.'"

CHAPTER TWENTY-EIGHT

THE NEVER-ENDING STRETCHES OF SUMMER LIGHT—with its bright days and glowing twilights—were long gone. They were replaced now with dreary winter gray and nearly continual darkness. When she went outdoors, Kathleen could not stay warm, no matter how tightly she tied her kerchief and how often she slapped her hands together. The snow fell in silence but crunched and squeaked with each footstep. This was the time of the bitter cold, the cold that burned.

Everyone lingered near the fire, and such closeness led to the transmission of disease. Among the dead were small infants and children and many thralls as well—the weak and the very young. Even the wild animals barely endured this time of suffering. Hungry deer and moose wandered close to the town in search of forage.

Ragnhild first felt the pangs of childbirth one especially cold day, when buckets of water left outside the longhouses froze quickly to stone. Worry immediately crossed her face like a shadow, for the pains were too early.

The midwives flew into action, but it was clear from the beginning that all would not go as normal. Though Ragnhild struggled and struggled to the point of exhaustion and beads of sweat poured from her, no progress was being made.

Aud, the oldest midwife, administered herbs, but still the birth process stalled.

One of the younger midwives cried out, "Loosen all the knots! All of them! If we loosen the knots, the delivery will be easier!"

The women immediately untied any knots on their clothing—even the careful knots of hair at the napes of their necks.

Aud and Kathleen hurried to see Grimkell. Panting, Aud went directly to the point. "She asks for the priest."

"But no men are allowed to be present during the birth process!" Grimkell answered.

"Nevertheless, she asks for the priest."

Grimkell looked first at Aud, then at Kathleen, and noted the expressions on their faces. Within minutes, Brand was in the women's building, standing at Ragnhild's bedside.

Ragnhild labored long and suffered great pain. Two perfectly formed infants were brought in succession into the prayer-filled air. But their lungs never took a breath of it. Brand made the sign of the cross over each, then the midwives quickly removed them.

Fever came over the exhausted Ragnhild. Kathleen kept vigil at her mother's sickbed for two days and nights. In the flickering candlelight, Brand led prayers murmured by fervent voices.

"Mother, drink this," Kathleen would urge, offering willow bark tea. But her mother was too weak to drink. She took her daughter's hand and slowly brought Kathleen's fingers to rest on the cross lying atop the linen at her throat.

"Take this," Ragnhild whispered.

Kathleen understood the request but made no move. Her mother closed her eyes, tightly, then opened them and looked intently at Kathleen, waiting.

"She wants you to take the cross. She wants you to have it," urged Brand.

Reluctantly Kathleen reached to take the cross. Her mother's eyelids were barely open now.

The last thing Ragnhild saw was her daughter's face moving toward her own. The last thing she felt was her daughter's soft kiss. And with all her mind and strength, Ragnhildr smiled one last smile and passed into the spirit world.

CHAPTER TWENTY-NINE

B RAND DID HIS BEST TO COMFORT KATHLEEN. He sat with her for many hours, reminding her of the promises of life after death that the followers of the White Kristr would attain. She heard the words, but her heart was still full of grief and longing for the scent and sound and touch of her mother. With her father away, she was indeed nearly an orphan, and she felt the loss deeply.

Brand struggled to find some way to bring her out of her deep mourning. Hallfredr, ever the observer, offered a suggestion.

"It is something small, something from above," he said.

The next day, Brand followed Hallfredr's advice and asked Kathleen to meet with him after morning Mass. She still was unable to control her longing for her mother, and she poured her heart out to her priest and teacher.

"Oh, Father Brand," she said, her voice raw from frequent tears. "I miss my mother so much. I want to sit with her and tell her everything that is happening with me. But she is gone now, and all I have left of her is this." She lightly touched the cross at her throat.

"I know, Kathleen. But I have brought you something that may make you feel less lonely."

He reached deep inside his priestly robe and pulled out a squirming kitten. It was covered in luxurious fur. When full grown, a magnificent mane would cover her neck and chest, like a miniature lion.

"This little one has no mother. She was found, alone, high in a tree near the edge of town. Her eyes have opened, and she can drink milk from a bowl. She needs someone to look after her."

He offered the small bit of warm fur to Kathleen. "Take her."

Kathleen heard but her heart was frozen. The cloud over her spirit was so deep that even the offering of a living gift hardly moved her.

Brand softly repeated, "Take her."

Kathleen stared at the mewling kitten. She slowly opened her arms and took the soft feline. She pressed the little animal to her chest, and it immediately settled in, enjoying the embrace.

"She has no mother?" Kathleen asked.

"She has no mother."

"Does she have a name?"

"That is for you to decide."

At first, Kathleen did not know what to name the kitten. Days went by, and she merely called it *skogkat*, or forest cat.

There was another cat in the court, and the skogkat constantly provoked it to play. It was Queen Thyre's cat, a rare pet that was said to have come all the way from Paris. It had a wavy coat of yellow fur, so the queen called it Bygul, for surely it did look like bee gold, or honey. Bygul was much indulged with cream and had grown quite fat and content. It was utterly disinterested in the little skogkat.

Then one day, as Kathleen watched her curious kitten tumble and jump and leap on Bygul's tail, she laughed. Out loud. It was the first since the day her mother died. She stopped mid-laugh, surprised at herself.

"All right, little skogkat. You shall finally have a name." She picked up the cat by the nape and looked directly into its face. "You shall be called Hlatr, for you and only you have made me laugh again."

Hlatr proved to be an excellent name, for the kitten was full of insatiable curiosity that brought laughter to everyone around. All the world and everything in it was a toy made just for her pleasure. No one could watch the tumbling, jumping, and stalking without a smile coming to his or her face. Hlatr she was called, and laughter she created.

Once a week, the little beast was made to suffer the indignity of a saltwater bath, followed by a soap bath, followed by a lanolin rubdown with sheep's wool to keep her coat shiny. Her fur was brushed daily with dried mint, tansy, and pyrethrum herbs. To keep the biting insects at bay, a sack of cedarwood chips was placed on her favorite daytime sleeping spot.

At night, the small four-footed creature would spend a few minutes kneading Kathleen's chest, then she would sprawl herself over Kathleen as they slept. They warmed and comforted one another. Motherlessness melted into motherlessness. Together, the two kept the away the black shadows of loneliness that cold and sad winter.

CHAPTER THIRTY

ABOUT A MONTH AFTER THE DEATH OF HER MOTHER, Kathleen and the rest of the court observed a most unusual scene. Strangers had come seeking audience with Olaf. There was a flurry of activity as Olaf's bondsmen carefully removed the petitioners' weapons, guarding them under lock outside the hall.

Kathleen watched, as wide-eyed as the rest of the court. Thirteen men entered the main hall. They had come overland, through forests thick with ice and snow. She had never seen men such as these. Their leader was fantastically ugly. His eyes were black, and his eyebrows joined in the middle. Thick dark hair covered his head, and his jaw was densely bearded. Little could be seen of his face except the nose, teeth, and eyes. He was more monster than man. Thick pelts of black and silver wolves hung around his enormous frame. The other men wore cloaks of heavy brown bearskin around their shoulders.

Despite the fact that the visitors were weaponless, the king's bondsmen were alert and ready. Leif and the Greenlanders were at high attention as well. Tension filled the air as palpably as did the smoke from the hearth.

The leader began to speak to the king. "Olaf, son of Tryggve, we salute you," he said, stiffly bowing before the king in the great hall. "I am Ogmund—"

"I know who you are," interrupted Olaf. "I know well your kind. Your reputation as a berserker precedes you."

All the populace knew that the berserkers were followers of Odinn, the god of fury. They were used as shock troops, who preceded the main body of warriors in battle, displaying great rage and violence. Some said they were shape-changers, taking the form of beasts such as wolves or bears. Or maybe they just took the souls of the animals.

Again Ogmund began to speak. "We have come—"

At that moment, Kathleen's kitten, which had been settled loosely in her arms, caught a glimpse of a frantic mouse running across the floor of the great hall. Hlatr had grown stronger, and Kathleen could not contain her. Instinctively, the long-tailed feline leapt from Kathleen's arms and scampered after the fat rodent as it disappeared under the heavy tapestry hanging behind Olaf's chair.

Kathleen knew such a chase would not be well received by the others in the hall.

"Oh no! Come, little *kis-kis*!" she cried.

Kathleen dashed to collect her errant pet from behind the heavy tapestry. She swiftly scooped the feline into her arms and returned to her place at the side of the hall, avoiding the disapproving eyes of the elders.

Ogmund stared at Kathleen as she retrieved the fluffy offender, but not with amusement or irritation.

At that moment, a change came over Ogmund. It may have been admiration for her beauty, a desire to possess her, plain lust, or all of these. A poet would describe it thus: Ogmund fell in love.

"Ogmund!" said Olaf impatiently.

Redirecting his gaze, Ogmund continued. "King Olaf, you know our reputation as warriors attached to the armies of both King Harald and King Halfdan. Your exploits are well known. We come to offer services—"

Once again, Olaf interrupted the visitor. "I and all the men bonded to me follow the White Kristr. Will you turn away from your worship of Odinn? Will you let our bishop baptize you and your men?"

Ogmund knew there had been talk of conversion in all the regions Olaf ruled. But, he thought, conversion stories were often exaggerated.

"My god is mighty, more powerful than Odinn," Olaf said. "If you do not agree to baptism, then you must leave at once."

For all his fearsomeness, Ogmund's reply was unusually quiet.

"Old Thor has always helped us in vengeance and victory, and gentle Freyja for many years has given us fair and fertile summers. Odinn has given us power and has always served us well. I will not give them up for the White Kristr, whom I have never seen and of whom I know nothing."

Ogmund stared solemnly at Olaf. "Not to the god who forgives nor to the god who suffered will I make my vows. I bow to Odinn, the god who makes men strong, the god who is the never-dying and all-powerful lord." He bowed stiffly again and stepped back. "We will withdraw from Trondheim."

As he turned to leave, his gaze fell on Kathleen. It was only an instant.

Kathleen was unaware of the heat in it. But Brand took note. Some of the elder women had also sensed what had taken place. They were relieved that Ogmund would never see her again.

CHAPTER THIRTY-ONE

AT LAST THE SPRING SUN WAS STRONG ENOUGH to warm the air in Trondheim. Spirits rose with new beginnings. For the first time since the waning warmth of the previous autumn, Olaf and Leif were playing chess outside the confines of wood walls. Vige found a patch of sun near his master and lay watching them, his eyes bright and wise.

"Leif, you soon will return to Greenland?" asked Olaf.

"Yes, King Olaf."

"I have a special commission for you."

Leif waited to hear what was to come next.

Olaf moved a chess piece. "When you reach the settlement, you will preach the word of the White Kristr to the heathens of Greenland."

This was not what Leif had expected, but he showed none of this surprise in his face. Was this the request Hallfredr had implied would come?

"My king, I will do whatever you bid me to do. But I am a farmer, a sailor, an explorer. I have no skill at preaching. The settlers are a stubborn and obstinate lot—none more so than my father, Erik."

"Perhaps," replied Olaf, "you would have been happier if I had asked you to kill a traitorous chieftain. Or perhaps to sail beyond the western edges of the sea, into the unknown of the unknown. But I know of no man better fitted for a difficult task. And I believe you will carry good luck with you."

"That can only be," said Leif, "if I carry yours with me."

"Good! It is settled."

Leif made another move on the board. He had bested Olaf yet again.

Olaf smiled. "Well, today at least, luck was with you!"

They both laughed.

Olaf motioned to a thrall, who brought an object wrapped in soft leather.

"Bishop Grimkell has asked that I send this copy of Holy Scripture with you, so that the Greenlanders may benefit from it. I promised him it would travel under your keeping."

Leif opened the book. It contained the four Gospels and some Psalms. Some of the pages were embellished with brightly colored letters and decoration in the margins. Leif could read only runes, not these Latin letters, but he knew the months of work scribes took to reproduce such a document. It was something so beautiful and so precious, he could scarcely believe it was in his hands.

"There is more," said Olaf.

Something in Olaf's tone made Leif look up from the book and listen expectantly.

"I have already made arrangements with Bishop Grimkell for Father Brand to serve as the priest for the farthest outposts of the Norse people. You will take him with you when you return to Greenland."

"Of course, King Olaf. This I will do."

"You must swear by your honor that you will allow no harm to come to him. This is of utmost importance to me. I want no one to say I sent this man away to his death."

Leif grasped the king's right hand and placed his left hand on the king's shoulder.

"I swear. I swear by my honor that I will allow no harm to come to Father Brand."

As soon as he heard this news, Hallfredr knew that payment on Olaf's gift had come due. The newly commissioned Leif and his crew would return to Greenland, accompanied by a handsome and stubborn priest who would irritate Olaf no more.

CHAPTER THIRTY-TWO

EIF'S CREW READIED THE SHIP for the long voyage to come. The air reeked of hot pitch as thralls repaired leaky floorboards. They filled the cargo areas with barrels of freshwater, sacks of grains, small and large tools, fish hooks and nets, and oiled clothing to protect against wind and water. They loaded mead for thirst and pleasure. Several bottles of precious wine and bags of wheat for the Eucharist meal were also stowed safely away. A special place was made for the sacred text. Leif surveyed everything—including Brand, who was easily the most precious cargo under his care.

Leif planned to set sail as soon as the winds were favorable and the waters calm. At last the time came. Leif announced they would sail the following day.

That night, Kathleen and Brand said their good-byes. He was certain he had kept his feelings hidden from her. Only Hallfredr knew his secret, and Hallfredr would never betray him. Hallfredr was a poet who felt Brand's pain and who understood his passion.

Kathleen said good-bye with gratitude and affection for her teacher, her shepherd.

"Thank you, Father Brand, for all you have taught me, all you have done for me. I shall never forget you."

"And I shall never forget you, Kathleen."

As he spoke, she reached out and embraced him. He could barely contain the urge to pull her closer and hold her there forever.

Brand felt immense sadness, as he was certain he would never see her again. And at the same time, he felt intense relief. He would no longer see her day after day and feel the pain of the unattainable. He fervently hoped he would never dream of her again either.

After Mass the next day, Grimkell insisted on attending to all ceremony to see the explorers off. The travelers assembled on board. In addition to Brand, Leif, Thryker, and crew, others were sailing with them as far as Iceland.

The *Sea Deer* was tied close to the town's longest wharf. There, Olaf and Thyre stood together. Next to them were Grimkell and Hallfredr, with Kathleen and Jórunn standing near. Nearly every inhabitant of Trondheim crowded the wharf and the edge of town. They gathered in honor and awe of what lay ahead for the travelers.

Leif stood proudly at the steering oar. He wore a scarlet cloak, a gift from the king's own hand. Olaf's other gift to him, the remarkable sword, hung at his side. Grimkell began the blessing. On the wharf lit candles were handed to the royal family, and thralls brought out burning pans of incense. The flames were carefully watched, and buckets were at the ready, lest a fire destroy the wharf, the ship, or even the town.

Grimkell moved forward to the prow of the *Sea Deer*. He set a crucifix upon the vessel, read from John the Evangelist, and said many prayers. He slowly sprinkled the length of the entire ship and all the travelers upon it with holy water.

Grimkell nodded to Brand, who loudly began to pray a final blessing for the mariners. "Jesu, master most pure, we beseech you, shield our journey. And may the Lord of Heaven bless us and stretch forth his hand in protection upon us."

Amid cheers and shouts of farewell, the *Sea Deer* began its homeward voyage to Iceland, then beyond to Greenland. The rowers confidently began their labors. Drops of crystal water fell from the wooden oars.

Brand stood at the side of the moving ship with the rest of the mariners, but he did not wave as they did. Gazing at the crowd, his eyes searched for a last look at Kathleen. Hallfredr had moved close to her, his arm held protectively around her shoulders.

When Brand's eyes found her in the crowd, the rest of the world faded away until he saw nothing but her, the sunlight glinting off her face and hair. He watched as she receded farther and farther into the distance. Against his will, his throat ached with unshed tears.

Leif's crew soon rowed into the narrow fjord that passed into the sea. Salt breezes covered their faces and hair. The sail caught a favorable wind and swelled in thanksgiving. The vast water and sky surrounded them, becoming the world for the vessel and those cradled within its wooden confines.

CHAPTER THIRTY-THREE

T HE *SEA DEER* SAILED EASILY FROM Trondheim to Iceland. The trip
from Iceland to Greenland, however, was more difficult. At times,
the fog shrouded them and the seas were too still. At other times,
the wind blew so viciously that extraordinary effort was needed to keep the
vessel from capsizing.

There were murmurings among the men. They had all been baptized, but the veneer was thin. They wondered why a priest traveled with
them. Although they had sworn allegiance to Olaf and to Leif, they were
discomfited. Everyone knew a priest aboard a ship was bad luck. Many an
English missionary had been thrown overboard during sudden squalls in
the North Sea, to appease the sea god Ægir and Rán, his wife.

When Leif heard the crew's complaints, he threatened severe punishment for whoever repeated these thoughts. No more words were said
against the priest.

Their final destination was Brattahlid, the outpost farm of Leif's
outlawed father. After settling in Greenland, Erik had briefly returned
to Iceland to persuade people that there was new and bountiful land to
the west. Erik enticed them with his stories and the attractive name of
Greenland.

All the good land in Iceland was nearly gone, so land-hungry
settlers had set out from Iceland in the summer of 986. Of the twenty-four boatloads of Icelanders who began the journey to Greenland, only
fourteen ships made it to their destination. The others were forced back
or lost at sea.

But the surviving colonists prospered. When Erik had first explored Greenland, all that could be found were weather-hardy fauna such as foxes, mice, arctic tern, eider ducks, hawks, and puffins. Soon the land was populated not only with native wildlife but also with sheep, pigs, cattle, and even some ponies, their hair shaggy and thick against the cold.

Because Erik was the first to settle in Greenland, he owned the best of all the land. In addition to his farm, Erik owned many fishing stations as well as small outposts on several islands, where men gathered wild bird eggs and whatever precious driftwood they could find.

The Greenlanders traded the skins of the white bear, narwhal tusks, and walrus ivory and hides for their precious imported necessities—iron, tools, and wood. And sometimes they even obtained a few luxuries, such as the fruits of the grape—raisins and wine—and fruits of the European nut trees.

When Leif reached the southern tip of Greenland, he began to sail north, up the western edge of the land mass. Early one morning, the crew sighted a dark channel. They entered into the waterway known as Erik's Fjord. On either side, towering walls hemmed them in. The highest cliffs were icebound and shrouded with clouds. The low cliffs were home to green and black lichen.

They navigated for hours in the bleakness. They passed nothing more inviting than a cluster of rocky islands with small patches of berry bushes huddling close to the ground.

Without warning, the frosty easterly winds ceased. The fog disappeared, and the air became pleasantly warm. The travelers noted that the green patches had overtaken the barren spots. Vegetation crept up the slopes until it met the snow line. The occasional waterfall tumbled down the cliffs—icy cold and foaming.

They passed tall thickets of yellow-green willows, birch, and alder, then pastures dotted with grazing sheep and cattle contentedly chewing their cud. The sailors knew they were close to their destination, located on the inner end of Erik's Fjord, inland from the sea. Deep within the narrow fjord, the farm was protected from cold, foggy weather and the icy waters of the coast. This small pocket of land was good for growing sweet grass as hay to feed cattle and sheep. The light-green pastures contrasted with the dun-colored rocks surrounding the blue water of the fjord, where white icebergs floated, even in deepest summer.

"There! There!" shouted Leif. "There is my father's home!" He pointed to a place ahead where smoke rose into the sky and people were gathering to greet the travelers. "We have arrived at Brattahlid!"

The exultation and thrill of safely reaching their destination overtook the shipmates. Smiles graced every face, and pulses beat faster and faster as they neared the crowd. Exuberant shouts of welcome echoed across the water before they even dropped anchor. Wives and children, fairly leaping with joy, waved to the returning Greenlanders.

Leif shouted, "Make ready to go ashore!"

Leif and Brand were in the first boat to ferry from the ship to the waiting crowd. A roar of delight rose up when Leif stepped onto the land, his arms high to the skies.

"Leif! Leif! Leif!" the settlers shouted to one of their own who had safely returned from afar.

Leif greeted them all warmly, with rough embraces and handshakes all around. The air was filled with the slapping of broad shoulders by men who could not contain their gladness.

Leif searched for two people in the crowd: his wild, impetuous father and his long-suffering mother. Erik stood tall among the men, his face red and his flaming hair flowing to his shoulders. Thjodhild waited until she could stand it no longer, then she rushed to embrace Leif. Her cheeks, still rosy at her age, flushed even more with mother's warmth. The keys at her waist jingled as her arms encircled her son. She touched his face with excited hands, her eyes shining moist with relief and pride.

Leif's brothers, Thorstein and Thorvald, also rushed to greet their sibling. But one was missing from this familial reunion. In addition to his three sons, Erik had a daughter, but not by his wife. Thjodhild had all but forbidden her family to even speak the daughter's name, so Leif felt it best not to inquire publicly about his half-sister, Freydis.

But first, there was another matter that could not wait. As the head man of the outpost, Erik was responsible for greeting newcomers.

"Leif, tell me—who are your fellow travelers?"

Leif began where he knew trouble would lie. "This is Father Brand. He has been sent here at the command of King Olaf, whom I am honor bound to obey."

At that point, Brand's robe shifted, and Erik noted the cross he wore.

"He is a priest of the White Kristr?" asked Erik, his eyes narrow with suspicion.

"Yes."

Others in the crowd looked on in amazement as well. "Leif has turned to the White Kristr?" they asked themselves. "Now I understand how much has changed since Leif first sailed to the east and gained favor with King Olaf."

Erik stepped back, away from Brand. "Olaf made a mistake in sending him here. We have no need of a White Kristr priest." His voice was cold.

"Father, let us discuss this later."

"Yes, let us discuss this later," implored Thjodhild. "First, let us have time to celebrate the return of our son and his crew."

Erik nodded his assent. But he turned and bellowed for all to hear, "*We have no need!*"

CHAPTER THIRTY-FOUR

WITH THE APPROACH OF AUTUMN, SHIPS WERE NOT an uncommon sight in Erik's fjord. Some had left Greenland in summer to make trading voyages or to spear whales in the more northern waters. For every returning traveler, kinsmen and friends made a feast of welcome. Usually, these celebrations lasted a day. For Leif and his men, Thjodhild would have wanted at least three days. But with tensions already rising between him and his father, she thought better of a lengthy and extravagant celebration. Instead, she planned a more modest homecoming.

Thjodhild sent messengers to spread the news of Leif's return and the upcoming feast. She intentionally dispatched the slowest and most incompetent messenger to the settlement at Gardar, where Freydis lived with her weak-willed but wealthy husband. Thjodhild certainly never accepted Freydis, and Erik barely so. There was something strange and frightening about Freydis, and she was both hated and hateful at the same time. Her wealth created the only interest for other settlers.

Eventually, a dozen chieftains and their families arrived. Between the many households and thralls, nearly two hundred people filled the great hall in Brattahlid.

Painted shields hung on the hall's inner walls, like beads on a necklace. Tables were spread with sun-bleached linen, then covered with platters of grilled mutton, pork, and beef. Horns were filled as soon as they emptied. There were games of intellect, speed, and strength, and small gifts were exchanged.

According to the custom of social order, Erik sat in his high seat between two exquisitely carved pillars, with Thjodhild next to him. The highborn men sat on benches close to Erik's right; the highborn women at Thjodhild's side to the left. As the guest of honor and his father's eldest son, Leif was seated opposite his parents in another high seat. Thryker sat next to his foster son. The crew of the *Sea Deer* was seated on benches extending on both sides from the front to the very back of the large room. Brand came at the very end of the line, in the lowest seat by the door.

The compound at Brattahlid was unvaryingly similar to the layout of all settlements of the Norse people. There were the predictable kitchens and storehouses, the women's house with herb gardens, and gesta hus. For the animal inhabitants of the outpost, there were stables, hog pens, sheep houses, and cow sheds.

In one way, however, this hall was unlike the great halls of Norway. Instead of being built with huge logs, it was built of rock. Three sides were built of blocks of red sandstone quarried nearby. The fourth wall was formed by a steep natural cliff, nearly vertical and approximately twelve feet high. These rock outcrops were the reason the place was called Brattahlid, or "steep slopes."

Toward the end of the day, the unavoidable conversation began. Leif spoke boldly for all to hear.

"Father, I was baptized while at the court of King Olaf Tryggvason.—I and all the Greenlanders there with me." Leif lifted his chin. "I have become a true follower of the White Kristr."

There was a small but audible hum among the people.

Brand also felt surprise when he heard Leif utter these words. He had spent many hours with Leif, instructing him in the values of the new faith, starting in Trondheim and continuing on during the long voyage to Iceland and on to Greenland. But he had never been entirely certain of Leif's commitment to Jesu until now.

"What?" exclaimed Erik. "A true follower? Why could you not just accept the white robe, then forget it? Many have done so."

"Because I am true to my word and will never break any oath."

Erik glared.

Leif continued, "Father Brand has come to help me convert all Greenlanders to the White Kristr faith."

At this pronouncement, the hall exploded into shouts of outrage and indignation. Leif waited until the hall quieted.

"While I was in Trondheim, I made a solemn oath with King Olaf, pledging to bring the White Kristr to the people here. King Olaf sent me back here to present this god to you, so you can accept this faith as the people of Trondheim have done."

Now Erik entered the verbal chaos with full force.

"We are not the people of Trondheim!" he said. "As I have told you, we have no need! We have done well enough without that god. Our gods have served us well. Why should we change?"

Others in the hall echoed Erik's words: "Yes. Why should we change?" "Who are you to tell us how and whom to worship?" "Why have you brought this priest here?" There was real anger and vehemence in the air. Words were thrown like rocks.

Leif was still calculating what tactics he could use to ensure the settlers' cooperation when Brand stepped into the verbal fray. He moved with deliberation to the center of the room. His voice was calm, and he spoke clearly so all could hear.

"I understand that my presence here confuses you—and perhaps angers you. But I have come to bring you peace. As you learn more, your hearts will be gladdened to know this is the True God among many, one who is both ever living and ever ready to help you with the cares and sufferings of this life."

Brand stretched out his hand to all those gathered. "If there is anyone, any person, here who is tired of conflict, who is tired of the way things are today, and who desires to learn how the love of Jesu can change hearts and minds, meet with me tomorrow after the midday meal, and we will begin our study."

Brand moved forward, without fear, and stood before Erik, directly in front of the high seat.

"May I have your word, Erik, that you will not impede any person who wishes to attend Mass or study the White Kristr?"

Erik had been placed publicly in a difficult spot. If he denied the request now, he would merely face it again and again with his son and with this priest. And what did it matter? Judging from the response in the hall, he was quite sure no one was interested in such learning.

"All right!" roared Erik. "You say you are here to bring peace. You may hold your worship and teach. Let anyone who wishes to learn be allowed to do so."

Erik avoided a deeper confrontation. But he miscalculated the interest in this foreign priest's theology. The next day, Brand began his class with Thjodhild—weary of conflict and as stubborn as her flame-haired spouse—sitting close and listening intently to every word.

CHAPTER THIRTY-FIVE

I T WAS NOT LONG BEFORE THE DAYS SHORTENED and long hours of darkness enveloped the settlement. During the winter the Norse hunkered down for serious storytelling.

Erik regaled listeners with stories of his explorations, first to Iceland and then to Greenland. Others told of their hunting expeditions and their encounters with the dangerous white bears. Leif told and retold of his journey to Olaf's court. And he told them of his beautiful Thorgunna and how he hoped someday to see her and claim their child as his own.

New to Brand was the curious tale of Bjarni Herjólfsson. Several years before, Bjarni had been blown off course on his way to Greenland. His parents lived in Iceland, and he spent his winters alternatively with them or in Norway. One year, he sailed to Iceland only to discover that his parents had gone with other settlers to Erik's new outpost in Greenland. Bjarni made the precipitous decision to sail on to Greenland to be with them, though he had no maps and had never sailed there before. Bjarni was gone for over a year, seeing strange lands, before he finally made landfall in Greenland. He told his story many times, always to a rapt audience.

"Mist had covered the North Star," he would say, "so we could not navigate. We sailed for many days, and finally we saw land. But it was not Greenland. It had no glaciers. It was green with grass. We did not go ashore. We kept sailing, for we were intent on returning reaching Greenland without more delay. Then we spotted another mass of land, this time with many flat rocks. Again, we did not land. Finally, we sailed up Erik's fjord, our ship battered but still sailable."

Some dismissed Bjarni's tale of this mystery land as the exaggeration of an attention seeker. Others thought it was a delusion brought on by a weak and sickened captain and crew. Yet others—including Erik and Leif—believed it could be true and were intrigued. Indeed, had the Greenlanders known to look and had they recognized what they saw, they would have seen banks of clouds hovering over a great land mass to the west.

That winter, Brand had his own stories to tell as well. With Erik's grudging consent, Thjodhild and a small group of women now attended Brand's instructional classes on the White Kristr faith. Thjodhild was an intelligent and ready student.

"Tell me, Brother Brand—how is the White Kristr god different from other gods?"

"This god is the only god who cares for you. He is a god of peace, not of war."

Thjodhild sighed. "I am tired of conflict. I am tired of violence. Erik has been twice outlawed because he has killed a man. And twice I have followed him, even to this place so far from home."

Still, she felt she needed more time to understand this new god. This was acceptable to Brand, who knew more of patience than the Greenlanders would ever have imagined.

Leif was not as patient, however. Despite some progress, the goal of converting Greenlanders was coming along far too slowly for him. He often traveled away from Brattahlid to talk with chieftains of other settlement outposts. He implied that serious measures might be taken to force conversion, and he was met with equally serious opposition.

Brand first learned of Leif's visits when he overheard some of Leif's thralls discussing it. Like all enslaved people, their eyes and ears were as alert as chickens in the shadow of a hawk. They were focused on every detail of their master's lives.

"I was surprised to see Leif was not at the feast last night," said one.

"Did you not know?" asked the other. "He will be away two days yet. He has gone south with a band of men to convert a chief to follow the

White Kristr. I have heard there have even been threats of death against Leif because of the pressure he puts on the people."

When he heard of these visits, Brand knew he had to intervene. As soon as Leif returned, he confronted him immediately. He found Leif sitting with a few of his bondsmen, cleaning their swords and comparing the various benefits of each type.

"Leif!" said Brand, interrupting the conversation. "I must speak with you now." He paused. "Alone."

The bondsmen looked at Leif. When he nodded, they slowly picked up their weapons and left.

Leif looked at Brand and continued polishing his sword, waiting.

"I have heard you have been spreading the Gospel of Jesu through threats and that some of those you pressure now want to harm you. Is this true?

"Yes, Father Brand. I have done what I felt needed to be done. And the threats against me cause me no concern. Have you not instructed me yourself on the many martyrs of the faith—the saints, you call them—and how they entered heaven for their suffering?"

Brand hated how easy it was for recent converts to misunderstand the truth of the faith.

"Yes, Leif. Some of these ideas are true. There have been great saints who died for their faith. But you must understand, you *must* understand, that you may not make converts by force. I will have no part of such coercion."

Leif put down his sword and stood facing the priest. He extended his arm and placed his right hand on Brand's left shoulder. "Yes, I will do as you say. I will no longer pressure the chieftains." Leif shook his head. "But I know no other way to change their heathen ways."

"Leave that to God in heaven. Pray that you can be strong in your faith, so that force will not be needed.

"Yes, Father, that I will do."

The two prayed together after this discussion, though Leif had his doubts about the effectiveness of such activity. Brand also worried that the dissention in Brattahlid would continue, whether from Erik's opposition or Leif's tactics.

Winter deepened. The time for celebration of Yule Eve arrived. There was no permanent temple in Brattahlid for the heathen rituals. The place for worship depended on the health and wealth of the community and the nature of the rites. This year, Erik decided it should be held away from his own longhouse, both to curry favor and to reduce the omnipresent tension in the settlement. The alternate building was ablaze with light and the sound of celebration. The idols of Freyr, Odinn, and Thor were prominently displayed and shining in the firelight. All those in attendance raised consecrated horns and drank sacred toasts.

"To Odinn—for victory and power!"

"To Freyr, for a fertile year!"

Erik laid his hands on the bristles of the atonement boar before it was sacrificed. He made a solemn vow to treat all men with justice, no matter what their crimes.

The mood was considerably less festive at the main hall in Brattahlid. There were no tables heaped high with good food and drink; there were no blazing fires. The long benches were empty except for Leif's bondsmen and Thjodhild and her loyal band of women. Brand sat apart, as always, and waited to see if he would be asked to share a story from the Holy Book.

Leif sat in his high seat, his jaw fixed in a scowl as he stared at their meager fire. He said nothing, but everyone sensed his frustration was growing, and no one wished to become the inadvertent recipient of his wrath. The best they hoped for was that with sufficient wine or mead, they would all settle into a stupor until morning. Occasionally, one or another of the thralls offered Leif food or drink, but he dismissed them with a growl.

Thjodhild leaned on the arm of her chair and studied her son closely in the dim light. Her ears were still sharp, and she could hear the whispers of the women: "He is angry because his father keeps up the heathen sacrifice."

She knew it was true, and her heart ached to help her son. Of all her children, Leif she loved the most. His absence to the court of King Olaf Tryggvason had seemed an eternity to her.

Her fingers tapped lightly on the arm of her chair. More time passed with nothing said in the great hall. Finally, she motioned to Brand. He came to her side, but when she spoke, it was with a voice loud enough to fill the empty hall.

"My teacher, I am ready to become a follower of the White Kristr. I am ready to have the waters of baptism sprinkled over me."

Thanks be to God for this little miracle, thought Brand. *Thanks be to God.*

CHAPTER THIRTY-SIX

B RAND HAD PRAYED FERVENTLY FOR his first convert in Greenland. He was grateful his prayers had been answered. He was even more grateful that the convert was someone of high status. He wasted no time. Thjodhild was baptized the next morning.

Erik was outraged at Thjodhild's decision. He approached her immediately after the baptism.

"What have you done?" he demanded. "Is this true, that you have had the waters sprinkled over you?"

"Yes, I have decided to follow the White Kristr," was her resolute reply. Then she took a deep breath to ready herself for her husband's response.

"*What?*" Erik sputtered. "Follow that weak god?"

"Yes. Father Brand has explained to me how weakness is really strength."

"What does he know of strength?" scoffed Erik. "For all we know, he is like the others—an argr man, effeminate. And hiding it."

"I do not think that is the case," said Thjodhild, calm in the face of Erik's anger.

"What do we really know of him and this god?"

"I know enough. And I tell you one more thing . . ."

Erik, who was unable to understand her decision to be baptized, was completely unprepared for what she said next.

"Until you are able to accept the White Kristr, you shall not be welcome in my bed."

Erik stared at her, his eyes wide with disbelief. They had had many differences in their marriage, but never anything like this.

"What? You would deny me?"

"Yes."

Erik glared and countered with a warning. "There are other beds that will warm me."

Still resolute, she replied, "I know. I have always known."

Erik stomped out with all the energy of a summer thunderstorm. He immediately set up a small sleeping place in a little building near the far end of the settlement. In the days to come, he found comfort there, in the arms of other women.

But his heart still yearned for Thjodhild. He entreated and cajoled her, but she was immovable. The stubborn Erik and the equally stubborn Thjodhild could not agree.

Erik complained bitterly to his son. "That man—that man you brought to us—is a trickster. He says he is a man of peace. But ever since he arrived here, there has been none!"

It was true. There was no peace in the settlement. Leif and Erik both began to do what many men do when confronted with an intractable problem—they dreamed of a way to escape.

The darkest days of winter had passed. The settlement was moving toward spring, when once again the ships could venture out into waters known and unknown.

Leif, especially, had grown restless. He had listened over and over to the story of Bjarni Herjólfsson. He was filled with a desire to repeat the adventure. And he sensed that tension between him and the other settlers might subside if he were to leave for a while. He hoped to make the journey with his father. Perhaps it would ease the discord between them and even open up his father to the White Kristr ways.

One dark afternoon, when the clouds were as thick and gray as the belly of a field mouse, father and son sat by the fire, talking. All winter long, Erik's joints had been a source of pain. He shifted often to try to find a comfortable spot.

A thrall took a red-hot iron from the fire, plunged it into a cup of water and herbs, then handed the warm mixture to Erik.

"Father," said Leif, "I have thought of starting a new expedition. This time to follow Bjarni's route, to sail not east but west."

Erik took a long drink, then swallowed slowly. He waited for what was to come next.

"And I want you to sail with me as well."

"Me? Sail with you?" Erik was intrigued. "Who else would go?"

"All my bondsmen. And Thryker, of course."

Erik's eyes narrowed slightly. *Of course Thryker.* For so many years, Thryker had been more father to Leif than Erik had been. And Leif's bondsmen would be more than sufficient crew for the expedition.

"Then why do you need me?"

"Because you have the courage and strength to lead us as no one else can."

Erik pondered this compliment. While flattering, his son's words merely spoke of a ceremonial leadership. Erik knew Leif would be the true leader of this expedition.

"What ship will you sail?" he finally asked.

"I am negotiating with Bjarni to purchase his ship."

"And why his ship and not the *Sea Deer* or my own?"

"I want to use Bjarni's ship because we know it can sail out into the unknown and safely return."

Erik was interested; he could not deny it. His blood was always filled with the urge to explore new places. But he was uncertain whether he could go on an expedition without being the leader.

"Not my ship? Not my men? Again, I say, what need to do you have of me?"

"There are none so good at handling the *styrbord* as you, Father. Did you not lead us settlers here, to this outpost, by your own skill?"

"And luck."

"Well, then, we need your skill. And your luck." Leif then used his best argument to persuade his father: "And the priest will stay here—not sail with us."

At this revelation, Erik's countenance brightened.

"I think, Leif, you are right. It would be good for us to sail together, to see if there is any truth to Bjarni's story."

And so Leif successfully negotiated with Bjarni for his ship. All that late winter, they organized and made ready to sail with a crew of thirty-five men. They would also bring aboard four cows, each soon to give birth.

By late March, all was ready. On sailing day, Brand made every attempt to replicate the blessing ceremony Grimkell had performed for the departing travelers back in Trondheim. Most of the Greenlanders looked on with simultaneous fascination and scorn.

Erik, wishing to avoid the ritual, mounted his horse. He went up the hills as high as possible for one last look at his settlement. He surveyed, with pride, the outpost he had founded. Then he slowly made his way down to the waterline of the fjord. As he neared, the settlers cheered with shouts and calls for good luck.

Suddenly, Erik was on the ground, writing with pain. He had either lost his balance or had been thrown from his horse—both versions later circulated among the people. At any rate, the injuries to Erik's ribs and shoulder were serious. He cried out in agony.

He was taken in great pain to his great hall, where he lay scowling. Leif followed with great concern for the patriarch.

"Father, how are you? We can wait until you are mended and well."

"No," said the elder, trying to hide the extent of his injuries and the pain he felt. "This is an omen. This shows that my exploration days are over. I will not sail with you. No right-minded man would do so with an ominous sign like that. I will stay home."

Leif truly was disappointed but decided any protest would be futile.

"Yes, Father." Then Leif added, with more brightness in his voice, "The sooner we sail, the sooner we shall return from our explorations."

"You shall return if you have luck, my son." Erik extended the arm of his good shoulder and held out his hand in blessing. "May you have luck."

CHAPTER THIRTY-SEVEN

To Vinland in what is now L'Anse aux Meadows, Newfoundland, Canada

L EIF FOLLOWED BJARNI'S ROUTE, SAILING west beyond the Greenland coast line. The explorers came first to a rocky land with high glaciers. It was a disappointing and desolate place. Leif named it Helluland for the flat rocks that seemed to cover the land.

After venturing farther south, they landed a second time. When he went ashore, Leif found the land to be flat with white beaches and trees. He decided to call this place Markland for the forest there.

From Markland, Leif sailed southeast for two days. Their small, tender boat crunched on rock as they clambered out to explore.

"Look! Look at this sweet grass!" cried Thryker.

The dew was heavy that morning. He ran his hands on the long strands of green until they were wet with water. He rubbed it all over his face and was refreshed.

Upon further exploration, they found that the rich pasture land was extensive, but thick stands of trees were not far. When they followed the creeks that flowed into the sea, they discovered salmon bigger than any they had ever before seen.

Basic tents were quickly erected. Leif sent out small groups daily to explore the surrounding lands. Leif's rules were clear: the group must stay together and must return to the shelter by nightfall.

After men returned from one of these day expeditions, they reported that Thryker had gone off on his own and was now missing. That night was a long one for the explorers.

Thryker did not appear until the next morning. He ran into camp, very happy and babbling in his mother tongue. Everyone immediately surrounded him, relieved he was alive.

Leif was also relieved. But even more, he was displeased. "Thryker, why did you separate yourself from us?" he asked, hardly able to contain his anger. "And why did you remain away so long against my orders?"

Thryker could barely speak in his excitement. He finally calmed himself and blurted out his explanation.

"I did not go much farther from the encampment than the others did. But I found something you have not seen—and which you may find it difficult to believe."

"Get to the point!" said Leif in exasperation. "What is this fantastic thing?"

"Grapevines!"

"Grapevines?"

"Yes, the very same grape plants I knew from my boyhood among the Germanic tribes."

"Are you sure, Foster Father?" asked Leif, still unconvinced. Thryker's demeanor suggested the possibility that he was hallucinating.

"Yes, I am sure. I know them well. There was no lack of grapevines in the land where I was born."

The explorers verified Thryker's story. It was an impressive find. The Norse people lived in climes too cold for grapes to thrive. This discovery opened new possibilities for the explorers.

They had built only temporary shelters, planning to depart before winter. But seeing the richness of the land—especially the discovery of grapevines—they decided to stay the winter in this grand wilderness. Soon they built a sturdy wooden building. They calculated that within two weeks of harvest, they would have new wine to drink. And new wine meant they could endure whatever winter should bring.

They observed that winter there was very peculiar. No frost covered the grasses, so their cattle grazed all winter long, with no need for fodder. And the days and nights seemed to be of more equal length than at home in

Greenland, or Iceland, or even in Norway. Even on the shortest day of the winter, the sun was up at morning meal and still in the sky at midafternoon.

When spring came again, Leif and his men filled Bjarni's ship with as much timber as it could hold. They made ready and sailed away to Greenland.

They were just off the western coast of home when Thryker noticed Leif was steering the vessel off course.

"What are you doing, Leif? Why are you sailing so far north?" asked Thryker.

"I see something," he replied, nodding up ahead.

Everyone rushed to the edge of the ship and peered into the distance. All they saw was a small rocky outcrop in the water.

"I see nothing!" various men protested.

Still, Leif would not change course. But soon enough, everyone could see a wrecked ship marooned on the tiny bit of land surrounded by water. And there were survivors. Men were in great peril and near death, clinging onto the shattered hull of their ship. When Leif's ship drew near, the shipwrecked men were hastily hauled in and given food and warm clothing.

It was the end of summer when Leif returned to Brattahlid with Thryker, the bondsmen, the survivors of the wreck, and plenty of tales to share. Within hours, people began to call him "Leif the Lucky," for he had returned safely from the unknown places and had made claim to a fine new land.

But Erik was not entirely impressed. It was true that his son had done great deeds. But it was also true that Leif had brought a trickster to Greenland. While Leif had been off on a thrilling journey, Erik had been left at home with a troublesome priest and a stubborn wife.

CHAPTER THIRTY-EIGHT

I T WAS TRUE THAT SOME of the tension in Brattahlid had calmed while Leif was gone on his expedition. In particular, tension toward conversion lessened. It was not that Brand had diminished his efforts in Leif's absence. Rather, it was that Brand's style was to be a quiet example. Coercion was anathema to him. So he had continued his work in his own way, teaching and listening.

Thjodhild had been his first convert, but she was not the last. Little by little, the small congregation was growing. Now, almost always a dozen or more people gathered for prayers, and two infant baptisms had been performed.

When Brand had left Trondheim as a missionary to Greenland, Grimkell had sent an altar stone with him. It was made of polished jasper, about an inch thick and the size of a large man's hand. The stone was set in an oak frame, and on one side, five crosses had been etched in the wood. With this consecrated stone, it was permissible to create an altar anywhere—on another stone or even a table.

Grimkell had also sent Brand off with a supply of wheat and grape wine so Brand could celebrate Holy Eucharist with Christians far from Trondheim. The requirements of the church were clear: the only permitted substances were wine made from grapes and bread made from wheat. And as bishop, Grimkell did not grant permission for Brand to use anything but both wheat bread and grape wine for Eucharist. There could be no substitutions. So when the supply of grape wine gave out, Brand could only sing the liturgy— the Kyrie, the Sanctus, and the Agnus Dei—to his flock of Greenlanders. The Eucharist, the most precious ritual of all, would have to wait.

Brand had a lot to keep him occupied: teaching, leading worship, visiting the sick. Yet sometimes, even during his prayers, his thoughts wandered back to the young maiden whose spirit still called so softly and incessantly to his own soul. Brand never ceased to wonder about Kathleen, if she were happier now, whether Arn had returned from the east that spring as he had promised, and if she had married. Brand was certain she would have no trouble finding suitors.

Kathleen was never really out of his mind, except when singing the Mass or leading the liturgy. The rituals always centered him; a deep peace would come over him. There was comfort in the familiar words and the flow of the prayers. But otherwise, she was nearly always there, just below the surface of his conscious. A constant background noise, like the sigh of the wind in thick woods or the bubbling of water in a stony brook.

In a similar way, Thjodhild was never really out of Erik's mind. True to his word, Erik had not interfered with Brand and his work. And true to her word, Thjodhild had not allowed him in her bed. Instead, other women spent hours with Erik in the relative privacy of his small hut at the edge of the settlement. He was even visited by Freydis's mother, his longtime consort.

Still, when Erik played with other women's hair, it was Thjodhild's locks he stroked. When he felt warm breasts against him, it was Thjodhild's body he recalled. He cursed her for having banned him from their bed, and he cursed himself for being unable to give in to her demand. He spent much time thinking of a way to appease her, short of converting.

Brand was surprised and a little curious when a thrall said he had a message from Erik. It was simple: "Meet me at my sleeping place at midday tomorrow." It was most mysterious, for Erik generally did everything he could to be as far away from Brand as possible. And when Erik did need to see Brand, it was usually before the high seat. It was unusual for Erik to bid Brand to come to his sleeping place.

Brand prayed as he walked: *Help me support this man to grow in the true faith. Whatever he asks of me, help me with the strength to do it.*

Erik began the conversation by stating the obvious: "Things have not been good between Thjodhild and me."

Brand nodded his understanding.

"Father Brand, I want to give Thjodhild a gift. Will you help?"

"Yes, of course I will help you if I can. But what is it you want from me?"

"I want you to design and build a chapel."

For a moment, Brand could not speak.

"A chapel. To the White Kristr?" Brand finally asked, uncertain if he understood.

"Yes."

Silently, Brand marveled to himself how the ways of God were mysterious.

"Yes, I will do what you ask," he answered.

Erik barely made time for Brand's reply before continuing his requirements. "Place it far enough from my main house, so it will not always be in my sight. I have enough to antagonize me without this too!"

Almost immediately, construction of Thjodhild's chapel began. It was to be part stone and part wood. Haki, Thjodhild's male thrall, did much of the work. He was a small and wiry man, with strength beyond his size. He scoured every shoreline near and far for precious wood. And when it was decided that a low rock wall should surround it to keep out errant cattle and sheep, it was Haki who selected and placed each stone.

Brand designed the last and most impressive piece of the site—a wooden pergola formed in an opening in the rock wall. The archway framed the entrance to the chapel. Every element of the simple design helped remind all who entered that they must pass from this present world into sacred space.

When completed, the chapel was a mere twelve feet wide and thirty-six feet long but large enough to hold twenty to thirty worshipers. But one important item was missing.

"I wish we had a bell for our little chapel," Thjodhild explained to Brand. "To call the faithful to worship. And to cleanse the air of unholy spirits."

She knew, of course, that to the heathen members of the settlement, the presence of a church bell would have been considered unlawful, an unacceptable disruption to the community. The bells so loved by the White Kristr folk would offend the very spirits the heathens protected and honored. And at any rate, no metal bell could be had in all of Greenland.

Thjodhild also wanted a small cow barn built nearby, so the priest would always have milk, butter, and cheese. She instructed Haki to begin work on the structure. It was to be made of stone and sod blocks, as were most buildings in the outpost.

It was not long before the cow barn was complete. Haki suggested they use the shoulder blades of whales to form the stalls. The bones worked exceedingly well, and Thjodhild complimented Haki on his resourcefulness.

On the day the chapel was consecrated, Thjodhild and the small group of new converts all gathered, with Brand officiating. Erik, of course, would not make an appearance. But he observed, from a distance, with a hopeful heart.

When Brand finished the consecration, tears filled Thjodhild's eyes. It was the most beautiful building she had ever seen. She hoped that someday her bones and those of her sons—even Erik's bones—would rest together under its eaves, waiting for judgement day.

She called her thrall aside. "Haki, you have been a most intelligent and resourceful thrall to me. I have been thinking of giving you in service to Father Brand. I have no need to ask your desire in this matter, but I am wondering, how would this sit with you?"

"I will do whatever you ask of me, and I would be pleased to serve the White Kristr priest. But I will not abandon the old gods."

Thjodhild reflected on this response. "I think that will be all right with Father Brand. He seems able to forgive us when we resist accepting the love the White Kristr offers us," answered Haki's kind mistress.

And that night, there was another who needed forgiveness. Erik walked into the main hall, to the sleeping place where Thjodhild waited. Without a word, she lifted up the bed furs, and he wrapped himself around her once again.

CHAPTER THIRTY-NINE

Trondheim

TIME HAD PASSED SINCE LEIF and Brand had left Olaf Tryggvason's stronghold and made their way to Greenland. The weather had been warm for their departure then, and it was warm for other travelers' arrival now. As he had promised, Arn sailed triumphantly back into Trondheim.

Delicate linnaea flowers were just beginning to bloom. Soft breezes, redolent with the scent of new bud and flower, washed through Arn's hair, now grown long. It flowed behind him in fluttering waves. He had kept his vow of faithfulness and wanted his unshorn hair to be the first thing Ragnhild would see.

The expedition had been phenomenally successful. The trunks on his ship held an abundance of luxury goods. They had exchanged furs, walrus ivory, and amber beads for silver arm and finger rings, fragrant spices, and shimmering silk.

Within minutes of sailing into the harbor, Arn was on land. A small crowd had gathered. Everyone was curious to greet the voyager and learn what goods he carried and what news he brought from the faraway lands.

His eyes searched for Ragnhild, and he was puzzled when he did not see her. Kathleen came running to him, flinging herself into his arms.

"Kathleen! My dear daughter!" Arn clasped her to his chest with fierce emotion, then asked, "Your mother—where is your mother?"

"She is not here, Father. She . . . she . . ." Tears welled up in her eyes and overflowed.

It was then that Arn looked more closely at his daughter. She had matured and was lovelier than ever. But when his eyes fell upon her throat, his breath stopped. The White Kristr cross he had last seen on the neck of his beloved wife now hung on the neck of his precious daughter. He knew it would have never left Ragnhild's slender throat if she were still alive.

Soon he learned it all: the difficult pregnancy, the birth and death of the twins, and Ragnhild's failed struggle to survive. When there was no more to learn, Arn immediately went to Olaf and requested permission to ride the fleetest of the king's steeds. He rode furiously into the deep forest, yelling the name of his dead wife into the unresponsive sky.

He thought of her faith in the White Kristr. *A weak god. A useless god.*

During the next days and weeks, he struggled with his own grief and did not know how to comfort Kathleen. Now she was all to her father. She was his past and his future, his hope and his life. Yet she remained sad and seldom spoke. The light was gone from her.

One morning, Arn took Kathleen to a nearby warehouse. He had directed that some of his goods be stored before they would be traded away for the best possible prices. He opened a wooden chest and pulled out the contents. He bade her to choose from the silken shawls he had carried with him from the East. They fluttered with the beauty of butterfly wings as he pulled them out, one by one. They dazzled the eye with their brilliant colors.

"Kathleen, these are the finest of silks. They are spun not from the fleece of sheep or the fibers of flax. No one knows how they are made, but legends say they are made from enchanted worms."

Kathleen made no response.

"I think that is impossible," he continued.

Again no response.

"But do you not agree that they are very beautiful?" he said enticingly as he spread them one atop the other across her lap.

"Yes, they are beautiful," she finally answered with a dull voice. Then her voice grew with emotion. "But I do not want them!" she shouted, flinging the colorful garments away as if they were plague-filled rags.

Kathleen collapsed into his arms, tears running down her cheeks. He cradled her as if she were a small child, not a young woman. He patted her back and intoned "*yaaa, yaaaa, yaaaa*" to soothe her. He stroked her hair gently. But all the while, his eyes stared out in sadness and helplessness, for he did not know how to help her.

Finally, he said with all earnestness, "Daughter, it is clear you do not want the things I have offered you." He held her tenderly by her shoulders and looked straight at her tear-stained face. "What *do* you want?"

"Father, you must promise me that you will never leave me. Never leave me again, as you left me and Mother before."

Arn's hands flew away from her in surprise. He had not anticipated this request. He stood, walked to the doorway, and looked out. Then he turned back to her.

"Daughter, you do not understand. I am a trader. I can never stay here—"

"I am not asking you to stay. I am asking you to never leave me. Take me with you. Wherever you go, I want to go with you."

"Take you with me?" he repeated.

"Yes. Do not leave me behind ever again."

"Daughter, you do not know what you are asking. The knarrs are open to whatever weather the gods send us. The seas, even the well-known ones, are unpredictable.

"Yes, I know." She lifted her chin. "Father, you see my tears and think me a child. But I am strong in my heart, and I can be strong against the wind and the rain. Take me with you."

"And it is crowded with animals and cargo—there will be little privacy," he countered.

"Yes, I know. Take me with you."

"Oh my child, there are dangers too. Pirates and other raiders can overcome us, and you would surely be sold into slavery. Even Olaf Tryggvason himself was bought and sold as a child in the markets of Estonia."

His words did not deter her. She replied with conviction. "You know that the mother of my mother, my own namesake, was sold into slavery from the Orkney Islands, and she survived. If I stayed here, I would also be in danger. I have heard of young girls being taken captive by Hákon Jarl—he made them his concubines. So you see, there is no place without danger. Take me with you."

Arn was running out of arguments against his strong-willed daughter. "You know I have never traveled with family," he finally offered.

The unhappy truth of that comment pierced her heart as surely as an arrow.

She stood up and moved next to him, her arm around his waist. They looked out the doorway together, out over the blue-green harbor waters.

"But wives and sometimes children travel on expeditions," she said.

She was right. Knowing he had lost the argument, Arn sighed. He looked at his stubborn daughter with exasperation and love.

"All right. You are bone of my bone, flesh of my flesh. Wherever I go, from now on, you will go with me. To the ends of the earth."

"Yes. Until the ends of the earth, my father, we shall be together," she said, smiling broadly.

Despite what she had told her father, Kathleen did not really know what life on the knarr would be like. She did not care. She had done something her mother had never done: she had won a concession from Arn. And she had also made a promise to herself: she vowed that never in her life would she stay behind and wait on the shore while a loved one sailed away.

She lifted the cross from her neck. "Now swear by the White Kristr god," she demanded.

"Yes, I swear," he replied, "by the White Kristr."

But in his heart, he silently swore to the gods of his youth, the heathen spirits, to make it a true vow.

CHAPTER FORTY

To Dublin, Ireland

A FTER THAT DAY IN THE warehouse with his sorrowful daughter, Arn gave his next expedition much thought. He was still uncomfortable with the idea of her sailing with him, but he had given his word.

He decided his next trip should be a new voyage, a new destination, to mark the new phase of their lives. They would not travel east to his usual trading routes. He had heard much of the settlements to the west—Iceland and even the new settlement in Greenland. When he shared this notion with Kathleen, she became more alive—enthusiastic even—for she would see Leif and the other Greenlanders, and her teacher Father Brand.

Finally, preparations were complete and the weather cooperated. It was a good sailing day. Arn's crew members were well and looking forward to the voyage. The sun had warmed their bodies, and they were in high spirits. They waited for just the right combination of wind and tide to bring them out of Trondheim. When the travelers left the safety of the harbor, the sparkle in Kathleen's eyes rivaled the glint of the sun on the Nidelva as it poured into the sea.

Kathleen insisted that Hlatr make the voyage with them. Of course, the young cat refused to be held in Kathleen's arms for more than a minute. The feline sniffed smells both mysterious and enticing. Her tail twitched with excitement as she explored every nook and cranny of the vessel. Hlatr had become sexually mature in the previous months, with more than a few encounters with interested males. Kathleen hoped the curious pet would have kittens soon.

"To Dublin!" shouted Arn.

"To Dublin!" echoed Kathleen.

And they were off on the whales' highway.

Kathleen had never before been on her father's ship, except when anchored or in calm waters close to the coast. She was unprepared for the unceasing sensation of movement as they sailed into deeper waters. She refused to allow her father to see her sickened by the life on the sea she had so eagerly pursued. She used every possible contrivance to avoid him, which was difficult with the confines of the vessel. Eventually, she could tolerate it no more. Over the side went her head. After this, she felt somewhat better.

They had been at sail for most of the afternoon when she called out excitedly, "Father, look!"

A small pod of pilot whales had surrounded the boat. They followed the vessel for several more hours, gliding up and down through the billowing waves.

"A good omen," said Arn. "We shall have luck now, for certain."

Indeed, the voyage went very smoothly. They arrived in Dublin a day earlier than anticipated. As their ship slowly neared the town, they sailed past rows and rows of longships and knarrs bobbing in the harbor. There was movement everywhere, and more people than Kathleen had ever seen in her life.

At one end of the wharf, women knelt over mounds of soiled clothing and linens. They scooped river water into their basins and vigorously slapped and pounded the laundry, their hair coming undone with exertion. Hairpins fell and floated down in silence through murky water to rest in the mud below.

Kathleen watched in astonishment as mariners, to keep up strength and for sport, ran in circles around the longships, never touching the water. The men moved confidently on oars poised horizontally over the waters, like the stiff wings of a dragonfly.

Arn quickly found an empty building not too far from the wharf.

After haggling over its fee, he and Kathleen settled into their new living space.

Arn also wasted no time in his next task. He asked others to direct him to the best shipbuilder. They quickly pointed him toward the sheds at the edge of town.

Arn approached the craftsman with confidence. "Ketill, they tell me you are a master shipbuilder, the best in all of Dublin." Arn knew flattery would serve him well.

Ketill, a man of few words, nodded in assent, feeling no need to keep up the pretense of humility.

Arn continued. "We are in need of a deep-water knarr, something that will withstand not only the coastal storms but also the strongest anger of Ægir and Rán. And I want the finest of instruments to guide us."

"Where are you bound?"

"We are bound for Iceland, then on to Greenland to meet with Erik the Red and his son Leif, whom my daughter knows as a friend. We will bring news and goods to the Greenlanders."

Arn produced a wooden model of the ship he desired, each tiny detail carved into it. When complete, it would measure fifty-four feet long and fifteen feet wide. The model showed half decks in stern and bow.

"You lose cargo space with the *lyftingar*," said Ketill, pointing to the half decks. "Are you sure you want them?"

"Yes, I want them. It will help protect fragile cargo. And it will be a special place for my daughter, Kathleen, to keep her things, for her to sleep away from wind and rain and to provide a bit of privacy."

The remainder of ship was simply an open hold with floorboards laid on the foundation timbers. Ketill inspected the model carefully.

"This is no ordinary ship." He paused. "It will be expensive."

"I want only the best. Tell me what you want to build it, and we will come to terms on price."

And they did. Arn agreed to sell Ketill his ship and give an additional amount of danegeld to satisfy both.

Arn and Kathleen settled into their temporary home and began to meet the leaders of the town. After much turmoil with the Irish kings,

Sigtrygg Silkbeard was once again the king of Dublin. When Sigtrygg heard that Arn and Kathleen had traveled from Trondheim, he instantly welcomed the two into his life at court. The Dubliners wanted to know everything about life in the new town to the north that Olaf Tryggvason had founded.

Sigtrygg enthusiastically showed Kathleen and Arn his family's lucrative horse-trading business. Arn recognized the signs of superior horse husbandry. Kathleen loved watching the foals as they gamboled and played. The heart of the young woman was healing as she walked in the green glowing countryside of Dublin.

Each day, Kathleen kept a close eye on Hlatr, waiting to see her belly grow. The cat had certainly had many encounters with toms, yet with no result. Kathleen began to wonder if Hlatr was barren.

Kathleen's days in Dublin were filled with activities of all kinds. She attended Mass daily with other members of the court, though heathen ideas were still powerful among the people.

There was only one part of Dublin that Kathleen avoided—the thrall market. It brought to mind too many memories of the grandmother she had not known and the mother she had known and lost.

Ketill lived up to his reputation. The master shipbuilder immediately set to work to assemble and direct the shipbuilding team: tree fellers, laborers, plank cutters, and ironsmiths. Ketill had a very clear mental image of the completed ship throughout the construction process. At every stage, he used plumb lines together with staves and strings to lay out the ship.

Arn spent every day at the shipyard. At first, Ketill's jaw worked in silent resentment every time he saw Arn nearby. The trader's constant presence was an irritant. But after a while, when Arn made no attempt to direct or intervene, Ketill realized Arn was merely studying every aspect of the ship so he could pilot her with complete confidence.

Oak was used throughout the ship. Tall, straight trees were selected for masts and planks. The tree men were dispatched to search the dark wooded hills for elusive specimens of sufficient size and quality. The sound of long-shafted axes rang out as the men felled the trees, then dragged them through the forest, meadows, and streams to the shipyard of Dublin.

Once the premium trees arrived in the shipyard, Arn watched the expert plank cutters fall to their work. The cutters drove wedges to split the trunks from the outside into their centers, resulting in long, thin planks with a wider edge tapering to fine edge. From a typical trunk, perhaps twenty planks—each approximately one foot wide and as long as the tree itself—could be created. These fine strakes were strong and would withstand splitting, warping, or shrinking.

The ironsmiths came next. They used the clinker technique, in which the lower edge of each hull plank overlapped the upper edge of the one below, like scales on a giant fish. This technique would allow the ship to give with the waves instead of breaking apart, as a stiffer hull would do. The strakes were joined together with iron rivets. Tarred woolen yarn was forced into the joints between the strakes to make them as watertight as possible.

Construction on the sea craft continued all through the winter, and Arn never missed a day. After the hull was completed, the fittings were next. Oiled skins were sown together to make a tent roof used as needed to keep spray, wind, or snow from the open areas of the knarr. The tent roof was made to overlap the sides of the ship for drainage. Small wooden pegs held it in place.

Tough walrus-hide ropes were installed to rig the precious and expensive sail. A fine-oak water cache was installed near the mast. It could be replenished with rainwater caught in the tent roof.

Chests for personal belongings were also used as benches and sleeping spaces for the crew. Each crew member would bring a two-person leather sleep sack, or *húdfat,* in which to sleep at night and to store gear for easy access during the day.

Arn was pleased. He was pleased with how the building of his new ship was progressing. And he was pleased with the new happiness he saw in his daughter. He even wondered if perhaps Kathleen had been right, that it would be good to sail together.

CHAPTER FORTY-ONE

As the construction of Arn's knarr neared completion, he looked for the most critical crew member of all: the navigator. He had used many navigators on his trading voyages, always with good luck. He knew that only a skilled, knowledgeable navigator could bring him through the treacherous and stormy waters that lay between Dublin and Greenland.

Arn went to the meeting place of all sailors waiting for work. The hall was modest, but the hearth fire crackled and burned hot to chase away the chill of late winter. The mead flowed as easily as the mariners' tales. Older men—their hair white and hands gnarled with painful, swollen joints—recalled days when they sailed the seas of the north and beyond.

After he finished a horn of mead, Arn stood up and announced his planned voyage to Iceland and then to Greenland.

"Who is the best navigator?" he asked.

"That would be Helgi. He has been to Greenland," the mariners replied. "*Twice.*"

That single word carried huge import. Everyone knew the main qualification for a Norse navigator was that he had been to the destination and returned to tell of it.

"And where do I find this man named Helgi?"

All heads turned to a corner of the hall, where three men sat. One of the men rose and said in a booming voice, "I am Helgi. And these are my friends, Patrekr and Gunnar."

Everything about Helgi exuded strength. The size of his strong neck was nearly the same as the substantial head that rested on it. On some men, this would have looked odd, but his muscular neck suited his broad face and easy, wide grin. Whatever the problem, Helgi attacked it with the optimism and enthusiasm of a beaver biting into the heart of an ancient aspen tree. He was as subtle as an avalanche.

The two other men also rose. Patrekr was nearly as tall as Helgi, but with exceptionally strong shoulders. Even in the dim light of the hall, you could see his eyes were as sharp as a hungry eagle's. Gunnar was the same in height, but his powerful body was uniform, with shoulders and legs equally well muscled.

After the introductions, Helgi asked Arn if they could walk alone together. "The air in here is thick. I need some fresh breezes to get my blood flowing."

Arn nodded and carried another horn of mead with him into the brisk air.

They walked in silence for some time. They were past the end of the wharf, away from crowds, and nearly to the shipyards when Helgi began to speak.

"The first thing you must understand, Arn, is that I will only navigate with the men I know I can trust."

"I understand. Just so you know, I have not made final agreement, but I have found six men who will act as bailers and rowers. They are traveling with their wives."

"All with their wives?" asked Helgi, a little puzzled.

"Yes, all. Will your wife travel with you?"

"I must ask her. Gudrun and I have been married long enough to know that she alone can make this decision for herself. But I believe she will say yes."

Such a marital decision-making process was unfamiliar to Arn. He said, "I understand," even though he did not.

"And for lookouts and sail handlers?" asked Helgi.

"No agreement yet for them," Arn responded, quickly gulping a swallow of mead.

"If I am to be your navigator, there are only two men for these duties: Gunnar and Patrekr."

"Do they have wives?" Arn quickly asked. "I am only taking married men and their wives on this voyage."

Again, Helgi was puzzled. "Only married men? That is most unusual, Arn. Why?"

"Because I want no man to return home to a dead wife, as I did. And I want no single man to be distracted with desire," he added, thinking of Kathleen.

There was a pause before Helgi answered. "Well, with Gunnar and Patrekr, that is no problem."

"They are married?"

"No. But your fears will not be justified with them."

Arn turned his face to look directly at Helgi. "What are you saying?"

"I am saying that Gunnar and Patrekr—they will not grow restless for female company."

A slow realization crept over Arn's face like a crack on a lake of ice. He replied with scorn, "I want no argr men with me."

Helgi expected this reaction and had no patience for it.

"Then you are a fool! I have made seven voyages with these men. Have you heard of the great waves, the monster waves that come on without warning in our seas? Some say they are merely stories, but I can tell you they are true. We were one day's sail out of Dublin when our ship was engulfed by such a wave. I was knocked into the sea. Have you ever spent time in the water of the sea?"

Helgi made no pause for Arn to respond.

"For a brief moment, you feel nothing, then a thousand needles prick unceasingly into your skin. I struggled back toward the ship. But my mind was becoming weak, and my legs and arms refused to move. Gunnar tied a rope around his body and leapt into the icy waters to pull me back aboard. Only, the rope was too short by a few feet. I tried and tried but could not reach it. I could hardly move anymore. It was then that Patrekr jumped into the sea. He extended the distance of the safety rope. All three of us were saved."

Arn refused to be impressed. "Well, it is all the decision of the Norns," he said. "When a man's time to die comes, there is nothing he can do to prevent it. And if it is not his time, there is nothing intentional or unintentional that will hasten the end of his life."

Helgi stared at Arn. "I know that is what many men believe. It heightens their bravery. But I do not think it is so true. Men can change the outcome when danger approaches, as Patrekr and Gunnar did for me."

Helgi continued, his great voice speaking so softly now that he could scarce be heard.

"These are men of courage and loyalty. I do not care what happens in the night when they climb into their sleep sack. If you do not accept them, you can find another navigator!"

CHAPTER FORTY-TWO

THE DUBLIN WINTER FINALLY YIELDED to welcome spring. After nearly a year of construction, Arn's ship was ready for her first trial under sail. Ketill and Arn, as builder and owner, took their places on the prow. And back on the styrbord side, handling the tiller, was Helgi, flanked by Patrekr and Gunnar.

The ship handled wonderfully well. "Yes!" Ketill exclaimed when they safely returned to harbor. "She is as fine a ship as any in the north, and nimbler than a goat."

"That's it!" said Arn, punching Ketill's shoulder in excitement. "That's what I will name her. This ship will be called the *Sea Goat*, for she will be as confident on the sea as the nimblest of goats in the mountains. In this ship, we will glide from wave top to wave top."

The *Sea Goat* was beautiful, with her sail reinforced with walrus rope in a crosshatch pattern. Though its purpose was to stabilize the wool in the wind, the pattern also gave the sail visual impact and drama. It had taken three women four years to spin and weave sufficient quantity of wool for the sail, so the sail cost Arn nearly as much as the hull of the ship. When completed, the precious sail had been coated with animal fats and oils to protect it from the elements.

Arn had insisted that an intricately carved wooden dragon head grace her prow. Usually such decoration was only for drakkar, the long-ships of war, and not the broad-bottomed, practical knarr. But Arn felt it would bring him luck. However, laws in many ports of call prohibited ships with dragon-head prows from entering harbor, lest the frightening appearance threaten the tranquility of the landvættir, the land spirits. So Arn had ordered that the carving be removable. That way, the land spirits would not become fearful and his trading partners uncooperative.

Arn had also insisted upon another feature for the dragon head. On one of his travels, he had seen a group of men from the hot lands in the south who had with them many exotic animals. One they called a lion, and it was fierce. Arn remembered the magnificent mane that swelled out from its neck and framed the face of the ferocious feline. He wanted his dragon to sport the same wild mane. Arn's dragon had flowing waves circling its neck and framing its head.

The ornament was placed, and the ship was finished. She was ready for her maiden voyage. Arn, in consultation with Helgi, waited several days for just the right conditions before setting sail. Along with six other knarr, they set off for Iceland on Wednesday—Odinn's Day.

On board were Arn and Kathleen, Helgi and Gudrun, Patrekr and Gunnar, and the other sailors and their wives. On this voyage, only Helgi, Patrekr, and Gunnar would share in Arn's profits. The others were earning their passage to Iceland.

Everything about Gudrun was soft and pink. Her cheeks were perpetually rosy and as soft as tiny pillows. Her breasts were as round and full as the underbelly of the knarr. Kathleen immediately fell in love with her, and the feeling was mutual.

The ship was outfitted along the floorboards with chests that doubled as benches. Some chests held items needed collectively for the voyage. In addition, each mariner had his own sea chest for personal items.

Gudrun was in charge of minding the food stores. Before the voyage began, Gudrun knelt beside before the food stores chest. She carefully placed in it her wooden and iron cooking tools as well as many small wooden boxes and bags of dried herbs and berries for flavoring. Monotony was often a guest on a voyage, so she would do her best to keep the food interesting as well as nourishing.

Kathleen also took extra care with the items for her personal chest. She carefully folded a blue cloak to match her father's, some extra linen underdresses, several overdresses, some woolen scarves, a woolen shawl, a pair of fur-lined mittens, two pairs of leather ankle boots, a half dozen wool socks, and two blankets. She also made room for a hooded cape, oiled to keep out wind and rain. She added some jewelry and a comb set Queen Thyre had given her at Olaf's court, all placed together in an embroidered crimson drawstring bag. The last things she added were a dozen bars of tawny lye soap. It was harsh on the skin and not always completely effective at removing oily dirt, but it was an item she never wanted to be without.

In other chests, the crew placed communal items: drinking horns, bowls and cups, bows and arrows, and fishing hooks and nets. The mariners also carried a bronze cooking pot for the days when they were on land. For sleeping on shore, they carried tent material and heavily carved poles to form an X shape to hold up tent roofs and walls. Sometimes sleeping hammocks were used, both on shore and at sea. There were also containers of grain plus metal tools and artifacts of all kinds to trade in Iceland and Greenland. A large cage of three squawking ravens completed the cargo.

As far as memory ran back in time, the launching of a Norse ship had always begun with a blood ritual to appease the gods of the sea. Arn chose a goat for the sacrificial animal, so his ship would be infused with the spirit of the animal. Kathleen tolerated the ritual in silence, as she was sure her mother would have been uncomfortable with it.

As blood spattered red on the oaken prow of the ship, a priest of Odinn intoned: "Unharmed go forth, unharmed return, unharmed back home!"

Just as they had during the voyage to Dublin, a cluster of pilot whales followed alongside the boat for nearly the whole morning. This was another sign of good luck, which pleased Arn very much.

That evening, all on board settled in for their first night at sea together. The winds and waters were calm, and in the semidarkness, the full moon cast a luminous pale sheen. Hearts and heads were filled with a mixture of excitement and fear and dreams of what was to come.

As grand a ship as the *Sea Goat* was, life was still difficult for the travelers. There was no cooking on board, for fear of fire. They ate meat and fish that had been dried and salted prior to the trip. There was butter, cheese, and a little bread at the beginning of the voyage. For thirst, they had rainwater collected in the tent top or sail, mead, and skyr, a special kind of soured milk. Gudrun kept after the others to chew on dried rose hips and dried berries. She did not know why, but she had heard it protected against the sailor's illness that harmed so many on long voyages.

The ship was small and cramped with people and animals. To maintain a little dignity, the group created a small degree of privacy for one another by simply *not seeing* and *not hearing*. They would turn their heads away or fix their eyes on a spot on the horizon. In that way, they did not feel so much a part of every private conversation and bodily function of their fellow passengers.

Arn had insisted the *Sea Goat* be built with the newest techniques, and he had also insisted it be outfitted with the newest technology. So Helgi had filled his chest with every navigational tool he had ever used plus some tools new to him but highly recommended by other mariners.

Arn had agreed, only reluctantly, to sail with Patrekr and Gunnar. For one thing, he was sure he would be revulsed if he saw them say or do anything remotely intimate. But Helgi had assured him that the men would be extremely careful and that no one else aboard would know the truth. And it was true. The men had lived many years hiding their true feelings from outsiders. It came naturally and easily to them—but not without pain.

Helgi had further explained that if any question should arise, Arn could tell the questioner that Patrekr and Gunnar were foster brothers. Arn had heard of the foster brother ritual, but knew little about it.

"Two men cut runes into the handles of a special spear," Helgi explained. "The runes include the promises they will make to each other as foster brothers. At the site of the ceremony, they place the spear into the ground with the blade pointing up. They then cut two long strips of turf from the earth, one on each side of the spear. They leave one end of each turf piece on the ground and secure the other end to the spear, piercing it with the blade. This way, the turf pieces create two sloping sides with the spear in the middle, in a kind of an arch.

"On the day of the ceremony, the men must first declare to their friends and family that they desire to become foster brothers. The two men walk under this arch, and each makes a little cut in his palm. They kneel and clasp hands, so that the blood of the two flows together. They say, 'Now we are of one blood.'

"Then each makes this vow: 'I will fight for and protect my foster brother whenever he shall need me. If he is killed before I am, I will exact revenge on the person who killed him. Whatever things I own belong to my foster brother as much as they belong to me. I will love this man until I die. I call upon Odinn and Thor and all the gods to hear my vow. May they punish me if ever I break it!'"

"And Patrekr and Gunnar have had such a ceremony?" asked Arn.

"Yes, several years ago. I should know. Gudrun and I were there."

CHAPTER FORTY-THREE

I T DID NOT TAKE LONG for Kathleen to grow somewhat bored within the confines of the ship. With nothing to do but ponder the endless sky and sea, her mind soon overflowed with thoughts and questions. But she found an eager partner willing to answer all her queries.

"Helgi, why have you brought the ravens?"

Helgi grinned. He had never sailed before with a young woman, and he loved answering her questions.

"If you are so far from land that you cannot see any landmarks, then you can release ravens or other seabirds. You closely watch the direction they fly. If they do not return, this is a sign land is near. If they return to the ship, then you know land is far off."

"What do you mean, landmarks?" asked Kathleen, not fully understanding.

"The land always tells a story. It marks the way for those who are sharp eyed and who can remember. There are mountain peaks with special shapes. And you can note the color and size of rocks, fjords, and rivers. Using landmarks is the most reliable method of navigation."

"But what if you cannot see the landmarks?"

"There are other signs too—things my father taught me. Sometimes you can tell if land is near by the type of seaweed floating in the sea. Also by the type of birds flying overhead and the kinds of sea animals, such as whales or seals. I have even heard that some men can tell where they are by the color of the mud at the bottom of the sea. They send sinkers down to pull some mud into ship. Many things, even the rhythm of the swells, can tell you something. And then there are the sun and the stars."

"How can the sun and stars guide you?"

"During the day, the sun guides us with her rising and setting."

Helgi pulled out the shadow board, a circular piece of wood engraved with concentric circles. He pushed a stick through the center of the board.

"Look at the shadow, Kathleen. By keeping the shadow in the same circle at successive sightings, we know we are heading due east or due west. We also measure the height of the sun above the horizon to guide us."

"And at night?" she asked. She expected him to tell her to stop pestering, but he did not.

"Then the night sky guides you. The North Star is a friend to every navigator. By measuring her height above the horizon at set intervals, you can tell in which of the four directions you are heading. If the North Star rises or falls, we are traveling north or south; if she remains steady, west or east. To sail west at night, we keep the North Star at ninety degrees to styrbord and ensure that her height remains constant."

"But Helgi, what do you do when the weather is cloudy?" Kathleen had heard of ships that had become sea-bewildered, unable to find the proper course for days and even weeks.

"Wait until the sun is obscured, and I will show you." With a wink, he refocused his attention on the styrbord.

And true enough, thick clouds rolled over the knarr as the day waned. Soon the sun was hidden in deep fog.

Helgi beckoned Kathleen to his side. He reached into the small leather sack he always kept tied around his neck.

"Here is the *sólarsteinn*. Its magic will tell us where the sun is, even when the weather is cloudy and the sun is weak and obscured."

Helgi pulled the precious crystal out of the sack. He held the sun-stone up to the sky and slowly rotated it.

"Watch, Kathleen."

She looked intently as the stone suddenly turned bright blue. She gasped in utter surprise and delight.

"See—when it turns color, you know the exact point of the sun in the sky, even if it is very near the horizon."

Kathleen learned much from Helgi. When he was not navigating, he passed the time with wood carving. He had brought with him several pieces of alder, beechwood, maple, and willow. His chest also contained his tools: a small sharp knife, a hammer, a chisel, and several files and rasps.

He was skilled at carving, but he was not alone. Most Norse men were as handy with a hammer and chisel as with a sword and battle-ax. From Helgi's strong fingers, figures both familiar and fantastical emerged from the pieces of wood. Sometimes he carved imaginary animals, all twisted and braided together in a tight, asymmetric arabesque. Sometimes he made practical objects, such as a spare tiller, but then embellished them. It was hard for him to leave anything plain when it could be made beautiful.

Kathleen learned his techniques by watching and experimenting on her own carvings. She would never be as skillful as Helgi; her hands were not so strong. But she worked on small pieces.

Helgi showed her a most marvelous little carving for her to copy. It was a deer, small enough to be held in her hand. But instead of hooves, Helgi carefully carved small wheels within the toy's legs, so it could be raced along a smooth surface.

At night, the arctic air—cold, clean, and beautiful—surrounded the voyagers. The seas darkened to black, and the stars appeared. Sometimes the northern lights, beautiful shimmering curtains of purple and green, kept them entertained.

Kathleen still yearned for her mother, but her heart was full and the deep loneliness was no more. She found in Gudrun everything she missed without her mother: someone to talk to, someone to learn from, someone to help her not be afraid.

Kathleen was curious about one subject in particular, and she was sure Gudrun could explain it. Before her mother's fateful pregnancy with the twins, Kathleen knew her parents had tried for a child for years. She knew what that entailed. But she did not know how women handled the opposite situation.

"Tell me, Gudrun—how do you keep from becoming with child?"

Gudrun motioned that the two should move to the far side of the vessel, away from the others. "We women have ways of dealing with these things. We have knowledge. But we must be very careful with that knowledge."

The way she said *careful* made it clear to Kathleen that she meant *secret.*

Gudrun took a small linen pouch from her storage trunk. "Seed for seed," she said, smiling to herself. "Put out your hand."

Kathleen obeyed. Gudrun reached into the sack and sprinkled a teaspoonful of small brown seeds into Kathleen's palm.

"Do you know what these are?"

Kathleen inspected the seeds closely and observed their curved form. She gently shook her head.

"They are the seeds of the wild carrot."

Kathleen envisioned the plant. Its stems were hairy, and its flat cluster of delicate white flowers had a single dark-crimson spot in the center, like an errant drop of blood. In fall, the flower head curled into an elongated bird nest shape.

"Try them. They will not harm you."

Kathleen hesitated, then took the seeds into her mouth and began to chew. As the volatile oils released into her mouth, she could not help but grimace with disgust.

"Keep chewing!" admonished Gudrun.

The seeds tasted truly awful. Kathleen wanted to spit out the heavy and oily mass but did not, to avoid offense. As Kathleen grimly kept chewing, Gudrun continued with the lesson.

"There are specific rules that must be followed. The seeds must be gathered in late summer or early autumn, when they have matured. The seeds must be chewed, not swallowed whole. To keep from becoming pregnant, you must take a spoonful of these within one day after you couple with your man. If you wait more than that time, it will do no good. And you should not take the seeds every day. Of course, this could be difficult if your man is particularly desirous. But I have found that can be managed with carefully timed arguments," she added with a sly nod. "When you want to become pregnant, you simply stop taking the seeds."

"Is that why you have no children, Gudrun, because you take the seeds?"

"No, Kathleen," she said, giving the young woman a hug. "When Helgi and I first married, we hoped for children. We tried!" She smiled a little at the memory. "But the years passed, and no child came. I told Helgi he could divorce me. But he never would. He never would."

CHAPTER FORTY-FOUR

Greenland

O N THE SAME SPRING DAY Arn and his daughter sailed out of Dublin, Leif and his men began their return trip from Vinland east to Brattahlid. Bjarni's former ship was loaded with wood and a few small grape plants carefully planted in rabbit-skin sacks filled with Vinland soil, to see if they might thrive in Greenland. And Leif brought a few casks of the new wine as well. He knew this would please Brand. If there was still a small supply of wheat in Brattahlid, and now the wine from Vinland, the priest would finally be able to celebrate the Eucharist once again.

The returning explorers arrived in Greenland in late spring, exuberant and excited to share the good news of the lands they had found. But immediately they discovered that many things had changed in Brattahlid.

During the winter before, a frightening sickness had broken out after people had crowded into Erik's longhouse for Yule celebrations. Erik himself became extremely ill. Thjodhild had stayed by his side, day and night. But the sickness was too much. After all she had endured with Erik, Thjodhild was now a widow.

Leif was surprised to see the small chapel that had been built for his mother—and more than astonished to learn his father had directed that it be made. While there was still tension in Brattahlid, Leif's absence and Erik's death had made a calmer atmosphere for everyone. Some still opposed Leif for his White Kristr ways, but it was mostly psychological rather than physical resistance. And there were many people waiting for the priest to become frustrated and leave them in peace.

For his part, Brand had continued his preaching and teaching. He held many classes, teaching the stories of the Gospels and the ancient writings of the Hebrew people. He was impressed with how quickly the Greenlanders learned, especially some of the women.

During this time of teaching the Gospel stories, Brand had made one difficult decision. He was not certain it would be well received if it were known by his bishop. Back in England, only the very highborn and men and women of religious orders were taught to read and write. But Brand had decided to teach the new converts how to read prayers and some of the holy words.

He did not come to this decision lightly, but after much prayer. Brand knew the people of Greenland would always need to hear the Good News of the man Jesu. He worried that if something should happen to him, it would be a long time before another priest would come to this far-flung outpost and care for the little flock of Christians. If the Greenlanders could read, the little flock would at least have the help of the holy words to carry on.

Brand's decision to teach reading and writing was met with much enthusiasm. And no one was more enthusiastic than Thjodhild, an eager learner. Brand started with the Pater Noster, the Our Father, and very slowly introduced new verses and prayers.

Leif took steps to quickly consolidate his power and establish himself as the new head man. As his father's son, no one was too surprised. He found little time to devote to the White Kristr priest and the issue of conversion.

Leif was vaguely aware that his mother, though still mourning, had turned her grief into learning as much as she could of the new god of love and suffering. He knew of her skill at reading the words, and he was proud of her for it.

Within a few weeks of Leif's return, word spread up the fjord that another trade ship was making its way to Brattahlid. No one recognized the ship, as it had never before visited the settlement. But the vessel had already garnered much approval, with its magnificent sail and the exquisitely carved and somewhat strange-looking dragon on its prow.

Excitement was running high, for so many goods were needed. The settlers were constantly tree starved and iron starved.

Brand was among those waiting on shore, ready to greet the visitors. All were eager to find out who they were. If they had come from Norway, they would have news of King Olaf Tryggvason and the others back in Trondheim. Brand's mind was filled with memories of those days: his arguments with Olaf, his exile to faraway Greenland with Leif and the bondsmen, and Kathleen. Always Kathleen.

With only a few rowers, the ship moved slowly to the landing. Standing at the bow was a group of people waving and shouting. As they neared the shoreline, individual faces could be made out.

Thjodhild clasped her hands in joy when she recognized Helgi. To have a visitor come to such a remote outpost was one thing, but to have a return visitor was even more cause for celebration.

Brand waved enthusiastically in broad arcs of welcome. Then suddenly everything within him stopped.

There she was. She. Waving and calling out Brand's own name— and not in a dream.

As soon as she stepped onto shore, Kathleen ran to Brand and hugged him with enthusiasm.

"Father Brand, Father Brand! My teacher!"

Brand embraced her, his mind overwhelmed. An enormous force hit his body and transformed him to stone. How could this be? How could this young woman be here before him? Surely she should be a wife back in Trondheim or Bergen, with a small child or two clinging to her skirt. Yet here she was, returned to him, at this outpost at the edge of their world.

Arn grabbed Brand next. "How good it is to see you. Well, of course, Kathleen had told me you and Leif had sailed west to Greenland. We made the decision to journey west also. We have been on our journey to Brattahlid for the last two years."

"I am surprised beyond all telling," said Brand, his heart pounding. He looked from father to daughter. "And Kathleen has sailed with you, all this way?"

"She would have it no other way. She is stubborn. Like me, I guess," answered Arn with a sheepish grin.

The rest of the crew was quickly introduced to the settlers. Arn explained that the *Sea Goat* and her crew would spend several weeks at Brattahlid, then begin their return voyage.

Thjodhild and Gudrun immediately moved to the side so Thjodhild could hear all the news of Trondheim, Dublin, and Iceland from a woman's point of view.

"Tell me, Thjodhild," Gudrun carefully asked, "how does the handsome priest get along with the people of this place?"

"He struggles to teach us all he can of the White Kristr. Many are hard of heart, but he refuses to let anyone compel conversion."

"No. I mean as a man," Gudrun clarified.

Helgi may have been good at navigating the seas, but Gudrun was even better at navigating people. Something had caught her eye about Brand, something she could not describe, which made her curious.

"Oh!" said Thjodhild, surprised she had missed the intent of Gudrun's question. "Well, you know, he has vowed to take no wife and to live a chaste life. I have never seen him do or heard him say anything that would violate that promise. And the nights here are long and cold! More than one woman threw herself at him with looks and sly words, but nothing came of their attempts."

Gudrun nodded her understanding. But Thjodhild's answer still left her with questions.

While the voyagers mingled with the settlers and news and gossip flew through the air, Brand found himself nearly unable to take in what had happened. The person he longed to be near had come back to him—yet she was still unattainable, untouchable, and always would be so.

As soon as he could get away, Brand fled to the chapel, fell to his knees, and prayed for God to help him with this terrible and beautiful temptation.

"Lord, were you not also tempted? Lord, did you not also feel alone?"

All Brand could do was console himself that the trader's visit would be brief.

The next morning, Kathleen met with the other followers of the White Kristr in Thjodhild's chapel. The *Sea Goat* had carried a small quantity of grape wine and a little wheat flour, which Father Brand used to celebrate the Holy Eucharist with his Greenlander flock.

Arn soon began engaging with the landowners for items to buy and items to sell. He also arranged for the ship to have needed inspections and normal repairs after the battering of the north seas.

Kathleen easily took to life at the settlement. After morning prayers, she often started her day in the dairy. There the women would talk, and Kathleen listened to all the gossip.

At the moment, much of the gossip was about Freydis, Leif's half-sister. She had come from Gardar to make sure nothing in Brattahlid had happened without her knowledge.

Something about Freydis made Kathleen feel uncomfortable. She had heard stories that Freydis was fierce and strong-willed and unpredictable, more like a warrior than a weaver of cloth. Everyone knew the contempt Freydis held for her weak-willed husband.

And even more notorious was her obsession with all outward signs of wealth. She was unrelentingly covetous. She wore the most outrageous brooches that hung like large gaudy half-moons at each shoulder of her overdress. They were not elegant or finely worked. Their only redemption was size. They resembled metal drinking bowls rather than personal jewelry.

Each morning, Kathleen also visited the small barn near the chapel, where Haki would be milking. Of all the cows, Bloma was her favorite. Bloma was a caramel-colored bovine with a distinctly gentle disposition. She was far into pregnancy. Kathleen loved her sweet brown eyes and gentle moos. She cradled Bloma's head in her arms and stroked Bloma's sides.

Haki watched in amusement. "Kathleen, you love that cow horn to hoof!" he teased.

"Why would I not love Bloma?" she responded indignantly. "She will give quite enough milk for her calf and enough more for milk and butter for us."

A harrumph was Haki's only reply. He kept on moving his strong hands, filling the milk pail. He knew she was right, but was not inclined to let her know it, for he already cared more for the trader's daughter than he could ever show.

After her morning visits with Haki and Bloma, Kathleen would run like a *dyr* to sit in on the lessons Brand had organized for his converts. She quickly made the connection that the Latin letters were not so different from the runes her mother had taught her.

Later in the day, Kathleen would explore the green pastures and often climb to the highest vistas in search of flowers and herbs. After the confines of the long watery journey, Kathleen reveled in the sheer space of the settlement on the fjord. She loved to roam all over the outpost and the surrounding meadows.

Sometimes Brand would see her there walking among the wild-flowers. He would imagine talking with her there, under the blue canopy of sky, with the lush meadows for their bed. Hearts beating fast. Hearts beating faster.

CHAPTER FORTY-FIVE

ONE SUNNY MORNING, KATHLEEN STOPPED at the chapel dairy and found Haki just finishing the early milking. Bloma was nowhere to be seen. Before she could ask about her, Haki made a request.

"Kathleen," said Haki, "I need your help. I think Bloma has calved. She and the young one need to be herded back. When I saw her yesterday, she had gone to the high pasture, where the grass is long. Will you go retrieve her?"

"Yes, yes!" said Kathleen excitedly.

Haki was right; in the high meadow, there were many patches of long grass. Kathleen found Bloma rather quickly. Bloma was contently chewing mouthfuls of the sweet grass. The afterbirth had not yet been completely expelled.

But it took Kathleen some time before she found the calf. It was lying flat like a newborn fawn in a thick patch of grass with its legs tucked under it. Its slender chin pushed close to the soft earth, its ancient blood telling it to hide, lest a predator find it. Though a domestic animal, the calf was following its primal instincts.

Kathleen gently pushed the calf to its wobbly knees. The three started the descent down to Brattahlid, first a slow ambling Bloma, then the vulnerable calf, followed by the attentive young woman.

Kathleen was happy. She had traveled this far with her father and had made new friends. She had shown her strength. She was learning so much. And she was with Brand again. She wished he would not be so distant with her. But then, perhaps that was how all priests were, she guessed. Or maybe it was the pressure of his many responsibilities. She would talk to Gudrun about it.

From her high vantage point, Kathleen could see far down the fjord. From the corner of her eye, Kathleen saw another ship making its way up the fjord. She was curious to find out who these travelers were and what they would bring to the settlement.

The newborn calf was still unsteady on its feet but could walk slowly. By the time Kathleen had made it down from the high meadow and left Bloma and the calf with Haki, most of the visitors on the ship had come ashore.

Kathleen saw her father talking with a huge man. The man turned around, and her eyes opened wide with surprise. It was Ogmund, the strange and frightening berserker she had met back in Trondheim years before.

Her heart began to race with apprehension. Had he followed her there? She ran toward her father, to warn him this was a dangerous person.

Just as she neared, her father raised his voice and stated very clearly to the newcomer, "No!"

Ogmund's face was already bright red, but it now turned a purple shade. "You would insult me by not taking the usual three days to reject my offer?"

"That's right. The answer is no. I do not need any time to consider this offer of marriage." Arn looked at Ogmund with revulsion. "You must be mad."

Ogmund breathed heavily. "Then we shall find out who is truly mad. You have insulted me. You have dishonored me. And for this, I challenge you to holmgang combat."

"I accept!" Arn immediately replied, taking a step toward Ogmund and thumping his own chest once with a fist.

"Father, no!" Kathleen begged, but Arn ignored her pleading.

It was common for a berserker to challenge men of property to holmgang combat, or duels, with sword and shield. A man so challenged had to accept the duel or have a champion fight for him. If not, he would be named a coward. And to be known as such among the people was near enough to being dead.

However, accepting the holmgang challenge placed the victim in a difficult position as well. Upon wounding or slaying the unfortunate target, the berserker would take possession of his victim's goods, wealth, and women.

And berserkers were no ordinary warriors. The royal courts used them as shock troops attached to the king's army. Rumor had it that the berserkers entered battle in a state of trance. It may have been due to their consumption of special potions made with amanita mushrooms, as part of the berserkers' worship of Odinnn. Or maybe they were possessed by demon spirits, the same as those cast out by the White Kristr when healing people in Galilee.

Kathleen was beside herself with panic. She tried again and again to dissuade her father, but he would have none of it. The duel was set for the next day at dawn. Ogmund stomped off, and Arn turned and walked away from her in another direction.

She ran immediately back to Haki.

"Where is Father Brand? Where I can find him? I must see him now!"

"I am sorry, Kathleen," said the thrall. "He left early this morning. I do not know when he will return."

Next, she ran to the great house of Leif. She passed by the kitchen house and saw Leif's half-sister, Freydis, slicing up a large piece of halibut on a small wooden table.

Freydis glanced down at the fish in front of her. "Yes, Kathleen. I know you are wondering why I am doing such work. It is because the thralls constantly contrive to be away from me. Even if they did not, I like how the blade feels in my hands."

Her face was thin and angular. Her eyes were a faded green and as cold and lifeless as the dead halibut she was eviscerating. Freydis stared at the silk shawl covering Kathleen's shoulders and the amber-and-silver necklace intertwined with the White Kristr cross on her neck.

"Why does the spoiled daughter of the merchant approach me today?"

Kathleen ignored the insult.

"Freydis, where is Leif? Please, do you know where he is? I must talk with him!"

At first, the only reply was the sound of the knife as it sliced through the flesh of the fish and came into contact with the wood. *Ka-thunk. Ka-thunk.*

Finally, Freydis paused from her task and said wearily, "Leif and several of his men have gone hunting for walrus. They will not return for many days."

It was true that the hunters were in pursuit of prey. But it was not true that they would be gone so long. Freydis knew they were due to return later that day or the next morning at the latest. So when worry showed even more clearly on Kathleen's face, Freydis took silent pleasure in it.

Then Kathleen had a thought. It was only a thought—and unlikely. But it was worth trying.

"Freydis, I need help. There is to be a holmgang tomorrow. My father and Ogmund, the newly arrived berserker."

Freydis had not yet heard this news, but it pleased her. It excited her. She enjoyed watching men as they engaged in violent combat. Somehow, she found it soothing. And fulfilling.

"I have heard that in some places, the women are able to stop the holmgang," Kathleen continued. "They throw their clothing onto the men, catching on their swords and feet, so they are unable to fight. They do this as a group. The men cannot stop them all. Also, then no one woman can be punished. Freydis, can you help me? Do you think we could do this?"

"I would rather be food for the ravens myself."

"But, Freydis—"

"You stupid fool!" Freydis's voice grew louder and louder. "Have you no understanding of what the holmgang means? It is about honor! Anyone who does not understand this does not deserve to live!"

She was standing very close to Kathleen now, shrieking and waving her carving knife in her hand.

"Now get away from me, you worthless girl, before I show how well a woman can use a blade!"

Kathleen retreated from the frightening Freydis. She went on her way, seeking out other women across the settlement and pleading for their help. They all listened, but not one agreed to intervene on her behalf. Even Thjodhild would not help her. She was sympathetic, but she stressed, not unlike Freydis had, that the holmgang was a matter of honor and that it must take place.

Some women were just frightened. Others were resentful of Arn and Kathleen's wealth. And some women were heathen and not inclined to help the distraught Christian girl.

"It is none of our business," some said.

"We do not want to make enemies," others responded, looking away.

"I understand," said Kathleen, struggling to keep her emotion in control. "But I will not stop hoping that the spirit will move you. Perhaps you will come to see that now my little family is in peril, but tomorrow it may be your own!"

That was not out of the realm of possibility. Away from the battle-field, the berserkers were known as a predatory group of brawlers and killers who disrupted many Norse communities. They were often unrestrained in their pillage of goods and belongings, and they would sometimes take an unmarried daughter, only to return her a month later.

A weary Kathleen walked slowly back to the chapel in search of Father Brand. It was now very late. The rays of daylight were turning into the fragile blue twilight of summer familiar to those who lived so near the top of the earth. The light at the edge of the horizon softly illuminated the stark and extreme beauty of the landscape surrounding Eriksfjord. Although it was an unusually warm night, Kathleen shivered. Her hair gleamed nearly white in the half light. She pulled her silk shawl closer.

She found Haki sleeping on a pallet filled with sweet grass near the entrance of the chapel. She woke him.

"Haki? Do you know where Father Brand may be?"

The slave looked at her with concern. "I am sorry. I waited all day here for Father Brand, but I must have fallen asleep."

At that moment, Brand came into the chapel. His green eyes widened when he saw her standing in the midsummer night. Even in the semi-darkness, he could see the fear in her.

"Father Brand, I have been looking for you all day!"

He looked at her gravely. "What is wrong?"

"There is a man called Ogmund who just arrived. He has followed us—all the way from Trondheim. He asked my father for permission to take me as his wife."

That a man could be obsessed with Kathleen did not surprise Brand.

"He is a berserker and a duel fighter."

At this revelation, Brand understood the panic in her voice.

"But Father rejected the offer and insulted Ogmund," Kathleen continued. "So Ogmund challenged Father to combat. He has to fight the holmgang tomorrow at dawn! Oh, Father Brand!" she cried. "I will never go with this man, but my father cannot die trying to save me! I have gone to everyone in the settlement. None of them will do anything to help us."

"What does Leif say?"

"He has gone hunting. I am told he will not return in time to help."

In desperation, she knelt down on the hard stone floor of the chapel. "You are the White Kristr priest of the court of King Olaf. You must help us!"

Brand lifted her hand and raised her up onto her feet. She was tall for a maiden, so their eyes were nearly even.

"Father Brand, you must convince them that the holmgang should not take place. Please, Father—my faith in the power of the White Kristr is strong." She touched the amulet corded around her neck. "It must be strong enough to stop this evil thing."

Brand did not answer right away. He wanted to protect her, to protect her completely, to promise that nothing and no one would harm her.

She misunderstood his hesitation as refusal. She pleaded again, "Please, Father Brand," she sobbed, taking both his hands and kissing them.

The moment she did so, his breath stopped short.

"I will try," he said. "I will speak to your father. I will do . . . I will do whatever I can, Kathleen. Let us pray to the One God that I may succeed."

Immediately after the brief prayer, Brand went to Arn and spoke most intensely with him. But it was no good.

Arn merely told him, in a way that signaled the conversation was over, "Wealth dies. Kinsmen die. Cattle die. And the wheat too. But this one thing never dies: a man's honor. Honor never dies for a man who shows it well."

Brand could hardly contain his frustration. Arn was just like Brand's own father. The same stubborn resignation!

Brand returned to the chapel for the rest of the night. Thoughts tumbled in his mind as he prayed for strength to meet the morrow.

Many times he had seen how the customs of the old ways favored the physically strong over the weak. He kept the hope that somehow the hand of God would intervene to stop the slaughter of Arn and the bondage of Kathleen.

CHAPTER FORTY-SIX

A HOLMGANG NORMALLY TOOK PLACE on an island, but because Brattahlid had no island near, an isolated meadow would have to do. The circle of short-cropped grass was high above the settlement and still shrouded in the cloudy mist of early morning. Two dark ravens circled above in the mushroom-colored sky. They occasionally took rest in a trio of nearby alders, whose branches were covered in exuberant green. The birds were restless, and from time to time they accented the air with raucous croaking.

Like the ravens, the people of the settlement had gathered on the lonely meadow. Men and women, White Kristr followers and heathen—all were curious to see what would unfold. Thjodhild stood among the women and as far from Freydis as she could place herself. Helgi and Gudrun, feeling helpless and impotent, stood waiting with the rest.

The settlers were surprised to see that Ogmund had only one other berserker with him, when usually they traveled in a band of twelve. The settlers soon learned that the berserkers had set out from Iceland in a flotilla of trading ships. Two ships made it as far as the southern tip of Greenland. Repairs were needed on one. Ogmund, impatient to find Kathleen and take her as his wife, opted to continue on to Brattahlid with only one fellow berserker. The rest of his men would come in a few days. Ogmund did not need them to capture his prize.

Arn, Kathleen, and Brand entered the meadow together. Ogmund stared at Kathleen. Kathleen stared back. She thought him unchanged from the day she had seen him in the court of King Olaf. For his part, Ogmund found that the years had only made Kathleen more attractive and his unmet desire for her more intense.

Before the holmgang ritual began, Ogmund announced to all the spectators that he had a poem to share. This resulted in much excitement and anticipation, for the settlers loved poetry almost as much as the combat to come.

For his size and demeanor, Ogmund's voice was surprisingly high when he stepped to the center of the crowd and began his poem. All conversation stopped so they could listen to the lovesick berserker.

"Consider well this woman.

She is worth the whole of Iceland, of Greenland,

Of Norway, and of Denmark.

My heart is heavy with love for her.

Not for all of England, not for all of earth's kingdoms

Would I forswear the woman of sunlight hair."

The poetry of the Norse was complex, with precise rhythm and rules. Ogmund's poem was perfect. In particular, it was about his love for Kathleen yet not addressed to her, so he avoided the scandal of mansǫngr.

The crowd hooted and hollered.

"Well done, poet!"

"Tell us more of your love!"

Ogmund looked at Kathleen for some sign but saw only his fantasy and not the contempt and fear in her eyes.

Brand, on the other hand, clearly saw Kathleen's fear. He turned to the crowd and in a loud voice said, "This holmgang must not take place. We must stay the slaughter of men!"

Both Arn and Ogmund ignored him, continuing to inspect their swords and adjust their clothing.

Brand confronted Arn and beseeched, "There must be another way."

As she observed the priest, Freydis turned to a woman at her side. "He knows nothing," she declared to the woman, though loudly enough for all to hear. "It is about honor—taking it away from the other man to keep your own."

Brand continued to press Arn, which made Ogmund more and more impatient.

"Do you think you can get the merchant out of defending his honor merely by talking?" Ogmund asked Brand. "Go back to your cowardly god. Take care and do not interfere, or you may find yourself playing the woman, argr man."

The berserker began to laugh, his large yellow teeth exposed and his head thrown back—like the braying of a donkey.

The heathens in the group snickered at this sexual insult, and the Kristr folk were embarrassed for their priest. To accuse another man of being argr was considered a most serious defamation. This insult alone had been the source of more than one challenge to holmgang.

Arn turned to Brand, his voice filled with unrestrained and uncharacteristic anger. "Get out of here! This does not concern you!"

Brand stepped back, futile to prevent the drama about to ensue.

Ogmund's fellow berserker began the rite by explaining the rules and invoking Odinn to grant victory to the man who showed the most courage and honor. Then a leather hide was unfolded and fastened to the ground with a pole at each corner. The hide acted as a mat to mark the fighting area for the combatants. It was not large—easily traversed in a few long strides. According to the rules, all the combat must be contained within its bounds. Combat would be carried out with swords and shields, and it would stop when the loser's blood was shed onto the hide.

Arn offered a change in the rules. "You, Ogmund, have challenged me to the holmgang. I offer to you that we fight in simple swordplay—no shields."

"As you wish," said Ogmund, setting aside his shield. He then glared at Arn and demanded, "Do you yield?"

Arn was overmatched in every way but still defiant. "You will not harm me nor take my daughter. I am a trader of precious cargo, but nothing is more precious to me than Kathleen. I will not yield."

Kathleen too replied to the berserker. "I would rather die here than live one minute as your plaything!" Her face flushed pink with anger and fear.

Ogmund said nothing. Instead, he calmly took the chalice the other berserker presented to him. "Blood of the wolf!" he declared, punctuating his words with a large gulp from the cup.

Ogmund slowly walked toward his end of the leather mat. When he turned around again, his face contorted and turned dark. Even the color of his eyes seemed to change. He howled, like a wild animal, and bit down on the edge of his sword.

They crowd murmured in awe, but Arn showed no fear.

The combatants began with tentative strikes, testing each other's speed and reach. Ogmund quickly took the offense, but Arn successfully defended each thrust of Ogmund's sword.

Minutes passed by. Arn's breathing grew louder and more labored. He was tiring.

Ogmund raised his sword aloft and cut at Arn's arm. There was an enormous clatter of metal upon metal, for it hit Arn's mantle ring and nearly cut it through. The blow was so great that it temporarily paralyzed Arn's right arm. His sword fell.

But Arn had no wound and no blood was shed, so the sword fight continued.

Arn quickly gripped his sword in his left hand, but Ogmund easily struck it out with another powerful blow. The sword flew across the leather mat and landed directly in front of Brand.

From the opposite side of leather mat, Ogmund stared at Arn. The trader was now completely defenseless.

"Yield!"

"No! Never!" shouted Arn.

Within a moment, Arn's blood would be spilled and Kathleen would be taken as the prize.

Brand looked down at the sword lying at his feet. On impulse, he picked it up. He stepped onto the leather mat, placing himself between Arn and the fury of Ogmund.

The crowd gave out a collective gasp.

Lifting the sword aloft, Brand heard himself shout, "*I am your true enemy!*" He then lowered the weapon into a defensive stance, its point directed at Ogmund.

"As you wish!" roared Ogmund.

Kathleen stared in terror as Ogmund now threatened her unarmed father and her priest. Without thinking, she rushed toward the fight arena. Instantly, she felt Freydis's arms restraining her.

"Be still!" threatened Freydis.

"Prepare for your death, argr man!" Ogmund laughed again. He took up his sword, two-handed, and raised it above his head for the final, fatal blow.

The crowd was thoroughly excited now. The air was filled with shouts, insults, and encouragements for the combatants.

Freydis's arms were strong, but Kathleen's emotion was stronger still. She twisted and struggled. With an anguished scream, Kathleen broke free. As she stumbled forward, she crashed against Ogmund's back so violently and so unexpectedly that he could not retain his balance.

Ogmund fell forward, skewered onto the sword held in Brand's strong hands.

The entire crowd went silent.

Ogmund stood for a moment, bewildered. He pulled the sword from his own belly and threw it aside. Then his whole body crumpled to the ground with a thud. Blood seeped onto the hide.

"You stupid girl!" hissed Freydis.

Arn stared incredulously at the scene before him, his arms limp at his sides. A curious, stunned look crossed his face. Kathleen rushed to embrace him.

Brand sat down beside the fallen berserker's body. He cradled Ogmund's head in his lap.

"Ogmund! Ogmund, confess! Accept the love of the White Kristr. It is not too late."

Ogmund's lips began to move. Brand put his ear close to Ogmund's mouth.

Ogmund's eyes moved toward Kathleen. Foamy blood gurgled from his mouth with each breath. He gasped each word, whispered but understandable. It was not an oath to Odinn. Nor a confession to the White Kristr or another god. Nor a curse on them all. No, the huge warrior surprised all those close enough to hear his final words.

"Can you blame me for wanting her?" he said to the priest. "She is so beautiful . . . and brave."

His eyes rolled back. His labored breaths became intermittent, then ceased.

In the somber sky, the two ravens took flight from their elevated vantage point. They croaked and cawed, punctuating the air with their farewell to Ogmund.

CHAPTER FORTY-SEVEN

THE REMAINING BERSERKER GATHERED OGMUND'S shield and sword. He set the shield at his fallen companion's feet and the sword at his head, then spread Ogmund's cloak over his body.

"Foul cowards!" he yelled at them all. "You have not seen the last of us. This death will be avenged!"

At that moment, Leif came running up to the meadow with other members of his hunting party. He saw the slain giant first. Then he saw that another man was menacing Brand. The crowd was agitated.

"All right!" he shouted. "All of you! Back to your homes!"

Slowly, reluctantly, the crowd dispersed. Several of Leif's bondsmen stepped toward the threatening berserker and surrounded him so he could not move without engaging them all in a struggle.

Leif immediately escorted Brand, Arn, and Kathleen back to his great house. Brand and Arn walked in silence, still in shock over what had taken place. Kathleen walked in silence too, her heart still frozen with fear.

Leif demanded that everyone leave them, even Thjodhild. But his mother refused.

"I will not leave until you all drink a special preparation I will make for you. It will calm you and help you think."

She stayed until they had drunk the hot liquid infused with chamomile and mint. Finally, she left the great house, and the four were alone.

Thjodhild was right; drinking the herbs had given Leif time to collect his thoughts. He began to calculate the number of men he could count on in a battle with the berserkers. It was not good. Many of his bondsmen were on sailing ventures of their own or on extended hunting trips. One or two of the dominant settlers might even back the berserkers out of a perverse dislike for the White Kristr god and in the hopes that they might become the new head man.

Long ago in Trondheim, Leif had promised to protect the stubborn priest. But it was quite clear to him that in a fight with the berserkers, he could not realistically do so.

Then an idea, an outrageous idea, came to him.

"Father Brand, I do not know if I can protect you or Arn from the rest of the berserkers who will be coming soon."

Leif put his hands on the table and leaned forward.

"You must leave here."

"Leave?" asked Arn. "What are you saying?"

"I am saying you must leave. You must sail, but not back to Iceland."

Everyone wondered at this curious statement.

"You must sail west. To Vinland."

There was a brief moment of stunned silence while they took this in. Then Arn tried to object, but Leif ignored him.

"I will tell the berserkers you have returned to Iceland," Leif continued. "When you do not arrive there by the end of summer, they will assume you have been lost at sea. Perhaps it would be safe to return later, next spring . . ."

Leif's words trailed, but everyone knew the unspoken message: perhaps it would *not* be safe to return in spring. Perhaps they would need to remain in exile for the rest of their lives.

Arn firmly shook his head in opposition. "Leif, you are a man of courage, honored by King Olaf himself. You of all people surely understand that if I run like a coward, I will have no honor, no life. I cannot do what you suggest."

"You *must!*" Leif said, his voice rising.

"Why?" Arn implored.

"Because you have a daughter," Brand interjected. "Look at her. *Look at her!*"

Arn looked at Kathleen, her face pale with fear. It was if he were seeing her for the first time. He had been so focused on his own honor that he had all but forgotten what could become of her.

They all waited. For a long time, no one said a word.

Finally, Arn spoke. "Vinland. We shall go to Vinland."

"And you, Father Brand?" Leif asked. He worried that the priest too would surely be killed if he stayed.

"Oh, Father, you must go with us," Kathleen said. "We cannot go without you."

Brand looked first to Leif, then to Arn, and finally to Kathleen. They could all see his mind whirling with thoughts. Once or twice they thought he was ready to speak, but then he would cast his eyes around them again, searching for an answer.

When at last he spoke, it was with conviction. "I have a flock to tend here. But . . . it is because of me that Arn and Kathleen need to flee. I will not desert them. I too will sail with them to Vinland."

A kind of relief came over them all, especially Leif. Kathleen embraced the priest, who, like the rest, had not yet come to fully comprehend the dramatic events of the day.

Several practical matters needed to be taken care of immediately. First, Leif took care to ensure that Ogmund's man was kept drunk nearly all the time. They could not risk him discovering the exiles' true destination.

Second, the crew. They would not need many men; rather, they needed men of utmost reliability. One by one, Leif called the *Sea Goat* sailors into a private area.

First, he made them all swear—on their honor—to total secrecy regarding his proposition for them sail to Vinland with Arn on the *Sea Goat*. Anyone who did not want to go did not have to do so. But the secret must be kept either way.

Patrekr and Gunnar came together to talk with Leif. When Leif asked if they would sail west, they said yes. Though they did not share it with Leif, they were tired of living among the Norse, where their every word and action had to be weighed to prevent discovery. *Maybe it will be better elsewhere*, they thought.

Helgi and Gudrun also said yes.

Brand went to Haki and told him the news. "Haki, I free you to make your own decision. You may stay here, if you wish. It is your choice."

"Then, Father Brand, I choose to go with you."

"Are you sure, Haki?"

"Yes, I am sure."

"Then I am glad," said Brand with some relief.

The next concern was the ship's stores. They needed the settlers to believe they were headed back to Iceland and then to Norway, but they had no need for the normal cargo for such a journey. Very stealthily, they filled barrels and boxes inside Leif's storerooms, then carried and rolled them to the ship. Leif gave them everything that might be of use: small tools, fish hooks, knives, axes, sealskin rope, a tinderbox, peat. Leif even gave Father Brand the red cloak he had received from the hand of King Olaf back in Trondheim. Haki brought his tom-tom and drum beater.

They took animals as well: Bloma, who would provide milk; Hlatr the cat; and a male cat named Sprettr. He was a jumper, as his name implied, renowned for his excellent mousing skills.

Arn brought goods not yet traded to the Brattahlid settlers: some cloth and smaller kitchen items. Kathleen insisted on bringing her soap, her mirror and comb, and all her clothing.

The exiles were ready within a day. Leif urged them to act quickly, for it was possible they would encounter the rest of the berserkers coming up the fjord as they sailed out. That would be very dangerous indeed.

On the morning of their departure, Brand stood in the chapel, holding in his hands the Gospel book Bishop Grimkell had sent to Greenland. The faint, early-morning light barely illuminated the letters on its pages. It was the most precious object Brand's fingers had ever touched. He wanted to linger, to hold it a while longer, before replacing it in its wooden storage chest. It would stay there to guide the small flock through the unknown number of days in which they would be without a priest.

Thjodhild came to say farewell. She observed his reverie and guessed at his inner turmoil.

"You must take it with you."

He looked at her in surprise. "No, I can never do that. It must stay here."

"No, Father Brand. Where your journey will take you, I do not know. But this book and your faith in its message may be more important with you than with us here."

Thjodhild's words were persuasive. His work there in Greenland had already borne fruit. And surely another priest would be dispatched for the worshippers there. Reluctantly, Brand took the book. He placed it in a small storage chest with other precious contents for the journey.

He embraced the widow Thjodhild as if it was to be the last time. He walked away but turned for one last look at his first convert as she stood in the improbable chapel they had built together.

Leif came down to the water to send the mariners off. No one knew the departure was so imminent, and many nervous settlers stayed away, so there was no grand farewell.

Leif admonished them, "Remember all I have told you. Watch for the signs, and use your instruments. After Vinland, there is no habitable land in the ocean. All that emerges is icebound and wrapped in impenetrable mist."

They all nodded in understanding his warning.

"Father Brand, there is one more thing," Leif said.

Leif removed the sword from his side. Brand was surprised to see it was the precious gift from King Olaf, inscribed with INOMINEDOMINE. Leif carefully placed it in Brand's hands and would not take it back.

He stood facing the priest. "Father Brand, I have done what I swore to do—and that is protect you. I pray it is enough."

Leif gave a quick embrace to Arn and kissed Kathleen on each cheek. To all of them he whispered, "Godspeed."

The *Sea Goat* sailed south down the fjord without incident. When it met the sea, they sailed out and to the right—to the west, as Leif had instructed them.

A few hours later, the ship carrying the rest of the berserkers entered the fjord. The incoming ship sailed up to Brattahlid, expecting to be met by Ogmund and the other berserker.

When they heard how Ogmund had died, they were enraged. As planned, Leif told them that Arn and Father Brand had fled back to Iceland. If any settlers suspected otherwise, they kept their silence. Among those Leif had propositioned, no man broke his promise of secrecy. And Ogmund's comrade had been kept entirely away from all the stealthy preparations for the voyage west.

The rest of the berserkers left Brattahlid and went in search of Brand and Arn in Iceland. Finding them not, they gave thanks to Odinn. This was a sign that Odinn and the sea gods had dealt appropriately with the treacherous priest and cowardly Arn. They believed the *Sea Goat* had undoubtedly slipped into the cold and dark sea, and all upon it had vanished from this world.

CHAPTER FORTY-EIGHT

To Vinland and beyond

T HE EXILES FOLLOWED LEIF'S DIRECTIONS, orienting themselves to the wind and the waves and the horizon. For four days, they held to a westerly route, past Helluland, flat and stony; past the Markland woods.

In truth, it was Helgi who captained them and Patrekr and Gunnar who did the sailing. Arn, Kathleen, and Brand operated in a kind of inner fog, thicker and darker than any sea mist. They needed time to understand what had transpired back in Brattahlid.

But Gudrun would not let Kathleen remain disoriented for long. Gudrun helped the maiden dress, combed her hair, and let her sleep in her arms. She made her eat and gave her tasks to perform that did not take any thinking.

So Kathleen was the first to return to herself. She knew that what had happened had deeply affected her father and the priest, yet she was still grateful, for Ogmund had not taken her away and her father had lived.

For a while, Brand struggled with his own demons. Guilt ate at him like a hungry wolf. But he knew what to do to keep the beast from devouring him. He prayed for many hours during the day and also during the night. He remembered that the White Kristr promised forgiveness of sins, no matter how dark. He confessed his lack of discipline. And he felt some comfort in the fact that Arn had not been killed.

And though Brand could never have Kathleen nor even let her know of his love, she too had lived because of him. She lived. Because of him. *Because of him.* And that was enough to fill him with gratitude in this most strange of situations.

It was Arn who struggled and struggled. He imagined his name was being despised back in Greenland, Iceland, and even the fjords and forests of Norway. He felt he could never overcome his shame.

Helgi tried to reason with him. "Do you not realize, Arn, that many men have overcome acts that were reckless or bad luck? Leif's father, Erik, had to flee not once but twice when he killed a man and was outlawed. So it will be with you, in time. You will have another chance."

But nothing seemed to make a difference. Arn was prone to long periods of silence, and everyone soon learned there was no point in trying to break his unhappy brooding.

They sailed farther, and at last they found the ellipse of beach, just as Leif said they would. There was the shelter he had built. There was the rich earth, with berries of scarlet and blue, ripening to sweetness. There was the bay where seals played and the abundant streams of water where salmon and huge trout leapt. There were the meadows of winter forage and the woods of fine timber. There was the place, just as Leif had said it would be. It was not a fantasy.

They immediately inspected and repaired the log shelter, then investigated their surroundings. Midsummer had already come and gone. They had to work hard to prepare themselves for the cold months ahead in this new settlement.

They gathered as many berries as possible and dried them. They dried the grapes to make raisins and set jars of grape juice to ferment to wine. They had sacks of rye and barley grown in Brattahlid. They also brought a small amount of wheat, set aside for only one purpose: Eucharist, the holy supper of Christ's passion.

They had just finished repairing the *Sea Goat* and were ready for her winter storage when Arn asked them all to meet. They gathered together early that evening, waiting to hear what he was so anxious to tell. A low flickering fire made dancing shadows, and on the spit a large salmon sizzled.

"I have something to say, something important," he began.

The entire group quieted; something about Arn's tone indicated a serious attitude was required.

"Ever since the events that day in Brattahlid, I have not been myself. I did not want to lose my honor. But lost it I have." He turned and looked at Kathleen. "Even so, I did not lose my daughter."

He turned again to address them all. "And I think I have come up with a way to help regain my honor. Not by another holmgang. Not by any trickery. But by doing something no one else has yet done. If Leif's plan succeeded, then the berserkers believe us dead. We could winter here, then consider returning to Greenland next spring. But I want to do something else, something more. I want to explore further this land we are in."

"What do you mean?" asked Helgi.

"By sailing south. We need to leave now, before the winter sets in."

Sail south? At such a proposition, no one could find words.

"I swear to you, I am not a mad man," Arn said to fill the silence.

"But, Arn," Helgi finally said, "remember Leif's warning. He said there is nothing but ice and mist beyond Vinland. How can you be sure what we will find?"

"I believe we will find warmer regions south, just as there are warmer regions when we sail south back home. We shall follow the shore. All I know is that I must do something to regain my honor. I must sail *toward* something, not *away from* something."

Arn could just imagine it. They would sail south and see horizons no eyes had ever seen. After a year, they could return to Greenland, then they could sail back to Iceland and to Norway. He would tell everyone of the great new land Bjarni and Leif had discovered, but that he—he, Arn of Bergen—had explored.

"Are you with me?" he asked.

One by one, they pondered his idea. For some, it did not matter much, as they had already set out so far into the unknown. For others, the additional adventure was enticing. Still others could not bear to think of what Arn would do if they said no.

And so, one by one, they all said, "Yes, we are with you."

Once they started south, their mood was light. Arn became himself again. He started to think of the events in Brattahlid as a kind of luck. Not bad luck, but good luck, for those events would bring him great honor and maybe even fortune.

They followed the coastline, as do all sailors in unknown waters. The *Sea Goat* hugged the shore like a colt that runs free yet never strays far from its mother's flanks. She was a knarr and could sail in close. Had the *Sea Goat* been another type of ship, needing deeper water, sailing southward along the coast would have been a constant trial. The normal currents and winds would have pressed hard on them, pushing them aground. And though the crew of the *Sea Goat* did not know it, they had chosen the best time to sail south. In the waters they sailed, autumn is usually a brief window of calm from storms.

To pass the time, the travelers filled the air around them with singing. Sometimes Arn would start in his low baritone, then Kathleen would add her bright soprano. And then Brand and the others would join in, with Haki providing the percussion on his tom-tom.

When they were feeling less boisterous, they would play riddle games. All the Norse loved poetry, and they loved the little kennings woven into the best poems. The phrases were a way to describe something without saying the word itself.

"Breaker of trees . . ." said Haki, starting the game.

"That is easy!" replied Arn. "The wind." It was now Arn's turn. "Stead of the seas . . ."

"I know!" said Kathleen. "That is a ship. Dragon's lair . . ." she prompted.

"That one is harder," said Gudrun. "But the answer is gold, for everyone knows that dragons lie upon gold in their nests!"

"Yes," said Arn. "And perhaps we shall find a dragon's lair someday."

The little group continued to sail south, their intrepid captain at the helm of the *Sea Goat*. No one knew if they would find only icy mist or the warmer climes as Arn suspected. But as each day of the ever-emerging autumn passed, they left behind the lands of seasons and snows and came closer to lands of perpetual summer.

Arn always made the decision of whether and where to put ashore. No one was certain if the lands were inhabited or not. Sometimes they sailed for long periods sighting nothing but wildlife on the shore. Other times the lookouts thought they saw movement in the trees, unsure if it were human eyes watching them from the lush wilderness.

When they did go ashore, they put up their portable tents and set the large kettle to cook hot grains for nourishment. Before leaving, they always took aboard a generous supply of fresh water.

The felines turned out to be excellent traveling companions. Once on shore, Hlatr and Sprettr immediately began to explore and perhaps to find a small wild creature to eat. Yet they always returned when Kathleen called them. They would come jumping and leaping out of the trees and brush, more canine than feline in their temperament.

And a most remarkable thing had happened. Hlatr's belly had become more and more round. Gudrun had confirmed it: the barren cat had somehow managed to become pregnant.

CHAPTER FORTY-NINE

THE MARINERS CONTINUED SOUTHWARD, PAST inlets and coves, bays and woodlands. They were astonished at the variety and great beauty that each day brought. Many times they saw animals along the shoreline—numerous deer and moose, sometimes a bear of brown or black. Then one day it happened—a group of figures emerged from the trees as they sailed past. People *did* live in these lands!

The people they saw looked quite different from themselves. From a distance, the Norse could see the people wore the skins of animals for clothing. Their hair was dark as a raven's wing. Some wore feathers in their hair, and some appeared to have elaborate paint applied to their faces and bodies. It was hard to estimate height; some seemed smaller than the Norse, and some seemed as tall or even taller.

The travelers were unsure how to deal with these people, whom they now encountered more and more often. Arn's years of experience as a trader helped him make decisions about whether to land, where to land, and how long to stay.

In some places, natives stood on shore, weapons ready. In those cases, Arn and his crew just sailed on. It seemed that the people did not have any vessels like the knarr, only smaller craft made of what appeared to be white bark or hollowed tree trunks. Although they had never been pursued, the travelers knew it would not be difficult to outrun any craft that approached them.

In other cases, a chief would let his curiosity overcome his fear. The natives would slowly paddle their canoes out to the knarr. As the natives held up items for barter, the two sides traded. The red cloth of Leif's cloak, given to Father Brand, was cut into strips for trade. The natives tied it around their heads as a sort of decoration.

Once when the travelers had made camp on shore, a small group of hunters and gatherers approached them peacefully from the woodlands. Using signs, the two sides showed techniques for hunting and fishing. The men shared examples of snares and compared fish hooks.

The women were very curious about Gudrun and Kathleen. The Norse noted that they had broad cheeks and large dark eyes. One robust woman, the obvious leader of the women, approached. Her breasts hung low to her waist, and she had the worn look of a woman who had lived through many pregnancies. Small shells had been braided into her long hair.

She reached out her hand to touch Kathleen's unadorned braids. Kathleen nodded her consent. A small, shy smile immediately appeared on the older woman's face. The golden braids felt the same as the woman's own; only the color was different. She smiled again when Kathleen reached out and stroked her hair as well. Then all the women began to stroke one another's hair and clothing, and general chaos ensued.

The next event was the inspection of Gudrun's cooking utensils and food stores. The women noted that some obvious food sources were missing. Two of the women left and entered a nearby marsh. They returned with arms loaded with the roots of a tall green grass with broad, flat leaves that looked like straps. They showed Gudrun how to clean and mash the roots to make a carbohydrate-rich gruel—the gift of the cattails. In return, Gudrun gave them two small silver spoons.

When the trading occurred, Brand tried mightily to understand the language being spoken. It did not take him long to realize that each group had its own language. In the end, though, there was not enough time for Brand to learn the new tongues. He was reduced to using signs and gestures, just as the other Norse did.

He thought often of his days of captivity with Ibn Beshir and how Latin had saved them both from isolation. He longed to share a word, just a word, with these natives about his faith. While others saw the natives as potential trading partners or as threats, he saw them as souls. *Precious souls.*

But not every encounter was peaceful. One day the travelers encamped on a small bay. They set up their tents and cooking pots. Kathleen shook out clothing for washing. Hlatr and Sprettr had started to explore.

Brand was the first to notice. "There are eyes upon us," he said very quietly to Arn.

Sharp-eyed Patrekr looked up and saw, indeed, at least a dozen warriors in the woods around them.

Arn said calmly to them all, "We must go now. Slowly. Pick up everything. We will go without confrontation."

The others did as he said. As Kathleen scooped up the clothing, she kept glancing about—not looking at the warriors but looking for Hlatr and Sprettr.

Arn read his daughter's concern. "Kathleen, we must hurry," he said sternly.

"Yes, Father," she replied. Then she immediately started calling for her cat. "Hlatr! *Hlatrrrrrrr!*" But no cat appeared.

Soon, nearly everything had been gathered and readied for retreat to the knarr. No attack had been made, but no one knew when one might begin. Everyone was already sweating in the heat. Arn wiped his brow.

"We must go *now*, Kathleen," he repeated.

"But I cannot find Hlatr!" she said in growing panic.

Arn spoke one final time: "We must go. *Now!*"

Once they were back on the boat and sailing into safety, Gudrun did her best to comfort the heartbroken young woman.

"But what will become of her?" Kathleen cried. "She will have kittens. How will she survive?"

"She is smart," Gudrun reassured. "She knows how to find mice and other small animals. And she knows how to fish. She will find a place in the hollow of a tree to have her kittens. They will be fine. She will be a good mother. Sprettr is there too, so she will not be lonely." Gudrun sighed as she held Kathleen. "We never know the future—for Hlatr or for us. We must believe the best."

Kathleen stared at the shore a long time as they sailed away. Brand looked on helplessly, the woman he loved again encountering loss.

And for many days, Kathleen thought she heard Hlatr's meows and squeaks and trills, and it would sadden her to turn and find her dear companion was not there.

CHAPTER FIFTY

Near present-day Chesapeake Bay

THE STURDY KNARR CONTINUED ITS southward journey down the coast. The weather no longer informed the travelers as it did back home, but by reckoning of days, all agreed it was mid-autumn.

On a day thick with gray clouds, they reached a large bay where numerous sweet water streams flowed into the saltwater. It appeared no different from the many shores and inlets they had already sailed past. They were about to move on when a most astonishing thing happened.

Dim but incessant at first, it evolved into the loudest, most overwhelming chorus of bird calls they had ever heard. The sky filled black with tens of thousands of the largest and most elegant geese they had ever seen. The sound was tremendous when the honking birds flew in from the northwest and landed, feet forward and splayed out, into the waiting waters. The cacophony was jubilant. The geese seemed to be saying, "We have arrived! We have arrived!" The birds were mostly gray and dun colored, with black tails and long black necks. Under their chins and reaching almost all around their necks was a collar of purest white. It looked as though someone had fashioned tiny bibs for them.

The mariners decided to stay awhile to restock with water and make some minor repairs. Also, they were sick of fish, and everyone wondered how the goose flesh compared to the birds' flesh at home.

Although the sky was threatening, no rain came. Patrekr and Gunnar set out to see if they would have hunting luck. The men were both sharp eyed but not so accurate with a bow, so the first shots missed their mark. It was hard work. Each time they shot and missed, they had to retrieve the precious arrows. By late afternoon, they considered whether nets would be a better way to capture one of the magnificent birds.

On one last try with the bow, Patrekr's arrow sliced through the air and into the breast of a feeding goose. She cried out in pain and alarm, then made her way to a dry hummock surrounded by deep water. The two men paused, deciding whether the arrow and their quarry were worth wading into the unknown waters and encountering the creatures that might lurk there.

At that moment, an even larger goose landed softly on the hummock and walked awkwardly toward the dying bird. He slowly circled her. Then he called to her with his wildest, most piercing cry. With his beak, he urged her to get up, spread her wings, and fly away with him. Though she did not move, he would not leave her.

Eventually, he hung his head, his body hunched in loneliness. He remained this way a long time, in quiet, complete, and utter devotion.

The two men sat down and watched the scene from afar. Finally, Gunnar broke the silence.

"Clearly, they were mates."

Patrekr replied quietly, "I wish my arrow had missed its mark."

He brushed his hand over his eyes and without averting his gaze, reached his arm around Gunnar's waist. Gunnar slipped his arm around Patrekr's broad shoulders and pulled him close.

And so they stayed, sitting vigil with the mourning goose, until the daylight was nearly gone and the sorrowful scene had faded almost to blackness.

Brand was dispatched to look for them. When he approached and saw the two men seated together, something moved within him. He was sure that what he saw in that dim light was love.

CHAPTER FIFTY-ONE

On the coastline of present-day Florida

A FTER A FEW DAYS, ARN decided it was time to leave the great bay with the geese without number. They continued to follow the coastline, sailing ever more to the south. The knarr sailed past enormous forests of mangrove trees, their spiny roots grasping the salty mud like gnarled fingers.

The Norse were amazed at the varieties of plants and animals they encountered. They all recognized the familiar deer, bear, and fox. But so much more astonished the eyes: birds the color of pink sunset, small lizards that hid shyly in the forest floor, snakes with fangs and snakes without fangs, shelled creatures that scuttled across or embedded themselves in the sand. And then there were vicious lizards, as large as men. They lay hidden like logs in water, their huge teeth outlining each side of their narrow snouts.

In addition to exploring, there was learning occurring on the *Sea Goat*. Kathleen could read and write the Latin prayers—the Pater Noster and more. She had memorized many of them as well. She and Brand often sat on the shores together. Brand used a twig to write words in the sand. Once the waves had obliterated his letters, Kathleen would re-create them on her own.

The travelers had sufficient food. Ever the inventive cook, Gudrun decided that if other animals ate a certain plant or animal, then it must be good enough for the Norse to eat. She herself tested each item before anyone else. All plants with any bitterness were summarily avoided, for bitterness often coincided with poisonous. If the raw plant was not bitter, she cooked it. By constant experimentation and the gift of the cattails, she expanded the small group's chances of survival far beyond what their stores, snares, and bows would have brought them.

Brand insisted that each meal begin with thanks to the Triune God. And truth be told, each person was grateful for whatever food they had, no matter what god lived in their hearts.

Haki proved his worth as well. Haki's hands were small and dexterous but strong. He was clever with them, fashioning nets and sharp hooks for catching fish. While the others were men of the sea, he was a man of the land. His eyes could see the smallest animal sign, be it a trail in the grass or a small track. He easily created and placed snares so he nearly always had a rabbit to add to the cooking pot.

And of course, when Helgi's large hands were not occupied with navigation, sails, or oars, they were busy with his other special skill. One day when the knarr was anchored near a calm shoreline, Helgi called Kathleen to him. Gudrun stood close by, her face almost bursting with anticipation. Everyone else on board also crowded around. Kathleen knew something was afoot.

Helgi stood with his hands behind him, hiding some sort of object. "Now choose which hand, Kathleen."

She pointed to his right, for she always thought of Helgi on the *styrbord* side of the ship. With a dramatic flourish, he swept a wooden object from behind him and placed it in her waiting hands. On it he had carved the likeness of a face: a smiling cat with cunning little ears and large eyes.

"Oh, Helgi! You have put Hlatr's face into the wood. I love it. I shall keep it forever!"

She danced around the deck, holding the object up in her arms. Everyone grinned at her exuberant happiness.

"How did you ever keep it so secret?" she asked.

Gudrun replied, "Well, Helgi had been experimenting with ways to ornament the arm of a chair he had in mind for me. But soon he knew he had to capture the spirit of Hlatr instead. Every time you asked about what he was carving, we told you it was for the chair. And if you hovered too near, the others stood in your way so you had no chance to see what was really being made."

"Actually, the carving was Father Brand's idea," Helgi interjected.

Kathleen looked at Brand, and her face shone with happiness.

Brand responded with a smile. Yes, the idea had been his, he thought. But he needed Helgi. Through his great skill, Helgi had done what Brand could not: help Kathleen heal.

One day, they found a small bay where a sweet water stream flowed into the sea. Arn decided it was a favorable place to anchor the knarr. They put to land with the usual items for rest and restoration.

They settled in for the night. It was Haki's turn to tend the campfire and keep the watch while the others slept. There were no suspicious sounds or any other disturbance during the night. All seemed calm.

But that changed as soon as the sun began to light the dark waters. An ominous sign appeared.

"It is blood!" Haki shouted. "The sea has turned to blood!"

They all heard but did not understand what had so alarmed Haki. They looked out at the water in astonishment. The sea had indeed turned to crimson. And more, thousands of dead fish floated atop the waves and gathered along on the shoreline.

The travelers were frightened to touch or taste the sea water, as it had perhaps poisoned the fish. They stood for several minutes, struggling to figure out what the red tide meant.

Arn called them all into a circle to discuss the phenomena. He thought it might be a sign from the sea gods Ægir and Rán. Helgi thought it could be the blood of a sea dragon. Practical Gudrun was perplexed. She looked very closely at the water. She had often seen seas and other waters green with tiny plants. But these seas were a dull red.

"Father Brand," asked Arn, "do you know the meaning of this sign?"

"I am not sure. In the stories of the Hebrews, a prophet named Moses turned a river to blood to force a king to let his people—an enslaved people—live in freedom." Brand shook his head in frustration. "I am sorry. I do not understand this sign."

As they talked, everyone agreed what they were seeing was so serious that it might force a change in their journey.

"Tell me, what should we do with our journey from this day forward?" Arn asked the others.

One by one, each mariner, free or slave, female or male, said what was on his or her mind and heart. It was not unlike the democratic Things held in Norway. Except here in this place, women and even Haki were given a voice.

Kathleen was the last to speak.

Brand watched her rise and move to the center of the circle. For the last year and a half, he had studied her without revealing—ever—his feelings for her. He was shepherd and teacher to her. That was all anyone knew.

Kathleen spoke clearly and with feeling. "Let us return again to the north. I long to feel a cool breeze on my face. It is time to go home, to sail again under the shimmering northern lights."

Arn was proud of his daughter. She had experienced much on their voyages together, and he had come to know her as she grew into a strong woman. But he sometimes wondered if he had been right to allow her to sail with him. If she were at home in Bergen or even in Trondheim, she would be living the life of a merchant's daughter, content with her weaving.

"Well, then," said Arn. "Everyone has spoken on the matter of a course change. Although some of you—Patrekr, Gunnar, and Haki—are willing to continue south, no one objects to turning around now. On that matter, we seem to be of one accord. So tomorrow we shall no longer sail south. We shall return to the north, to Vinland and then back to Brattahlid." Arn paused and then added with a wide grin, "They will never believe the stories we shall have to tell!"

Not too far away, another circle was meeting.

A chief with black hair sat in the center of the tribal lodge, listening to his captains. He was dressed in animal skins, and his body was decorated with black paint. A smoky fire smoldered, and drums beat a soft, solemn cadence.

Everyone in the tribe was familiar with the red tide. It came some years and not others. When it came, it always brought poisonous devastation. They all believed it was the work of some evil thing or force that had entered their tribe.

For some time, they had known of the unfamiliar vessel sailing past their lands. They called it the "great canoe" and had been content to watch it from afar. But now the captains told the chief that something had to be done about the strangers. The chief was unsure, but the warriors persisted and clamored to be heard. The strangers had brought the curse of the red tide with them.

Something had to be done!

CHAPTER FIFTY-TWO

D AWN WAS STRANGELY DARK. Low on the horizon, a glint of sunlight was visible. But above the thin slice of gold, layer after layer of heavy steel-colored clouds blocked the sun.

Kathleen, ever the early riser, emerged from her tent. She was dressed in her simple linen underdress, as she needed nothing more in the moist heat. As the travelers had ventured south, they progressively shed the clothing they used to wear in the cold of the north.

She greeted Helgi as he stood outside the tent shelter. She noted that he looked pensively at the sky.

"What is it, Helgi?"

"I wish I knew, Kathleen," he said, scanning the horizon. "At home, I could read the sky like the face of my mother. I knew what was to come. The color of the sunset, the number and kind of whales, the familiar seabirds, the direction and scent of the wind, even the ravens' flight —it told me all I needed. Here, I am useless."

"Oh no, Helgi. That is not true! You have been our able guide though all the unknown seas."

Helgi responded by giving her a huge bear hug. He lifted her up until her toes left the sand.

"Helgi, put me down!" she demanded with a laugh.

He did so immediately and smiled at her as she headed to a nearby sweet water stream. Then he turned his eyes again to the sky. *The Norns*, he thought. *What fate have the three sisters woven for us today?*

Some of the crew were still asleep in their shore tents. Others had started their morning ablutions and personal care. Gudrun had started the cauldron to boil the day's cattail mush. She hummed as she stoked the fire.

Everyone's mood had brightened. *Going home. Going home!*

The nearby stream was clear and warm. Kathleen decided that a face wash was not enough, so she waded into the rippling water to cleanse her body. The water was not quite deep enough for a proper swim, so she did not remove her dress. A quick dip in the fresh water would be a convenient way to give it a good rinse.

Droplets sparkled as she exuberantly splashed water all over herself. She had a small supply of soap left. She held it in her hand as she calculated how much longer this precious luxury would last.

In the next instant, a volley of arrows split the morning air.

The first arrows were aimed at the men. But for some inexplicable reason, all missed their mark. Instead Gudrun was the first to fall. The arrow's stone point pierced her chest. A strange, surprised look fell across her face like a shadow. A red blot seeped onto her white apron before she hit the ground.

"*No!*" Kathleen screamed.

All the men rushed for their weapons. There was no time for bow and arrow. Swords were quickly in hand. But there was little place to hide from the barrage of arrows that continued.

Attackers entered the camp from out of the dense green. Frenzy erupted. Amid the chaos, Brand looked desperately for Kathleen.

Helgi went rushing into the fray, swinging his sword in a great arc, catching an attacker above the ear, and removing half the warrior's brain.

Haki showed the courage of a man twice his size. He was able to repel several warriors before he fell to the ground.

Patrekr and Gunnar, seeing their comrades skewered with arrows, fought like madmen. They struck as many blows as possible but were overwhelmed by numbers. Patrekr fell to his knees as an arrow pierced his back and lodged in a lung. Blood spurted from his mouth like a fountain.

Gunnar fell next, a few feet away, an arrow in his neck. Contorted with pain, they crawled toward one another. They pushed and struggled, until finally, finally, their fingers touched. Then their struggling breaths ceased.

"Oh God! Oh God, help us!" Kathleen cried out. She picked up Gunnar's sword and ran to Brand and her father.

Arn and Brand fended off individual attackers. They were pushed backward into the sea, toward the moored knarr.

Helgi waded to his waist into the surf. He lifted the *Sea Goat's* anchor. With extreme effort, he flung it inside the craft. Then he grabbed Kathleen and lifted her up into the knarr.

Arn and Brand clambered into the ship and fell heavily onto the oak floorboards.

Two natives leaped upon Helgi and began stabbing him. He threw them off. With a yell, he gave the untethered craft a mighty push.

It was the final effort of his life.

A current swept the ship toward open sea as rapidly as a white-water river. The sky was a dark swirling vortex. Angry winds shifted.

Arn, Brand, and Kathleen—alone in the bobbing craft, without their shipmates, without provisions, and lost in unknown waters—prepared for the struggle of their lives.

BOOK TWO

Chaos and Order

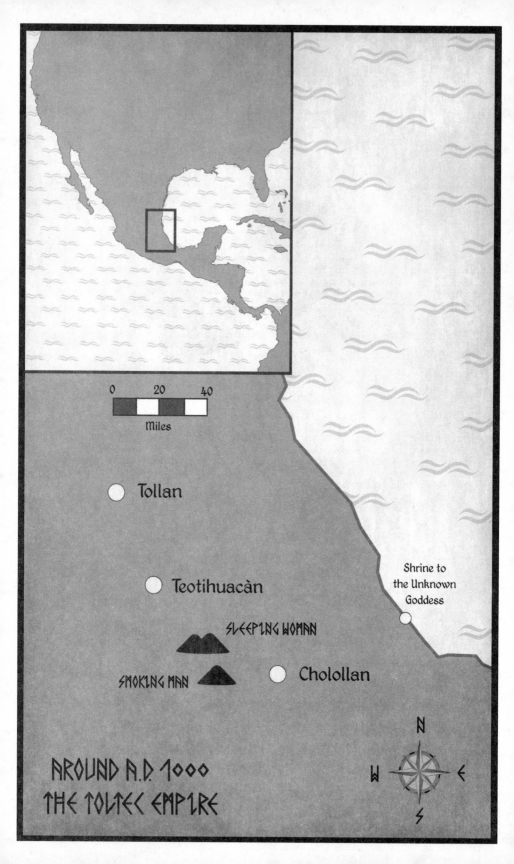

Miles

Tollan

Teotihuacàn

Shrine to
the Unknown
Goddess

SLEEPING WOMAN

SMOKING MAN

Cholollan

AROUND A.D. 1000
THE TOLTEC EMPIRE

CHAPTER ONE

On a beach near present-day Veracruz, Mexico

KATHLEEN WAS IN THAT HALF-AWAKE, half-asleep world where the conscious mind is there yet not there. What brought her unto herself was not touch but sound—the sound of waves quietly sweeping the shore.

I am alive, she thought, rousing herself from the sleep of exhaustion.

She did not know how long she had been unconscious. When she tried to move, her muscles forced a low moan. The agonies of the previous days—the torments of the wind, sea, and rain—were reflected in her worn and bruised body. Wind and rain. More wind and rain. Bailing water. Exhausted. Bailing. Bailing awake. Bailing asleep.

But *where* was she? She looked down and saw a rope tied to her waist. It was tethered to the mast of the oaken trader that had carried her to shore. She slowly untied the rope and pushed herself to a sitting position. With dazed effort, she forced the fog from her mind.

Suddenly, thoughts and memories burst like a flood. What of her companions?

She crawled to the closest body on the wooden floorboards and rolled it to her. She saw the beloved face of her father. And yes, yes, he was breathing!

"Father, wake up!" Her extreme thirst made her voice a weak whisper.

She shook him gently. Her father groaned a reply. She noticed the wound on his side, under his ribs, deep and crusted with blood. His clothing was stained a frightening red-brown.

At that moment, Brand began to rouse as well. He was lying a few feet away, close to the styrbord. He began to crawl to her. Kathleen noticed he had wounds on each of his forearms.

"Father Brand, you are hurt!"

"Kathleen, you are alive! Are you all right?" He held her face in his hand, every cell of his body longing to embrace her.

"I am unhurt, but my father is badly wounded."

Brand glanced at Arn and saw his wound. Then he quickly scanned the landscape. Their ship was aground on a gentle shore. The entire area looked as if the plants and trees had been shredded by ten thousand knives. Not by an ordinary wind; maybe by something else. He could see no village and no people. But a river emptied into the sea very near them. He grabbed a small water cask and ran to the river.

Kathleen studied her father. She remembered the attack now. Her father's wound was deep. A great quantity of blood had undoubtedly poured from it.

Brand quickly returned, splashing the sweet water as he hurried back. He and Kathleen took a long drink, and they brought the cask to Arn's lips as well. It refreshed Arn somewhat. He roused from his weakened state. He motioned for Kathleen to move her ear close to his mouth.

"I am dying, Kathleen."

"No, no—it is not true!" Placing her hands on his head, she frantically began to pray but stopped when her father continued speaking.

"Yes, Kathleen. No man—no matter how rich, how strong, how wise, or how powerful—can escape death when the Norns have cut the threads of his life. I will go with courage to my death."

He struggled for more air.

"Back in Brattahlid, fate took my chance to show my honor and protect my name. But I have since shown that I do not lack courage. I have met all the challenges of this voyage. Now I can go with confidence away from this life. I can go, with honor, to the sleep of the sword."

Kathleen looked imploringly at Brand and then at her father. "Please, tell Father Brand your confession," she begged.

Arn ignored her pleas. "Kathleen, my dear daughter, I have one thing to ask of you. Promise me"—he paused for strength—"promise me you will do whatever is necessary to survive. And that you will have children."

"Yes, Father, I give you my word. I will survive. I will have children. Now please confess. It is not too late. Father Brand is here. Please."

Again, he did not comply. "Later," he said. "Now let me talk to Brand. Alone."

Kathleen moved to the prow of the battered knarr. She felt strangely relieved to see that even though the ship was damaged, its mast still stood tall and unbroken.

Arn looked directly into Brand's face.

"Take care of her. I know you will. *Eigi leyna augu ef ann manni kona.*"

Brand understood these words. *The eyes cannot hide it if a man loves a woman.* He began to protest but stopped. There was no point when Arn was so close to dying.

Brand called for Kathleen. She gathered up her father's body, cradling his head in her lap. He moved his lips, but Kathleen and Brand struggled to hear.

"What? Father, what are you saying? Do you accept the White Kristr? Father!"

His lips moved, and she put her face closer to his. She heard the word *I*. But each breath became weaker and further apart until a small, strange sound came from deep within him. She watched his mouth and waited for another word until the faint pink in his lips disappeared.

She never knew her father's last words. But she knew his spirit had begun its journey. The Arn of this earth was no more.

A cry of anguish burst from Kathleen's throat. Hot tears flooded her eyes in an instant. She beat her breast a single time with a clenched fist, as if by a physical blow she could keep the beating heart within her from bursting forth and breaking.

CHAPTER TWO

THE SUN WAS LOWERING ON the horizon as they prepared Arn's body for burial. Kathleen gathered more freshwater from the river and washed his face and the bloody wounds on his body. She tore out some hairs from her head and gently closed his fingers around them, so that a part of her would always be with him.

Without proper tools, they struggled to dig a grave deep enough to receive his body. It was dug east to west, in the Christian manner. They wrapped Arn in a piece of linen cloth and lowered him down into his resting place, placing him on his right side, his feet drawn up into a fetal position. Kathleen carefully laid his drinking horn in his hand and covered his head with a cloth.

Brand held Arn's sword in his hands, waiting. They both knew Arn would want to be buried with it. Finally, Kathleen spoke.

"I know my father would want his sword with him. But I promised him I would survive. And he knows we may need it more."

Brand nodded in agreement.

They filled in the shallow grave as best they could to keep away hungry wild things.

"Father Brand," asked Kathleen, her eyes red with tears, "could we not at least make an outline of a ship with rocks, to mark the place where he sleeps?"

Brand understood her wishes, but his analytical mind had already calculated the risks. Although the area had first appeared to be deserted, he had since noticed what appeared to be a small stone altar just up from the shore. He guessed that other people had visited the area.

"Kathleen, even if we could find enough rocks, we do not know what the people here might do if they discover the grave."

Reluctantly, they covered the spot with broken branches, leaves, and other plant litter so no one but themselves could perceive that a body lay buried there. It was the best they could do. They did not want someone in this unknown land to discover and disturb Arn's sleep.

At last, the burial was done. The two stood beside Arn's resting place. Brand recalled what he could of the ritual of the commendation of the dead. He modified it, given the uncertainty of the state of Arn's soul at the moment of his death.

"Arn, we entrust you to God, who created you. May you be surrounded by angels and triumphant saints. May the Lord grant you a holy rest and peace at last. May you enjoy the sight of God forever."

Brand continued with a prayer for the living. Finally, together, they made the sign of the cross and recited the Pater Noster.

That night, the moon was full. The rabbit on its face was clear for all to see. The survivors clung to each other in the knarr. Brand was grateful that they had been exhausted in every way imaginable to make his chaste embrace possible.

"Brand, I feel so alone!" Kathleen cried, her tears falling so hard, her fingertips could not contain them.

Tenderly, he wiped away her tears. "No," he answered. "When God is with us, we are never lost, never truly abandoned."

And it was true; they were not alone. The stars and the moon above were not the only ones that watched them.

CHAPTER THREE

ARLIER THAT DAY, HOURS BEFORE the knarr came ashore, a small child and her mother had begun their annual pilgrimage to the small altar at the beach. The two had trudged along together. In one hand, the mother carried a basket. In the other, she held the little girl's hand. A headband kept the sweat off the mother's brow and kept her dark wavy hair out of her eyes. She wore a round disk of iridescent shell at her neck, attached with a leather cord.

The five-year-old child wore her hair in braids at each side of her ears. She was small and delicate, so she was called Nenetl, for she was like a little doll.

Each wore a simple cotton shift, made soft by many washings. Once brightly colored with plant dyes, the garments had been lightened by drying in the sun.

For many years, the twice-widowed mother had made pilgrimage to put flowers and offerings of fruit on the small stone altar and to ask for blessing. It was a half day's walk from the village.

Only women knew of this place. Nearly all the known gods were male and warlike and cruel. But this altar, this place of worship and supplication, was to the goddess with no name. Any leader who knew of its existence would surely destroy it.

The woman's mother had brought her here years ago. When she became a mother herself, the woman brought her young son, in secret—until he was taken away to the city of Tollan. There he trained as an athlete for the ball game. That was many years ago.

This year, however, the woman was especially grateful. Word had come that her son was coming to see her. When the woman told her daughter that Tizoc was on his way, the little girl could hardly contain her excitement at meeting the half brother she had never known.

The woman placed flowers on the altar. She prayed for the well-being of her girl child and her boy child, now a young man, whom she had not seen in so many years.

Suddenly, a tremor shook the ground under her knees. A strong wind scattered the flowers.

She looked up and out to the sea. Anxiety rose in her like a dreadful flame. Far in the distance, she saw a wave rushing toward them. It was larger than any she had ever seen, and it was approaching fast.

"Nenetl, come here!" she said, looking at her daughter with fierce intensity. "You must listen very, very carefully." She fought to hide the strain in her voice.

Like all children of her village, Nenetl had been reared to be obedient. She listened closely to her mother, her sweet, small face somewhat quizzical.

"A big wave is coming. I am going to put you high in a tree."

The mother quickly scanned the thicket of palms and mangrove trees and selected one. She pulled a rope from her basket and looped it around the handle. She carried Nenetl and the basket as high as she could up the curved trunk of a palm. She reached the topknot of the tree.

Nenetl whimpered. Her small arms clenched tighter to her mother's neck.

The mother kissed her daughter's cheeks and hands. Taking the shell amulet from around her neck, she placed it over her daughter's head.

"Nenetl, always remember me when you look at his. And always remember that I love you."

She climbed back down the tree, listening to Nenetl's whimpering grow louder.

"I am scared. Scared, Mama."

"I know, Nenetl, but you must be brave," she called. "No matter what happens, what you may see or hear, you must not leave the basket until I tell you. Nenetl, I am here! I am right here. I am with you!"

There was no rope left for Nenetl's mother. So she determined to watch as a sentinel at the base of the tree and to cling to it. She hoped she and the tree would be strong enough.

"Mama!" Nenetl called.

But the sound of the wave was so strong, her voice was carried far off. It never reached her mother below.

The waters came. They were more powerful than Nenetl's mother. But not more powerful than the nest she had made for her eaglet. Nenetl huddled like a baby bird in the top of the huge palm tree. She called out to her mother until her voice was hoarse and she was exhausted. She fell asleep, then woke and repeated her anguished cries. But there was silence.

Hours passed. Nenetl looked down and saw that her mother was not there. Her voice was nearly gone. She tried to call out again, but the sound was barely a whisper.

Suddenly, her eyes fixed on movement on the beach. *Maybe my mama is there!* she thought. But the longer she looked, the clearer it became that the figures were unlike any she had seen before. *They look so strange*, she thought. When she saw that her mother was not among these strange people, another tear rolled down her cheek.

Then she thought, *Maybe the people have seen Mama.* And then a new thought struck her: *Maybe they are gods. And if they are gods, maybe they will help me!*

The night passed with Nenetl alone in the treetop and the strangers in the shipwrecked knarr.

At the half light of dawn, the child resolved to disobey her mother, who had said not to come down from the tree until her command. Nenetl slowly climbed out of the basket, her little legs weak and cramping. She descended slowly down the curve of the palm tree. The ground was littered thick with leaves and branches. She stumbled many times as she ran to plead with the gods.

Kathleen awoke from a fitful sleep. Then it hit her like a powerful, unexpected blow. Her heart was again stunned by the reality. Her father—gone. And all the others. Patrekr and Gunnar. Haki. Sweet Helgi and Gudrun. Even Hlatr's softness. Gone, all gone now.

She decided not to wake Father Brand, lying next to her. She left the knarr and headed to land. She stood for some moments there on the shore, facing the rising sun, her mind lost in a brief reverie. Then she turned around and froze midstep.

Her gaze fell downward as she stared at a small child, a child kneeling before her with bowed head. Kathleen looked around wildly—was the child alone? She scanned in every direction but saw no one.

In a tongue Kathleen could not understand, Nenetl began to implore the goddess: "Have you seen my mother? Please, tell me where my mother has gone." The words came out only as whispers.

The tiny child was shaking, and tears were falling. She did not dare to look up. She had nothing to give as an offering. Maybe the goddess would not listen.

Kathleen called out to Brand.

"What is it?" he asked, hearing the urgency in her voice.

Then he saw the child. Like Kathleen, he quickly looked all around.

In an instant, Brand stood next to her. "Where did she come from?" he asked.

"I do not know. She just appeared. But she seems to be alone. And so frightened."

Kathleen's heart, so raw with grief, responded to the child's distress.

Nenetl continued her petitions. Suddenly, the strange goddess took her into her arms, stroked her hair, and made sounds that felt good to hear. Up close, Nenetl was certain these beings *were* gods. The goddess who cradled her had eyes the color of the sky, and the god had eyes the color of jade. The strange sounds from their mouths made no sense to her.

"Father Brand, what shall we do?"

Brand looked at the child. Her skin was coppery, and her eyes and hair were black or nearly so. She did not look that much different from the men who had so savagely attacked and killed their companions and mortally wounded Arn. To Brand, however, there was only one way to answer Kathleen's question.

"We must take care of her," he said without hesitation.

Kathleen offered a cup of water, which Nenetl greedily drank.

Nenetl noted that the gods had not answered her pleadings to produce her mother. But she would stay with them if they would keep her.

She had nowhere else to go.

CHAPTER FOUR

Two strong figures moved relentlessly along the wind-ravaged and water-soaked landscape. Tizoc and Patli were close friends, closer even than brothers, and inseparable. They had been born in the same village, only a few moon cycles apart.

They passed awkwardly yet quickly over downed trees and other wet forest debris. Tizoc moved with unflagging energy over the obstacles, pushing ever forward. Patli struggled somewhat to keep up.

Tizoc's eyes were as dark and shining as wet black ink. They were framed with lashes straight and thick as pine needles. Wide set and alert, his eyes gave him an aura of intelligence, even before he said a word. When he smiled, which was often, his even, white teeth gleamed.

He wore a loincloth made of woven cotton fibers. A soft cotton cape fell across his strong shoulders and across his body. His feet were shod with sandals made of twisted henequen plant fibers. No hair grew on his face or chest, but black hair curled in slight waves behind his ears and at the nape of his neck.

His companion, though somewhat smaller in stature, was likewise well muscled and dressed in the same mantle, loincloth, and sandals. Patli's straight black hair was cut in a bowl shape just above his ears.

Each young man carried a sort of knapsack over his shoulders. Patli carried another bag, filled with his traveling medicines and supplies: cotton strips to staunch blood, herbs for pain, and herbs for healing wounds.

Although they had been born in a nearby village, they had not spent all their childhood there. For as long as anyone could remember, representatives from the warrior kingdom of Tollan had scoured the land for recruits for *ollama*, the ball game played everywhere. The boys were only eight years old when scouts from the city determined they might indeed have the speed and stamina to be outstanding athletes.

Neither boy had a father to protect him when soldiers arrived. In any case, a father's protest or defiance would have been futile. The soldiers of Tollan were powerful and could enforce whatever their rulers asked of them. The mothers wept when their sons were taken away, for it was well known that they may never see them again.

The boys were taken to Tollan, where they joined other young athletes and began a long and rigorous training. Tizoc matured and excelled, just as the scouts believed he would. Patli stopped growing at an earlier age, and he was never as fast as they had hoped. That did not separate their lives, though. Patli had an interest in and aptitude for medicine. He started training to be part of the medical team that cared for the players.

Sometimes, the boys received messages from their home village. Tizoc knew his widowed mother had remarried but was then widowed again. He knew he had a little sister. A girl as tiny as a doll at birth, and therefore was called Nenetl.

After more than a decade, Tizoc and Patli had been granted a chance to briefly visit their home village once again. They were wild with anticipation. But when their reached the place of their birth, they were met with a scene of disaster. Everyone moved slowly and walked and talked as if they were in a dream.

"Just before you arrived," the villagers said, "the storm hit the area, like a fist from the rain god. And then the earth moved, and an immense wave washed far inland."

Worse still, no one was able to find Tizoc's mother and little Nenetl. The chief elder stood dazed and swaying with fatigue. He wanted to help Tizoc but said he had no idea where his family was.

In desperation, they went to Patli's mother. They suspected she knew something but was reluctant to speak. Patli and Tizoc implored her, and at last she relented. Tizoc's mother and sister had gone to a special place, she said, to make offering to the goddess with no name. It was hidden and secret, so she could only give them a general idea of where it was.

"It is an isolated place. It is beside the spot where the little river meets the sea," she told them.

Tizoc had a vague memory of this place he had visited so long ago. It was considered somewhat dangerous to go there—no one knew exactly why.

Leaving the village, the two young men started out into the devastation. First they found the river and followed it to the sea. In normal times, they would have traversed the distance in half the time or less. But after the storm, nothing was normal. Trails had eroded, and the shredded jungle offered few clues to help them in the search. Even the birds were silent.

"Do you think we are getting close?" Patli asked, shifting his pack and the medicine bag.

"I think so," Tizoc replied, though he was far less certain than he wanted to admit.

At last, they emerged from the tangled green veil of the forest onto the edge of the beach. They stopped in their tracks, like figures in a stone mural.

Before them were two beings like no other. They appeared to be a male and a female. They were both taller than any person, male or female, they had ever seen. The beings were speaking—at least, it seemed to be some form of language—and singing. Beyond the figures the searchers saw a great canoe, larger than they had ever seen, beached on the shore.

And between them, sitting on a fallen tree trunk, was a little girl.

The young men's presence had not been noted. Patli tapped Tizoc on the shoulder and motioned with his head to turn back into the obscurity of the jungle. Tizoc did not immediately respond, but he knew what Patli had in mind. The forest had been badly damaged by the water and wind, yet there was still enough foliage to keep them somewhat hidden. They could confer in secret and decide what to do next.

Hidden in the forest, Tizoc spoke first, in hushed and breathless tones.

"I am sure that is my sister. I recognize the amulet. Nenetl is alive! But I did not see my mother. Did you see her, Patli?"

"I saw only the child. And she seemed fine." Patli saw the anxiety in Tizoc's eyes. "Maybe your mother is nearby," he said quietly.

"Who are those people? I have never seen a great canoe like that one. And how did Nenetl come to be with them?"

Tizoc and Patli were full of questions with no obvious answers.

They peered across the sand toward the trio. Nenetl seemed calm, relaxed, and in no immediate danger. The pair decided to spend some time observing the strange little group so they could plan how to safely secure Nenetl from the strangers.

Each young man carried a knife with obsidian blade and knew how to use it. But they were not warriors, only an athlete and doctor in training. They needed to ascertain what weapons the strangers possessed and whether more strangers had yet to be discovered.

Nenetl was unrestrained. Tizoc and Patli decided it would be safest if they approached as near as possible, then beckon her to them by name.

"And if they threaten or restrain her, we slay them," said Patli without emotion.

Tizoc could not stop himself from staring at the strangers. The man and woman got down on their knees. The male began talking as if reciting something from memory, his eyes closed but his face to the sky.

The male had a beard covering nearly all his face. The color of his hair was not dark but light and reddish. But the female—her hair was light and tawny. He had never seen a woman such as her.

The strangers stood up. Tizoc and Patli watched as the woman offered something for the child to drink.

Patli urged Tizoc, "We can wait no longer. We do not know what that liquid is. Maybe an evil sorcerer's potion."

Tizoc nodded.

In the next moment, Patli and Tizoc stepped out of the shadows of the glade. "Nenetl! Nenetl, come here!" they called out.

The child immediately recognized the sound of her own language and ran toward them, her fleet feet leaving small imprints in the sand.

Kathleen gasped at the sudden appearance of the strangers. Brand felt the adrenalin rush of danger flow in his blood. He quickly plucked his sword from the edge of the campsite and stood, all muscles tensed, waiting to see what the two young men would do next.

But with Nenetl now safe, Tizoc was somewhat unsure of what to do. He and Patli had not really taken into consideration what would happen after they had obtained the small child.

"Nenetl, I am your brother, Tizoc," he said, taking her into his arms.

Her mother had told her Tizoc was coming for a visit. Still, Nenetl was bewildered to suddenly see him.

He sensed her confusion and gently placed her down. "Nenetl, where is our mother? Do you know?"

She sadly shook her head.

Before he had more time to reflect, Nenetl began pulling him toward the strangers.

"Tizoc, Tizoc—you must talk to the gods," Nenetl insisted. "They can help us."

Brand and Kathleen watched from the short distance separating them as the little girl tugged on the taller man's arm. Brand moved protectively between Kathleen and the strangers. The men did not appear aggressive, but Brand could not ignore the knife the smaller man so obviously displayed.

Tizoc admonished Nenetl to quiet down. But instead of acting as the obedient child she had been trained to be, she suddenly broke free from him and ran *toward* the strangers. None of the adults had anticipated this.

"Nenetl!" scolded Tizoc.

She did not stop. She continued to run. When she reached Kathleen, she grabbed her hand and began pulling the tall woman closer to Tizoc and Patli.

Brand hesitated, not knowing what to do. Any threatening move might precipitate reprisal, and he had only a sword against two men armed with weapons that appeared to have well-fashioned cutting edges.

Kathleen felt the little hand pull her closer and closer to the men until she was face-to-face with the taller one, with little Nenetl beside her.

"Tizoc," Nenetl said, looking up at her older brother, "this is the goddess who gave me water and food. She *must* be a goddess. Tizoc, look at her eyes."

Tizoc looked. He made a short, quick breath, as if he had been struck. Sometimes a mysterious wind can catch the heart off guard and blow it open.

For a moment, no one moved.

Brand recalled that day back in Brattahlid, when his taking up the sword had brought about turbulence and chaos and forever changed the lives of Kathleen and her father. Something within him told him to try another tactic.

He slowly lowered the elegant sword and placed it on the sand. Then, in a moment of audacity that came from instinct rather than calculation, Brand motioned for the men to do the same.

"Tizoc, look! He wants us to put down our weapons!" said Patli incredulously. "The gods must have taken his mind!"

"No, he is not crazy. He is brave. Put down your knife, Patli."

Patli looked at Tizoc as if his friend were now the crazy one, rather than the pale stranger. But he complied.

When all weapons were placed gently on the sandy shore, the pale man again moved protectively between the woman and the ball players.

Who is the man with the woman? Tizoc thought with unaccustomed feelings of jealousy. *Her husband? Some sort of kin?*

Kathleen knew the taller man was staring at her, but not with the determined violence and hostility she had seen in other dark eyes the day of the ambush. And each time she met his gaze, he quickly turned away.

"What kind of woman is this?" he asked with such astonishment that he spoke the words aloud.

Patli had already noted that his friend was looking at the female a little too intensely and was trying to hide it. Patli was not nearly as awe-struck as his companion. He responded in a matter-of-fact tone.

"Once," said the man of medicine, "I saw a woman whose skin and hair were as white as the snow of Smoking Mountain. But her eyes were pink, and the sun god made her suffer so that her eyes watered continuously and the sun's rays turned the white skin into horrible burns."

"But surely, this woman is not the same," Tizoc countered.

"You are right, Tizoc. The skin seems healthy, though it is a most unusual color."

Tizoc nodded in agreement. "Patli, did you notice the man has wounds? We must help him."

Patli frowned. He had noticed the wounds. "We do not know how those wounds were inflicted. Why should we help?"

"We must help. They protected my sister."

CHAPTER FIVE

TIZOC MADE A GESTURE THAT they should all sit down together on the sand. Kathleen and Brand remained quiet and still while the two searchers conversed, trying to determine what to do next.

Patli studied Brand's arms. He asked, with gestures, to look at the wounds. Brand held out his forearms.

Patli could see the festering in the gashes was advanced. He pantomimed that Brand should wash the wounds with his own urine. But that message only led to complete confusion.

Instead, Patli poured freshwater over the wounds. He took a leather packet from his pack and sprinkled dried herbs on the infection. Then he wrapped the area with clean cotton strips.

When he finished, Kathleen bowed her head and crossed her thumb over her right index finger. She moved her hand from her forehead down to her waist, then up to her left shoulder and across her chest to her right shoulder. She repeated the same movement over Brand. When she began to make the motion across Patli, he jumped away.

"What is she doing?" exclaimed Patli.

"What's the matter, Patli—are you afraid of her magic?" Tizoc laughed, his white teeth flashing. "Let's wait to see what else she can do to irritate you."

Patli was not amused. "We came looking for your mother and your little your sister," he retorted. "We passed through destroyed villages, swollen rivers, forests without leaves, dead animals. And what do we find?" He paused to give the right amount of emphasis. "The ugliest people on earth!"

For the rest of the day, Tizoc and Patli spent time talking with Nenetl and searching the immediate area for any sign of the missing mother. They found nothing.

Light soon began to fade to purple shadows. For safety, it was clear they should all sleep together on the ship. Tizoc and Patli took turns standing watch with a fire on the beach.

In the semidarkness, Kathleen could discretely study every detail of the men's appearance. She noted that Tizoc's skin was like the smooth shell of autumn *akarns,* maybe a little lighter.

Brand also watched the men and carefully noted every glance between Tizoc and Kathleen.

Over the next few days, the group settled into a routine where Tizoc and Patli left each morning to search for the missing mother while Brand and Kathleen stayed with Nenetl. Every day, Tizoc and Patli searched an ever-larger area and returned at late day to the knarr for rest.

When they were not foraging for food, hauling water, or kneeling at prayer, Brand and Kathleen spent their time trying to decode language. For her part, Kathleen could only struggle with gestures. But Brand was picking up some words and their meanings. He listened intently to every word. He knew that someday their very lives might depend on how much of the words he could understand.

Already, Brand determined that *nehhuatl* meant "I," and *tehuātl* meant "you." *Amo* meant "no," and *quema* meant "yes." *Cualli* meant "good," and *huel cualli* meant "very good."

After three days, Patli knew the time had come to have a difficult conversation with Tizoc. He gestured to his friend, and they walked to a quiet spot near the river.

"Tizoc, we cannot continue to look for your mother." Patli took a big breath. "She is not here. Or at least, we cannot find her."

Tizoc was quick to respond. "I must continue looking. There are places we have not yet looked. Places that are still close. She could be lying under a mound of leaves or too weak to walk."

Patli placed his hand on Tizoc's shoulder, but Tizoc flung it aside.

"I must continue looking!"

"I know, Tizoc. I know. But we are nearly starving. What if we search for one more day? Maybe tomorrow we will find her. One more day."

Tizoc's breathing became regular, and he embraced his friend in silent gratitude.

The next morning dawned quiet and calm. At sunrise, Brand and Kathleen rose to sing and pray. Tizoc and Patli watched and listened, one transfixed and the other appalled.

"Have you ever heard such noise?" said Patli. "The sounds are like the screech of a wounded monkey or a dying rabbit."

But to Tizoc, the sounds were compelling and fascinating. Of all the musicians he had heard, none sounded remotely like this. Whether with voices or flutes, even the most accomplished musicians never made sounds that were apart yet together. Instead of singing together in one melody, the voices moved to distinct and separate tones. Tizoc was so moved that his skin responded with involuntary bumps, like emotion spilling out of his own body. It was the first harmony that had ever risen in their land. It floated into the warm and humid air, like turquoise smoke.

They all shared a meager breakfast of scavenged fruits and fish, then Tizoc and Patli set off, for one last time, on their search.

The sun rose higher into the sky. It was nearing midday when Kathleen gave Nenetl a container and pantomimed the action to fetch more freshwater from the river. Eager to please, Nenetl ran ahead and disappeared from sight around a large tangle of trees.

Kathleen watched Brand as he stood near a tide pool, waiting to catch some food for their next meal. He missed fifty times for every morsel he caught, but he never gave up.

She began to remember days back in Bergen, the hours she and her mother spent near the water. She recalled the court at Trondheim and the people there. She even missed the cold and snowy weather. Without words, she asked herself, *Will I ever feel a cool breeze again or watch whales or the shimmering northern lights?*

She was uncertain how long she had been lost in her memories when she realized Nenetl had not returned. She had taken only one step toward the river when there was a chilling shriek from the opposite direction. At the sound, she turned. In an instant, a spear struck the ground in front of her. She heard the threatening shouts of a group of warriors.

Kathleen was defenseless, and Brand had no weapon against their numbers. They were subdued completely. The warriors roughly shoved them to the ground and onto their knees.

The warrior in charge had a nose that jutted out with the fierce angles of an eagle's beak and had piercing eyes that seemed never to blink. He looked intently at Brand and Kathleen. He had never seen anything like them.

He called to all his men. "I want no marks on them. They may be the most prized of all prisoners ever to be brought to the king."

He gave orders to some soldiers who then boarded the knarr and began to ransack what was left on the ship. They gave excited shouts, examining everything intently.

From the river, Nenetl heard the shouts and cries of the warriors. The water container fell from her hands with a thud. She started to run back to the camp. Then she stopped short and dropped to the ground just behind the barrier of trees and sand. She kept her small body low, watching without sound or movement.

The warriors looked for evidence of other people. But the footprints of Patli, Tizoc and Nenetl had been trodden upon or swept away by the waves. And because the warriors were not looking for it, they did not see one special thing. Arn's grave, so carefully hidden, was not disturbed.

The soldiers, with captives in tow, moved on. The strangers and the large canoe were an unexpected, stupendous find. But they were not their prime quarry. They needed to continue their search for their true objective: a valuable ball player and his friend.

Once again Nenetl was alone. She summoned all the courage within her and resolved to wait until her brother returned. Tears came once or twice, but she swallowed hard and forced them back.

Patli and Tizoc returned toward dusk, as they had before. And as before, they had not found the missing mother.

Tizoc's mood was low. But his faced changed immediately to alarm when he saw Nenetl standing alone on the shore.

"What happened, little sister? Where are the others?"

Nenetl explained how she had hid and how the men had taken away the gods and many of the gods' things.

"Nenetl, what did the men look like?"

"They were scary. They carried spear-throwers and knives."

"What were they wearing?"

"They wore vests with a butterfly painted on the front—here," she said, pointing to her chest.

Tizoc's heart shuddered with cold fear. He knew these symbols, the sign of eternal victory for the warrior cult from Tollan.

"Patli, we must return to Tollan. Immediately."

"But why?"

"We must protect the strange people, the way they protected Nenetl." And to justify it even more, he added, "And these captives belong to us, not the soldiers."

Patli was not fooled but said no more.

They began the slow trek back to Tollan. When Nenetl could not keep up, Tizoc carried her on his back. Her small weight had no effect; he still moved with all the urgency of a man fighting to prevent the inevitable.

CHAPTER SIX

THE LEADER OF THE MILITARY squad sent a runner ahead to update his superiors on the mission. The unit had been unable to find Tizoc and Patli, who were urgently needed to return to Tollan for an upcoming ball game. He knew this news would be met with anger. So he was pleased to send word instead that he had captured prisoners of a great and unique nature. He hoped this would diminish his superiors' wrath.

The group moved at forced-march pace. At first the captives' wrists were tied together, and a rope was tethered around their waists. But the terrain was so uneven and the struggle over downed trees, around roots, and through water so difficult that the captives could not maintain their balance. First the tether was removed, then the wrist bindings.

In the early afternoon, rain began to fall. The caravan was called to a temporary halt. Kathleen and Brand were allowed to rest under the shelter of a giant tree. Brand slowly reached for Kathleen's hand. Using his index finger to trace into the palm of her hand, he could communicate with her in silence.

He recalled the lessons in Latin during their time together. She knew some prayers. Slowly, he traced "*O-R-E-M-U-S*" for "let us pray."

With only her eyes, Kathleen said yes, then turned them away before the exchange was detected. As long as they made no sound nor expression, the guards took no notice of them.

Brand continued with the familiar words of the Lord's Prayer. "*Pater noster, qui es in caelis.*"

"*Sanctificetur nomen tuum,*" she traced back, not looking at him.

They continued through the prayer, staring into the distance without emotion as their captors moved about. Brand finished with *"Sed libera nos a malo."*

Deliver us from evil.

"Sed libera nos a malo," she repeated into his palm. Then she looked in Brand's eyes and silently communicated the amen.

Oh, how Brand wished he had taught her some more practical words that might help them right now—not just the words of the Pater Noster and other prayers. But then, maybe it was best that she knew only words of faith and hopefulness.

As the rain cleared, the captors ordered them to their feet. The trek continued. Finally, they encountered a small path.

Brand watched Kathleen carefully. After so many months of relative confinement in the knarr, it was a change to be walking for hours. It was clear to Brand that Kathleen was weak. He wondered how long she would be able to continue the march.

When the travelers finally stopped for the night, the exhausted Norse could barely walk. In the dark, with only a few campfires for protection, the jungle came alive with new sounds. Some smaller creatures scurried close in the darkness. And there was much roaring of jaguars and ocelots, whose screams punctuated the air all through the night until dawn.

During the next few days, they moved out of the devastation near the shore into a new kind of land. They passed through almost impervious thickets of aromatic shrubs and colorful flowers. In the midst of this green splendor, trees of magnificent growth reached toward the sky. The whistling, chirping, and trilling of birds of all kinds was constant. The thicket of plants, vines, and trees surrounding them was alive with animals of the daylight. They saw foraging tapirs, hoglike and grunting. They also saw hungry foxes and slithering snakes.

As they trudged along with the soldiers, Brand noted the hierarchy in the group. The identity of the leader was clear. He wore arm rings, and jade rested in his earlobes. His leg and arm muscles were strong beneath his skin. His manner was imperious but not imperious enough to be a *jarl*, or chieftain. Brand concluded he must be an intermediate leader of some kind. The others must be bondmen of a king.

Kathleen also observed the members of the group. Tizoc was nearly as tall as Kathleen, but not these men. They were Patli's size. She towered over nearly all of them.

At least they have not yet slain us, she thought. She often touched the White Kristr symbol at her throat and recited the prayers her mother had taught her.

As they marched, people from villages sometimes joined them, to travel in the protection of a group. Then they would go their own way again. Along the trail, occasionally there were stopping places and small stalls where travelers could purchase items to eat and drink. Vendors called out persistently and displayed their wares until they made a sale.

At dusk, women with painted faces and teeth dyed bright orange appeared by the side of the road. The women spoke quietly to the men. Sometimes the men pretended not to hear. Sometimes they responded with a brief word or grunt, and they disappeared into the darkness with the women. Kathleen recalled the women at the port in Dublin and thought that these creatures must be performing the same desperate acts.

With each passing day, the heavy, oppressive air of the tropics gave way to the less humid air of the tableland. The sultry heat and intoxicating perfumes of the lowlands disappeared. Brand and Kathleen breathed more freely in the clearer atmosphere. The land now surrounding the pathway was thickly covered with oak, cypress, juniper, and pine, some with extravagant proportions.

The path swept along the base of mountains capped with mantles of snow. It was the first mountain snow Brand and Kathleen had seen in some time. In a small way, it made this land less strange to them. They passed through microclimates, where in some places the wind blew soft warm breezes. In others, bursts of cold air pulsed through the forests and hills. And in some places, the air was still as a sleeping sloth.

From time to time, the caravan would pass through small villages and towns. Brand and Kathleen immediately recognized the marketplaces and even some familiar goods: foodstuffs such as venison, rabbit, fish, turtles, eggs, and honey. Just as in the markets of home, there were street vendors working on crafts—a basketmaker, a leatherworker, a broom maker, a jewelry artisan, a woodworker, and potters.

Other items mystified them. They mistook the vast array of chilies—fresh, dried, large, small, green, yellow, and smoked—as some sort of medicinal herbs. They stared at the bright-red prickly-pear cactus fruits and the pale-green paddles that also came from the spikey plant. And there were the ever-present three sisters—corn, squash, and beans—that were as familiar in this land as oats, rye, and barley were at home.

They saw small dogs in cages—nothing at all like the hounds back home. At first, they thought they might be puppies. But on closer look, they saw that the animals were being fattened, then butchered. Brand and Kathleen both recalled Vige, King Olaf's sagacious hound, from their days in the court in Trondheim.

They observed what they thought were small brown trade beads being used as currency. They could not know the items were high-quality cacao beans. The low-quality beans would be used to make an intoxicating and stimulating beverage, available only to the elites, such as priests and government and military officials.

They passed by the stalls of the feather merchants. Kathleen was fascinated by the unimaginable color and artistry of the capes and tapestries. She recalled the day long ago when she had flung the multicolored silks to the floor of her father's warehouse. She noticed the painted women were here also, walking back and forth among the market stall, circling constantly, like birds of prey.

The travelers had now been on the trail for fourteen days. Brand's and Kathleen's linen garments were soiled and worn, hanging like rags on their tired bodies. In a small gesture of kindness and practicality, the soldiers gave them sandals when Brand's and Kathleen's own shoes had fallen away.

They continued the journey and entered a wider road. Brand noted it was broad enough for horses and oxen and their cartage to easily pass abreast. But where were the horses? Where were the carts? With his eyes and nose, he detected no pungent traces that any pack animals had passed through.

Instead, sturdy porters passed singly or in groups. With tumplines tight against their sweating foreheads, they trudged steadily despite the obvious weight of the packs upon their backs. Brand supposed these bearers were the thralls of this land.

They then entered a broad valley. Tall trees covered the hills above them. Kathleen often saw families of deer with spotted coats. As the column of marchers passed, the fawns and their mother would halt in rigid stillness. Then, certain there was no immediate threat, they would slowly move away and disappear into the forest undergrowth. At times, the column passed close by a great river, where fisherman flung nets that returned full of quivering, silvery bounty. All morning long, the pathway became more and more crowded.

"Brand," Kathleen whispered, "I think we are nearing a city."

"I think you are right, Kathleen. Do not be afraid. God is with us, no matter what. There is a reason we have survived."

A guard, displeased with their talking, raised his arm as if to strike Brand with the back of his hand but stopped midair.

"Tollan!" shouted the soldiers at the head of the column, quickening their steps. "Tollan!"

CHAPTER SEVEN

In Tollan, present-day city of Tula, Mexico

TONAUAC HAD RISEN EARLY THAT morning, unable to sleep. The people of Tollan had not yet begun their daily activities. He had acquired a habitual darkness under his eyes. He moved dully through his activities.

He was thirty-five years old and normally had the energy of a much younger man. But he was anxious about serious matters. For one, as priest to the city's ollama players, he was concerned about Tizoc and Patli. He knew they had gone to see Tizoc's mother, but word came that a huge wave had destroyed much of the area. Now they were overdue to return to the city.

And that was not all. Conflict among King Huemac's advisors was increasing. General Yaotl and others with military power kept pressing for more conquest and more human sacrifice. Tezcatlipoca, the god of the smoking mirror, demanded it.

Tonauac believed that such a path would lead to destruction. He followed the god Quetzalcoatl, who hated human sacrifice. Eventually, Tonauac knew, one side would destroy the other.

And more than all this, Tonauac desperately sought to escape the general malaise and unrest he had been feeling. For the last month, his meditations had always ended with the impulse to prepare himself for a prophetic vision. He could resist the idea no longer. The only way to prepare was with fasting and the aid of the sacred mushroom.

He had been fasting for several days in the temple at Tollan. His stomach was shrunken and flat. The only hunger he felt was for *teonanácatl*, the flesh of the gods. Tonauac took a small piece of the sacred mushroom and dipped it into a saucer of golden honey. He solemnly chewed and swallowed the morsel.

It was not long before his vision began.

He was present at a sacrifice. The victims had all been slain and were now united with the gods. Their blood was sprinkled generously on a bowl of crushed amaranth seed, which he kneaded with his own hands into *tzoalli* dough. Then this was broken up into small fragments.

Beginning with the elders, everyone present received and ate the tzoalli—old and young, men and women, infants and children. All received it with reverence, awe, joy and wonder.

"We have eaten the flesh and bones of the gods, though we are unworthy," they murmured one after the other.

And when all had partaken, Tonauac heard himself say to them: "Receive the stranger who comes from the east, whose face is covered, who brings a sign from God, who comes to us in mercy and pity. The time of change is coming."

All the people crowded around him and began to ask him questions. "What do you mean, our priest? What change is coming? For what stranger shall we prepare?"

Tonauac's vision ended before he could offer any answers.

Tonauac thought long and hard about this vision, but it remained a mystery. He then went to the stone altar outside the priest's quarters, prayed, and made burnt offerings of paper, incense, and rubber to Quetzalcoatl.

CHAPTER EIGHT

THE SEARCH UNIT AND ITS strange and valuable prisoners approached the city from the south. Rows of small houses made of daubed mud bricks gave way to larger buildings with roofs made of wood.

The captives and their guards had not quite entered the city proper when they came upon a crowd surrounding a small shrine. The leader ordered the travelers to stop. From their vantage point, they could see the entire event.

Built of stone and about as tall as a man, the shrine was comprised of steep steps rising into a pyramid. At its summit was a platform large enough for three or four people to stand. Marigolds of yellow and orange had been strewn up and down the steps and on the summit of the pyramid. Bas-relief artwork had been chiseled around the edge of the platform and painted with bright colors. There were serpents and the face of a humanlike figure painted blue with goggles around each eye.

Drumbeats announced that something of import was about to happen. The crowd of onlookers was so intent on watching the activity surrounding the shrine that, for once, virtually no one made immediate notice of Brand's or Kathleen's exotic appearance.

Even from a distance, Brand noted that there seemed to be one group of leaders. By their clothing and bearing, he suspected they were priests of some sort.

The crowd chanted one word over and over: "Tlaloc. Tlaloc. Tlaloc." Everyone gathered in the crowd believed Tlaloc was the bringer of rain and that these sacrifices would ensure it.

The crowd parted. A separate group was herded toward the base of the shrine. They were naked, and their bodies had been painted a glistening blue. Marigolds had been carefully plaited in their hair.

"Oh, Father Brand—they are children!" exclaimed Kathleen with alarm.

Two dozen children, from about age five to fifteen, now gathered at the shrine. Their eyes were unseeing, as if they were in a trance or stupor.

In addition to their vacant stares, Brand also noted they were very thin and possibly ill. They moved slowly, as if in pain or perhaps just in weakness. To Kathleen, they looked as if a sorcerer had enchanted them.

One of the priests made a series of incantations. Whenever he said "Tlaloc," everyone in the crowd repeated the word in a single, unified response.

Brand had a sense of foreboding as he observed the scene. It felt familiar—too familiar. The altar. The drums. The priests. The sounds of the crowd. No one in the crowd looked away. Brand deduced that any sign of fear or grief might be punished.

He wondered whether these were the sons and daughters of local people. Or perhaps they were captives, like Brand and Kathleen themselves, transported in a forced march from some other kingdom. Or perhaps they were enslaved and expendable, no matter where their home.

Since being taken captive, Brand had known there would be no ransom to be paid for him or Kathleen. He had been hoping in his heart that he and Kathleen would at least be spared to live as slaves. Now he was not so sure what fate might become them.

The drumbeats were pounding more quickly now. Their rhythm matched the frantic beating of Kathleen's own pulse.

"Father Brand! What is happening?"

The first child was led before the chief priest. An axe was raised to the azure sky, its edge of dark obsidian glittering in the sun.

"Look away!" Brand shouted.

But it was too late. Her eyes saw what she would never forget.

Child after child was dispatched with a single slice across their delicate necks, the blade so sharp the decapitation was instantaneous. The crowd roared at the thrill of the sight.

The cadence of the drums began anew as a fresh victim was lead up to the summit. Again, the awful ritual was repeated. The dark axe swung, a new blade for each child, until twenty-four children were dead.

The priests then placed the remains in a nearby pit. All the bodies were carefully laid out in the same position, facing east. A figurine of the same goggle-eyed sculpture on the shrine was placed in the pit with the small corpses.

Overcome by the sights, sounds, and smells, Kathleen began to vomit. After the first spasm, there was nothing left in her. But her body refused to stop, as if the retching could rid herself of the horror she had witnessed.

Finally, it ended. She repeated her silent pleas for help from the White Kristr. She settled herself into the deepest well her soul had ever known, and she wondered when the time would come for her own walk up the flowery stairway to her death.

The leader of the soldiers took note of Kathleen's distress. Her fear showed her to be an unworthy sacrifice. The male, however, was a different story. He was stoic, without emotion, no outward sign of fear. This pleased the soldier. The greater the prisoner's bravery, the greater the capturer's honor. He already anticipated how his notoriety would soar. No one knew yet exactly who or what these strange beings were. But everyone would remember that it was he who had brought them for public spectacle—he was sure of it.

Tizoc heard the drumbeats as he neared the city center. He had traveled for weeks, always a half day behind the ones he sought. He recognized the familiar repetitive crescendos and the noise of the crowd. He knew a public sacrifice was underway. He ran faster and faster.

He entered the plaza and pushed past the tightly packed crowds. He frantically scanned the scene. *Where is she? Where is she? Had her heart already been offered up to Tlaloc, the rain god, or to Tonatiuh, the sun god?*

His eyes darted. He spun in every direction, searching, searching. His panic rose with each passing moment. *Why does this woman mean so much to me?*

Suddenly, his eyes caught a movement near the shrine. His breath stopped short. A group of city security soldiers were herding two prisoners *away* from the plaza. He saw a glimpse of long flaxen hair.

It is not too late! It is not too late! His heart pulsed into his brain in utter relief and joy.

He had to speak with Tonauac. Tonauac would be his only chance.

CHAPTER NINE

THE TRAVELERS CONTINUED WALKING TOWARD the center of the city. The main road gave way to stone steps and plazas of increasing height.

At last, they entered a large broad plaza nearly surrounded by immense stone structures. This was the heart of the city. Everything that occurred here—the petitions, the tributes, the ceremonies and sacrifices—was its official heartbeat. The structures were covered in white stucco and decorated with carved images painted red, blue, black, and yellow. The colors were so bright it nearly hurt the eyes to look upon them.

What world have we entered? thought Brand.

He and Kathleen were awestruck. The city was like nothing they had ever seen and nothing they could have imagined. On their right, they passed a huge pyramid with a flat top. Its stone walls were ledges, like steep stairs to the top. There were five levels in all. On their left, they passed a long crib filled with hundreds of human skulls glaring out in grotesque silence through the slats.

A small shrine had been built near the center of the plaza. It was a strange stone figure—half sitting and half reclining, with its head looking out over its right shoulder in an awkward pose. The abdomen of this *chacmool* was a shallow hollow meant to receive the still-beating hearts of sacrificed humans.

Looking ahead, up beyond a low hallway of columns, they saw another pyramid with a large flat top. At its summit, they could see tall stone columns twice as thick as the oldest oaks of the Trondheim forest.

The columns were fantastical carved warriors—as tall as three men. They were armed with shields and ready to attack. The unseeing eyes of the stone soldiers peered to the south.

They ascended into a large room filled with columns supporting a flat wooden roof. The walls here were ornamented with seashells of all conceivable hues. The square columns were adorned with the forms of monstrous and terrible images. They reminded Kathleen of the dragon at the prow of the *Sea Goat.*

Kathleen and Brand were led farther into a large hall. Some of its stone walls were covered with carvings of jaguars, coyotes, eagles, and serpents. Other walls were decorated with feathers woven into a kind of tapestry of elegant and entrancing beauty. Blue clouds of copal incense hung heavy in the air. The room was crowded, as everyone wanted to see the prisoners.

A small group of musicians was seated in one corner, softly playing on shells, small drums, and flutes. A troupe of dwarfs was engaged in a display of tumbling and acrobatics, their leaping and jumping accompanied by laughter and shouts from the members of court.

Xicotencatl, the court hunchback, was there. His name meant "angry bumblebee." This suited him, as he was perpetually agitated and never still. He moved excitedly among the crowd, hoping for a good look at the strangers.

The courtiers gasped when they viewed Brand and Kathleen close enough to touch. A murmuring buzz filled the air. Behind the prisoners came a string of slaves, each carrying an item or two taken from the knarr.

Kathleen and Brand kept silent as their eyes moved quickly and scanned the crowd. Their gaze stopped on the man seated on a low platform in the center of the room.

King Huemac sat on an armless chair, his arms crossed. In his left hand, he held a scepter made from a human femur, heavily crusted with turquoise mosaic. Heavy jade medallions hung from his neck on thick gold chains. Silver and gold bands circled his arms and wrists. Green jade spools adorned his earlobes, sagging from the weight of the gemstone.

The Norse captives noted that this platform was like the high seat of the rulers back in their homeland. They guessed that the man must be the supreme ruler of this city.

Two priests stood to the left of King Huemac: Tonauac and Toveyo. They both wore feathered capes that flowed extravagantly from their shoulders to the floor. Each represented one of the two most powerful gods in the region.

Toveyo was tall, and his face was handsome, as he well knew. He perpetually kept his chin raised slightly upward, which meant he, in fact, looked down at everyone around him. He served the powerful Tezcatlipoca, god of the smoking mirror. Dangling from his wrist by a leather cord was a small obsidian mirror, which he could hold in his hand. When he looked into it, he claimed he could see images of past and future that gave him knowledge unknown to others. He never went anywhere without it, and even kept it near when he slept.

Tonauac was smaller than Toveyo and commanded a different kind of respect. He served Quetzalcoatl, the feathered serpent, the god who joined heaven and earth in a single duality. Tonauac's face was solemn, and he focused entirely on the prisoners.

General Yaotl was there, along with his only daughter, Centehua. The leader of the squad had already briefed the general. He was ready to take credit for the unexpected find. But once he had served his purpose, the squad leader was quickly ordered away.

Tizoc had managed to gain entrance to the great hall as well. He struggled to get as near as possible to the strangers.

Centehua spotted Tizoc almost instantly and was pleased, for she had long wanted to get to know the handsome young athlete better.

Slaves led Kathleen and Brand to the center of the hall and pushed them forward until they were standing immediately below the high seat.

"Great King Huemac, look what I have brought you!" said General Yaotl with a sweeping gesture toward the captives.

"Indeed, what have you brought me, General? Are they human or animal? I have never seen a human whose face was covered with hair."

Indeed, no one had ever seen a man like Brand, whose beard was thick. At most, the males of Tollan had thin and sparse hair on their faces; a mother or wife could easily pluck it as part of normal grooming.

"My king, I agree they are most strange," answered the general. "But they are human, for they wear clothing has humans do, and they speak some gibberish as if it were a language."

"Yes, I can see they are wearing clothing," said King Huemac, staring at Kathleen.

The king rose from his dais and stepped down to where Kathleen stood. He moved very close to her and stared at her body, starting from the top of her head and moving down, slowly, pausing at her hips, and down her long legs to her dusty feet. Then he touched her hair with his hand, lightly brushing her shoulder, which caused Kathleen to shudder.

At the same instant, both Brand and Tizoc began to breathe faster, every part of them aching to protect her.

Everyone in the court knew of King Huemac's proclivity for large-hipped women, who were very rare. He often announced his desire for women who were extraordinarily wide across the buttocks. When a woman brought to him did not meet this standard, he became insulted and angry, sometimes to the point of continued attacks against the tribe who offered such an inadequate tribute.

He motioned with his bone scepter to two female slaves. "Remove those rags from her."

The women immediately approached Kathleen and pulled her ragged and filthy linen dress up and off her. Kathleen tried not to make a sound, but a small cry left her lips.

Her entire body flushed a light rose, and her legs trembled slightly. The only thing protecting her from the gaze of all was her long hair and her White Kristr cross. Her humiliation was more complete when she saw Brand turn his eyes away from her. Even on the confines of the small ship, Gudrun had taught her how to maintain modesty. No man had ever seen her completely naked.

Tizoc was stunned. Her skin, where the sun had not darkened it, was luminous. It seemed as if someone had taken the rays of the moon and rubbed them onto her breasts, torso, and thighs. Everyone present—male and female—took note that there was a soft triangle of kinky hair between her legs, slightly darker than the hair bleached to nearly white on her head.

King Huemac slowly walked around Kathleen in a circle, ignoring Brand for the moment. Then he returned to his throne chair. Kathleen's hips disappointed him, though her exotic looks still intrigued his mind.

"And what shall be done with these creatures?" he said as much to himself as to the assembled court.

"King Huemac," said the general, "I brought you these captives that they might be sacrificed at the next feast day of Tezcatlipoca." He tried not to smile as he said this, already relishing the increase in status such a sacrifice would bring.

But before King Huemac could answer, Tonauac stepped forward.

"My king," interjected Tonauac, walking closer to the dais, "these are not ordinary captives. We must consider carefully what may be . . . their greatest use for us."

The general frowned and stiffened slightly.

Even though they understood almost no words, Kathleen and Brand noted the unmistakable tension between the larger fierce man and the smaller man who stood next to the king.

"But King Huemac," said General Yaotl impatiently, his voice rising in volume, "it is my right to decide their fate. The capturer always holds the fate of his captives. And their fate is sacrifice." He quickly added, "For the glory of our great god Tezcatlipoca, of course."

Tonauac moved directly to King Huemac's side. "My king, when these beings came to our shore, the military scouts were not the *first* to discover them."

"What lie is this?" sputtered the general, shooting a fierce, angry glance toward Tonauac.

"Tizoc and Patli found them," said Tonauac rapidly, "when they were looking for Tizoc's mother and sister after the great wave. Tizoc informed me that these beings had befriended his little sister and protected her. They even shared their food with her."

Everyone looked at Tizoc. For the first time, Brand and Kathleen saw him in the crowd as well. Their next breaths came a little more freely. In a tiny way, they felt they had one friend in a sea of strangers.

The general continued to sputter, but King Huemac silenced him with a look.

Tonauac continued. "But that is not the reason why they should not be sacrificed. While Tizoc and Patli were with them, they saw that the strangers have symbols and other things we do not understand. Their knowledge may be very powerful. We must learn their secrets. It may help us against our enemies."

"No, King Huemac!" Toveyo blustered, now stepping in to support the general. "They *must* be sacrificed. They are a *danger*. Do we not always sacrifice the scribes of our enemies, first by removing their fingernails and then their hearts?"

King Huemac absentmindedly stroked the cool jade disk hanging around his neck. "Maybe," he said to taunt them all, "I should sell them to the king of Cholollan. He is always interested in curiosities. I would get an exceptional price for them."

Toveyo and General Yaotl began to speak at once, with voices growing louder and louder, their faces reddening.

"Enough! You are squabbling children!" King Huemac's insult silenced them all at once.

"Tonauac, you shall have three cycles of the moon to study this male being and his symbols. Then, I will decide his fate further."

"And what of the female?" asked the general, still hoping the king would allow him the glory for half of the capture.

"The female is to begin preparation as a temple priestess."

The general's countenance fell.

Tizoc's brain whirled. *I have saved her, but for what purpose?*

Centehua smiled to herself. Now this strange female would be out of the way, and she could concentrate on Tizoc without distraction. She had seen in his eyes his fascination with the light-haired female.

Two women stood at each side of Kathleen. They took her arms and guided her out. Kathleen turned in fear and called to Brand. Since Greenland, they had never been apart.

"Father Brand!" she screamed.

He moved toward her, but two guards quickly stepped in front of him and blocked his way. She disappeared behind the pillars, though it was several minutes before he could no longer hear her cries.

Although he had witnessed the ritual murder of children with no outward sign, Brand could not bear the separation from Kathleen. His whole body shook with anger and fear. He recalled his pledge to Arn to protect Kathleen. But his frustration and anguish were born of more than the failure of his pledge. The woman he loved was no longer in sight, and he did not know how to save her.

Somehow there must be a way. Somehow.

CHAPTER TEN

TONAUAC SAID A WORD TO the guards surrounding Brand, and they immediately stepped aside. Tonauac gestured for Brand to follow him.

Brand froze for a moment, considering whether he should try to run after Kathleen. But he quickly realized it was futile. All eyes were on him as he left the great hall with Tonauac. Brand saw Tizoc in the crowd. He sensed that somehow he and Kathleen were still alive because of him.

Brand made a resolution: more than ever, he would take note of everything around him—details of sight, sound, taste, and even texture. Maybe some small thing would save Kathleen. It helped that he knew a few words and phrases of the language.

Tonauac took Brand to a small room in the priests' quarters. The priests of the god Quetzalcoatl lived together in a small compound on the outskirts of the city. Five or six rooms surrounded a small courtyard with a shrine in the center. Some of the rooms were larger and some smaller. There was a room for bathing, and fresh running water ran in a ceramic pipe at the edge of the property.

Attendants gestured for Brand to remove his clothing and step into a small tank of warm water. They poured water over him with dried gourd scoops. It had been a long time since he had bathed. He luxuriated in the simple act of cleansing.

The attendants dried his skin with cotton cloth squares and rubbed the juice of medicinal plants over the partially healed wounds on his arms.

They gave him a new mantle, loincloth, and sandals. Slowly, he put the new clothes on his cleansed body.

Then Tonauac returned. He brought two glossy red earthenware plates piled high with food. He set the food on a low table. Once he smelled the aromas, Brand realized he was very hungry.

There were no utensils. Tonauac picked up a flat circular piece of food. It was the same food the guards had given them during their march to Tollan. Tonauac showed Brand how to fold the disk, then he deftly used it to move food around the plate and into his mouth. Brand did his best to mimic Tonauac.

They ate together in silence. It was the same silence as back in England, when Brand had first arrived as a stranger to the priory. Brand was ravenous. Though he struggled some to eat with only the food pusher disk, it was not long before all the food was gone.

Tonauac then led Brand to a small room with a cotton mat on the floor—a sort of sleeping place. Then Tonauac left the room. Brand wondered if he would ever see him again. It occurred to him that the bathing and food might be preparation for sacrifice. Yet he was not bound or shackled, and the door to the room was only covered by a curtain.

By then, the sun was setting. Brand prayed. He thanked God for having saved them thus far, and he asked for strength for whatever the next day would bring.

"Kathleen, where are you?" he said out loud.

He reproached himself. He felt he had failed her in so many ways— in Greenland and during the attack when the red tide appeared. Now they were separated here in this fantastical and violent world. And there was no way he could comfort or protect her.

The sounds of the day faded into the sounds of the night: chirping insects, the flutter of leaves in the breezes, the sudden call of a bird startled from its roost, the wind moving in tall pines. There was a small window, and from it, silvery moonlight streamed. Brand stared at the orb, so far away, not knowing that elsewhere in the city, Kathleen was doing the same.

Kathleen had also been bathed, clothed, then placed in a small room alone. She watched the moon and thought of home: the whiteness and purity of snow, freckled faces, snuggling into the warmth of eiderdown pillows, the taste of fresh butter.

So many dead now—her father, her mother, Helgi and Gudrun, Patrekr and Gunnar, and all the rest. Only Brand remained, but where was he? Was he alive?

She crumpled into a heap in a corner. Uncontrollable sobs filled the room with anguish. She could not think. She could not even pray the prayers she had been taught. All she could do was whisper hoarsely over and over, through her tears.

"Please help me. *Please.* Help me."

CHAPTER ELEVEN

T HE NEXT MORNING, THE CURTAIN to Brand's room moved. Tonauac entered, again with food. He sat down on the floor with Brand. This time, he did not eat with Brand but waited until Brand had eaten. He then led him out to a different courtyard.

It was a pleasant and special garden filled with plants of all types, including flowers and herbs that sweetly scented the air. Gardeners worked in silence in every corner: cutting, pruning, and watering the gorgeous lines and clusters of color.

The two sat down on stone benches a few feet apart, facing each other. Hummingbirds zoomed in and out of the courtyard. Brand heard them fly a few inches from his head, seeking sweet nectar from the abundant flowers.

Tonauac felt his anxiety rise as he looked at the man sitting across from him. Was this the man of his vision? Three moons. Only three cycles of time to teach the strange man to speak and understand!

Yet he knew he had to try. Tizoc had begged him to do whatever he could to save the strangers. Now Tonauac was convinced that there was something very special about this man, that this man would be important to the people of the city. Even so, Tonauac had no idea how that may be. He decided to start the lessons immediately.

"*Nehhuatl notoka Tonauac. Tonauac,*" he repeated and pointed to himself.

Brand was unsure if the word was his name, his function, or something else. He decided to repeat it.

"Tonauac," he said, a little hesitantly.

The teacher was relieved that the pupil was catching on so quickly. Tonauac pointed to Brand with his index finger, then waited.

Brand nodded to show he understood. He pointed to himself and said very slowly and distinctly, "My name is Father Brand. Father Brand. Father Brand."

Tonauac repeated the words but struggled to put together the sounds, especially the *r* sound, which did not exist in his mother tongue.

It was then that Brand realized Tonauac intended to be his teacher and that he would be Tonauac's teacher as well.

Before any more words were said, Brand bowed his head and closed his eyes. Tonauac watched, somewhat puzzled, as Brand prayed.

"My God, I most humbly ask you for wisdom. Did not the Holy Spirit come and grant the followers of Christ the ability to speak in tongues unknown to them? I am in great need to understand. May it please God that I may understand." He finished the prayer with a sign of the cross.

When Brand looked up, Tonauac waited a moment, then continued the lesson. He said the words for *I* and *you*. Brand immediately understood. He repeated the simple words and gestured to show he knew their meaning.

This greatly delighted Tonauac, for it helped lay a foundation. Brand began pointing at objects all around them. He waited for Tonauac to say the name, then repeated it as best he could. Brand got nearly everything right after hearing it only once. Tonauac beamed and said "*Huel cualli*," or "Very good."

Each day was filled with language lessons. And at the end of each day, both Tonauac and Brand were exhausted from the intensity of listening and learning.

Brand had deduced that the language was one where words were built upon words to give a specific new meaning. It was a challenge, for some words consisted of several words put together, resulting in a lengthy string of syllables to remember in the correct order. Many Norse words had one or two syllables, at most. But words in Tonauac's language required multiple sounds of extreme length.

As the days passed, Brand became more and more familiar with the language, mostly names, verbs, and common phrases. Sometimes when he knew a word but not its opposite, he would say the word with the prefix for *not*. So *not hot* meant *cold*. And sometimes he was able to construct meaning, albeit awkwardly. Instead of the word *hurt*, he said *to do harm*.

Tonauac was astonished at Brand's ability to learn. Slowly, Brand began to understand concepts. Every day, Brand showed that he understood some new idea or concept and applied it to his rapidly growing vocabulary and understanding of grammar. Tonauac realized that the pupil would go as far intellectually as the tutor cared to lead.

It was not long before Brand started asking Tonauac questions about things other than simple language.

"Tonauac, tell me about the people of this city."

"We are called Tolteca. We are known throughout the land for our fierce and mighty warriors." Then he added, "But also for our fine artistry and craftsmanship."

Like all people, the Tolteca were a mix of those who came before. Centuries earlier, the great nearby city of Teotihuacan had been abandoned. The refined people who had lived there assimilated with the invading Chichimeca, or "sons of dogs." Through the generations, the cultured and the violent engaged in an uneasy alliance, both needing each other to survive and thrive.

Brand wanted to know more, but Tonauac quickly reverted back to the vocabulary drills they were practicing. In truth, Tonauac was as eager to learn about Brand as Brand was to learn about Tonauac. *Who are you?* was the thought in each man's mind.

And at the end of every day, Brand asked about Kathleen, but Tonauac would only shake his head. Did it mean Tonauac did not know? Or did it mean he would not or could not say what had happened to her?

CHAPTER TWELVE

ATHLEEN WAS LOST. THE LANGUAGE of the people around her utterly confounded her. She had learned the simple words for *yes* and *no* during their time with Nenetl and the young men. She tried to understand and remember other words, but it was always too much. It exhausted her. She made gestures, and sometimes they worked, but often they did not. And no one showed her how to use the flat circle to make a food pusher, so she struggled to eat without feeling like a baby eating with her hands.

It appeared she had been given over to the supervision of an older woman who lived near the great buildings in the city center. Her name was Izel. It meant "unique," and she was.

Izel stood straight and upright and was nearly as tall as the tallest man in Tollan. She had the look of a pillar: strong but inflexible, to the point of breaking when bending would be a better choice. Her eyes were as dark as the deepest forest pool at dusk, and they flashed with energy.

Izel was a temple prostitute of the "third age." She was too old to be attractive to men, but she held great power and prestige and was in charge of all the temple priestesses.

She had even given birth—at a late age, when most thought it was impossible. Her son was born with strange facial features, and he never grew or learned normally. It was an accepted custom that any child born with a defect was never named and was quietly taken into the forest to die. She used every trick, threat, manipulation, and contrivance at her disposal to keep him. She named him Tlazohtlaloni, or "one who is loved," as he was her own, her beloved. She protected him like a mother jaguar.

Izel was in charge of training the sacred prostitutes. Essentially, the young women were available to any of the elite of the city—nobility, warriors, athletes—for sexual purposes. The women were specially chosen, often from highborn families. Occasionally, a girl of great beauty, though not noble, was selected.

Between the ages of twelve and fourteen, the girls left their homes and began their new life as holy virgins to be instructed in the nature of their duties. They tended the sacred fires and did some weaving, embroidery, and other artisan work. During this time of training and responsibility, they were cut off from family and friends. When they reached their late teens, many were married off to men of the most powerful families in the city.

When they first met, Izel had stared at Kathleen with venom in her eyes. She completely resented that this object of curiosity was her responsibility. She hated it when people stared at her son. Now this stranger would bring more curious and judgmental looks.

Kathleen had studied Izel as well. She noticed the gray streaks in her black hair, the matronly thickening of her waist. Izel reminded her of sweet, motherly Gudrun.

But then Izel suddenly raised her hand and slapped Kathleen's face so hard that Kathleen fell upon the floor. Izel snatched the cross from Kathleen's neck and ripped it away. The woman railed at her, spewing vile words Kathleen could not understand, though they conveyed a clear meaning.

Some of the other temple priestesses observed the incident with some concern.

"Is something bothering Izel?" one asked. "She seems upset."

"She was born upset," her companion replied dryly.

Kathleen, stunned by the violence, slowly rose up from the floor. She had thought Izel was a friend and possibly a protector. Now she knew she was an enemy.

That night, Izel brought Kathleen to a small building near the city center. Men sat on benches around the perimeter of the room. A small group of musicians sat in a corner and played a song nearly tuneless but with a compelling rhythm.

Izel called out, and dancers entered and stood in the center of the room. They were adorned with shell bracelets on their wrists and ankles and fresh flowers behind their ears—nothing else.

Izel signaled for the musicians and dancers to begin. The tempo started slowly, then it transitioned, become more and more rapid. The women leaped, arms and legs as graceful as red deer in flight, hair flying, and sweat glistening on their skin.

The women danced together, sometimes alone. But always with their eyes toward the men. At last the music reached its climax and ended. The women knelt before the men, eyes downcast.

Kathleen watched as Izel moved slowly to each man. She whispered a word or two. The man answered with a nod. Then Izel dispatched each woman to a predetermined room, where the man would shortly join the selected dancer.

It slowly dawned on Kathleen that someday she may be forced to participate in the wild dances, then disappear into a small dark room. And it was then, for the first time, that she felt there might be a fate worse than death.

CHAPTER THIRTEEN

ABOUT A MONTH HAD PASSED since Brand had begun his training with Tonauac. In addition to their sessions in the courtyard of flowers, they would sometimes walk in the city proper. Brand had a growing respect for the organization of the city. The scale and architecture of its buildings was astounding. The stone carvings were impressive, even if they seemed grotesque in their depiction of eagles and snakes devouring hearts.

Kathleen, however, still struggled to make sense of the sights, actions, and words surrounding her and the other women under Izel's supervision. The only thing that looked familiar to Kathleen was the women who sat with looms, creating cloth from colored strands. It was just as the women had done back in Trondheim and in Bergen.

Then, one morning, both Brand and Kathleen were awakened early. They knew something different was about to take place. Separately, they were bathed and their skin smoothed with scented ointments. They were dressed in fine, brightly colored cotton clothing, and necklaces of jade and carved shells were placed over their heads. Finally, sandals of soft deerskin were placed on their feet.

Kathleen wondered if she were being prepared for ritual death. When Brand tried to ask Tonauac what was happening, all he could comprehend was that it was something important but that he would not be hurt.

Tonauac led Brand to a part of the city where a large multitude of people were assembling. Izel brought Kathleen to the same place. And there, among the gathering crowd, they saw each other.

Before a second had passed, Brand and Kathleen had run to each other and flung themselves into each other's arms. Then they stood back, breathless, and smiled and laughed as they looked at each other once again. Words spilled out of them like waterfalls after a heavy rain. Surrounded by a throng of people, they might as well have been completely alone.

The occasion for their reunion was a great athletic contest, the game of ollama. Ollama was a kind of running game between two teams, played with a rubber ball. All morning long, the people had been assembling at the ball court, located west of the main plaza of the city. They gathered for the excitement and thrill of the competition. This contest was unlike the sacred ball game played at the other court in the city, where only priests were present and the game always concluded with death.

The ball field, or *tlachtli,* was rectangular, open at each end, and framed along its length by two parallel walls. Had they been able to view it from above, the tlachtli would have appeared to Brand and Kathleen to be shaped like a giant double-ended hammer of Thor.

The walls were divided into several sections, each with distinctive stonework and bright colors. Terraced stone seating led upward from each wall. A large stone disk with a hole in its middle jutted out at a ninety-degree angle from the center of each wall, about twenty feet above the floor of the court.

People filled the seats and spilled onto the opposite ends of the court, just outside the playing field. Vendors moved among the crowd, selling tortillas stuffed with savory venison or turkey, bowls of colorful papaya, and toasted squash seeds and fried grasshoppers flavored with chili powders. To drink, there were gourds of fruit-infused water and coconuts pierced to access the water within. Pungent smoke from censers filled with smoldering copal wafted into the air. Banners of bright feathers fluttered in the breeze.

Groups of musicians were scattered through the area. There was no place where the sound of drums and flutes could not be heard. Sometimes the music overlapped, resulting in an exuberant cacophony. Acrobats leaped and danced, their seedpod ankle bracelets adding another percussive voice to the drums' steady beating.

Then, conch shells were blown with a burst of sound. All other music stopped immediately. The crowd hushed.

"Brand, what do you think is happening?" said Kathleen.

"Maybe a festival or fair, like the trade and festivities at a Thing?" he surmised. "Maybe there will be a recitation of the laws and decisions made for the community as well?"

Brand's guess was partly right. Indeed, it was a festival and trade fair, but also something more. The elite of Chollollan, a rival city-state, had traveled to Tollan for the ball game. From opposite sides of the field came King Huemac and King Amapane of Chollollan, followed by their royal retinues. King Huemac looked strong and important and somewhat flamboyant. The king of Chollollan walked with straight and erect posture and exuded a quiet strength.

The royal groups took their reserved places in the terraced stone seating areas on opposite sides of the field. They rested on thick pillows shaded by tented curtains of fine cotton. Slaves slowly wafted fans of brilliant plumage to cool them.

General Yaotl was there, along with his daughter, Centehua. She had spent all morning trying on gowns of different-colored cotton and arranging and rearranging her earrings and other ornaments. She had already received numerous admiring looks from likely suitors, and she felt sure she would make a good impression on Tizoc.

Once the royals were seated, Kathleen and Brand were taken to the center of the ball court so the crowd could see them. Then they were made to walk close to the Chollollan side, so Amapane could see them better. Brand felt he was being viewed in a way not unlike cattle for sale back in Trondheim, although there were no cattle in this place.

King Huemac knew the king of Chollollan had never seen anything like these people. He swelled with pride knowing he had secured something the Chollollan king would never have.

But what King Huemac did not know was that within days of the *Sea Goat* landing on the shore, word had spread in the region that a large canoe had foundered on the beach. After Kathleen and Brand had been captured and Tizoc, Nenetl, and Patli had left to find them, the ship was left unguarded. King

Amapane had sent men to pull it into a secret place and keep it hidden, waiting until the time was right for him to use it for his own gain. Then he spread the rumor that it had become unmoored and had disappeared into the sea.

Even though the people of Tollan were fascinated with the strangers, their attention was diverted elsewhere. Much wagering was occurring among the crowd. There were trades as well: a strand of green stones for a pair of jade ear flares; a feather mantle for a quill of gold dust.

Each team was preparing for the game in separate halls near the ball court. There were twelve players on each team and one captain, for a total of thirteen. No substitutes were allowed during play.

The rules of the game were simple. A round rubber ball, slightly smaller than a human head, was to be kept in the air using all parts of the body but not hands. A player could use wrists, elbows, shoulders, hips, knees, and even his head to ricochet the ball onto different parts of the wall to score points. Using the head was risky, for the ball was heavy and hard. Serious injuries and even deaths were not uncommon.

The first team to score thirteen points would win. And in the unlikely event that a ball was propelled through the protruding stone hoop at the center of each opposite wall, that team would instantly win and all play would end. Before play began, the players would enter the arena wearing richly decorated headdresses, luxurious animal skins, and gold jewelry. They would carry small statues of eagles and jaguars. Later, they would change into the protective gear needed for the game.

Tizoc watched as his team members put on their finery. A plan, a possibility, was forming in his mind. Patli noted that Tizoc's concentration seemed to be elsewhere.

"Pull yourself together, Tizoc!" he admonished, almost certain it had to do with *that woman*.

Tonauac entered the players' hall and recited a brief prayer, asking Quetzalcoatl for victory. Now the athletes were ready to enter the arena.

The Cholollan players entered first, walked the ball court perimeter, and bowed before their own king. Then they turned to the opposite side and bowed to King Huemac.

The Tollan players entered next, with Tizoc entering last. Hidden under all the feathers and adornments, neither Kathleen nor Brand recognized him. When the Tollan players had all entered, they bowed before King Huemac and King Amapane. The Tollan crowd rose to its feet and cheered.

Aides removed the regalia from the athletes and replaced it with protective gear. Thick leather pads stuffed with cotton covered their shoulders, arms, and torsos down through the hips. All of this added significant weight but was needed to prevent injury once play began.

Kathleen's heart gladdened when she recognized the captain of the Tollan team. Tizoc did not see her at first, but when he did, he felt strangely excited, anxious, and relieved, all at the same time. Kathleen and Brand also saw Patli, who was seated along with the other team physicians.

King Huemac welcomed all to the game. He announced that the contest would be dedicated to Xochipilli—god of music and dance and patron of the ball game.

The crowd was on its feet, cheering and jumping, arms in the air in anticipation. Play began when a small flag, fashioned of bright-red feathers, was dropped onto the field. When it did, the crowd burst into an excited human roar.

The boisterous crowd watched the ball go spinning by as players rushed to return serves and perhaps to score. The players began to sweat in the heat, and soon their bodies glistened in the sun. Short breaks were taken to allow the players to rest and take water.

It was not long before there were crashes between ball and player and between players. Bruising injuries occurred. Patli and the other healers attended to them. Some players had to have blood drawn from bruises on their calves and thighs.

Kathleen and Brand had never before seen an athletic contest where groups of athletes tested their collective skills. They were familiar with wrestling and archery and even the poetic sparring of the skalds. They recalled the orchestrated baiting of dogs or stallions for the amusement of the people. But never had they seen or heard of groups of men facing against other men, except on the battlefield.

Tizoc realized early on that the teams were equally matched. A win would not come easily. With each score, the crowd would rise to its feet and either boo or cheer as appropriate. But to the players, the sound of the crowd was mere background; the beating of their own hearts was louder.

The game was fast paced. It seemed that almost no time had passed when the score was tied at ten to ten. On the next play, one of Tizoc's teammates did not see the ball as it hurled toward his head. The ball struck him near his temple. He fell to the ground. The crowds gasped as one person.

His teammates surrounded the fallen player, anxious looks on their faces. Patli and the other physicians hurried to remove him from the playing field and to tend to him, but he was already dead. Tizoc knew the player well, but there was no time to think about it.

The Tollan team was now without one player. Tizoc pushed and pushed himself and his teammates, their legs and lungs tiring. The Cholollan team quickly scored another two points. If they scored another, the game would be over.

Despite his training to remain calm, anxiety rose in Tizoc's chest like a wave. His team had to win. Had to win, for her.

On the next play, the crowd waited expectantly as a teammate fed the ball to him. Tizoc found himself near the edge of the Tollan side of the court, facing away from the goal and about to step out of bounds. He let out a deep breath as he ricocheted the ball up and backward off his shoulder.

Tizoc turned and the crowd watched as the ball soared upward. Somehow it impossibly entered and then exited the stone goal in a single, perfectly placed arc.

CHAPTER FOURTEEN

THE CROWD WENT WILD—JUMPING, HOOTING, and screaming like excited bands of monkeys. The roar of their voices reached high into the sky.

The Cholollan spectators were dejected, stunned. They loudly groaned their disappointment.

The home team supporters immediately rushed to collect on their wagers. The guards struggled to keep back the onslaught of spectators who tried to press onto the field. The drummers beat furiously on their instruments.

Tizoc's teammates leapt and shouted in celebration. They hoisted Tizoc upon their shoulders and transported him in victory around the perimeter of the ball field. Brand and Kathleen watched in excitement as the teammates set him down before the king of Cholollan.

In an obligatory sign of respect, King Amapane placed a necklace of carved jade and jaguar claws around Tizoc's neck. As he did, he leaned forward and whispered, "You and I will meet again."

Tizoc did not have time to ponder the mysterious message, for the players again hoisted him up over their shoulders and placed him this time before King Huemac. The noise reached up and over all the people and into the heavens. Tizoc's face and body were shining with perspiration. His heart was racing. Tizoc knelt down and raised his arm in salute to Huemac.

The plan he had built was now unfolding. Did she see him? Did she know what he had done, what he was trying to do?

King Huemac's courtiers signaled for the crowd to quiet down.

"Well done! Well done!" King Huemac exclaimed with satisfaction. He took a circle of golden leaves and placed them on Tizoc's head. "I crown you prince of the ball game."

Again the crowd roared. While the noise continued, King Huemac motioned for Tizoc to move closer.

"What desire can I grant to you?" the king spoke into his ear.

Tizoc knew exactly what he wished for. But it was so outrageous that he would need to prepare King Huemac for it.

"Thank you, King Huemac. To answer such a question, I will need time to think. I request that you give me until tomorrow, so I may make the wisest decision regarding your generosity."

King Huemac was somewhat taken aback, but he answered, "All right then, Prince. Until tomorrow."

With the ball game now ended, Brand and Kathleen were again separated and returned to their respective quarters. At least they had been allowed to be together, if only for a short time. Each one felt relief for the sake of the other. They hoped they would see each other again, and soon.

Kathleen surprised herself a little as she recalled the day's events. In particular, seeing Tizoc again made her feel happier than she had anticipated. He was obviously held in high esteem as an athlete. But something else, something she was uncertain of, was very attractive about him.

That night, Tizoc could scarcely contain his excitement. Sleep would not come. His mind raced from one thought to the next. The improbable had happened; perhaps his desire would become possible as well.

The next morning, when the sun was just beginning to slide into the brightening sky, Tizoc walked to the *temazcalli* for healing and his meeting with the king. Tizoc had bathed and received a rubdown immediately after the ball game. But this was a special temazcalli, for healing. And for the chance to talk with King Huemac.

Patli was already there with the elder physicians, preparing the herbs and heat for the medicinal steam bath. The healers worked in front of a low domed structure made of clay. To enter the structure, one had to nearly crawl on hands and knees. The area for the steam bath was connected by a small passage to another smaller structure with a chimney. A fire there heated carefully selected rocks. When all was ready, the assistants poured water onto the heated rocks, producing the curative and cleansing steam. Because they were volcanic, the rocks would not explode.

Everyone bowed head to ground as King Huemac and his entourage approached the temazcalli. Both the king and Tizoc had fasted that morning. They crawled through the low structure and sat down on a bench near the heated rocks. The floor of the steam bath was covered with a thick mat woven of banana leaves.

Patli poured water infused with herbs over the rocks to create the steam. Leafy branches of herbs were gently patted down the bathers' backs to help the sweat flow better. Patli watched carefully so the heat was optimal for the desired effects. When it became too hot, he lifted open a small curtain. When more herbal steam was needed, he poured more of the fragrant water.

After the healers calculated the correct amount of time, Tizoc and Huemac exited the bath by crawling out backward. Outside, attendants covered them with cotton mantles. They walked a few steps to another area to cool down before the healing massage could begin. The cooldown process took twice as long as the bath itself. Copious amounts of herbal infusions were poured over the men and offered as drink.

Finally, King Huemac and Tizoc were ready for the massage. A solitary musician played soothing notes on a flute. King Huemac's physician massaged him, and Patli massaged Tizoc with fragrant oils and the juice of the maguey plant. Patli was somewhat puzzled; Tizoc's muscles were still tight, as if he could not really relax.

King Huemac was anxious to complete his promise to Tizoc. He sat up from the massage table.

"Tizoc, you have brought much honor to me and the people of Tollan. They wagered very heavily on you, and you have brought them new wealth. I am in excellent position to negotiate extremely good terms with the king of Cholollan. As a result of your prowess, he has delivered to me one hundred sacks of high-quality cacao beans as well as one hundred turkey quills filled with gold flakes and five hundred fine-cotton mantles.

What do you want? Name it. Jewels? A princess to take to wife? A large home on the hill of Palpan?"

Tizoc did not answer, so Huemac continued.

"Work has just been completed on several new houses with numerous rooms. The artists have ensured that the houses have beautiful frescoes and columns. But the builders have outdone themselves with practicality. They have installed a system of water pipes and cisterns so the clearest and cleanest of water is available to you at all times, with no effort."

King Huemac paused, pleased with himself that he could offer such extravagant gifts.

"Name the thing you desire, and it is yours."

Patli waited with some apprehension for Tizoc to answer Huemac, though his hands continued the healing massage.

"Tell me, King Huemac," Tizoc finally replied, "are the two strangers married?"

Huemac was a little surprised at this question. But he answered as best he could.

"The two strangers? My informants do not think so, Tizoc." The king paused a moment, then added, "But it is confusing. She addresses him as 'father,' but he does not call her 'daughter.'"

On hearing this answer, Tizoc felt he was at last ready. He sat up and turned his head toward the king. He spoke slowly and very deliberately, preparing himself for the king's reaction.

"King Huemac, here is my answer to your question: that the priestess services of the captive woman be reserved only for me. Me alone."

"What?" King Huemac said sharply.

Even the flutist ceased playing.

Patli stopped the healing massage, but only for a second. He waited to see what would happen next.

King Huemac was unprepared for this request. A slight frown appeared. He too wanted to experiment with the mysterious woman.

"Tizoc, it is unheard of for a temple priestess to be available to only one man."

"It is what I want, King Huemac."

Patli observed this conversation with growing unease. He was uncomfortable with Tizoc's obsession with Kathleen. But he was loyal to Tizoc and wished for his happiness.

Tizoc was about to say more, but Patli caught his eye and indicated that he should be silent.

Then Patli leaned close to the king's ear. "Of course, she is intriguing," he whispered. "But with that unknown comes the chance that she carries bad magic or even sickness."

King Huemac leaned forward to hear more of Patli's message.

"Better that this should befall just one athlete," Patli said, "rather than many temple visitors—or you, my king."

Patli's logic was appealing. King Huemac was now pleased to grant as a gift something he no longer wanted.

"Of course, Tizoc," he said, smiling broadly. "Your desire is granted."

In an instant, the tense muscles in Tizoc's back relaxed. Patli could continue with the deep and healing massage.

CHAPTER FIFTEEN

NOTHER CYCLE OF THE MOON passed. Tonauac was relentless in his education of Brand. They began study when the rays of the morning sun cast long shadows and continued until the orb had weakened nearly to sunset. Ever the eager learner, Brand listened to and learned as much language as Tonauac could impart.

But Tonauac had one more step in Brand's preparation. And it did not have to do with listening, but *seeing*.

Tollan's history, culture, and religion were oral, not written. However, for a few select men, the responsibility of keeping the oral tradition was aided by the use of written symbols. Tonauac decided that the time had come to reveal these secrets. Brand was ready to understand the work of the scribes.

He brought Brand to a special patio. It was located so sunlight filtered through overhanging trees or through netting to lessen the glare. All around the patio, men sat cross-legged. They worked intently with fine turkey quills and with inks of the deepest hues: red, yellow, and blue as well as midnight black. They wrote on thin sheets made of either maguey plant fibers or delicately tanned skins of newborn fawns.

The Toltecs had an arithmetic system of numbers—bars and dots. Some scribes used this system to record the tribute extracted from subservient tribes. Other scribes worked only on astronomy and created manuscripts to mark events for the calendars. Some created brief records of the reigns of kings past and present. All the men were related, for being a scribe was passed on from generation to generation.

Brand thought they looked not unlike the scribes at the priory back in England, painstakingly copying words from the Holy Scriptures and illuminating them with exquisite decorative letters inked in bright colors. In Winchester, the monks had all been taught that the blood of Christ was life, but that ink was the lifeblood of civilization.

Tonauac motioned for Brand to come near and look at a finished manuscript. Brand inspected it closely as Tonauac held it in front of him. He saw small pictures and some symbols formed into rows across the document. None of them were like the letters he knew so well—the runes and the Latin letters. But his excitement was high when he recognized some of the symbols were the same as those carved into the stone decoration throughout the city.

What Tonauac displayed for Brand was a combination of pictograms, hieroglyphs, and phonetic symbols. But it would take much effort for a learner to recognize these distinctions.

The pictograms, at first, seemed the easiest to understand. Tonauac pointed to a realistic drawing of a plaited reed mat, outlined in black and inked in a brilliant green.

Brand said the word for reed mat, and Tonauac nodded.

Then Tonauac began to explain, "Sometimes an image can mean what it looks like. So, this picture can represent exactly that—a reed mat." With some difficulty, Tonauac explained further, "But other times, Father Brand, the image is not a thing, but something else."

Brand waited, which Tonauac took as an indication that he was following the concept.

"Because chieftains and kings often sit on reed mats," Tonauac continued, "sometimes this symbol refers to power, to authority. The picture is not of a thing, then, but of an idea."

Ah, thought Brand, *I understand*. It was like the cross: a thing but also a symbol of something greater, of the White Kristr faith. He thought of the thousand times he had glanced at the cherished cross Kathleen had worn at her throat.

Tonauac showed Brand another small pictogram. This time it was a pyramid, and at the top, a temple was aflame with red and orange ink.

"This," said Tonauac, "means victory over an enemy."

"I do not understand," said Brand.

Tonauac explained that whenever a king had victory over an enemy, he destroyed the gods of the conquered people. That meant destroying the defeated enemy's temples and god images. It did not take Brand long to recall King Olaf Trygvasson and his systematic destruction of the images of Thor and Odinn.

In the next phase of the lessons, Tonauac explained that sometimes the symbols were phonetic. The drawing of an obsidian arrowhead, or *itz*, plus a drawing of a pot, or *ko*, plus the symbol for water, *atl*, together became the symbol for a person called Itzcoatl. Or the same meaning could be made by putting together the arrowhead drawing along with the drawing for a serpent, or *coatl*. Either way, it meant the name of a long-ago king known as "Obsidian Serpent."

All these rules had to be memorized and understood in context. Even with his great gifts of language and intelligence, Brand struggled to understand when a drawing or symbol referred to a thing, an idea, or some phonetic clue about a person or thing.

But before long, Brand noted that the scribes' writing was elemental. It was used to mark the beginning and ending dates of the reigns of various kings and sometimes to mark other extraordinary events. But it was very limited in the kind of information that could be recorded.

Then one day, Tonauac carried a carefully wrapped object into the patio of the scribes. Brand looked up from the symbols he was studying. Tonauac slowly unwrapped the object and let the wrapping fall to the ground.

Could it be? Could it possibly be?

Brand started to shake with excitement and relief. His eyes became moist with joy. He could scarcely endure it. He walked toward Tonauac, his gaze fixed on the precious object in Tonauac's outstretched hands.

It was the Gospel book created in England, then sent to Trondheim, then carried across the north seas to Brattahlid, and now residing here. It had not been destroyed. It still existed.

Tonauac placed it in Brand's trembling hands. Brand's eyes looked to the sky in gratitude.

They moved to a quiet corner of the patio. Brand opened the book and carefully began to turn its fragile pages.

"What is this thing?" Tonauac asked.

"It is a book," Brand explained. "It is a way to group together many symbols."

Tonauac took the book and hesitantly turned one of the pages himself. He looked very intently and closely at the marks on the pages.

Tonauac said slowly, "Tell me what these symbols mean. I want to understand."

Brand did not quite know where to begin. He started by telling Tonauac that these marks were the words of the One God. The words that God spoke to the people, so the people understand that God loves them and how God wants them to live.

"Your god has writing?" said Tonauac, incredulous. "Does not your god speak through the wind or through the rain? Or the mountains? Or the blood of the sacrificed?"

Brand knew what he was saying was difficult for Tonauac to understand.

"The spirit of God entered the humans. It was with them and in them when they made these symbols," he answered.

Tonauac did not understand how such a thing could be. But he decided not to pursue questions about it. He was eager to ask Brand other things about the symbols. He drew the symbol for god, *teotl,* in the ground before them.

"Do you have a sign for your god in this book?"

"Yes," Brand replied.

"Show me."

Brand opened the book, quickly found the word *Deo,* and pointed to it with his finger. Tonauac looked at the small letters, curved and straight, written on the linen pages. His eyes widened. The little symbols were complex. There were no colored inks to help understand the meaning. There were no obvious comparisons to real objects, as in the symbol language he knew.

Tonauac looked up from the book, his eyes staring straight ahead. He saw nothing; he saw *everything*.

The next day, the lessons began when Brand carefully wrote his name in Latin letters in the dirt before them. He pointed to the writing, then repeated his name. Then he reversed the order, saying his name, then touching the writing with his index finger.

Tonauac looked at the letters, then at Brand, then once again at the letters.

He pointed to the letters written in the dirt.

"Father Brand?" he asked. Was this how the name Father Brand was written?

"Yes!" said Brand, full of excitement.

Next, Tonauac pointed to himself. Brand pondered a minute, unsure of how to use the Latin alphabet to approximate the sound of Tonauac's name. Then he wrote it out in the sandy soil.

"My name?" asked Tonauac.

"Yes. Your name."

Tonauac was so delighted he laughed out loud. Then a steady stream of questions began.

"Who wrote these symbols?"

Brand explained, "Special men, like the scribes, copied the books so other people might know the stories about the life and meaning of Jesu the White Kristr."

"These marks tell *stories*?"

"Yes, these marks tell how the One God loves us and how his son came down to earth to teach us how to live."

"A god who *loves*," said Tonauac, another quizzical look on his face. "The marks can talk of love?"

"Yes. And other feelings too."

It took a while for Tonauac to take this in.

"Who can write them and understand them?"

"Usually only priests who have been trained to write and understand them. But sometimes other men. And sometimes women too."

"*Women?*"

Brand pondered how to explain the concept of women's holy orders, then decided to leave that for another time. "Well, yes, a very few women."

"Can Kathleen write and understand these marks?"

Brand paused before he answered. He was unsure how much to reveal of Kathleen's knowledge. If he said yes, it may increase her value and safeguard her. Or maybe it would entwine her in more problems.

Tonauac waited.

Brand decided to take a chance. "Yes, Tonauac. Kathleen can understand these little signs."

Tonauac sat for a moment, silently holding the book. He formed an idea for a test, a kind of way to truly understand the power of the little marks.

"I must send her a message," Tonauac said. "Something she could learn only from the message, not any other way. And the message must tell a story."

Brand looked at Tonauac somewhat strangely, his head slightly cocked to one side.

"All right," Brand finally said. "But it must be a simple message. I have not seen Kathleen since the day of the ball game. I do not know how much of your language she has learned nor what she remembers of these words and letters."

Tonauac gathered a quill, a clay bottle of ink, and a piece of pressed paper. He gave them to Brand.

"This is what the message should say: 'I had a brother. His name was Ollin. He was a dancer. I loved him, and he loved me. He died. I was sad.'"

Brand struggled somewhat to write the words in Latin. The message was simple. But he was unsure of some things, such as how to write the name of Tonauac's brother, so he made some phonetic guesses. For good measure, he wrote the message in runes as well.

Then, at the end he wrote, "Kathleen, I am well. I pray you also are well."

The next morning, Tonauac went to Izel, carrying with him the message so painstakingly written by Brand. "I must speak with the woman called Kathleen."

Izel motioned him to follow her to where the temple priestesses were gathered.

During the month Brand was learning from Tonauac, Kathleen spent her time only with Izel and the other temple priestesses. Some of the young women took their cues from Izel and treated Kathleen rudely. Some just ignored her. Some pushed her and called her names. But others, seeing the sadness in Kathleen mirrored in their own hearts, took her as a friend.

Kathleen accepted their friendship; it helped ease her loneliness. She asked to learn words Izel would never teach her. Words like *friend* and *please* and *thank you*.

There was one word Kathleen especially wanted to learn. She turned to her friends, folded her hands over her chest, hugged herself, and smiled. Her friends laughed and said the Nahuatl word she needed. Kathleen repeated the word many times to memorize it.

It greatly upset Izel that her charge was to be treated differently from the other young girls. All the young women began with a period of sequestration, followed by gradual introduction into their rites and practices, with eventual service to the nobility and others permitted to participate in the temple activities.

Kathleen was sitting with a group of the young women who had befriended her, and they were trying to teach Kathleen to dance in their style. Kathleen's arms and legs were so long and unaccustomed to the movements that her attempts prompted much laughter. They all looked up together, as one, when Tonauac entered the area.

Izel gestured to Kathleen. Kathleen stood up, looked back at the other women, and walked slowly to where Izel and Tonauac stood. Tonauac dismissed Izel, and the two then moved to another part of the compound. Kathleen's heart was racing, for once more, she did not know what was about to take place, whether she should fear or give thanks.

Tonauac handed Kathleen the written message. She opened it, hoping it would contain some news of Brand. She quickly read, and her eyes opened wide as she did. She understood the words completely, though why she had been given the message was a mystery. Her heart leaped when she read Brand's small personal note at the end. He was alive! He was well!

"Tell me. Tell me," said Tonauac, using simple Nahuatl words. "Do you know what these marks mean?"

"Yes." She began to read the message, translating it into her halting Nahuatl. "I had a brother. His name was Ollin. He was a dancer. I . . ." Here she made the gesture and said the word she had learned from the other women. "*Loved* Ollin. Ollin *loved* me. Ollin died. I was sad." Her hand, clutching the message, fell to her side. She looked at Tonauac and waited for his response.

Tonauac stood quite still for several moments. He swallowed hard, unsure if he had heard correctly. He placed his hand on his forehead to take it all in. It was the most marvelous thing he had ever dreamed of. The symbols conveyed data and facts. But even more, the symbols could convey feelings. *Feelings.*

CHAPTER SIXTEEN

Ing Huemac's chief administrator had told Izel that Tizoc, and only Tizoc, would be allowed to spend time with the strange woman.

With grudging obedience, Izel did as she was told. Kathleen was given a blue cotton gown that made her blue eyes look even more like a bright sky. Her hair was washed, and sweet-smelling plant oils were lightly rubbed onto her long locks. Finally, a necklace of carved coral beads was put around her neck. The women who helped her dress told her she was stunning. But Kathleen did not understand.

Izel led Kathleen to a secluded courtyard near the residence of the king. Izel motioned for her to sit at a small table with leather stools at opposite sides. Then Izel crossed over to the edge of the courtyard and waited.

Kathleen did not know what was to happen next. She bowed her head in uncertainty and closed her eyes. When she looked up, Tizoc suddenly was there, moving toward her, his eyes only on her. Tizoc. A friend!

He sat down across from her. He stared at her, smiling from his heart.

He was dressed as befitted a prince—much different than the day they had first met along the shore. His mantle was the finest cotton, dyed a deep green. Over this he had a cloak of ocelot skin held with a gold pin in the shape of a frog. On his feet, he wore sandals of softest deerskin decorated with tiny gold braid. His eyes were shining with anticipation.

Kathleen looked first to Izel, then to Tizoc.

"Father Brand?" she asked, hoping Tizoc would know something.

But Tizoc could only shake his head slowly. Kathleen was unsure if this meant Brand was dead or that Tizoc did not know what had happened to him.

Then she asked, "Nenetl?"

This time, Tizoc smiled so she would know Nenetl was well.

They sat there in silence for a while as Izel's hawklike eyes pierced the air around them. Tizoc ached to say more, to learn more. But he waited. And Kathleen waited. Language was a chasm between them.

Finally, he got up and moved toward the edge of the courtyard. Dahlias grew there in wild and lush profusion. He plucked a deep-red flower—crimson, like heart's blood. He sat down across from her again.

"This flower is called *chichipatl*," he said almost in a whisper. He offered the colorful bloom to her. "Take it. For you."

She was surprised at the intensity of emotions flowing through her and did not know what to do. When she did not respond, Tizoc leaned closer across the table and very gently brushed her hair away from her face. He placed the flower behind her ear, then let her long straight hair fall back into place, like a curtain.

She shivered when his hand grazed her shoulder.

Then he leaned back, looked at her, and smiled again.

She was unsure of what to do, so again she bowed her head and closed her eyes. When she raised her head and looked, he was gone.

Her hand moved cautiously toward the dahlia and felt it. This is how she knew he had been there with her. This was not a dream.

Brand's own dreams had been the ordinary, usual dreams for a long time. For years, he had dreamed of the unknown young woman who so mesmerized him, then he met her that fateful day back in Trondheim. Since then, his dreams had been no different from other dreams.

That is, until one night in Tollan, when a vivid, unforgettable dream entered his sleeping mind. He was alone in his dream, and in the bizarre way of some dreams, he was both actor and observer. In it, he stood alone on a shore, facing water of unknown name and origin. He spoke words aloud, to an invisible audience.

Spirit of invention, am I.
Spirit of learning, am I.
Creator of books, am I.
I am the Lord of the Star of the Dawn.
I am the priest of the one true sacrifice.
I am the priest of offerings of jade, birds, and butterflies.
I am the priest of true light.
The wanderer, am I.
The departed, am I.
The spirit of peace, am I.

He had no idea of its meaning, only that it somehow foretold the future. He dreamed it many more times. But he told no one about it.

CHAPTER SEVENTEEN

E ARLY ONE MORNING, BRAND AND Tonauac sat together in the scribes' patio. The air was still cool, and they were finishing a light breakfast of fruit and *tlaxcalli*. Tonauac noted that Brand had become quite adept at using the warm, soft, and fragrant disks.

Tonauac explained that the tlaxcalli were made from the seeds of *elotl*. The seeds grew in tightly formed linear rows along a thick core. The mature seeds were removed from the core, dried, then soaked in water made alkaline with wood ash when needed. No one really knew how the process had evolved. Perhaps an absent-minded cook had carelessly dropped ash into a soaking vessel. And perhaps a sharp-eyed cook had noticed that the seeds were then easier to prepare. Whether the result of trial and error over centuries or a gift of insight from the gods, the strange alchemy of wood ash in the water resulted in a more nutritious fare.

Brand had often seen women bending over grindstones to trans-form the soaked seeds into coarse particles. Water was added to the ground seeds to form a soft, doughy mass. The dough was colored according to the color of the dried seeds used.

The women deftly formed the dough into thin, even disks by quickly moving a small ball of dough back and forth between their flat hands. Then they placed the disks on a hot earthenware platter, or comal, placed over the open flames of a hearth fire.

Tlaxcalli was eaten every day, at each meal, in one form or another, by everyone in the city. Brand knew this food was as important to these people as was the chewy rye bread and steaming pots of oats, peas, and barley in the land of his birth.

Tonauac studied Brand as they ate. He was more than pleased with how Brand's language training was progressing. They still had one more moon before they had to report to King Huemac. And the writing! The writing would be a source of disbelief and awe.

For his part, Brand understood that the power of writing meant a great deal to Tonauac. He decided to make a proposal.

"Tonauac," said Brand, "would you like to learn the symbols faster?"

"Of course," said Tonauac with interest.

"Kathleen and I, we both can teach you about these symbols. You could have two teachers instead of only one."

Tonauac did not believe there was any real advantage in having two teachers. Still, he did not need to think long on Brand's proposal. He knew why Brand had offered it. Brand was lonely for the woman's companionship.

"Yes, Father Brand. I will do what I can."

That afternoon, Tonauac went to King Huemac and petitioned him in private. He explained that Kathleen's presence was required for a few hours a day. Preoccupied with a recent skirmish on their northern border, the king was not interested in any distraction. He summarily granted the request.

The next day, Kathleen joined the morning lessons between Brand and Tonauac. Both she and Brand were overcome with joy at seeing each other. It was true that Kathleen's participation did not increase Tonauac's learning to any great degree. But sometimes she and Brand would talk, then Brand would incorporate her ideas into the lessons of the day.

Every night at evening prayers, Brand thanked God for the opportunity to teach Tonauac. And he thanked God that he could now see Kathleen every morning and know she was well.

It was still unclear to Brand what happened to Kathleen during the afternoon and evenings. He asked Kathleen one day, but all she could tell him was: "I am with Izel and Tizoc."

Izel insisted that Kathleen rejoin the other temple priestesses in the afternoons, but never again did she bring Kathleen to the House of Dancing and Pleasure in the evenings.

Tizoc did not miss a single opportunity to be with Kathleen in the afternoons. Every morning, he practiced with the ollama players, as required. But it was his afternoons that he now lived for.

Sometimes he brought Nenetl with him. The three would sit in the temple gardens, always out of sight of others. Nenetl would help teach Kathleen new Nahuatl words or show her little games the other children had taught her.

Kathleen had begun to teach the Latin alphabet to Nenetl, who thought it was a fun little memory game. Nenetl would perch and cuddle on Kathleen's lap. Kathleen recalled her own mother's arms, Gudrun's generous embrace, even the comfort of Hlatr's soft, dense fur.

During their time together, Tizoc never attempted to touch Kathleen without being thoroughly certain it would not alarm her. Most of the time, he just watched her, his eyes soft. Once or twice he touched her arm. And one day, he rested his hand on hers as they watched Nenetl attempt to tumble like the palace dwarfs. He waited for Kathleen to withdraw her hand, but she did not.

While Kathleen and Tizoc sat together in the temple gardens, Brand and Tonauac filled their afternoons with discussion of religion and culture in the scribes' patio. Each struggled to understand the reality of the other's world. For Brand, these conversations were not so different from the discussions he had engaged in with the heathen Norse. For one thing, both the Toltecs and the Norse had a multitude of gods and goddesses, with some more important and powerful than others.

"Tell me, Tonauac, who are the important gods?"

"There is Tezcatlipoca, the Smoking Mirror; and there is Quetzalcoatl, the Feathered Serpent."

Brand had heard the names of these gods and had seen the image of the Feathered Serpent throughout the city. Seeing that Brand understood, Tonauac continued his explanation.

"The priest Toveyo serves Smoking Mirror."

Brand knew who Toveyo was; he had been in the court when he and Kathleen were first brought to the city. He remembered the shiny dark obsidian disk Toveyo wore on his chest and the other disk that hung from his wrist.

"At one time, Quetzalcoatl and Tezcatlipoca cooperated to create the world," Tonauac explained. "But now they are opposites. Tezcatlipoca is the god of conflict. Tezcatlipoca's followers are many, including the military. If you see priests wearing white turkey feather headdresses or covered in black soot, you will know they have been engaged in worship of Tezcatlipoca. Tezcatlipoca requires human sacrifice from time to time and requires all to show respect. Even the king must stand before his image and say, 'We are your slaves.'"

"And Quetzalcoatl?"

"The Feathered Serpent, Quetzalcoatl is of earth and sky, the human and the divine. The great Quetzalcoatl connects and builds the two worlds. This god has given us many gifts: knowledge of all kinds and the importance of transmitting this knowledge from one generation to the other. I serve this god."

"Tonauac, who taught you about Quetzalcoatl?"

"My fathers, the priests who came before me. Is it not the same with you?"

Brand considered for a moment how he had disavowed the gods of his own father, Sören. He had an impulse to tell Tonauac how he had abandoned the gods of his father when he found faith in Jesu.

"I can explain another time," Brand finally said, hoping Tonauac would not press him on the issue.

"The ancient people of Teotihuacan worshipped Quetzalcoatl," Tonauac continued. "They made many images of him throughout that city." He looked in the direction of the abandoned metropolis. "But no one has lived there for many, many years."

"What else can you tell me, Tonauac?"

"Quetzalcoatl was born of a virgin mother, named Chimalman."

301

A virgin birth! The very notion surprised Brand. He made a mental note to learn more of this.

"And when the gods were creating the sun, the moon, earth, water, and many other things, it was Quetzalcoatl who created the calendar."

"Are there other gods?"

"Yes, many. There is Tlaloc, who gives us rain. And Xochipilli, the god of music, dancing, and ollama. And many other lesser gods."

Brand sat for a minute or two, taking in all this information. Then he took a breath.

"Tonauac, when I first came into the city, there was a group of priests of Tlaloc. They sacrificed children. Why? Was it to grant a specific need? Was it part of a regular event? Had the parents of these children done something that deserved punishment?"

"It was all and none of these things. Tlaloc requires the sacrifice of children to ensure the rains will come. If we do not serve the gods and give them sacrifice, then the whole world will come spinning apart. We are taught that without human sacrifice, there will be no order to the universe, only chaos."

"And does the god you serve demand human sacrifice?"

"No. Quetzalcoatl abhors human sacrifice. Rather, we burn offerings of rubber, paper, flowers, and butterflies before his image to show sincerity and loyalty."

"I agree, Tonauac. There is no reason for men to be sacrificed. The god I serve wants our hearts. But he wants our *living* hearts—our loyalty and our adoration."

Then Tonauac asked solemnly, "Father Brand, tell me of your gods."

Brand recalled the difficulties he had in explaining his faith to Ibn Beshir and to the Greenlander folk. And here in this place, things were so different from Winchester. How could he tell the story of the Good Shepherd? There were no shepherds, for there were no sheep! How could he tell of the land of milk and honey, when there was no milk? Brand longed for the wisdom of Bishop Ælfheah and Prior Simeon. He would have to rely on the Holy Spirit to help him. Yes, the Holy Spirit would help him. Somehow.

He took a deep breath.

"I worship one god."

"Only one god?" Tonauac interrupted.

"Yes," Brand answered. "One god who has three ways to be with us. There is a creator. The creator of all that is. This creator saw that men were sinful and disobedient and deserved to be punished. So the creator god sent his son to earth to tell the people of the love of the creator god. The son told them there was a way to avoid punishment. The son spent time on earth teaching and healing people. But the people hated him because he told the truth about God. And he was killed on . . . on . . ."

Brand struggled to find the right words.

"On a kind of a wooden stake. We call it a cross and use it as a symbol for our god."

He thought of drawing the symbol in the earth but decided to continue with his explanation.

"But the son did not remain dead. He rose again, then went to be with the creator god. And everyone who believes in the son, called Jesu Kristr, will also go to be with the creator god and the son when they die. And in the other world, there will be no sorrow or pain or tears—only happiness." Brand paused. "And there is also a spirit god, who helps people believe and comforts and protects those here in this world."

"So, you worship *three* gods," said Tonauac, thinking he was correcting Brand's earlier statement.

"Not three gods. One god with three ways to speak to us and be with us. The creator and the son and the spirit."

Tonauac's eyes narrowed as he struggled with this concept. He knew many gods who expressed duality, including Quetzalcoatl, who incorporated earth and sky, human and spirit. But a god with *three* aspects—that was more complicated.

Brand decided that a full explanation of the Holy Trinity could wait until later. He moved on to his next point instead.

"And you must understand that the creator, the son, and the spirit all love human beings. The creator made each person who lives on the earth, and he loves all of them equally."

Tonauac looked up into the sky, his mouth slightly open as he reflected on what he was hearing. Brand had seen this intellectual struggle before. The notion of a loving god, a god who knew you and who asked for your love in return, was just as radical to the Toltecan priest as it had been to the Norse. Of all the pantheon of gods, both here and in the cold lands to the north, no god had ever said, "I will call you by name; you are mine."

"Of all our gods," Tonauac stated after some reflection, "I think your god is most like the god I serve, Quetzalcoatl. And I want to learn more."

CHAPTER EIGHTEEN

THAT NIGHT, AT THE SAME time Brand was saying his evening prayers, Tonauac sat before smoldering incense, turning things over in his mind. There was only one more moon before King Huemac would demand an account of Brand's education. Tonauac had been giddy to share the news of the Brand and Kathleen's special writing. But now he was not so sure.

Just like the incense, a grave conflict smoldered in Tollan. It was possibly about to burst into flame. Toveyo and the Tezcatlipoca followers were increasingly hostile to the followers of Quetzalcoatl. Toveyo and the other worshippers believed that military strength and fear were necessary to keep Tollan strong.

But the Quetzalcoatl followers were artisans and scribes and astronomers. They believed that a people united only by fear and force would eventually crumble from within.

Tonauac knew that spies followed all his activities. They probably knew of his decision to show Brand the symbols of the Toltecan scribes. But he was fairly certain they did not know of Brand and Kathleen's astonishing writing.

The ultimate outcome of the conflict might not be known in his lifetime, but Tonauac resolved to do whatever he could, whenever he could, to save the lives of the strangers from the east.

A few days later, Brand requested that they hold their morning lessons at the river. Dawn had broken that day into a beautiful sky. The air was warm yet cooler by the flowing water.

A group of women were a little downriver, washing cotton clothing and gossiping. Izel and her son were there as well. With his short legs, Tlazohtlaloni walked into the water to his knees. He laughed with his whole body as Izel splashed water on his chest and back.

The river thoroughly delighted Kathleen. Wearing only her simple cotton shift, she dove in and disappeared into the rushing waters. The river was running quite fast after a recent rain, and it was a little muddy, but she did not care. She laughed, turned somersaults, and swam on her back. Rivers were a source of sweet memories for her—memories of days with her mother, who also loved the water.

"It is wonderful!" she shouted to Brand.

After Kathleen swam to shore and dried off, she joined Brand and Tonauac for their lesson. Brand began a discussion of baptism. It was the reason he had wanted to meet by the river. He described the baptism of Jesus in the River Jordan. Brand recited from the Gospel of Luke.

"And a dove from heaven came down, and a voice said, 'You are my beloved Son in whom I am well pleased.'"

Suddenly a scream jolted them all.

Izel was shouting, "Help me! Help me! My son, my son!"

Tlazohtlaloni had waded too far into the river. In a twinkling, the current had taken him.

Everyone went running to Izel. The washerwomen abandoned their clothing to the rushing waters. It got caught in the current and moved rapidly downstream.

"Where? Where?" Kathleen shouted to Izel.

As soon as Izel pointed, Kathleen dove into the murky depths. She quickly calculated that the current may have forced Tlazohtlaloni, like the clothing, downstream.

Minutes passed. Three times she came up for air, her hands empty. Finally, on the fourth dive, she felt something. She caught Tlazohtlaloni by his small hand, then tucked his body, face upward, into the crook of her arm. She struggled back to the riverbank with her precious find.

Everyone gathered around Tlazohtlaloni, their faces frozen in fear. Izel took him into her arms, shook him, and begged him to wake up. His lips were bluish. He neither shivered nor breathed. All the washerwomen began to weep. Some murmured that the boy was dead.

Izel sunk into a heap of devastation. A sound came out of her—half wail, half howl.

"Kathleen, *pray!*" Brand ordered as he quickly pulled the boy out of Izel's arms.

He placed the boy on the ground and rolled him on his side. A small amount of water dribbled from his mouth. Then Brand rolled the child onto his back and tilted the small chin sharply upward.

He remembered the day Ibn Beshir saved the fellow slave who had fallen overboard. He remembered how later Ibn Beshir explained the life-saving technique: *You must place the mouth so it faces the sky, so that the life spirit can enter again into the body. Use your breath and your hands to force it back.*

Brand placed his fingers over the child's tiny nostrils, put his mouth onto the blue lips, puffed gently for a second, then stopped. Then he pressed his hands over Tlazohtlaloni's heart and gave a forceful push downward.

"Keep praying, Kathleen!"

Her lips moved rapidly as she feverishly repeated the words of the Pater Noster.

Brand did a rapid series of chest pushes, twelve in all, one for each Apostle. At the end of each series, he listened and watched for a sign of life. He blew air into the child's mouth, then started the compressions again. Beads of sweat fell off Brand's face and splashed onto the face of the child. Still, Brand would not give up.

Suddenly the boy began to cough. He took a long, shuddering rush of air into his lungs on his own. Then came the breaths that moved his chest slowly up and down.

The washerwomen gasped as one. Izel took her living son back into her arms and covered him with kisses.

"Tlazohtlaloni, oh Tlazohtlaloni—my child!"

She looked up at Brand, her face filled with relief and gratitude. "Thank you, Father Brand."

"It is a miracle," Kathleen said softly, gazing at the boy and his mother.

"Yes," replied Brand, sitting in the river sand, still panting from the exertions. "A miracle."

Brand thought of the path that had brought him to this moment: the journey to Rome, the enslavement with Ibn Beshir, the arguments with Olaf Trygvasson in Trondheim, the voyage to Brattahlid and the west beyond. *Yes*, he thought, *God has granted me the grace to help me save this small child, in this place, so far away from all that has been before. Yes, a miracle.*

Still clutching her son, Izel reached out her hand toward Kathleen, the same hand that had never touched Kathleen except to hurt and to punish. Kathleen took Izel's hand into her own.

Izel moved it to her face and kissed it.

"Thank you," she whispered, her voice hoarse from tears.

Then Izel looked back at Brand. "Will you be my teacher? I want to learn about your god."

The next morning, Brand, Kathleen, and Tonauac gathered by the river for another lesson. Only this time, Izel, Tlazohtlaloni, and the washerwomen all joined them.

Allahu kebir, thought Brand. *God is great.*

CHAPTER NINETEEN

THE THREE MOONS' TIME KING Huemac had granted to Tonauac passed quickly, especially the final month. Brand's ability to learn the language had been nothing short of astonishing. But Tonauac had not told Brand about the reality of the deadline or that he might not be able to protect Brand in the end. He told Brand only that it would be best to learn and share as much knowledge as possible, as quickly as possible.

He also made sure to bring Brand out among the people often, so they might see him and grow to like him. In that he was successful, for every time Brand interacted with the citizens of Tollan, he charmed them all. Tonauac had advised Brand to share simple phrases with them, and they were surprised and flattered when he did. Still, Tonauac knew there was a possibility that Toveyo and his followers could persuade the king that Brand's heart should be offered up to Tezcatlipoca as a special sacrifice.

The final day of the three-moon period came at last. Tonauac and Brand had very carefully rehearsed all that they would say and do when Brand appeared before the king. Still, anything could happen. Brand prayed that the Holy Spirit would be with them. Tonauac prayed to Quetzalcoatl and made burnt offerings of precious leaves of paper.

Brand and Tonauac entered the great hall together. The courtiers made way for them, creating a temporary corridor among the multitude of people. Copal smoke wafted everywhere. The room hummed.

Brand had asked to wear his priestly robe for this appearance before the king. It had been carefully wrapped and stored in the knarr when they had left Vinland. The Toltecan guards had removed it from the knarr at the time of capture. It was black wool, somewhat moth-eaten and tattered, with red crosses embroidered on the front. Simply wearing it again was comforting to Brand.

The king's dwarfs climbed up on benches and chairs to get a better look as the two men walked into the room. Some of them had begun to visit Brand, along with Izel and the washerwomen, to learn more about the new god. They had sat somewhat apart from the rest of the followers at the lessons. But they listened intently, hanging onto every word that Brand spoke. Even Xicotencatl, the court hunchback, came, although he could never sit still for more than a few minutes.

The king sat on his dais, as normal. Toveyo and the general were already in the great hall, standing next to one another near the king. Toveyo had a thick black stripe painted horizontally across his face, from his nose back to his ears. The general wore a large obsidian knife at his side, and his shoulders were covered with the skin of the spotted jaguar, the large predator cat that prowled the area. Each man had the look of a hungry coyote in his eyes.

Izel brought Kathleen in from a separate entry. The members of the court had often seen Brand since their entry into the city, but many had not seen Kathleen since the day she stood, rudely stripped of her clothing, before them all. She was dressed now in a cotton gown of reds and blues, and her hair fell pleasingly down her back. Her pewter cross was once again around her neck, where Izel had tenderly placed it in gratitude after Tlazohtlaloni had been revived.

Tizoc stood in the crowd and watched Kathleen with eyes alert with concern. She had never seemed more beautiful to him.

Brand and Kathleen followed Tonauac's and Izel's lead and bowed low before King Huemac, then moved to the side. Brand's sword, the gift from Leif, rested on a small table next to the king.

"It has been three moons' time, Tonauac," said the king. "What have you learned about our prisoner and the strange symbols he possessed when he was captured?"

Tonauac and Brand had rehearsed what do at this point. Instead of Tonauac, Brand answered—in flawless Nahuatl.

"It is poetry, King Huemac. Poetry."

Everyone in the room, including the king, turned to one another, surprised that Brand understood the king and to hear Brand speaking their language so perfectly.

"Poetry?" said the king, his eyes widening.

"Yes, King Huemac. Poetry and a kind of storytelling."

"Continue."

Now Tonauac answered. "My king, you know well how your scribes use our symbols to help them recall the poetry they have learned, the poetry their ancestors taught them."

"Yes, of course."

"Well, it is something like that."

"So, the marks on the pages are not what you had thought? They do not contain powerful secrets to conquer and destroy our enemies?"

"No, King Huemac," Tonauac said. *Truthfully.*

King Huemac and the others seemed to accept this explanation. Of course, it was easy for the people of Tollan to believe that Brand's symbols might be used to recall an oral tradition of poetry or stories. The ruse was working!

"But Father Brand does have many skills that have been and will be helpful to us," Tonauac said. "Already he has visited our silversmiths and showed them how to make a better bellows to process the metal."

King Huemac held Brand's sword aloft. He spoke directly to Brand. "Can you instruct us how to make this weapon?"

"I am sorry," Brand answered. "I cannot help you with that request. The special metal used to make such things is not available here. I have spoken with the weaponsmiths and the metallurgists, and they know of no place where the special metal it requires can be mined."

"Father Brand is also working with our astronomers to better help them understand the night sky far to our north," Tonauac quickly interjected, to divert the king's obvious disappointment.

Tonauac had encouraged Brand to meet with the Toltecan astronomers. Brand shared with them the lessons his foster father, Rolf, had taught him as a young child back in Hedeby. And he tried to describe to them Helgi's precious sólarsteinn and how it remained on the navigator's neck at all times.

Upon hearing of Brand's involvement with the astronomers, Toveyo stiffened even more. Tonauac had underestimated how deeply this news would anger Toveyo. The night sky, especially the constant star in the north, was the realm of Tezcatlipoca, *his* god.

"So," the king said to Tonauac, "you believe that this man has valuable knowledge and skills from which we can learn, even if the marks have only minimal use?"

"Yes, King Huemac."

The king took a moment to reflect on this revelation. "What else do you have to show me?"

Tonauac reached into his robe and brought out a small carved object. It also had been taken from the knarr. He held it aloft so everyone in the room could see.

When she saw it, Kathleen smiled broadly.

It was the little wheeled deer Helgi had taught her to make. Tonauac bent low and ran it across the smooth surface of the great hall's stone floor. It sped quickly and bounced off the general's foot. He roughly kicked it away. Xicotencatl laughed out loud. Several of the members of the court tried to stifle their snickers.

"What is it? A child's toy?" grumbled the general. "Of what use is a toy to us?" he said, derision dripping from his words.

"Yes, it is a toy, General Yaotl, but also much more," Tonauac countered. He pointed to the small wheels. "With such round devices connected to a box, we could move many things. Goods. Even people."

"And how would we do that?" Toveyo interjected with scorn. "Our trade routes are too narrow, and they are not smooth. And what of the porters? What would they do? How would they make a living if such devices were in common use? We do not need such a thing. Save it for the children."

"I think Toveyo and General Yaotl are right," the king said, nodding to them. "We have no need for the disks that move."

Tonauac knew it would be folly to press the issue further. He picked up the little carving and placed it back underneath his robe.

"You are wise, King Huemac," said the general, bowing his head. At least he had won this argument against Tonauac. But it was a minor skirmish compared to his real objective.

"And, my king, what is your decision regarding the man? Shall he be sacrificed?"

The king fingered the gold and jade rings on his left hand. "I have thought it over carefully."

Everyone in the hall waited. Even Xicotencatl was still.

When the king spoke, it was with finality.

"It is clear to me that this man is of more use to us living rather than dead."

Silent relief crept over the stoic faces of Tonauac and Brand.

Toveyo's jaw clenched with this frustration. But there was one more possibility for his faction to be rewarded.

"And what shall be done with the woman?" he asked expectantly.

Without realizing, Brand and Tizoc both stopped breathing. Kathleen could not understand many words, but she knew intuitively that her fate was being decided.

"What does the teacher of the temple priestesses have to say?" asked the king, turning toward Izel.

Izel moved gracefully to the center of the room, head held high. Izel was prepared to do whatever it took to protect the woman who had saved her son.

She simply said, truthfully, "My king, she has done all the temple priestess duties I have asked her to do." She bowed her head and waited.

"I have heard enough," the king suddenly declared without asking more questions. "Tonauac! The man, Brand, may continue with you as an assistant. Izel! The woman shall continue her training with you. This matter is now closed."

In the same moment, Brand and Tizoc both breathed a sigh. The crowd murmured. Kathleen had understood only half of what was said, but she relaxed when Izel smiled at her.

Toveyo leaned to whisper close to General Yaotl's ear. "No, this matter is *not* closed."

CHAPTER TWENTY

A FTER THE MOMENTOUS APPEARANCE BEFORE the king, Toveyo and General Yaotl met at the general's compound. They needed to plan their next move.

"This cannot go on!" said Toveyo, his face red with anger and frustration. "The king has become enamored of these beings. And many of the people have as well. Even the king's hunchback and the dwarfs! Tonauac protects the strangers. And I think Izel too!"

"You are right," said the general. "Once this man has a toehold, he will then have a foothold, and eventually a stronghold."

Toveyo and General Yaotl were correct in their assumptions. The popularity of Father Brand and his teachings was growing ever greater. One by one, people came to him. Many were widows, fed up with the warfare that killed their husbands and their sons. They said to Brand, "Teach us. Teach us of this new god who does not demand our blood and the sacrifice of our hearts. Teach us of the god who loves us."

Toveyo nodded in agreement. "We need someone who can act as an observer, to tell us what is going on."

"I know someone who can help in that way," said the general. "In fact, I have already summoned him. He is waiting to speak with us."

"Who?"

"Cuetzpali. He is a former trader. He knows how to make people believe he is sincere, but wealth will always be his true master."

General Yaotl waved his hand, and a slave went to bring Cuetzpali into the room. The trader was named for the lizard, and it was an apt name.

He was shorter than most men in Tollan, but his belly was considerably rounder. The lids of his almond-shaped eyes only half opened, even when he was awake, so he looked like a fat reptile warming itself in the sun. Large turquoise disks weighed down his earlobes, so stretched that they reached the top of his shoulders. His full lips seemed flabby, not sensuous.

The visitor bowed to both the men. "Why have you summoned me, Lord High Priest of Tezcatlipoca?"

"We have heard, Cuetzpali, that you are a man who knows how to learn things about others, even when they do not know you are doing so."

Cuetzpali's narrow eyes narrowed even more. "I have learned many skills, Lord Toveyo, in my work as a trader. It is always best to have the most knowledge and to make sure that others do not harbor suspicions."

Even when Cuetzpali described his work as a spy, he sounded positively benign. His answer reassured Toveyo and the general that he had the skills they needed.

"There is a matter that needs your expertise," said Toveyo. "It concerns the stranger, whom they call Father Brand. You will be well rewarded for your efforts. We will meet each week to hear your reports. Each report will be worth three cotton mantles; more if the information is extremely useful."

Cuetzpali did not take long to consider this offer. "Of course, Lord Toveyo. I will begin immediately." He slowly backed away, then turned and left the room, his fat feet padding on the stone floor.

It did not seem unusual when Cuetzpali showed up for instruction the next day with Father Brand. Many new students were coming.

Cuetzpali approached Brand and announced, "I am here to learn."

Had Arn, himself a trader, been there alongside Brand, he would have detected something suspicious in Cuetzpali. Being able to intuit whom to trust and whom not to trust was a special skill Arn had so successfully honed on his many trade journeys. But Brand did not possess such an ability. Brand was never able to discern an enemy posing as a friend. Moreover, the Benedictine Rule from his training in the monastery required that he treat each stranger as he would treat the Christ.

Only Izel sensed something was not right. *That man makes my teeth itch!* she thought but kept her reservations to herself.

"Welcome!" said Brand to the new student.

In this simple word, the stage was set for the followers of blood-hungry Tezcatlipoca to continue their quest to control, and if necessary, destroy the people who chose not to follow their ways.

CHAPTER TWENTY-ONE

ANOTHER MOON PASSED. LIFE WAS settling into a kind of routine for all. Brand continued to work with Tonauac to learn and share knowledge. He kept up his personal prayers and preached to his growing little flock.

Kathleen was learning more from Izel. She saw Tizoc and Brand every day. Tizoc continued to train with the other athletes. He had become a close and affectionate brother to Nenetl. Whenever she saw him, she ran to him, her little face lit up with a broad smile. And of course, he cherished his time with Kathleen.

Then news came that caused an excited stir throughout the city. King Amapane of Cholollan had sent messengers to the court of Tollan.

It was not unexpected. The messengers informed King Huemac that King Amapane wished to have an ollama rematch, this time in his city of Cholollan. In reality, it was not politically possible for King Huemac to refuse such an invitation. And the messengers arrived with gifts—numerous bags of high-quality cacao beans, cages of brightly colored birds, and many fine cotton mantles, some colored with expensive purple dye. King Huemac promptly agreed to the rematch.

There was an additional, somewhat unusual request as well. King Amapane also asked that Brand accompany Tizoc and the athletic delegation. Tonauac urged the king to agree, and he did.

The athletes and officials immediately began preparations for the journey to the rival city. This journey would mean Brand would be away from Kathleen once again, and he was already anxious about it. Tizoc, for his part, had similar anxiety.

The travelers set out from Tollan early in the morning. Mist still hung in the air above the river waters and low-lying areas. Tizoc and the players were there, as well as Patli and the other medical personnel. As priest to the ball players, Tonauac was especially excited to travel to Cholollan, for it was there that even more followers of the peaceful Quetzalcoatl could be found.

Brand walked along as well, usually at Tonauac's side, taking in all that he saw and heard. At least this time on the trail, he was less uncertain whether he would live or die.

One hundred porters walked along at the end of the column, tumplines straining. Some were laden with food, others with trade goods. Still others carried heavy packs filled with athletic regalia and equipment.

At the outskirts of Cholollan, King Amapane sent official greeters to welcome the Toltecs. As they approached the city center, the travelers' jaws dropped in wordless awe at the sight of a giant four-sided stone pyramid.

It dominated every other structure in Cholollan in size and majesty. Thirty men standing on one another's shoulders would not reach the summit. And its footprint was even greater than its height would indicate.

For over five hundred years, inhabitants of the area had built up the pyramid in four successive stages of construction, until it was the dominant feature in the surrounding plain.

As the Toltecs moved through the city, they passed by brightly colored murals showing scenes from Cholollan's history. One mural showed men who appeared to be dazed and stumbling.

Brand studied it. "What is happening in this scene?"

"I believe they are drunk, Father Brand," Tonauac answered. "Drunk from drinking *octli*."

"Tell me more about this octli." He wondered if it might be a kind of wine made from grapes. If so, he might use it someday as part of Holy Eucharist.

"It is made from the juices of the *metl* plant," explained Tonauac. "It takes twelve years for the plant to be ready for harvest. A single stalk bearing flowers grows straight up from the plant, so tall that you think it will pierce the sky. Then the heart of the plant is removed, and the sap collects in the empty space in the center of the plant. The plant must die to provide the sap. Those who are permitted to drink it are strictly limited."

The travelers from Tollan were housed in a special compound. As guests, they were given access to every type of food and entertainment, although the athletes strictly adhered to the regimen their trainers mandated. There was no temptation for Tizoc. Since the day he had met Kathleen, he had no appetite for other women's caresses.

The evening before the competition, a small group of visitors came to the compound, all carefully shrouded in dark mantles. Pine-pitch torches hissed and crackled, illuminating the area with circles of yellow light. In the dim torchlight, with hoods over their heads, the faces of the visitors were difficult to see.

"We are emissaries from King Amapane," one said. "We are here to meet with Tonauac, your priest, and with the one called Father Brand. Alone."

The emissaries then moved to a more isolated courtyard and waited.

Tonauac reflected on the request. He decided to meet with the group, though with caution. Brand and Tonauac carefully approached the Cholollans.

When the leader of the group let down his hood, Brand and Tonauac both took an inward breath. It was no less than King Amapane himself. Before they could speak, the king made a most extraordinary pronouncement.

"I have heard much about you. More than you may realize. I know that you, Tonauac, Bringer of Light, are a follower of Quetzalcoatl. And I know that you, Father Brand, teach about a god who is peaceful. And even more, who loves the people he has created. And that those who worship your god can gain eternal life. They need not die on a battlefield to attain it."

319

Again, Brand and Tonauac looked at each other in surprise. The king's information and knowledge was accurate. It had traveled far.

"I also know that the followers of Tezcatlipoca, Smoking Mirror, are threatened by you and may someday try to destroy you. I want to warn you about this. You may come here for help, if you should ever need it. The name of this city means 'place of refuge,' and sanctuary will be offered to you."

There was no further explanation. As quickly as they had arrived, King Amapane and his small entourage disappeared into the darkness of the night.

The next day, the games were played with the usual enthusiastic and noisy crowds. This time, the Cholollan team won. Each team played well, but it was a pedestrian game. There were no spectacular plays or excitement because the teams were so well matched.

The return journey to Tollan also went without major incident. It gave Tizoc and Patli the opportunity to talk of many things. As they walked, they recalled their days in the village of their youth, the times they spent in training and in learning to heal, even the time they had gone searching for Tizoc's mother and had found his little sister. With this, the conversation turned to Kathleen.

As the group stopped by a small river, Patli poured himself a drink of water. He almost emptied his orange pottery cup in one gulp.

"You plan to marry her, do you not?" asked Patli, wiping his lip. He stared hard at Tizoc.

Tizoc knew his answer would upset Patli, yet he had to tell his friend the truth.

"The truth, Patli? Yes—if she will have me."

Patli threw his cup on the ground. It hit a rock and shattered as if it were an obsidian mirror.

"Forget her! Why are you obsessed with her?" Patli stomped around in frustration. "Marry a Toltecan girl. There are many who want you. General Yaotl's daughter wants you. Marry her—you will gain many advantages. If you do not, you may make enemies. Powerful enemies."

The show of such strong emotion was unusual for the normally jovial Patli.

"I understand what you are telling me Patli," Tizoc said. "And I understand why. But I cannot forget her. I cannot."

Patli took a moment to compose himself. "Tizoc, I can never accept this woman as being right for you. I fear what she will bring to you. But I will never stop being your friend, and I will do nothing to harm her or your relationship with her."

The two friends said nothing more of this all the way back to Tollan. Patli returned to his usual self, joking and making the time lively for everyone.

But Patli knew Tizoc had chosen a path. And that path would have to be walked, no matter what Patli wished for.

CHAPTER TWENTY-TWO

TIZOC AND BRAND WERE GONE for more than a full cycle of the moon on their journey to Cholollan and back. While they were away, Kathleen had fewer distractions from her own thoughts. She was lonely. Her appetite was small, despite Izel's gentle coaxing. She slept fitfully.

Kathleen keenly felt Brand's absence. There was no other person with whom she could talk of intimate things. And she had no one to comfort her when sorrows were too deep for words. She continued with her personal prayers, but she missed hearing Brand's voice mixed with her own during the recitation.

She missed Tizoc too. He was good and kind to her, and she enjoyed him very much. But there was less intensity in her longing for him. In fact, thinking about Tizoc's attentions toward her awakened in her new understanding—an understanding about Brand.

Tizoc often looked at her with affection and longing. Now she realized that Brand's gaze toward her was similar. But only when he thought she did not notice him watching her. She realized, with a jolt, how blind she had been. Blind to Brand's feelings toward her and blind to her own toward him. She was astonished at how unaware she had been.

She began to long for the time when Brand would show his true feelings and not turn away. Then her world would be complete. Then she would have someone to love her who understood her, someone who would be her lover and her friend.

She was flush with excitement when the travelers returned. She hoped fervently that she could influence Brand to see her as more than a student. She knew he felt something for her. *Something.*

When Brand returned from Cholollan, he immediately continued with his teaching. He was more than pleased that his little flock was growing. He thanked God for it. He began to teach at different places and at different times of the day, so more people might hear of God and come to believe.

Kathleen watched him closely. Brand loved her; she was sure of it. Yet even after such a long absence, there was no change in how he acted toward her—always controlled.

Tizoc treated her as he always did—with devotion and affection barely contained.

Days and then weeks passed. Kathleen prayed for a word, a gesture, some sign from Brand. It was by the river, very late one afternoon, when she finally received her wish.

Purple and gold shadows of twilight had just begun to tint the waters. The lesson of the day had been shared with the small band of followers, and the murmurs of the final prayers had ended.

Kathleen was there, as was Tonauac. Cuetzpali had attended, as did some of the court dwarfs and Xicotencatl, despite his inability to keep still during the lesson. A trio of astronomers had also come that day. A little cluster of cleaners, the men and women who each day collected human waste in the city, stood to the side. Though Brand welcomed them and encouraged them to come near, they would not. They knew their place and would not dare to come closer.

Many women were present as well, though several had already started the walk back to their homes. Izel was there with Tlazohtlaloni, her eyes watching so that if he wandered, it was never toward the river.

"Tell me, Father Brand, why have you never married?" asked Izel as she and Kathleen gathered up their belongings—a water flask, small reed mats for sitting, and a small basket of leftover tlaxcalli disks.

Brand opened his mouth as if to reply, then immediately closed it, as if rethinking his words. After a pause, he responded. "I had thought of taking a wife when I was very young. But I made a solemn promise to my teacher and leader that I would know no woman and take no wife for all my life."

"But *why*, Father Brand?" Izel persisted.

It was simply incomprehensible to her—and to many—that a man such as Brand would not have a wife or even an occasional woman to warm his bed at night.

Brand recalled that day back in England, when he made the promise to be celibate. How could he explain to these people the complex reasons why that had happened? Sometimes he did not fully understand it himself. He left it as a mystery of God. Yet he would never break that oath. He had been taught from childhood that a man's oath was unbreakable. His foster father, Rolf, had made that clear. But Brand was a long way from Hedeby now.

So Brand said simply, "Because it was a promise I made to make myself a better servant for the work of God."

But the questions would not stop.

Cuetzpali, who never missed a chance to stand near Brand's conversations, interjected, "Surely, Father Brand, it would be better if you would take a wife. Marriage is important for every man."

Brand sighed inwardly and searched his mind for a way to finally end the relentless questions.

"Well, someday I may marry."

Without realizing, Kathleen leaned in.

Brand continued, "But that will be when the *elote* plant sheds chili peppers, when one can cross a river with dry sandals, when hummingbirds grow beards, and when the sun rises in the west!"

Everyone chuckled at this outrageous declaration, then prepared to depart for the evening.

Kathleen had understood most of these words. Upon hearing them, she could no longer bear it. She suddenly rushed off into the deeper darkness of the riverbank trees.

Izel noted, "She has not been herself lately."

"I will go to her and make sure she is all right," Brand said reassuringly.

The rest of the group drifted off, eager to be back in their homes before dark. Cuetzpali lingered as the little assembly disbursed. Brand hurried after Kathleen, calling her name.

Finally, Brand caught up with her. They stood close together in an isolated glade in the waning sunlight. The full moon was just beginning to rise. They spoke in the language of their homeland.

Kathleen wasted no time. "We are alone here in this strange land. Why do you say you can never marry? I need you. You need me. Sometimes I think you love me. You have never said the words, but I feel it. Can you deny it?"

Standing so close to her, he felt the emotion of her words. A part of him wanted to walk away. But he did not move. Despite the stirring of feeling her words evoked, he would not answer her directly. "Kathleen, if you feel I love you, it is as a priest, not as a man. You must never think of me romantically."

"I do not believe you!" she replied, her hands wild with frustration and her voice rising in anguish.

Brand looked away for a moment. When he answered, he tried to keep his voice from wavering. "I have made a vow, a vow to my bishop. I cannot break it. If ever I would break this vow, I would no longer be a man, no longer be worthy of respect from anyone. I could not live with that."

"Yes, I know," said Kathleen, hearing but not accepting. "I know you made a vow. But that was long ago, in a faraway place. We are here now, and we will never leave. I am alone. I have to survive. I promised my father I would survive and have children." Her cheeks flushed a bright pink. She grabbed both his hands and held them. "And I *know* you love me! You love me as a man loves a woman."

She laid her head on his shoulder. He did not move away. He could feel each breath, fast and warm on his skin. The closeness overwhelmed his senses. Something deep in his soul broke. Or maybe it opened. He put his arms around her.

She could feel the warmth of his body and the pounding of his heart. Without a word, he moved his face closer to hers and kissed her cheek. She shivered as she felt his beard, surprisingly soft on her skin. Then his lips moved down to her neck, and he lingered there for a moment. Then, again without a word, he stopped and looked deep into her eyes.

Her heart and mind swirled. Was this a dream?

He held her head in his hands and tipped her face up to his.

"Oh, Kathleen, you are so beautiful."

He kissed her on her waiting mouth, then spoke words neither of them would ever forget.

"Yes. Yes, it is true. I dreamed you before I ever knew you. Kathleen, I love you."

He kissed her again, with all the passion he had kept hidden for so long. For an instant, Kathleen felt as if she might faint. She eagerly kissed him back. Emotions swept over them, like the powerful currents of the northern seas. At last, at last, both of them could express what had so long been contained.

Kathleen was about to speak, to profess her love to him. But as quickly as the kiss had begun, it abruptly stopped. Brand pulled away from her.

"I cannot do this."

"Why?" she demanded, her eyes wild with bewilderment. "You said you love me. Why can you not love me as a woman?"

"Kathleen. Kathleen, I was wrong to say that." His eyes were glossy with frustration. He looked up into the sky in desperation. "I wish I could make you understand."

"Your honor is more important than love?" she asked, disbelieving.

Brand did not reply, but she knew his answer.

Kathleen's breathing began to slow, but her heart still pounded. "And you and I—we can never be together as husband and wife?" she asked, waiting for some glimmer of hope.

"No, Kathleen. Never." He looked deep into her eyes and took her hands in his. "It just cannot be."

"But—" she pleaded, her heart breaking.

His voice was quiet and low as he tried to control the agony. "No, Kathleen, it cannot be."

She was very, very still. They stood only a few feet from one another, but it might as well have been an ocean. Then she turned her back on him and walked away.

Brand stood alone, his hands empty.

Nearby, the river waters quietly splashed and gurgled in a relentless flow. The silence was broken by an owl hooting softly, calling for a mate. It was Chalchiuhtecolotl, Precious Owl, the messenger of Tezcatlipoca.

Kathleen walked very slowly back to her living quarters, not noticing anything around her. She did not even notice Brand following from a distance, to ensure she was safe. Her mind whirled. Her body shook with adrenalin.

One thing she knew: Brand did love her! Yet because of his vow, he seemed able to control those feelings—or nearly so. It would be useless to seek any relationship with physical love between them.

Well, she thought, *if he can control his emotions, then so can I!*

If Brand could force himself to turn away from his true feelings, then she would also use her will to rule her emotions. She knew Tizoc wanted her. She was fond of him. She would *make* herself love Tizoc. It would be as simple as that.

When Kathleen returned to her quarters, Izel found her. "What is wrong? Why did you run away? You look like you have been crying."

"I am all right," said Kathleen, although she did not seem so.

"Very well," said Izel, gently rubbing Kathleen's back.

Izel knew that something had happened. She would figure it out. She always did.

The following morning, Cuetzpali was unable to contain himself. He could not wait until his appointed meeting time with Toveyo and General Yaotl. He had much to reveal about the scene he had observed the night before. He went to General Yaotl's family compound and insisted to meet. *Immediately.* When he was allowed entrance, Cuetzpali barged into the room, barely stopping to bow.

Toveyo and Yaotl were eating a late-morning meal. There were plates of colorful fruits of every kind. The general also had before him a platter of tlaxcalli disks filled with fried turkey eggs and an aromatic salsa made with chilies and tomatoes.

"Why have you insisted on meeting with us?" demanded Toveyo, sipping on a frothy cup of the bitter cacao beverage.

The general too chimed in. "Yes, why? What is so important?"

Cuetzpali wanted to increase the drama. He scanned the fruit platter for the choicest morsel and placed it in his mouth. He slowly chewed and smiled at its sweetness.

"Last night, by the river, I saw something. I know the weakness of the man who calls himself 'Father.' With it, we can destroy him."

At these words, Toveyo put down his cup and the general stopped chewing.

CHAPTER TWENTY-THREE

SEVERAL UNEASY DAYS PASSED. BRAND and Kathleen often successfully avoided one another. When they could not, they were civil. But their eyes hardly ever met, and if they did, they would quickly dart away, like startled birds.

One sultry night, Kathleen was sitting in the patio area, watching the other girls. The women were dancing to amuse themselves. They improvised new steps and poses with much enthusiasm and laughter. They tried to draw her in, but she declined. In the midst of the festivities, Izel approached her.

"Tizoc is waiting. He has asked to see you. What shall I tell him?"

It was unusual for Tizoc to see Kathleen in the evening. Izel was unsure of Kathleen's reply.

Kathleen did not hesitate. She spoke very deliberately. "Tell Tizoc I will see him."

Normally, such privacy and familiarity would not be allowed between a young man and a young woman. But Izel permitted it, within reason. She knew of Tizoc's love for Kathleen, and she was glad of it.

By the time Kathleen met with Tizoc in the outer patio, the moon was high in the sky. It was bright and round and framed by misty clouds that moved mysteriously across its face.

As soon as he saw her, Tizoc's face broke into a smile.

"Kathleen!" He spoke with simple words, so she would understand him. "I must speak with you. It is important."

"Yes, Tizoc. What is it?"

She approached him and lightly touched the top of his hand. With all his yearning for her, it seemed as if a tiny bolt of lightning had leapt from the tip of her fingers to Tizoc's waiting skin.

He leaned in to kiss her. She did not move or turn away. His kiss was warm on her lips. She decided not to think or analyze. She just fell into his arms. It was not anything like the electrifying embrace with Brand, but it was not unpleasant.

After the kiss, Tizoc looked directly into her eyes.

"I love you. I will love you forever and protect you and stay with you always."

Then he asked the question Kathleen knew was coming.

"Will you be my wife?"

Once again, Kathleen gathered her resolve. If Brand could tame and control and repress what he felt, so could she! *Yes*, she thought, *I can make myself love this man.*

"Yes, Tizoc, I will be your wife."

Tizoc did not notice that her answer was flat—forced, even. His face broke into a broad smile. He could barely contain his joy. He kissed her face, her lips, over and over.

"But first you must become a follower of Jesu," she added, pushing him slightly away.

"Yes, I will be a follower," he answered without hesitation.

"Are you *sure*?"

"Yes, Kathleen. Your god shall be my god." Tizoc embraced her, his whole body filled with happiness. "Shall I go to Father Brand?"

"Yes, Tizoc." Again, her voice was flat, without emotion.

Again, he did not notice. He kissed her again. She gave him a faint smile.

"I will go to him tomorrow," he said.

In the normal course of things, Toltecan parents arranged marriages, sometimes for economic or political considerations. Their children were expected to follow the decisions. These resulted in practical unions not known for passion. But many people knew of great loves that resulted in long and happy marriages as well.

Since Kathleen had no father, Tizoc went to Brand the following morning. He knew Father Brand and Kathleen were close. How could it be otherwise? And sometimes, he wondered what the depth of their feelings might be. But he put it aside and never let his mind wander there for long.

"Father Brand, I have asked Kathleen to marry me."

Brand waited for what was to come next.

"She said yes," said Tizoc, his voice slightly raised in excitement.

Brand tried hard to not feel a sting. After all, what could he expect of Kathleen after their conversation by the river? He knew Tizoc had been enamored of Kathleen every day since he first set eyes on her. It had been a source of internal conflict for Brand. All too frequently, jealously had slithered like a silent snake into Brand's heart. Now he longed to feel happiness for Tizoc—or at least feel nothing.

Tizoc took note of Brand's failure to react to this news. He attributed it to the fact that it was so sudden. And that Brand was a holy man.

"I can only marry persons who have been baptized in the White Kristr faith."

"Yes, I know," said Tizoc. "Kathleen too has said she will only marry a follower of Jesu. I am ready to accept her god as my own. Her god will be my god."

Brand recalled the story of Ruth from the scriptures he had studied and copied back in Winchester. Tizoc's words were nearly the same as Ruth's.

Tizoc continued, "I want to be baptized as soon as possible."

"You know you have only begun to learn the good news of the Gospel."

"I know." Tizoc put his hand on his forehead, as if to help in solving this obstacle. Then he asked, "Is there any way that does not involve waiting? Could I not be baptized once now so the marriage can proceed, and then again, after I have had more instruction?"

"We must honor the rite, and there is only one baptism." Brand could see and feel Tizoc's earnest desire. He continued with a theological explanation to help him. "But the baptism is not based on your understanding of God; it comes from the goodness of God. You can be baptized, even with your limited knowledge of the True God. After you have received the sacrament of the water, you must still continue learning to be a true follower of Jesu."

"Yes, yes—I will do whatever is required."

Brand assumed the conversation had ended, but he sensed Tizoc had something more to say.

"Is there something else on your mind, Tizoc?"

A nod was the reply.

"What is it?"

"I need . . . I need your help. Will you help me with a gift for Kathleen?"

CHAPTER TWENTY-FOUR

"W HAT KIND OF A GIFT?" asked Brand, not at all sure where this was leading.

"I have created a poem for her," said Tizoc. "But my language is too difficult for her, and I do not know how to speak the words of her language. As I speak it, can you write it—in the language she understands? Can you write, using the *feeling words*, for me?"

Brand was surprised at this revelation. Brand pondered how many other people now knew something of the Latin alphabet.

"How do you know about the feeling words?"

"Nenetl told me. She thought it was a game, but I understood the power in the little circles and lines."

Brand had never imagined such a request. He was uncertain how to respond.

"It is very important," Tizoc added, waiting for Brand's reply.

"Why is this so important?"

"*Why*, Father?" said Tizoc. He hesitated. "Father Brand, is it true that I can tell you anything and that you will not tell anyone what you hear?"

"Yes, that is true."

Tizoc placed two fingers on his lips, thinking before he replied to Brand's question. When he did speak, it was in a very quiet voice.

"I fear."

Brand heard the words but did not fully comprehend. What could this young man, famous and admired by so many, have to fear?

"I do not understand, Tizoc. What do you mean?"

The next words came with difficulty for Tizoc. "I fear she does not love me as much as I love her. But if I write her a poem of my love for her, maybe her heart will grow more warm to me."

Once again, it took a few seconds for the meaning of Tizoc's words to register. Tizoc's revelation took courage; it was not what Brand would ever have imagined. And more, Tizoc was doing the very thing Brand would have wanted to do: openly tell Kathleen of his love for her in a poem.

After a moment, though, Brand had only one thought: *What can I do to help Kathleen have a full and abundant life?*

"Yes, I will help you," answered the priest.

He got up and retrieved a small sheaf of maguey fiber paper along with a turkey quill and a clay bottle of charcoal ink from a wooden storage box. Brand took the quill in hand and dipped it into the black liquid. He sat, quill poised, prepared to write words he could never express except through another man's love letter to the woman both of them loved.

"I am ready," Brand said.

Tizoc had committed his message to memory. He closed his eyes and began to dictate his poem. He spoke slowly and repeated so Brand could turn the Nahuatl to Latin and then write the letters onto the paper leaves.

At times, Brand's hand shook. Each word was a dart in his aching heart. It was extraordinary, intimate, sensual, and confessional. Brand likened it instantly to mansǫngr, the secretive but powerful poetry of a young Norseman in love.

For a moment, Brand wondered if such poetry was unseemly and if as a priest he should refuse to participate. But then he remembered some of the poetry in the sacred texts. He recalled the Song of Solomon, with "Let him kiss me with the kisses of his mouth"—words of one lover to another.

Several times, Brand asked Tizoc to wait while he composed the letters and composed his emotions. But Brand continued through it. Tizoc waited as Brand completed that last of the mysterious symbols.

Brand silently read through the poem. Tears threatened to spill from his lashes.

I want to make you feel like a woman,
desired
and
that you feel my love
every minute of your life.
You made me fall in love with you.
You make me feel
what love is.
I would like to be with you,
see you, feel you, love you
by touching your face, your lips,
your eyes.
I want to
fill you with kisses,
caress your hair,
look into your eyes,
deeply,
and be together,
one next to the other,
to feel you profoundly
in your sky-blue eyes and
love you, love you
to give you all my love
and to receive it,
to feel it,
also from you.

When he finished, Brand took a moment and composed himself once more.

"It is very beautiful," he said to Tizoc.

"Thank you! Thank you, Father Brand. Will she understand the marks and what my message is to her?" Tizoc asked hopefully.

"Yes, Tizoc, I believe she will understand," said Brand, handing the precious leaves of paper to the author of the love poem.

CHAPTER TWENTY-FIVE

Immediately after the meeting with Brand, Tizoc went to Kathleen. He greeted her as he always did now, with an embrace and kisses that warmed them both. He handed her the leaves of paper.

"What is this? she asked, looking down at the rows of Latin letters.

"A poem. For you," said Tizoc expectantly.

A poem? she wondered. She had never seen a poem written down. Brand had told her that some parts of the Holy Scriptures were like poetry. All the poetry she knew was oral, such as the recitations of the clever court skalds in the great halls back home. Or the poetry spoken by Jórunn the Poet Maiden, the almond-eyed woman with the beautiful voice.

Tizoc saw the confusion on her face and explained. "Yes, I want you to read the poem first, so you understand. Then I will speak it to you."

Kathleen began to read, slowly, as she sought to understand the message. After she deciphered the first few words, she stopped.

"You wrote this?"

"I wrote it," Tizoc answered. Again he said, "For you."

"But you do not know how to communicate using the lines and circles."

"Yes, that is true. Father Brand helped me. I said the poem, and he wrote the words using the special symbols. That way you can read it and be reminded of my love always."

"I see," said Kathleen. She thought about the effort this process must have exacted on Brand. "Thank you."

Tizoc took the papers and placed them on a table. He drew her close to him. She placed her head on his shoulder. He began to recite. Kathleen listened to each word—all the while longing for it to be Brand's poem, not the poem of the beautiful and earnest young man who embraced her.

When Tizoc left her, he did not leave the compound. He went instead to visit with Izel. She was glad to see him. She had been thinking much about Tizoc and Kathleen. Izel was sure the marriage would not be easy. But then, she knew Tizoc loved Kathleen, and she knew Kathleen needed to be loved.

"Izel, I have a question," Tizoc said somewhat awkwardly. "About something that concerns women."

"What is it, Tizoc?"

"I want to know what pleases them." For all his notoriety and skill as an athlete, Tizoc had little experience with women.

Izel arched one eyebrow. "What do you mean, 'pleases them'?" she asked, knowing full well what he meant.

"How they like to be . . . touched."

"I see." Izel smiled to herself. She was enjoying Tizoc's slight discomfort.

"For my bride," Tizoc continued. "For Kathleen. I know what feels good to me, but I want to know how to please Kathleen."

"There are many priestesses who are highly trained in such things, as you know. They would be happy to show you what to do."

"No, I do not want that," he said with an emphatic wave of his hand.

"All right, Tizoc. Come closer. I will tell you the two things to remember when you are with her."

One month later, a small group gathered at a place about half an hour's walk from the city. It was a secret gathering, so people did not come together. They came alone or in groups of two or three. Kathleen had come with Nenetl. Izel and Tlazohtlaloni walked together, as had Tonauac and Brand. Tizoc walked there alone. Patli refused to come to the ceremony.

Izel had suggested the location. There was a small building for shelter and a garden area where a few dahlias struggled to bloom. Both the building and garden were in considerable disrepair. The place had been abandoned some years earlier, when the followers of Tezcatlipoca had said it was a cursed. People avoided it, for it was widely believed that evil spirits lived there. Yet even in its overgrown and untended state, it still held a quiet beauty.

Brand began the ceremony with prayers of thanksgiving and blessing. Izel had been secretly baptized some time before, so she acted as sponsor for Tizoc.

"Are you ready to be baptized?" asked Brand.

"Yes," said Tizoc.

"And do you declare your faith in the One True God and renounce all other gods?"

"I renounce them."

"Your new name will be Adam, for the first man of creation. And because you are the first man I have baptized here in Tollan."

Brand continued with the ceremony: "Tizoc, I baptize you Adam, *in nomine Patris*"—one scoop of water was sprinkled on Tizoc's bowed forehead—"*et Filii*"—another sprinkling of water—"*et Spiritus Sancti.*" More water, then the sign of the cross.

"Tizoc, your eternal life has begun," said Brand.

He smiled. He was always very happy at baptisms, and this moment was no different. It was the next ritual that he was dreading.

Immediately after the baptism came the marriage ceremony. Brand had prepared himself for this moment. And now that it had arrived, he could only get through it by focusing all his mind and emotions on his role as priest. Kathleen and Tizoc stood before him now, waiting to be made husband and wife.

The bride wore her mother's cross, the pendant Brand had seen so many times around her throat, the pendant that meant so much to her. Izel had carefully embroidered the hem of Kathleen's dress using a cactus-spine needle and brightly colored thread. She had incorporated the geometric patterns that appeared on so many stone buildings in Tollan. Then she added many tiny crosses.

Izel stood next to Kathleen, and Tonauac stood solemnly next to Tizoc. Tlazohtlaloni and Nenetl watched from the side, excited to be present at the special occasion.

Brand began with invocation to God, then proceeded to the vows.

"Tizoc, do you receive this woman as your wife? Do you promise before God and these witnesses to love her and care for her, and only her, for all of your life?"

"I receive her as mine." Tizoc's eyes shown with emotion.

Brand turned to Kathleen. "Kathleen, do you receive this man as your husband? Do you promise before God and these witnesses to love him and care for him, and only him, for all your life?"

Kathleen looked at Brand for the last time as an unmarried woman. She knew what she had to do. She would be a good and loyal wife to Tizoc, no matter what her feelings for another.

Brand waited, then everyone heard Kathleen's words of promise to Tizoc. "I receive him as mine."

"Please kneel for the blessing," Brand instructed the couple.

Tizoc took Kathleen's hand and helped her down to her knees. He knelt beside her, in front of Brand.

"May almighty God, the Creator of all that is, bless this union." Brand made the sign of the cross over them. "Let us pray together the Pater Noster."

Brand led the prayer, along with Kathleen, with Tonauac and Izel saying a few words, and Tizoc understanding nothing at all.

Brand left immediately after the ceremony. Walking alone, he used the time to settle his mind and the feelings that still overwhelmed him whenever he thought of Kathleen.

While the couple waited, Izel and Nenetl carefully swept an empty, roofless room free of debris and any biting thing that may have lived there. They made a small bed—a thick layer of sweet grasses and fragrant leaves covered with cotton blankets and small pillows they had carried there. Red dahlias were cut and strewn on the cotton, punctuating the whiteness of the sleeping place.

Finally, the couple was alone. The sun was just beginning to settle into the west, creating an orange and turquoise sky.

Tizoc took off his mantle and placed it over the bower. He held out his hand to Kathleen in invitation. He looked deep, deep into her eyes, as if he were seeing her for the first time. Her eyes seemed so blue to him, eyes the color of a passionate, tempestuous sea.

He was so overcome with emotion, and his body so ready to express his love, that he almost forgot the advice from Izel. It was simple: *ask her, go slow.*

He stood close, facing his bride. He began by stroking Kathleen's hair and caressing her shoulders. He traced the outline of her eyebrows with his fingertips and kissed her eyelids.

She pushed her dress to the side of her shoulder and let it slide down to her feet. He licked her nipples and breasts, surprised and pleased at the sweet and salty taste of her skin. He tenderly nipped her lips with his white teeth. He would have devoured her if he could, so anxious he was to commune with her, unite with her, and become one with her. His heart was pounding.

"I will try not to hurt you."

"You will not hurt me."

She lay down on the soft bed and pulled him down to her.

He touched her secret places gently, tenderly. "Like that, Kathleen?" he asked. "Like this? *Yuhquin?* And this?"

Yes, she said without words. *Quema. Yes.*

Yes, and again, *yes.*

He was intoxicated with her scent, her woman's perfume. Kathleen entwined her limbs around him. He felt surrounded by love in the most unimaginable way. She was his. At last, she was *his.* And he was *hers.*

Kathleen knew she had started a new life; there was no turning back. She had made her decision. She would love this man, love him with as much of her heart as possible, for as long as they lived.

Together they moved and arched their bodies, delirious with joy, until they reached the precipice and tumbled down into a valley of complete surrender. It was a long time before the two closed their eyes, shortly before the rays of morning penetrated the dark, sweet, and cool air that blessed their marriage bed.

CHAPTER TWENTY-SIX

LIFE SETTLED INTO SOMEWHAT OF a routine after the secret marriage. Tizoc and Kathleen met whenever they could, and Izel contrived to give them privacy as much as possible. Izel had become Nenetl's primary caretaker. The little girl adored Tizoc, and now she had innocent Tlazohtlaloni as a "brother" as well. And Kathleen loved Nenetl nearly as much as Tizoc did.

Brand and Tonauac continued with their efforts to know and understand each other. Tonauac watched Brand closely, more closely than Brand knew. Tonauac understood more than ever Brand's commitment to be a servant of his god—he understood the enormity of Brand's sacrifice. And after much meditation, he decided now was the time to speak to Brand about a powerful practice that would bring him closer to the people.

"Father Brand, you want to understand the people of Tollan, do you not?"

"Yes, Tonauac, of course. God has brought me here to this place, to these people, to be a servant to them. The more I understand, the better I can serve."

"Then you must partake of teonanácatl; you must eat of the flesh of the gods. You cannot truly understand us unless you have eaten the special mushrooms."

Brand gently raised his hand as if to prevent the conversation from continuing. "Tonauac," he replied, "you know I believe there is but one god—"

"Yes," interjected Tonauac, "in three persons. I know."

"And we eat the Body and drink the Blood of Christ in remembrance of his sacrifice for our sins. That is our ceremony. It is called Eucharist."

"Yes, Father Brand, I understand. But the partaking of teonanácatl will bring you closer to understanding the spirit of the people of Tollan. You will see and feel powerful visions."

Brand remembered the amanita mushrooms the berserkers used.

"I know of some people in my land, soldiers who serve whichever king pays them the most," he said. "They eat certain mushrooms. They gain no understanding. Rather, they become fierce and violent and fear nothing."

"No, Father Brand. That is not how teonanácatl affects us. However, you must be properly prepared. You must not partake of it as do some of the nobles, who use it for mere recreation. You must be prepared and have a guide. I will guide you."

"I use the practice of prayer and fasting to be closer to God," Brand said flatly.

Tonauac's jaw was also set. "Father Brand, again I say, if you are to understand us, you must partake of this ceremony. Then his face softened. "But only if you are prepared. Let me know when you are ready."

Tonauac did not bring up the subject again.

Another cycle of the moon passed. Often, after his prayers, Brand did think about the special mushrooms. He wished he were not so alone in this strange land. There was no bishop to advise him, no other priests who could share their personal insight. Would they say using these mushrooms was demonic?

Brand knew—clearly—that many practices in Tollan had to be regarded as evil. But was it not also true that evil was everywhere? He had seen it in Bergen, on the voyage to Rome, and in Greenland. Everywhere, really.

He pondered how, other than himself, no one had ever told the people of Tollan to turn away from evil. No one to tell them of the Gospel and the redemptive love of Christ for all people, as he so much wanted to do.

And now Kathleen was married. He often thought of those few moments with her by the river. He knew he had done the right thing. And yet—and yet—he could not think of his decision without a pang of regret. He prayed that someday he would have true peace.

Now, his time with her would become more limited. Now he could devote all of himself in service to the people. He decided Tonauac was right: to serve the people, he needed to understand them.

Within days, he and Tonauac began preparations.

"You may see the past. You may see the future. But," Tonauac warned, "it is not always possible to predict what will ensue after the mushrooms are eaten."

Despite this, Brand was determined to continue. They both fasted and prayed so that whatever happened, the ceremony would bring them insight and blessing.

They met one evening in Tonauac's room, where other priests of Quetzalcoatl could watch over them and keep them from any harm. The space was dimly lit and quiet.

They sat facing each other on soft cotton cushions. Tonauac prepared the mushrooms and poured honey over them. He carefully considered the amount to give to Brand. Too little, and the desired insight may never come. Too much, and Brand might never recover from its effects. He offered a small plate to Brand.

"May it please God," said Brand, taking the morsel and chewing it well before swallowing.

They sat together in stillness. After about twenty minutes, Brand began to feel the effects of the mushrooms. He felt a numbness, especially in his face. His heart began to beat faster, and his pupils dilated. Then he began to see visions. Brilliant, vivid colors swirled before him, unlike anything he had ever seen or could even describe. He rose to his feet and stood for a long time, his eyes open and transfixed on the immense beauty he beheld.

Then the visions changed. He began to perceive images he recognized. He saw serpents, but they were not frightening. He saw the seductive serpent of the Garden of Eden, which urged disobedience to God. It contrasted with the vision of the healing serpent of Moses, held high above the wandering Hebrew people.

Then once again, the images changed. The snakes became long lines of swirling strands, strings of information strung like pearls on a necklace of life. In his trance, Brand was looking into the deep act of creation, where strands of genetic material twisted like snakes in the beginning of all beginning.

Twice Tonauac reached out his right hand to Brand, seeking contact with his fingers in friendly greeting across the chasm of the language barrier, across the chasm of separateness, across the chasm of misunderstanding.

Then Brand lowered himself to the floor and slept. Several hours later he awoke. Tonauac was there, waiting.

"What did you see?"

"I saw many things I have not seen before," said Brand. "I saw snakes who speak to us though they have no voice. Snakes who move silently on the surface of the earth though they have no legs, no feet. And those who fly in our dreams though they have no wings."

Tonauac only nodded, his eyes bright. He had been right. The flesh of the gods had given Brand insight. Now Brand understood why the image of Quetzalcoatl, the improbable plumed serpent, was carved everywhere. Now he knew why the people kept this vision in their hearts and minds.

CHAPTER TWENTY-SEVEN

TOVEYO AND GENERAL YAOTL WERE most anxious to meet with King Huemac. They had been instructed to wait in the outer hall. The general sat while Toveyo drummed his fingers on a stone bench and periodically paced. They were surrounded by bas-relief carvings of serpents and humans in ferocious death scenes. This was the place where military strength was most concentrated into symbolic form.

For some time, the king had been away from the city, preoccupied with military affairs both strategic and defensive. Anything not directly related to these matters was deferred. Finally, they were granted an audience.

"King Huemac," began the general, "we are very concerned about what is happening with the man called Father Brand. There is a group of people who follow him as a teacher, and the group is growing larger."

Before he spoke, furrows of annoyance already appeared between the ruler's tired eyes. "Yes, I have heard that he has followers," the king replied. "But they are widows and others of little consequence."

"That is true, King Huemac. But there is more," said the general.

"He is teaching about a new god," Toveyo interjected.

Huemac rolled his eyes. "We have many lesser gods. What difference will this god make?"

This was not going well. Toveyo and General Yaotl both began to perspire though it was cool in the great room and the heat of the day was still hours away.

Toveyo continued. "King Huemac, the stranger is reciting poetry and songs from the marks on the pages he brought with him. But he is also teaching others to know what the marks mean. And Tonauac supports and conspires with him."

Now Huemac frowned. This allegation was disturbing. Knowledge of symbols was strictly limited to the scribes. This understanding had been passed from generation to generation. Even he, the king, did not understand all the scribes did.

"How do you know this?" Huemac asked.

"We have some people among the followers who help us understand, my king," said the general.

Of course, thought Huemac, *a general would always have spies in place.*

But before he could respond, Toveyo added the largest log to the growing fire of concerns.

"King Huemac, the man is conducting marriage ceremonies!"

"What do you mean?"

Huemac's face turned a reddish hue as Toveyo and Yaotl explained what had taken place in the abandoned compound. Marriages were arranged to perfect alliances, to strengthen power. The stranger's audacious decision to preside over marriage ceremonies was indeed dangerous.

"Yes, I agree this is a problem," said Huemac. He paused for reflection. "However, the people have begun to follow the stranger. Doing anything to him might provoke dissention. I have enough to contend with, with enemies all around us. I will do nothing, for now."

"But," asked Toveyo, "what if something should change? If the people no longer wanted the stranger to be their teacher? What if the people became angry with him? What then?"

King Huemac was uncertain what Toveyo meant. But he was tired and wanted to be done with this problem. "If the people turned against the stranger, he would be on his own. I would do nothing for him."

"So, may we take steps to stop the spread of the stranger's treasonous acts?" asked the general.

"Yes. But you must do nothing that the people would interpret as an act against him on my part. Other than that, do what you will to stop Tonauac and the stranger who dares defy our customs. But do not kill them."

King Huemac dismissed them with a slight nod of his head. They left his presence, backward on their knees, until they were sufficiently away from his sight.

Finally, the time for General Yaotl and Toveyo had come. The moment to put their plans into place had arrived. With the king's acquiescence, nothing would impede them now.

Soldiers under General Yaotl's command were immediately dispatched. They went first to Brand's quarters. Tonauc was there also.

The soldiers were large men. Six of them surrounded Brand, their faces and bodies fierce.

"What are you doing here?" Brand asked in alarm.

"You are hereby ordered: you may not leave these quarters for any reason."

"Ordered by whom?" Tonauac demanded.

"By a high authority."

"What does the king say about this?"

"The king does not care."

Tonauac began to protest.

"Be silent!" the largest soldier barked.

Brand and Tonauac looked at one another in confusion.

"You are forbidden to conduct any more rituals or ceremonies. You may not meet with the people anymore. And you, Tonauac, you also are forbidden to leave the temple area."

Next they went to Kathleen. She was sitting, talking with Izel and a few other women. As soon as the soldiers appeared, the other women scattered.

The soldiers surrounded Kathleen.

"You are to come with us," ordered the large soldier, who grabbed her arms.

"You have no authority here!" Izel shouted.

But they laughed at her. They forcibly took Kathleen away, both women screaming and crying in distress.

"Tell Tizoc what has happened!" Kathleen cried out, her arms straining against the soldiers who half walked, half dragged her away.

"Do not worry. He will know soon enough," growled the soldier on her left.

Lastly, they went to Tizoc. He was on the ball field, getting ready for practice. Patli was the first to see the soldiers. Immediately, he was overcome with a great fear.

The captain of the soldiers marched up to Tizoc. "By order of General Yaotl, you are hereby ordered to stay within the city and not leave without permission, until further instructions," he said bluntly.

"What? What do you mean?" asked Tizoc, confused and alarmed.

"If you have any questions, take it up with the general." Then he added, to finish the conversation, "Or with Toveyo, priest of the almighty Tezcatlipoca."

CHAPTER TWENTY-EIGHT

A WEEK WENT BY. TIZOC was beside himself, haunted with thoughts of Kathleen. Brand was as well but dared not show just how much he too was sick with worry for her. He was no longer permitted to meet with his little flock, and he was also concerned for all of them.

Tizoc was allowed to move about within the city. One afternoon, he went to the compound where Brand had been ordered to stay. Brand was pleased to see the athlete. They greeted each other warmly. The stress of the situation showed on the face of each man—even in their voices.

"How are you, Tizoc?"

"I am well enough, Father Brand. But I have been ordered not to leave the city."

"And Kathleen?"

"She is in a small town about an hour's walk from here. I am told she is unharmed."

Such news was a relief to Brand, although he still keenly felt helpless.

"Father Brand, I cannot go to where Kathleen has been taken. I need your help again."

"What help can I give you?" asked the priest.

"I have another poem. Will you write the marks for me?"

"Another poem?"

"It is about dreams, Father Brand."

Brand thought of his own dreams, which had been chaotic and without meaning as of late. Yet there was one image Brand had dreamed of many recent nights. It was brief; just a dark-haired faceless person gazing into a reflection and laughing, laughing a maniacal laugh.

Tizoc continued, "I cannot be with Kathleen, but I want her to come to me in my dreams. I want to tell her about this."

Brand could not believe his ears. He remembered all those years when he had dreamed of Kathleen, even before he met her. And now Tizoc was yearning for her in his own dreams.

"But how will you get the poem to her?"

"I have made arrangements for someone to help me."

Brand did not hesitate any longer. "Yes, I will help you."

As they had done before, Tizoc recited his poem while Brand sat listening with his head and his heart, turning Tizoc's recitation into lines and circles to create the feeling words.

To Dream of You
My beloved, we are only separated by a physical distance.
Only that,
A physical distance.
I think about you so much.
I do not know what to do, but I think of you.
I think of how to please you, how to love you.
I think of how to make you feel good.
I think of how to make you happy.
I think of what we have together.
I would like to dream of you every night.
And in that way, be with you.
I would like you to be with me every night,
at my side, holding each other,
loving each other.
I would like to touch you, to love you, to give you all my love
and receive your sweet caresses.
Come to me in my dreams, my beloved.
I want to dream of you and be close to you.
And I know that they will be sweet dreams.
Yes . . . sweet dreams.

Brand finished the last of the words, blew gently on the pages to dry them, then handed them to Tizoc.

And the next day, a reluctant yet determined Patli walked to the place where Kathleen was imprisoned and left the poem with her.

CHAPTER TWENTY-NINE

ENTEHUA SAT IN FRONT OF her mirror of obsidian and stared at her reflection in the dark surface. Her hair was black and shiny, like the sheen on a crow's wing when the sun glints off it. She adjusted the silver and gold bracelets on her wrists, then turned her head to admire the jade earrings that swung above her perfectly shaped shoulders. She could see nothing but beauty.

But beauty was becoming impatient. She practically flung herself at Tizoc at every opportunity, yet he ignored her. She was ready to do whatever would be necessary to obtain her prize.

"Father," she said, entering General Yaotl's quarters without being summoned. She stood before him, head held high. "I must talk with you. I am ready to be married."

Such talk from a daughter was more than unusual; it was stunning. Girls and women usually lived, married, and died without anyone seriously caring about their feelings in the matter.

But Centehua was a force to be reckoned with. She had inherited all the flintiness and ferocity of a warrior. But for her gender, she would have been one, like her brothers. One by one, the general's sons had died or been killed. And now his wife had died too. How he wished she were still alive and able to deal with this strong-willed daughter.

"I know *who* you want to marry," said the general, "but I am not sure you are ready. Just to be clear with you, I will consent only to a marriage that brings favor to you and to the family."

"Yes, Father, I know. I have already consulted with the soothsayers and the keeper of the calendars. They say a marriage with Tizoc would be favorable and must be done within the week."

"Is this true?"

"Yes, it is true. You can check with Toveyo if you do not believe me," she said, slyly turning her face away so her father would not see the cunning in her eyes.

"But Centehua, everyone is aware that Tizoc is bewitched by the strange woman."

This comment caused immediate anger in the beautiful woman. But she feigned indifference.

"Yes, I have heard rumors. But they may be exaggerated. Perhaps he could be persuaded? For me, can you do this for me?"

"And if I do not, there will be no peace—is that it?"

"You must give me what I desire, Father. I know you can. Give me—what I desire."

He knew he indulged his daughter. In this manner, he felt he could still pamper his long-dead wife, whom he had truly loved. And he would have peace.

The next day, Tizoc was summoned to meet with the general. The aging military man sat in a small chair surrounded by three house slaves. With their faces fixed in a blank stare, they used woven palm fronds to cool him. He looked relaxed, and he casually stroked a white bird held loosely in his left hand.

Tizoc was wary.

"Why have you summoned me?"

"You know my daughter, Centehua."

Tizoc nodded. He had a general sense of the beautiful and vain woman, but he neither knew nor cared about her. He recalled Patli once saying she would be a good match for him.

The general continued, "I do not know why, but she is sick with love for you. She will not be quiet about it."

Now Tizoc was even more uneasy. "I do not understand."

"The soothsayers and astronomers say a marriage between you and my daughter would be highly favored. It would be to your advantage to follow this advice."

An emphatic "No!" burst from the young man's mouth.

"Tizoc, you have no family to object to this match. And do not think to go to King Huemac. I have already met with him, and he is in favor of this marriage."

"No! I will not do it."

"Yes, you will," said the general with finality.

"No!"

The general was quite sure his next statement would result in acquiescence from the stubborn athlete.

"If you ever want to play ball again, you must agree. If not, you will have a terrible accident. You will never play again. You will never again step foot on a ball court."

Ollama! It meant everything to Tizoc. It had been his life, since childhood. He knew nothing else. His teammates, the crowd, the thrill of competition, even the discipline of training. He believed he had many years ahead before age or injury would end his play on the field. What would his life be without the ball game?

But if he did not play again, at least he would have Kathleen. With her love, he could figure out a new way to live. He was just beginning to learn of her god. There was so much he wanted to learn about being a good husband. And he had help—Tonauac, Izel, and Father Brand. Together, with her, he would still have a life, even without ollama.

"No. Even if it means I will never play again," Tizoc said emphatically. "I will not marry Centehua."

General Yaotl looked down at the bird in his hand and gently stroked its feathers.

"I see," he said. "You would give up your precious game? I had not expected that." He paused. "And the strange woman—what do they call her?"

"Do not bring her into this!"

"She is important to you?"

"I said, leave her out of this!"

"And you would not want her to be harmed in any way?"

Tizoc did not answer this time. He only glared at the general.

"Even as we speak, she is surrounded by my soldiers, who will obey any order given to them."

Tizoc knew this was undoubtedly true and that he was helpless to change it. His mouth became dry, and sweat beaded on his forehead.

The general pressed on. "You will do as I say and marry my daughter. If you want the stranger woman . . . to . . . *live*."

As he spoke these words, the general tightly clutched the white bird in one hand. Before it could make a sound, he casually wrung its neck. The general said nothing more but slowly opened his hand so Tizoc could see the bird, limp and unmoving.

Tizoc looked away, as if he were searching for something far in the distance.

When he finally spoke, it was in a barely audible voice.

"Yes. Yes, I will do as you want."

CHAPTER THIRTY

C ENTEHUA HAD TOLD THE TRUTH about the astronomers. Within a week, a favorable day for the wedding was selected. The ceremony took place in the late afternoon at the general's home in the elite residential section of the city. Copal incense burned in every corner, and there was standing room only for the guests.

The bride and groom wore new clothing. As part of the ritual, a mantle so fine, so gossamer you could see through it, was placed across both their shoulders. The officiant tied the ends of the cloth around their shoulders and declared before the witnesses, "You are now married."

The ceremony was followed by a grand feast. A multitude of servants served steaming tamales. There were platters piled high with roasted venison and turkey, tlaxcalli of yellow and blue corn, and sauces delicately seasoned with chilies of every variety. Sweets were offered as well: *tlalcacahuatl*, or peanuts, mixed with amaranth and boiled honey, pressed down, cooled, and cut into little squares. Octli, the cactus wine normally permitted to a limited few, flowed like a milky river to anyone who wanted to taste and feel its effects.

From the general's house, the bride and groom walked to Tizoc's home, followed by the wedding revelers. Torches burned bright in the night as the procession, like a giant glowing serpent, lit up the darkness.

From the roof of his living quarters, Brand watched the spectacle as it moved through the city. He had been shocked when he first heard that the ceremony was to take place. Patli had come to him and explained the unexplainable. Brand understood that Tizoc had no choice. He was glad Kathleen was not there to see it.

Tonauac and Izel watched too. They had tried to give Tizoc some hope that somehow he could endure. Someday he and Kathleen would be together again, and this time of trial would merely be a distant memory. But Tizoc seemed unable to grasp their heartfelt words.

At last, the ceremony and feast ended. The revelers returned to their own homes, some of them staggering in the night.

Centehua and Tizoc were alone in the sleeping room of his compound. Tizoc sat, silent as the stony walls of the room.

Centehua ignored his mood.

"All the world knows now that we are married," she declared in triumph.

"My heart belongs to another, as you well know."

"Your so-called wife? That strange creature? Yes, I have heard about the ceremony." She threw her head back. "It means nothing!"

He stood up and turned away, unable to bear looking at her. She stood behind him and put her arms around his waist. He did not move but his body recoiled from her touch.

She seductively rubbed her cheek along his back and pressed her body into his. "Do not be this way, Tizoc," she cooed. "You can have a great life with me at your side. You have your ball game. All of your wants and wishes will be fulfilled."

He did not answer. That infuriated and emboldened her. She released her hold on him and faced him directly.

"Make love to me, Tizoc." It was an order, not a request.

He still did not answer or move. She changed tactics.

She walked to a small table, where orange pottery cups and a pitcher had been set. A whitish liquid had been poured into a cup.

"Drink this," she said, offering the cup. "It will help you feel more relaxed. Drink it."

Tizoc took the cup of thick liquid and drunk until the vessel was empty. It was octli. As an athlete, he normally would not drink it. But he knew the liquid could make people feel differently and sometimes help them forget the pain in their lives. His cheeks soon turned pink with the flush of alcohol.

Next she told him to take off his clothing. He would not do it, so she slowly removed each item and dropped it on the floor. He stood before her, every muscle exposed. She admired the shape of his shoulders, his lean torso, and his strong, athletic legs.

Again she repeated, "Make love to me, Tizoc."

He stood completely still.

"Make love to me or Kathleen dies."

In an instant, he could have fled the room—or broken her neck. But doing those things would not save Kathleen. He *would* save Kathleen.

She pulled him down next to her on the pillow-covered sleeping mat. She rubbed her hands along his torso. As soon as she did so, his body began to respond.

"See, you are not as faithful as you wish to be!" she cackled.

He tried and tried to stop his body from responding, but he could not. She began kissing his mouth, stroking him with her hand. She mounted him, and he felt his body react. He could not stop. Could not stop. All the while, his heart was dying within him. Finally, it was over.

"It did not take much to make you forget her!" Centehua laughed, rolling away.

But she was wrong. He did not forget Kathleen then or anytime later. He quickly got up from the bed and washed himself, disbelieving what had happened. He grabbed the octli container and filled his cup again. Then he emptied it in one long drink and prepared another.

CHAPTER THIRTY-ONE

ATLI WATCHED HELPLESSLY AS TIZOC began to drink all day, every day. Nothing he said or did could stop his childhood friend from living in an alcoholic haze. Patli wished he had never mentioned the name of Centehua to him. But even more, he wished he and Tizoc had never met the strangers they found on the beach.

Patli rose very early one morning, before the sun had even begun to rim the horizon with light. He needed to speak privately with Tizoc before he had a chance to drink the octli he had begun to crave.

When he entered Tizoc's living quarters, he found his friend sitting in the patio. The change in his appearance was so great that Patli could hardly find words. Tizoc's eyes were sunken and circled in dark shadows. Patli stared at his friend in pity.

Tizoc saw Patli but did not greet him.

"Tizoc, you are not well. I want to help you."

"There is no help for me," said Tizoc, his voice hollow.

"Perhaps you could speak with Father Brand? I have heard that he listens to people's problems and can help them feel better."

How Patli had come by this information, Tizoc could not fathom.

"No, Patli. I cannot speak of my situation with Father Brand. Not now. Not ever."

Patli knew he had to do something to help Tizoc, so he offered an idea. It was dangerous, but he was desperate for his friend. Desperate acts were required.

"Tizoc, I think I know a way for you to see Kathleen again."

At these words, Tizoc looked up at his friend, jolted into the possibility of seeing his beloved wife again.

"How? She is guarded constantly, and I am forbidden to leave the city!" There was anger, pain, and sorrow in every word from Tizoc's mouth.

"I have a plan."

It was not complicated, but it required audacity. Once he heard the plan, Tizoc did not waver. "Yes, I will try it. Anything to see her again."

They discussed a few more details, then Patli hurried away before he would be missed by the other physicians.

Patli wanted to execute the plan as soon as possible. But there was another visit he had to make. The next day, he made his way to Brand's compound. He found Brand on his knees, alone, saying morning prayers.

Sensing someone was there, Brand looked up, a surprised and quizzical tilt to his head. Patli had never come to this spot before, yet now he stood before him. Brand quickly got up, but before he could greet Patli or even speak, the visitor began his petition.

"Please, Father Brand," said Patli. "I have come to you for help—to ask you to pray to your god. Not for me. For someone else."

That Patli was there before him was surprise enough. But that he was asking for prayer was even more puzzling to Brand.

Patli explained the plan. Brand understood the risks but also understood why Tizoc needed to take them. Ever since he had heard of the forced ceremony, Brand had been trying to process what it meant to Tizoc, to Brand himself, and especially to Kathleen. He hoped she did not know the ritual had taken place.

After Patli left, Brand prayed. He prayed that Tizoc might be successful. He prayed that Tizoc could leave the city and not be recognized.

"Almighty and merciful God, you are our sun and our shield. I beseech you: give Tizoc the skill of a shape-changer, so that he may pass without incident among those who would injure or punish him."

The next morning, Patli and Tizoc met at a predetermined vacant house in the city. Tizoc took a winding route, looking around often to ensure he was not being followed. Patli dressed Tizoc in the manner of a doctor, with the proper mantle and medicine sacks. They began their trek, knowing that the most difficult part would be getting past the soldiers standing guard at the main road.

Perhaps it was the different garb. The soldiers had always seen Tizoc on the ball field, dressed in his regalia or protective gear. The doctor disguise may have been enough to make him unfamiliar. Or perhaps it *was* Brand's prayers—perhaps Tizoc had truly changed shape. Whatever happened, the soldiers did not recognize Tizoc!

Patli and Tizoc walked together, not speaking, until they were well past the city proper. Walking quickly now, Patli led Tizoc to the town where Kathleen was being detained at a compound. The men easily gained entry, for everyone granted access to medical doctors; to refuse would bring harm to one's own health.

They entered her room together.

"Patli!" she cried out, seeing him first. Then, "Tizoc!"

She ran to Tizoc, flinging herself into his arms, overwhelmed with joy. Kathleen stepped back and looked at Tizoc, alarmed at what she saw.

"Tizoc, what has happened to you?"

"It is nothing, my love. Only that I have longed to see you."

Tizoc opened one of the medicine sacks he carried and offered her a blood-red dahlia. She accepted it, tears in her eyes.

Patli left them alone for several hours. In those brief hours, Tizoc loved Kathleen exactly, *exactly* as he had wanted to in his dreams.

When Patli returned, Kathleen grabbed his hands and thanked him.

"I know you do not like me, Patli. But I am in your debt forever."

Patli said nothing except, "Tizoc, we must go now."

Tizoc put his arms around his wife and embraced her with all his being.

"Until I see you again, Tizoc," said Kathleen, not wanting to move an inch from her husband.

"Until I see you again, my love."

Tizoc moved toward the doorway of the room, his hand extended, keeping his fingertips on hers until the moment when they could touch no more.

Tizoc and Patli repeated their disguised journey several times. Though Tizoc's hours with Kathleen were joyous, each return to Tolland and to Centehua's web became more and more unbearable.

CHAPTER THIRTY-TWO

C ENTEHUA TRIED ON SIX NECKLACES in quick succession: some were made of delicate gold pendants shaped into exotic animals, some of coral, and some of black-veined turquoise. All were flung onto the floor.

She stared into the dark mirror. Normally, her eyebrows swooped out like the graceful curve of butterfly wings. But now they were pinched downward and inward in a scowl.

In the few months since her wedding ceremony, she realized her marriage to Tizoc would never be what she wanted. He consistently made excuses to be away from her. And when he was at home in their living quarters, he was so intoxicated that he could barely walk, let alone satisfy her.

There had to be a way to rid herself of him.

She went to Toveyo, and he suggested a plan that pleased them both. The game of ollama had been played for millennia in the sultry regions surrounding Tollan. Dozens of playing fields had been painstakingly built of stone.

Within days, Centehua and Toveyo met with a small group of select people. They had assembled at Tollan's second ball court, for, in fact, there were two ball courts in Tollan. They were very similar in size and shape. One tlachtli was used for the raucous sporting contests so beloved by the rowdy crowds. The other was used exclusively for ball games of the spirit world.

The spirit world ball game was nothing at all like the crowd-pleasing spectacles held on the other tlachtli. There were no shouting, uproarious spectators. Only priests and the highest of the elite were permitted to attend. And now, the ultimate internal conflict in Tollan would be decided. This game would be a contest between the followers of Quetzalcoatl and the followers of Tezcatlipoca—the eternal conflict between opposite spiritual powers.

King Huemac had selected the two teams and their captains. He had been influenced by Toveyo, who convinced him this game would solidify the king's power.

Now all was ready for the spirit world contest. Marigold petals were strewn over the ball court. The flower of death signaled that the field was now a place for spiritual conflict, not a tournament of athletic skill alone.

At the exact moment the spirit world game began, soldiers entered the room where Kathleen had been imprisoned.

What is happening now? she thought with fear.

"You are to return to Tollan. Immediately," a soldier ordered.

She was beside herself with joy. She quickly gathered up her belongings and placed them in a cotton sack for the walk back to Tollan. She adjusted her sandals so her steps could be fast and light. She was filled with hope that maybe, perhaps, she would see Tizoc and the others again.

As Kathleen prepared for her journey, the two teams at the tlachtli initiated their contest. There were few witnesses that day: only Centehua; her father; Tonauac, Toveyo, and other priest advisors; and the teams' doctors. Most of those present believed the gods watched as well.

There were no cheers, no shouts, no cries of defeat or victory that day. The game was not close. One team captain seemed to hold back. Or not. It was unclear to most. In any event, the winning team was decided before long.

The winning captain wore a headband decorated with a small obsidian mirror representing Tezcatlipoca. He wielded a new obsidian knife, its edge razor sharp. He approached the losing captain. The defeated man fell to his knees.

Tonauac, Toveyo, and the other priests watched intently as Tizoc knelt before the captain of the opposing team. Patli looked on helplessly from the sideline, his heart bursting within him. How it had come to this, he did not know. Perhaps Tizoc had been forced to play. Perhaps he had volunteered. Patli could do nothing but bear witness.

Tonauac wanted to shout, to scream. But all he could do was stare at Toveyo, whom he was sure was the source of all the pain. There had been no need for this contest, except an unchecked thirst for power.

Centehua watched as well, interested only in confirming that her mistake in marrying Tizoc would disappear and she would be free to continue her life as she would like.

Tizoc showed no fear, no regret. Patli was close enough to hear Tizoc's last words before the deadly blade flew through the air.

As soon as he was able to compose himself and slip away, Patli informed Brand of what had happened at the spirit ball court. It fell upon Brand to tell Kathleen.

The soldiers had returned Kathleen to the compound of the priestesses. She was convinced she would soon see Tizoc again. She was playing with Nenetl and Tlazohtlaloni, teaching them a little song from her own childhood. She looked up, eager and happy, as Brand entered. As soon as she saw his face, her smile disappeared. She stood up.

"What is it, Father Brand? Tell me!"

"I must speak to you alone."

The children slowly left the room, absorbing the ominous tone in Brand's voice despite his efforts to conceal it.

"Kathleen, you must sit down."

She sat down again, waiting, her hands clenching.

Brand struggled. "I have no words."

"Tell me!"

"Tizoc's life has been taken from him."

Blood drained from Kathleen's face. She became pale as death.

Still struggling, Brand reached for her hand and looked into her eyes.

"Kathleen, he did not suffer pain. And Patli has told me his last words were of you."

"Of me?" she said weakly, still in shock. "What did he say?"

"He said your name. He said, 'Kathleen, I will see you again, in the heaven of your god.'"

Brand tried his best to comfort Kathleen, just as he had when she lost her mother and then her father to death's command. The body of Tizoc was not released to them, so no funerary rites would be possible.

It was decided that Kathleen would tell Nenetl of the death of her brother. Nenetl sank into Kathleen's loving embrace and wept tears of utter grief and loss.

"Do not worry, little sister," said Kathleen. "I am here. I am with you."

Nenetl nestled in Kathleen's embrace. Both of them cried until at last blessed sleep came.

Brand wanted to help Kathleen in her sorrow, but his words felt hollow. All he could do was remind her that Tizoc's last words were pro-phetic—she would see Tizoc again in heaven. But most of the time, he just sat with Kathleen in silence.

Brand sank deeper and deeper into his own despair, something new to him. Even the reading of the Psalms could not relieve his sadness.

His only comfort was the thought that, surely, nothing worse could happen to him and to Kathleen.

CHAPTER THIRTY-THREE

IMMEDIATELY FOLLOWING TIZOC'S DEATH, THE air was heavy with grief. It was as if no one could breathe. Kathleen recalled the few brief hours she had spent with Tizoc only a few days before his death. Now she was in deep mourning. Her sorrow was nearly matched by that of Nenetl, Patli, and Tonauac.

Brand struggled greatly. His teachers in Winchester had instructed him that suffering was a way to grow closer to Christ. But this was overwhelming. Tizoc had been Kathleen's husband for such a brief time and now he was suddenly gone. Brand knew he should comfort Kathleen, yet when he thought of her, the old conflicted emotions came flooding back.

Brand would not leave his sleeping room. Tonauac and others encouraged him to eat and drink and to sit in the sunshine, but he preferred the darkness. Brand's eyes were sunken. Dark shadows framed the skin under his eyes.

He was sitting alone, on a sleeping mat, trying to remember the verses of hope he had once known so well. Verses he needed for Kathleen—and for himself.

A voice coming from the other side of the curtained doorway surprised him.

"Father Brand?"

Brand recognized the voice. It was Cuetzpali.

"May I enter?"

Brand had no desire to see anyone, not even one of his followers. But he had no will to argue with the visitor.

"Yes, you may come in," he said wearily.

Cuetzpali, curiously, did not react to Brand's greatly changed appearance.

"I have heard you are ill. I have come to cheer you," he said, plopping down on a cushion next to Brand.

"Thank you, Cuetzpali. But no, I am not ill."

"But Father Brand, many have observed that you have become sad. There is little life within you. I have a medicine for you." He pulled a drinking gourd bottle out of his mantle and offered it to Brand. "If you drink it, it will calm you. It will heal you."

"No, Cuetzpali. I want nothing."

But Cuetzpali persisted.

"It will calm you and make you feel better. Drink it, Father Brand," insisted Cuetzpali. "At least lift this to your mouth and taste a single drop."

Brand reluctantly took a sip of the milky liquid. It was familiar yet different.

"If you drink it, it will soothe your heart. You will be transformed. You will become strong again. Strong again *for Kathleen.*"

When Brand heard her name, something changed within him. His heart stirred. Maybe he should drink of the medicine. He took a long swallow from the cup.

"Drink four times for the four directions," said Cuetzpali, lifting up the gourd.

He smiled as Brand drank the milky liquid to which he had added an infusion of *tlitlitzin*, made from the seeds of the morning glory plant. The heavenly blue flowers were allowed to go to seed. The seeds were ground to flour, then soaked with water and drained. The liquid potion would slow down time for Brand and distort his perceptions.

"And then drink once for the center of all," Cuetzpali urged again.

So altogether Brand drank five times. He felt the power of the liquid.

"What is this? What is in this drink?" Brand's words were slurred. He fell back onto his sleeping pallet.

Unnoticed, Toveyo stepped quietly into the room. "Cueztpali," he said, "it is time to summon Kathleen."

Cuetzpali immediately left the room and half walked, half waddled to where Kathleen had been staying. She was alone. Izel was not there to protect and guide her.

She looked up with surprise when Cuetzpali approached her. Like Brand, her eyes were hollow and dark with grief.

"Cuetzpali! What is it?" Her voice was anxious, like the voice of a sailor who sees a dark cloud on the horizon.

"Father Brand needs you. He asks that you come to him."

"Is something wrong? Is he ill?" Her eyes were now wild with alarm.

Cuetzpali did not explain but only said, "It is urgent that you come."

Kathleen instantly obeyed. All she knew was that Brand needed her. She hurried along with Cuetzpali to Brand's sleeping quarters, wondering what this unusual summons could mean.

"He is in there," said Cuetzpali. Then he stepped out of the room.

As soon as she saw Brand, Kathleen knew something was not right. He was sitting upright on his sleeping pallet, but leaning slightly to one side.

When Brand saw her he roused somewhat. "Please, sit here, Kathleen. Sit here beside me."

When he spoke, it was obvious he needed help.

"You are not yourself, Father Brand. What is wrong?"

He did not answer. He held out the cup with the liquid. "It is medicine, Kathleen," he urged. "Medicine for the heart. Take some. Cuetzpali has brought it to me. You must take it too." He implored her with his entire being. He wanted her to be well. "Please, take the medicine!"

"I will drink, but only if you promise you will not drink any more. You must promise me you will sleep and rest."

Normally, Brand was the one to take care of Kathleen. But in this strange moment, he did not resist her attentions.

"Yes, Kathleen. I promise."

She took Brand's cup. She assumed it was octli, the drink she had heard of. She knew that in enough quantity, it could induce drunkenness and then sleep. But she felt it was safe to take only a few sips.

Almost immediately, however, she felt its influence. At first, she felt strangely light and free from worry. She and Brand began to sing some of the songs of their homeland. Not songs of the White Kristr, but songs of their childhood, songs of the long winter nights. There were no prayers. Then the lightness transformed into heaviness, into nothingness. They soon sank asleep on the floor, Kathleen in Brand's arms.

Neither Brand nor Kathleen awakened when Toveyo's sorcerers entered the room. They pulled Kathleen from Brand's embrace.

First they removed her clothing. They then began to abuse her body. So evil were they that one could hardly wait until another had finished. They bruised her, without and within, yet she did not wake. Though unconscious, she called out for Tizoc and murmured Brand's name, but he did not hear her.

When they had finished, they flung her body on top of his. There she lay crazily spread, like a branch that had been blown by a violent windstorm onto a field.

Toveyo and Cuetzpali had watched the entire scene unfold, without saying a word. Then they exited the room.

CHAPTER THIRTY-FOUR

MANY HOURS PASSED. BRAND WAS the first to awaken, his body aware of an unaccustomed weight. When his eyes opened, he saw Kathleen so close, so close. He thought he was dreaming the dream he had so often experienced over many years. It was what he had so longed for—waking with Kathleen in his arms.

He reached to pull her closer. She moaned.

Instantly, he realized this was no dream. His mind was jumbled. How did she get here? He was half dressed and she was naked. What had happened?

At that moment, as he had planned, Toveyo burst back into the room.

"What have you done?" he shouted. "You have told all the people you were a chaste man. But look what you have done! You are a liar! You have slept with the woman who calls you father!"

Brand stared at Toveyo with utter confusion. Had he capitulated to the desires he had contained for so long? He could not answer Toveyo's accusation because he did not know how this scene before him had come to be. He pulled away from Kathleen, struggling to make sense of it all.

He remembered the visit from Cuetzpali. He somewhat recalled that Kathleen had come to him as well. But for the rest, his mind was blank. He had no memory of Cuetzpali's potion. No matter how hard he tried, he could remember nothing. He took a blanket from the sleeping area and placed it gently over Kathleen.

At Toveyo's shouting, Kathleen also began to rouse. She too could not remember what had happened. When she moved, she felt a bruising between her legs and wet stickiness down her thighs. The realization that she had been violated slowly came over her. She looked at Brand and saw nothing but confusion in him.

Toveyo surveyed the scene with silent pleasure. Surely, his well-crafted plan was playing out exactly as he wanted. Now he could move to the next phase.

Kathleen clutched the blanket. She searched Brand's eyes and face for answers. "Father Brand, what is—"

Brand began to speak, but at the same moment, Toveyo barked an order to his men.

"Take him away! Now!"

The men grabbed Brand by his arms, pulled him to his feet, then pushed him out through the curtained doorway.

"Father Brand! Do not leave me!" Kathleen called after him. When he was out of her sight, she put her hands over her face and began to sob in pain and fear.

Toveyo's assistants marched Brand toward the city center. Once they arrived there, they dressed Brand in stained clothing they had prepared for him. Though he still reeled from the potion, Brand knew the garments reeked of foul blood and excrement.

"Remember, there is no water anywhere with which you can wash and cleanse yourself!" Toveyo shouted, a final taunt and insult.

Toveyo sent men to begin to spread the rumor that Brand and Kathleen had copulated. Then he and his assistants pushed Brand onto a pallet and led him through the streets of Tollan for all to see. This was the next phase of the plan—a parade of shame. It was not enough for Kathleen to be violated. Toveyo had to be sure Brand would have no followers, no supporters, no one on his side ever again.

Almost at once, large crowds gathered as the procession slowly moved through the streets and the rumors passed from person to person. The people were at first shocked, but their shock soon turned to anger and scorn. They called Brand names and mocked him.

"You are a man of no honor!"

"You are no better than an animal!"

"You have no restraint!"

Brand made no reply. He said nothing in his own defense. He hung his head as waves of immense shame washed over him.

Tonauac came running through the crowd.

"Let him down! Let him down!" he shouted.

Toveyo was satisfied with his work. He nodded, and the bearers placed the pallet on the ground.

Tonauac took Brand quickly back to his quarters. He removed the soiled clothing and called for assistants to wash Brand and dress him in clean clothing.

Through it all, Brand was silent.

"Father Brand, you are ill," said Tonauac, looking into Brand's eyes with concern. "What happened?"

"I do not know, Tonauac."

"Toveyo is saying you have broken your vow. But I do not believe it. It is not true. It cannot be true."

The reply from the broken man was more plea than statement.

"Tonauc, may it please God that nothing happened. *But I do not know.*"

CHAPTER THIRTY-FIVE

A FTER SEEING THE SPECTACLE Toveyo had mounted to shame Brand, the priestesses found Kathleen in Brand's quarters and brought her home. Izel flew into the room where Kathleen lay.

She could see Kathleen's eyes were dilated and that she could not move without a cry of pain. Izel lifted the cotton cover that lay across Kathleen's hips and legs. She tried to mask her horror, but in an instant, she clasped her hand to her mouth and began to breathe even faster. Kathleen's delicate skin was red and swollen. Large purplish bruises were dark against her paleness.

"Kathleen, what happened?"

Kathleen recounted the story to the best of her knowledge, though she knew so little. She recalled being summoned by Cuetzpali, then taking a sip of the "medicine" to appease Brand, and then waking to the terrible confusion that she had been violated.

"When I awoke, Father Brand was lying beside me. Toveyo and his men were shouting at him. But he does not remember anything, either." Her eyes lowered. "Someone has done this to me, but I do not know who."

Izel called for the others' help. Within minutes, a priestess brought a bundle of herbs, a cup, and a pot of very hot water. Izel added the herbs to the pot and let it steep while she gently washed Kathleen. When the herbal infusion was ready, she poured a cup and offered it to her.

"Take this—it will help with the pain."

The injured and defiled young woman took a few sips. From deep within her, Kathleen had a memory of another time and a cold place, with a woman urging another woman to drink a healing liquid.

Izel stroked Kathleen's brow with tenderness. "I sense treachery, my dear. Something is very wrong."

Izel knew she had to investigate. Her mind began to form all the pieces.

She waited until Kathleen was asleep. Although it was forbidden for a woman, Izel knew where and how to quietly climb to the top of the tall pyramid, to the place where the little temple to Tezcatlipoca stood. It was dusk, and the lengthening shadows helped to hide her. She waited outside in stealth and listened to the conversation coming from inside the temple. She recognized Cuetzpali's voice and Toveyo's as well.

"Yes," said Toveyo, "we could have poisoned him as easily as drugging him. But creating a martyr would have served nothing. Rather, this victory is greater and sweeter now that we have placed him into humiliation."

From her hiding place around the corner of the temple wall, Izel watched as Toveyo exited and went down the steps of the pyramid. A minute later, Cuetzpali exited the little room, a small bag of gold rings and arm bands in his hand.

She decided to show herself and confront him.

"I know what you have done," she said, standing before him in defiance. "I know of this plot to humiliate Father Brand."

Cuetzpali looked at her blankly, his reptilian eyes not denying her accusation.

"I know you are part of a conspiracy to bring the generals to power. They want the people to be only slave workers and sacrifices. How could you be so disloyal to Father Brand?"

"I do what I must do. Loyalty has nothing to do with it."

"Who attacked Kathleen?"

"What difference does it make? Many. That is all I will tell you. Many."

At hearing these words, Izel's mind exploded with anger. Izel had never loathed anyone as much as she loathed Cuetzpali in that moment. She moved closer to strike him in all her fury. When she did, Cuetzpali lunged toward her as well. He reached out to push her from the summit.

Her eyes wide with fear and rage, Izel clutched him. They teetered on the high steps for a moment, but still she would not let go. Suddenly they fell, tangled together amidst cries of pain, tumbling on the steep rock steps, down and down to the bottom of the stone monument.

No movement came from Cuetzpali. He was dead. Izel lay next to him, alive but unconscious.

Many people heard the death battle and came running to the bottom of the temple. Torches were lit to illuminate the scene as the onlookers struggled to make sense of it. Soon King Huemac's soldiers arrived. They ordered the crowd to disburse.

The temple priestesses took Izel away. Patli was called and arrived quickly.

He gently felt her bones and looked into her eyes. Then he declared his diagnosis to the crowd of women surrounding Izel.

"She has no broken bones, only bruises. She has a slight injury to her head that must be watched. She must rest in bed for a least a day."

They waited for his next words.

"But she will recover."

Patli's training as a healer had consumed his first moments with Izel. He had seen many head injuries and broken bones. He knew when they were life threatening and when they were not. He knew she was fortunate to be alive.

It was only after he had examined Izel that his mind began to process all that had happened in recent days. His friend Tizoc was dead. Father Brand had been publicly shamed. Both Kathleen and Izel were shattered and wounded. And he had heard Cuetzpali was dead, possibly at Izel's doing. He could not make sense of any of it.

So he stayed by Izel and Kathleen, monitoring their resting and waking. Understanding would have to wait.

Toveyo's assistants collected Cuetzpali's corpulent body from the bottom of the pyramid. No one knew what became of it. Some heard rumors that, having served his purpose, he was cut into pieces and fed to the wild cats in the king's zoo.

CHAPTER THIRTY-SIX

I ZEL WAS TO STAY IN bed for two days, which required significant effort to accomplish. During her convalescence, she peppered everyone she saw with questions: How was Kathleen? Was she healing from the attack? How was Father Brand? Had he recovered from seeing Kathleen so wounded, followed by his condemnation from the people? She got some answers—partial answers.

After two days, Patli checked her eyes. Seeing no worrisome signs, he gave his reluctant consent for her to get up.

She immediately rose from her bed. In truth, though, it was a slow and painful process. The many bruises all over her body caused agony, but she said nothing. All Izel could think about was Kathleen. It was imperative that she speak with her, and soon.

Izel's heart fell when she saw her. The young woman had lost weight; her arms were twiglike, her face thin and ashen. The priestesses had placed herbal compresses on her skin to help with bruising. Both women wanted to embrace, but the pain forced them to be content with sitting close, holding hands.

"Izel, how is Father Brand?" Kathleen asked. "I know I was attacked, and somehow he blames himself. I know he was put to shame."

"He is getting better," said Izel, though she suspected he was not. It was merely what she needed to say in that moment to protect both Brand and Kathleen.

Kathleen seemed to accept this response. There was a pause, then she spoke, her fragile voice heavy with emotion.

"Izel?"

"Yes, Kathleen?"

"I know he did not harm me."

"You are correct, Kathleen. He did not harm you."

They both absorbed the import of this statement with another pause of silence.

Then Izel began to fuss about how Kathleen needed to eat. A platter had been placed on a small table nearby. She enticed her with delicious bits of crispy tapir meat, creamy avocado slices, atolli porridge, and peanut honey sweets. Kathleen viewed the food with indifference.

"Try some, Kathleen," said Izel, handing her a square of peanut candy. "Tlazohtlaloni always loves it. He asks about you. He wants you to eat."

Kathleen gingerly took a piece of the nut candy and began to munch on it with little enthusiasm.

Izel knew that what she was about to say would be difficult for Kathleen. Unconsciously, she took a deep breath.

"There is something we must talk about."

Kathleen stopped chewing and swallowed. She waited.

"It is possible that you may be pregnant," said Izel, trying to sound matter-of-fact.

"I know," said Kathleen dully.

"What . . . what do you want to do about it?" asked Izel gently.

"What do you mean?"

"There is a tea that will keep you from having a baby. It is called *cihuapatl,* women's medicine. But you must take it within six days of the expected beginning of your next moon cycle, or it will not be effective. Only we women know of this plant. The men, if they knew, might prevent us from using it. I can give you some of this plant to take."

Kathleen had heard some of the other temple women talking about the shrub with heart-shaped leaves that came from a region south of Tollan. They never spoke of it as something that affected a pregnancy; they just described it as a plant whose leaves can regulate a woman's moon cycle. She

378

supposed it was something like the special seeds Gudrun had told her about on the little knarr while sailing in the northern seas. That seemed so long ago now.

Izel waited while Kathleen thought.

"Does it kill the baby?" Kathleen finally asked.

"It stops the baby from growing and being born."

Kathleen could still feel the physical pain caused by those who attacked her. That pain, she knew, would pass. But the thought of giving birth to the child of her violators was too much for her heart. Each time she would look at the child, she would be reminded of this impossibly sad and difficult time.

"Izel, please prepare the plant for me. I will take it."

"Are you sure?"

"Yes, I am sure."

Izel called for one of the priestesses to bring boiling water. She mixed finely crushed cacao beans with the water. Then she used a spoon made from turtle shell to beat it to a frothy texture.

"The cacao will mask the taste of the tea," Izel explained.

She poured the liquid into a small orange clay jar. Then Izel took a handful of the special leaves and let the right amount fall into the hot mixture.

All the while, Kathleen sat and watched, wordless. The quiet outward pose belied the racing in her mind.

After a few minutes passed, Izel said, "It is ready now, if you are ready."

Kathleen took the jar into her trembling hands. She slowly moved it to her mouth and parted her lips.

Suddenly she exclaimed, "I cannot do this! Take it away!"

She pushed the jar back to Izel.

"I might be pregnant," she continued, "but I cannot get rid of it. I cannot!"

Her sudden resolve took Kathleen by surprise. She did not know from where it came. All she knew was that something deep inside her told her not to drink the tea.

Izel's face was very grave, yet she was relieved. She took the clay jar and set it aside.

"I am glad you have made this decision," she said, turning back to Kathleen. Once again Izel held Kathleen's hand. "When my son was born, many told me to abandon him in the jungle. How could one love an imperfect child, a deformed child, they said." She smiled a little. "But now I cannot imagine my life without him. And no matter how he came to be in this world or who his father was or what pain came with him, the joy he has brought me has far exceeded anything I could have imagined."

They both sat together for a long time, holding hands and thinking of what the future would bring.

CHAPTER THIRTY-SEVEN

RAND'S SENSES BEGAN TO RETURN a few hours after he had been rescued him from the jeering crowds. Immediately, guilt haunted him. He was uncertain what had happened between him and Kathleen.

Brand longed to hear the words of the absolution: *ego te absolvo a peccatis tuis in nomine Patris, et Filii, et Spiritus Sancti.* But there was no priest to hear his confession. And even if there were a priest, Brand did not know *what* to confess.

Brand sat in the corner of his sleeping room and would not leave. But Tonauac would not let Brand struggle alone. As soon as she was able, he brought Izel to him. Great gray thunderclouds filled the sky, keeping everything gloomy, even though it was afternoon.

"Father Brand, why do you hide yourself in the dark?" Tonauac asked as they stood outside his room. They got no answer but stepped inside.

Brand would not look at Tonauac or Izel. All he could see were the faces of the people who had laughed and jeered at him, all at Toveyo's urging. Brand's name, his reputation, his honor—this was all that mattered.

"I may have sinned. I do not know." Then he responded as a Viking would respond: "But I do know the stain on my name can never be erased."

"You are wrong to blame yourself!" protested Izel. "We suspected something was not right, and now we know for certain: Cuetzpali betrayed you. He was the one who lured Kathleen to your quarters. I heard Cuetzpali and Toveyo myself."

Tonauac looked at Izel, marveling at the high risk she took for this information, the price she was willing to pay to be a protector.

"They gave you drugs to alter your mind and make things that did not happen appear to have happened," she explained.

Tonauac continued. "And then Toveyo poured poison into the ears of the people. He has tried to destroy you by destroying what the people think of you."

Brand remained unresponsive to their words. They coaxed and urged and exhorted him, but he would not hear them.

Tonauac grew frustrated, throwing his hands into the air. "Have you not taught us that your god can forgive any error, any transgression, *any* sin? Did not the person called David commit great sin, to covet a man's wife and then ensure that her husband would be certain to die in battle?"

Even in his sadness, Brand smiled a little at the irony—the students were now teaching the teacher.

Finally, Brand spoke.

"You are right, Tonauac. I serve a god of forgiveness. Still, my reputation in this place will never be repaired."

The next words he said stunned both Tonauac and Izel.

"I must leave."

"Leave the city?" asked Tonauac.

"Yes, leave Tollan. To start anew somewhere else."

Tonauac hesitated for only a moment. "If you go, I will go too."

"As will I," said Izel definitively. "And Tlazohtlaloni as well. The sooner we can wipe the dust of Tollan from our sandals, the better!"

At that moment, a great thunderclap resounded throughout Tollan, and it began to rain.

CHAPTER THIRTY-EIGHT

Their decision now made, Izel and Tonauac prepared to leave Brand's quarters.

"I will let Kathleen know what we have discussed," said Izel.

When she said this, Tonauac noted a huge sense of relief washed over Brand. Brand was sure of his decision to leave Tollan, but he still worried about the reaction from the woman he loved when he would next see her.

Izel walked through the rain with determination, a protective circle of green woven fronds held above her head. She decided she would go right to Kathleen and convey their decision to leave in the only way she knew how—direct and to the point.

Kathleen took the news calmly, almost without reaction. A general cloud had enveloped her.

"You must come with us," said Izel.

"Of course," said Kathleen, her voice hollow.

So much had happened that nothing more seemed of great consequence to her. *What choice do I have?* she thought.

Slowly, over the next few days, word of Brand's departure began to spread through the city. Most of the people believed Toveyo's lies and therefore were happy to hear the disgraced man would no longer live among them. But many others were not sure.

Brand's small group of followers had been saddened and angered when they heard of Cuetzpali's treachery and Izel's near death. That one of their own, someone they trusted, had betrayed them was hard to understand.

Some fell away from the group and the faith, unable to reconcile Brand's lessons of hope with the destruction and disappointment all around them. Others talked among themselves.

The widows came to Izel and said, "We believe in Father Brand and his message. We want to leave Tollan with him."

Other Toltecs decided to leave as well. But it was not out of loyalty to Brand. They were artisans, the people who knew deep in their collective memory how to form the thin orange pottery, craft intricate metalwork, as well as recite beautiful poetry and make music. Many had observed that the fortunes of Quetzalcoatl's followers now waned in Tollan. The beginning of the end of the empire was underway. For them, it was a practical decision to leave, as no one was safe any longer.

The decision to leave was harder for some than for others. Was not Tollan their home? But then, they reasoned, "Before Tollan, we had another home, and after Tollan, we shall have another."

Brand's followers and many artisans began their preparations to leave the city. The artisans calculated which implements of their craft they would carry with them and what they could trade or barter along the way. Others considered what foods and household articles would be needed and began to organize their possessions for the journey. All had to be carefully thought through, for they could take with them only what could be carried on the back of a human. Those who had the means hired porters to assist them.

On seeing this activity, several advisors approached King Huemac in alarm. They insisted on seeing him immediately, even though he was in consultation with Toveyo.

"What is this commotion?" barked the king as the advisors rushed into the great hall of governance.

"King Huemac, how can you let these people leave?" asked one of his counselors.

"My king—" Toveyo interrupted before the king could speak.

The room fell silent at this impertinence, and the slaves gently fanning the king stopped in midair.

But Huemac had become so enthralled by Toveyo that he did not even noticed this rude behavior.

"These people are widows, old people, children, the sick," Toveyo declared. "Others are of no consequence at all. None of them can help with your military objectives. Let them go!" he said confidently.

Huemac quickly agreed. "I will follow your advice, Toveyo, for you have more knowledge of these matters than I."

It was true; those who planned to leave could not help with his military needs. What the king could not see, however, was that these people took with them the flower of the Toltecan culture. It was but one of many decisions that ensured the doom of his kingdom.

CHAPTER THIRTY-NINE

B RAND AND TONAUAC INSTRUCTED EVERYONE when and where to gather to begin the journey away from Tollan. When the day finally arrived, they met at the edge of the ceremonial center of the city. They planned to begin the journey as soon as the drums announced the beginning of morning rituals for Tezcatlipoca.

The morning was beautiful, with sunshine and blue skies graced only with high, thin clouds. The sun's rays shone brilliantly on the white-washed ceremonial buildings, causing the eyes to water unless one quickly looked away. Yet the brilliance of the sun could not completely hide the cold and cruel heart of Tollan, which had begun to rot from within. The people were firm in their resolve to leave.

Brand and Tonauac stood at the head of the assembled travelers. Brand was talking with Tonauac when he turned and suddenly saw Kathleen. He had known she was coming, but it was the first time he had seen her since that awful day when she was violated.

He froze, still unsure of himself and how she might greet him.

"Father Brand," she said. She stepped closer, opened her arms, and embraced him. "I am here."

"And I am glad you are here," said Brand, his heart full.

Nenetl, Izel, and Tlazohtlaloni joined the group as well, near the front of the moving column. The children wore little packs on their backs. Inside were water gourds, extra clothing and sandals, bags of dried fruits, and small blankets to soothe them.

Next came Xicotencatl, the court hunchback, and several members of the dwarf troupe. They had decided they would leave Tollan too. And they would leave in joy, not in shame or fear.

The beating of drums began, and the familiar and ominous sounds filled the ceremonial center. Brand quieted everyone, then said a prayer of gratitude and blessing over all of them. It was the same prayer he had said they day he sailed from Trondheim on his way to Greenland with Leif Eriksson.

"Jesu, master most pure, we beseech you, shield our journey. And may the Lord of Heaven bless us and stretch forth his hand in protection upon us."

Then the march began. Playing their flutes, young boys led the way for the exiles. Dwarfs skillfully tumbled behind them, even with their packs firmly strapped to their backs.

As the little group passed through the streets, people slowly came out of houses and workshops, one by one. Some were curious to confirm the rumors and to see the spectacle of the exiles. Others came to Brand and touched their hands to his. They hoisted their packs and joined the procession.

As they neared the outskirts of town, a young man stepped out along their path. Brand turned as he felt a hand on his. He saw, with surprise, someone he knew.

It was Patli.

"You will need a doctor," Patli said, patting his medicine pack. Without another word, he fell into line with the rest of the people.

They had started as a small group, a few dozen refugees. Now as they prepared to leave the edge of the city, Brand was astonished to see that their number had swelled into the hundreds.

Tonauac stood before the group and spoke in a loud voice that seemed to carry all the way back to the center of the city they had left behind.

"There is a place called Teotihuacan, an ancient, abandoned city of our heritage. No one lives there anymore. It is filled with stone monuments and pyramids of fantastic size. That is our destination. Our new life begins now."

They began their journey south, a column of unbowed people, toward Teotihuacan, the empty place of ancient gods.

CHAPTER FORTY

T HE EXILES HAD BEEN ON their journey only a half day when Toveyo and General Yaotl began to second-guess their strategy to destroy Brand. They met once again in the garden patio of the general's home.

"Things have not worked out as we had imagined," said the general reluctantly, slowly puffing on a smoldering pipe bowl of tobacco. He stared at Toveyo. "The public humiliation you suggested appears to have only been short lived. At least, with some of the people."

"It was the correct thing to do," retorted Toveyo indignantly. "But the void created by the artisans' absence may be greater than I had thought. Already, complaints are being made."

The general handed him the pipe, and he too took a puff.

"There must be some other way to punish and diminish that man and his followers," said the general in frustration.

The two began to talk in earnest and did not finish until the tobacco pipes had been filled and smoked several times.

Reluctantly, they decided they needed to appear yet again before King Huemac. Bowing lower than normal, they came before him.

"King Huemac," Toveyo began his petition, "there is one more thing that must be done with respect to the man Brand and the people who follow him."

"One more thing?" Huemac asked sarcastically. "What is it now?" He could scarcely contain his annoyance. "The people have only just left the city. I am tired of dealing with this!"

"Remember when Brand appeared before you and told you the special symbols were poetry?" Toveyo asked carefully. "My king, it was a lie. It is not poetry. Our informant told us it is writing about their god and what their god tells them to think and do. We must destroy the symbols. They will be helpless without them. Their god must never be a threat to Tezcatlipoca, who is the source of our military advantage, whom we must honor with reverence and sacrifice."

"Yes, yes—destroy the symbols," responded a weary and distracted Huemac. "But let this be the last I hear of this. I am done!"

Soldiers were immediately dispatched at double time, led by the same captain who had found Brand and Kathleen and the storm-tossed *Sea Goat*. *I should have received credit for such a discovery*, he thought. This slight still festered in his heart, like a deep, infected wound that would not heal.

It did not take long for the soldiers to catch up with the slow-moving exiles. The soldiers were dressed for battle: colored paints covered their bodies in wild distortion, and knives and spear-throwers were ready.

When the people had seen them coming, fear immobilized them. They were like rabbits exposed in an open field with a predator close at hand.

The soldiers moved quickly to the front of the group, blocking their way. At the head of the travelers, Brand and Tonauac stood together. Kathleen and Nenetl had been walking together, hand in hand, at the front of the group as well.

"What do you want?" Brand asked, sounding confident yet wary for the safety of the people.

The captain glared at Brand. "You have taken the special symbols with you. You must give them to us, on order of the king!"

Brand stared in confusion for a moment. Then he remembered that the "special symbols" meant his Gospel books. He tried to remain expressionless as he struggled to understand why the captain was asking for the books—and why now.

The captain continued his demand. "We will kill one child after another until you turn them over."

Before Brand could reply, the captain grabbed little Nenetl away from Kathleen. He placed an obsidian knife near the child's small neck.

"Stop!" exclaimed Brand, raising his hand protectively. "There is no need. Let her go."

"Not until we have the symbols!"

The captain held the razor-sharp blade so close to the child's neck that blood already appeared in small droplets on her delicate skin.

"Yes, yes! Do not harm her!" Brand pleaded.

He immediately reached into his own pack. Everyone watched in anxious silence as he pulled out the precious books, carefully wrapped in white cotton cloth, and handed them to the captain.

"Now release her," Brand said with authority.

As soon as the captain released his grip on Nenetl, she bit his forearm. Hard.

The captain winced in pain.

Nenetl ran back to Kathleen, who quickly pushed her back to shield her from any more danger.

The soldiers gathered grass and fallen branches. One soldier had fire-starting material in his pack: dry cotton lint and flint to create sparks. It was difficult to grow the fire with damp wood from the recent rain, but once sufficiently lit, it quickly grew hot.

Brand trembled as the Gospel books were thrown unceremoniously into the fire. The precious book of Matthew, telling of Jesus as the fulfillment of Hebrew prophecy. The book of Mark, with its stories of the emotions of Jesus. Luke with its stories of Jesus's concern for the poor. And Brand's favorite, the book of John, with its emphasis on the Word.

The flames began their slow destruction, first at the edges and then toward the center. The paper, with its beautiful decoration, flamed a bright yellow and red, then transformed to dull blackness.

Tonauac looked on, his face grim and disbelieving. The symbols— he had learned to love the symbols and all they could communicate.

The others watched in horrified silence as well. Some began to weep.

The soldiers watched as the books burned quickly down. Then the captain ordered them to attention. He turned back to glare at Brand, his hatred still as hot as the embers. They left as quickly as they had arrived.

"Father Brand, you must say something to the people," urged Tonauac. "You must speak to them."

Brand gathered himself and climbed up a small hillside. He looked out on the people and saw their pain. He spoke from his heart.

"They may burn our books, but they will never burn the truth from our hearts. There is a god who loves us. Even though we are wicked, Jesu was sent to us to tell us of this love. And though we may be destroyed by wind or flood or fire or blades of death, even so shall we live, if we believe."

That night, Brand had a dream. He knew it was prophetic. When the group gathered the next morning, he confided in Tonauac.

"Tonauac, I had a dream that foretold the future. I am certain it will come to pass."

"What happened in this dream?" asked Tonauac, who also respected the power of dreams.

"It was about books. And in two parts. In the first part, there was a great king—a descendent of your people, he looked like you. He ordered his followers to collect many of the painted pages throughout his kingdom—the painted pages telling of history. 'Destroy them!' he commanded. 'The history they tell is no longer acceptable to me.' And the pages were burned."

Tonauac reflected on this dream, a mystified look on his face. Surely, only a powerful king would dare burn the records of his predecessors. But such a king should also know the importance and value of the history of his people, and refrain from destroying them.

"And the second part?" he asked.

"The second part took place in yet another time, many years later," Brand replied. "Once again, painted pages were collected from many places in the land, placed into a huge pile, then set aflame. Only this time, the people ordering the burning looked like me. And the people who wept at the burning looked like you."

"Perhaps," said Tonauac, "the burning of the Gospels was the first book burning here but will not be not the last."

"It seems this may come to pass," said Brand, shaking his head. "Even though I do not understand it." He sighed. "Nevertheless, I will do whatever I can to tell the story of the Gospels, even without the books, no matter where I may be."

"Come, my friend," said Tonauac, taking up his walking stick.

"Yes," said Brand, picking up his own stick. "Let us continue our journey."

CHAPTER FORTY-ONE

THE SOJOURNERS CONTINUED ON TO Teotihuacan, a journey of approximately fifty miles. The group stopped at towns and villages along the way. In some places, they stayed only a day or two, to trade and refresh. In other places, they stayed longer, weeks at a time.

In exchange for shelter and food, the artisans gave demonstrations on metalwork and how to craft the thin orange pottery so coveted throughout the region. Patli shared his expertise with the local healers.

The people even bartered with the musicians for their songs. The younger musicians showed the people how to make clay flutes and how to make music—sometimes joyous, sometimes forlorn. And the dwarfs always pleased the crowds who gathered around for a performance. The villagers were generous with their payment for the entertainment.

The people in these towns were highly impressed with the knowledge and techniques the Toltecs shared. The exiles' fame preceded them in the countryside. Soon the word *Toltec* became a substitute term meaning "highly skilled person."

Usually, Brand and Tonauac, along with other men, led the exiles. Then came the women, children, and old people, followed at the end by more men. Some of the children and old ones needed frequent rest. In the beginning, even Izel and Kathleen both walked rather slowly, as their bruises were still healing. But the exiles had no timetable for the journey, so no one complained at the pace.

The group had no weapons, only obsidian blades used for cutting food and other items. But no one molested or harmed them. In an odd way, they felt more secure than they had in their homes in Tollan.

At night, they used their fire-making skills to keep wild animals away. That is when Brand would sit by the fire and try to recall the words of the Gospel books. Somehow Tonauac had managed to barter for some plant-fiber paper, turkey-quill pens, and ink. He gave them to Brand, who by the flickering light would write whatever he could recall. Tonauac sat close and continued to learn how to read the mysterious symbols that so fascinated him.

Kathleen often joined them and watched carefully as Brand created the words and sentences. She noted that he wrote the words first in Latin, then repeated them in the runes he had learned in his youth.

With each passing day, Kathleen was healing in body and spirit. Sometimes she sang little songs her mother had taught her to soothe young ones to sleep. She began to smile and even laugh again.

As always, Izel observed all and missed nothing. They had been traveling for about two months when she noted that Kathleen, though still in good spirits, seemed disinterested in food and was unusually tired again. She waited until they were alone to ask the question she needed to confirm her suspicions.

"Yes," said Kathleen. "I am with child. Say nothing to Father Brand. I am not ready to tell him."

CHAPTER FORTY-TWO

NOT LONG AFTER KATHLEEN AND Izel spoke, the exiles reached their destination—the magnificent and mysterious Teotihuacan. Many days before they entered the city proper, the travelers had gazed at the great pyramids rising out of the plain.

Tonauac and some of the Toltecs had heard of this fabled place, but none of the travelers had ever been there. The city had been built approximately nine hundred years before they walked into the city. At its height, it had one hundred thousand inhabitants, maybe more. Then it was mysteriously abandoned. Except for a few squatters eking a living near the outskirts of the city, no one had lived there for several centuries.

As they moved closer to the center of the city, the travelers passed abandoned houses—multilevel compounds with pebbled plaster walls. Some had remnants of beautifully painted murals. The people of Teotihuacan had lived well and had loved art.

It was midafternoon when they reached the heart of the ruins. Everything they saw evoked wonder and awe. Mostly, they walked in silence, with an occasional cry of a child or an audible exhalation of disbelief in response to what lay around them.

The procession moved past the second largest of three stone pyramids—the Pyramid of the Moon—and onto a wide stone avenue. The city was built at a nearly north orientation, and the avenue ran through the center of the city for more than two and a half miles. They walked along the avenue, to the south. They passed another stone pyramid to the east of the avenue—the Pyramid of the Sun. As the largest of the ruins, its size was overwhelming.

They reached the final and smallest of the pyramids, also built to the east of the avenue, when the western sun was beginning to cast shadows. It was clearly constructed in honor of Quetzalcoatl, the god Tonauac served.

The exiles rested that night among the gigantic stone remnants of the uninhabited city. Tonauac rose very early the next morning; he wanted to study the Quetzalcoatl pyramid alone.

Multiple carved stone images of the feathered serpent adorned the pyramid. He slowly walked its perimeter, observing the structure from every perspective in the morning light. Though the structure was long abandoned, he could see its exterior still held vestiges of blue paint.

As Tonauac rounded the last corner of the pyramid, he met Brand, who had completed his morning prayers.

"Have you eaten?" asked Brand, offering Tonauac a tlaxcalli disk folded and filled with beans.

"No," said Tonauac with a smile, taking the food and eating it with gusto.

"Now that you are nourished," said Brand, "shall we climb?"

With that, the two began the ascent of the pyramid, up 248 steps. With his longer legs, the climb was easier for Brand. But at times, he too needed to move from step to step at an angle. They were both glad for the stone platforms built into the pyramid at intervals, where they could rest.

Finally, they reached the top and were rewarded with a magnificent view. From their vantage, they could see for miles in every direction. A large azure butterfly—several inches across—flew over their heads, wafting high on a gentle breeze.

They sat together for a while, saying nothing. At length, Brand spoke.

"We cannot stay long here in Teotihuacan. It is a dead place."

Tonauac swept his eyes across the vista in front of them. "The ruins are a sign to all of us that people can rise up, civilization can flower, and then it can die."

"You *knew* there would be no people here, did you not?"

"Yes."

"Then why—?"

"Father Brand, during those last days in Tollan, all was in chaos. It was more important to start the journey than to know the final destination. I believed that if we could make our way here, we could make our way to any place. And I believed that once we reached Teotihuacan, the next phase of our journey would become clear."

Tonauac gazed now at Brand.

"Do you remember when we were in Cholollan for the ball game, and King Amapane made that mysterious visit?"

Brand recalled the journey to Cholollan. With a pang of grief, he remembered that Tizoc had been alive, so alive, when they were there. So much had happened since then.

"Yes, I remember."

"The king said it was a 'place of refuge,'" Tonauac continued. "We can go there. There are other people there who hate human sacrifice. In that city, we can live in peace and safety and share our knowledge with others."

Brand nodded. It was settled; they would continue their travels on to Cholollan.

Brand descended the steep steps, but Tonauac stayed awhile atop the pyramid. He needed time to think. The pyramid on which he rested had been built to honor Quetzalcoatl, the god he had been trained to serve. Quetzalcoatl was the creator of the universe. Yet Brand taught that all things had been created by the Father God—that out of darkness the land and waters, plants and animals, and finally humankind had been formed.

Tonauac had listened to all of Brand's lessons, and he had worked hard to understand the ideas. He knew Brand wanted him to accept the new god, to be baptized in water, and to reject his ancient gods. He had considered it. Yet he could not do it. It was too hard to leave behind all he had known, all he had understood to be true.

Brand would not force him—this he knew as well. Tonauac pondered the possibility that he could somehow combine the two religions and honor both. He knew Brand would not condone this; he would want

Tonauac to make a choice. Still, he pondered. He slowly began the climb down, resting a while on each of the platforms and taking in the view.

When Brand told the other travelers of their new destination, they were content with this decision. They prepared to leave the ancient and empty place named "where the gods were born."

When Brand told Kathleen of their new destination, she smiled.

"Why are you smiling?" he asked, sensing she had something to say.

"Only because of this, Father Brand: In Cholollan, my baby will be born. And in that city, my baby will be baptized."

She smiled again.

"Oh, Kathleen!"

He embraced her, then took a step back to look at her more carefully. He was relieved when he could see no trace of the horror she had been through, only her determination to face the future.

CHAPTER FORTY-THREE

THE EXILES LEFT TEOTIHUACAN AND traveled south and to the east. They had another fifty miles before they would reach Cholollan.

They stopped and spent more time than usual with the people of Tlaxcala, whom they met along the way. There were no grand pyramids in Tlaxcala, but there were several smaller stone monuments to Quetzalcoatl and other lesser gods.

The Tlaxcalans were shorter than any other people they had encountered, but very strong, physically and mentally. As usual, Brand and Kathleen were objects of curiosity. But once the Tlaxcalans spoke with the travelers—Brand conversing fluently and Kathleen more haltingly—the laughter came easily and mutual friendship was established. Nenetl found other little girls to play with and quickly learned new games.

One evening after a delicious roasted turkey meal, Brand, Tonauac, and the Tlaxcalan chief sat together, watching the Toltecan dwarfs perform. The night before, Brand had dreamed a dream about the Tlaxcalans, and he believed it was prophetic. Tonauac had advised him that it would be acceptable to share the dream with the Tlaxcalan leader.

Brand told the chief it was a dream about the future.

"In my dream," he began, "I could see that the Tlaxcalans are fierce warriors. They were being attacked by a conquering tribe—an empire of tribes—from the west."

The chief's eyes narrowed, and he frowned slightly.

"But the Tlaxcalans are a proud people, and in my dream, they resisted the stronger empire for many, many years. Then the Tlaxcalans were

399

joined in their struggle by visitors from the east. They made an alliance with the visitors. Eventually, they—together—utterly destroyed the empire to the west."

The chief relaxed. He was pleased with this dream, for it showed his people to be resilient, absolutely refusing to be conquered by an invading power.

"The strange thing is," Brand said, "though I cannot explain it, the visitors were men who looked like me. Bearded and with light skin."

All three men sat quietly for a moment, reflecting on what this dream might mean.

Tonauac broke the silence.

"Can you tell us what route we should take to reach Cholollan?"

"To get to Cholollan, you need to travel through the mountain pass by Iztaccihuatl, the Sleeping Woman and Popocatepetl, the Smoking Mountain. It will be difficult, but not dangerous," he explained, "for you will not be traveling during the season of snow and storm."

Soon, the Toltecs said good-bye to the Tlaxcalans. Some tears were shed between the new friends.

The Toltecs set off, a string of people ascending from the plains, into the highlands, and up into the mountains. They were weary, but they felt a strong sense of purpose: their goal was Cholollan. Cholollan would be their new home. Together they sang songs of hope and repeated chants of expectation.

CHAPTER FORTY-FOUR

HE TLAXCALANS WERE CORRECT THAT the trail would be difficult, but they were wrong that it would not be dangerous. The chief had said it was not the season for storms, but the mountains did not agree.

The travelers had reached the middle of the pass when suddenly the wind came up and snowflakes began to fall. At first, Kathleen was happy to see the white flakes, stirring memories of Bergen and the winters of her childhood. She showed Nenetl and Tlazohtlaloni how to catch them on their tongues.

But then it became obvious that this was no benign snowfall. The wind became a bone-chilling howl.

The refugees knew nothing of survival in such cold. They had little clothing to protect from the wind and snow. They wrapped their cotton mantles around themselves and wrapped their feet and hands with cotton strips. The snow fell so steadily that it soon covered their bodies, as if they were wearing white shrouds. The travelers' eyes watered, and their noses and fingertips reddened.

"Father Brand, help us!" they cried out in fear.

Brand surveyed the scene and decided there was only one choice— they must hunker down and wait out the storm. He sent men to hack off low branches from nearby pine trees. Then he showed them how to use their packs to build low walls with an opening away from the blowing winds. They placed the branches on top of the packs to create a kind of roof for the shelter. Brand instructed everyone that from time to time they would need to push away the snow from the shelter entrance, lest they suffocate in their sleep.

The drifts grew ever deeper around them. Brand ran up and down the column.

"You must build shelters! You must crawl inside and wait until the storm ends."

Many believed him and created the makeshift shelters so they could huddle together out of the biting wind. But some refused. Xicotencatl, the court hunchback, was one who chose to face the wind and snow. He paced back and forth in the gathering drifts and sometimes walked in little circles.

"Xicotencatl, you must come inside," pleaded Brand at the entrance to one of the little shelters. "You must come inside!"

"No, it is cold inside the snow. It is better out here."

"No, no—you must come inside!" shouted Brand through the wind.

"I cannot! It is too small in there!" He pointed at the low shelter as if it were a tomb.

Everyone knew of Xicotencatl's fear of small places and how he constantly needed to move about in any room he was in.

Finally, Brand realized he could do no more for him.

Brand found Izel just as she was finishing a shelter. He told her to move to the rear of the shelter with her back to the wall of packs. Then Tlazohtlaloni crawled in after her. Brand told him to snuggle next to his mother with his back to her. Izel protectively put her arms around her child.

Next came Kathleen, then Nenetl, and finally Brand, all spooned together with the young ones' feet and hands protected. They all huddled together like wolf pups in a den.

Several times during the night, Brand had to brush away snow from the opening to their shelter. He was anxious for dawn, when he could emerge and check on the exiles. He believed he had done his best, but he feared what daylight might reveal.

When the sun emerged again, the snow and wind had stopped. The sky was surprisingly blue, and the sun was shining clear and strong. Everyone in the shelters seemed to have survived. But no one could find Xicotencatl. And there were others who were missing—the dwarfs. Everyone thought they had made their own little shelter, but now they too could not be found.

Suddenly a shout came up. A silversmith had found Xicotencatl half buried in snow. But there was no life there, for he had succumbed to the cold.

"We must find the dwarfs," said Brand. "They may yet live!"

The strongest men frantically searched. Finally they found a drift that seemed to have an unnatural mound. They dug in. Under the layer of snow, they found the dwarfs. The bodies that had so joyously moved and delighted all were now perfectly still. Even Patli, with his medicine and skill, could do nothing.

Fires had been started to melt snow to drink. Many people had frostbite, especially on their hands and feet. They wanted to rub the affected areas and hold them to the fire.

"No!" Brand cried out.

He showed them how to very gently warm the frostbitten skin with their own breath. He sternly cautioned them to warm their hands and feet by the fire only after all feeling had returned to their extremities.

By midday, the people were ready to pick up their belongings as well as the bodies of the dead. It was time to move on. The bodies of the dead were small and light.

As soon as they could find a suitable place, they stopped. They said prayers for the dead and committed their bodies to the earth and their souls to God's care. Brand struggled through the words of hope and eternal life. He saw the question in the eyes of the people: *Why?* He had no answers to give them. He longed for another priest, someone who could help him to support the faith of the people. He was tired in every way it was possible to be tired—physically, emotionally, mentally, and spiritually.

The loss of these gentle friends affected the exiles greatly. Many wept. Mournful songs accompanied their steps. They traveled until they reached a place called Quauhtitlan, where there was a lofty and spreading tree.

The events of the last days had taken a toll on Brand. He threw small stones at the tree with such force that they lodged in the wood. Tonauac and Kathleen quickly moved him aside, out of sight of the others.

"What is wrong, Father Brand?" asked Tonauac.

"I could not protect them!" he shouted in anger.

"You tried to tell Xicotencatl to seek shelter," Tonauac said gently, "but he—"

"No! I could not protect any of them—not one!" He clenched his hands in frustration. "I could not protect *you* or Kathleen. I could not protect Tizoc. I could not save the others who died in the cold."

Brand began to weep—not tears of petty loss but of deep grief.

Kathleen could not bear it.

"Stop it, Father Brand. Stop it! Have you not always told me never to lose heart, that God is always with us? Well, God is with us now."

Tonauac knew he had to speak up as well.

"Father Brand, you have given the people hope. They have not lost that hope. You must not lose it either."

"I am sorry. It is just that the tears would not be contained," said Brand, calming himself.

"A man who sheds no tears has no heart," Tonauac said quietly. "Can you not see what others see? The people would not have left Tollan if they did not trust you. They trust you more for your compassion, not less."

CHAPTER FORTY-FIVE

AFTER THEIR TERRIBLE ORDEAL IN the mountain pass, the travelers continued to Cholollan more or less without incident. Again, they saw a massive stone pyramid long before they entered this metropolis. Unlike Teotihuacan, however, this city was alive with people.

King Amapane greeted them all warmly, assuring them that in Cholollan they would find a place of refuge. The Cholollans were eager to integrate the artisans into their own ranks and did so within days.

Tonauac persuaded King Amapane to permit Brand to teach and keep his worship practices. The converts from Tollan were faithful worshipers with Brand. Soon some of the Cholollans also showed interest in his classes.

Izel tended to Kathleen's pregnancy, banishing Patli, whom she believed knew nothing at all about babies and birth. Nenetl was especially attentive and could not wait until the birth. After so much loss in her short life, the idea of a baby allowed a flicker of hope in her weary little heart.

Izel, Tlazohtlaloni, Kathleen, and Nenetl spent many hours in a weaving room in the king's compound. A special space had been made for them in a corner. Kathleen felt especially good there, as it reminded her of a place where women gathered to weave and converse back in Trondheim and Bergen.

Izel kept a close eye on Kathleen as her delivery drew near. One day, Izel watched closely as the pregnant woman stretched her back, then she asked Kathleen to lie down. Izel leaned over and carefully pressed on Kathleen's abdomen. She sat back on her knees and reflected.

"I think you will have twins," Izel declared.

"Oh no!" Kathleen cried out, covering her eyes.

"You are not happy? What is the matter, Kathleen?"

She lowered her hands and looked at Izel, her face filled with worry. "My mother died after giving birth to twins. And they died too."

"We will not allow that to happen to you." Izel took Kathleen's hands. "The women here and I—we will take care of you." Izel helped her up. "Come, Kathleen—walk with me. It will help you to be strong when your labor begins."

When Kathleen's time came one moon later, the women first gave her herbs to help with the pain, then other herbs to ease her labor. Before long, they gently ushered Nenetl out of the birthing room because she could not contain her excitement. She would not cease asking questions and sometimes hopped from one foot to another. The women knew Kathleen needed calm and quiet to bring her babies into the world. As the moment grew near, however, the intensity in the room increased.

"Push!" ordered Izel.

Kathleen pushed and pushed, perspiration covering her face and body. Finally, a baby emerged—a boy.

"Push again!" Izel commanded after a pause.

Again, Kathleen labored through her exhaustion. Another baby left her body and breathed air for the first time. It was a girl.

Kathleen immediately demanded to see the babies. They were somewhat small, but each was perfect. When their squalling filled the air, Kathleen finally smiled—in relief more than happiness.

Kathleen delighted in the infants. But when she looked at them, she deliberately fixed her mind only on the features that reminded her of herself. If she allowed herself to do otherwise, she worried she might be overcome by memories of events she would rather forget.

Both the babies' heads were covered in thick dark hair about an inch long. The boy child had very dark eyes and hair the color of a sea otter, rich and brown. The little girl's eyes were a warmer brown, and her hair was lighter than her brother's. Although the color was not alike, the little girl's eyes were shaped exactly like her mother's.

When Nenetl was finally allowed to see the babies, she was cautioned to be calm. She touched the tiny babies tenderly. A huge grin broke her face open in wonder and love. She kissed Kathleen on each cheek.

The midwives gave Kathleen herbs to stop bleeding and to help her rest. They kept visitors away until they were satisfied Kathleen was strong enough.

At length, Brand was permitted to enter the room where Kathleen was recovering with the babies. When he saw Kathleen's face, he thought she had never looked more beautiful.

He tenderly took her hand. "Are you well?"

"Yes, Father Brand. I am well. And my children."

He looked over at the midwives, who held the swaddled infants in their arms.

"What will you name them?"

Kathleen had decided to follow the Norse way and name them for deceased relatives. But it was too painful to name them after her own father and mother.

"The boy will be called Ulf and the girl Signy, after my father's parents."

"You have made good choices, Kathleen. Arn would be pleased."

The Toltecs were also pleased when they heard the names and what they meant. Ulf meant *cuetlachtli*, or "wolf." It was deemed an auspicious name. Signy meant "new victory." It was also thought to be an acceptable name for the tiny girl, though rather strange and unusual.

Within days, the infants were baptized in Cholollan, just as Kathleen had said they would be. Each day, they grew in strength and health and became the source of immeasurable joy to all.

CHAPTER FORTY-SIX

TWO MOONS PASSED. ALL THE exiles settled in to what they believed would be their new home. They had kept together and supported each other as one people. They had survived.

Kathleen was busy with her tiny twins. She had regained much of her strength. Brand continued his teaching with Tonauac attentively at his side, observing all. Patli found friends with the physicians who looked after the Cholollan ball players.

One morning, Brand received an unexpected summons. A messenger said Brand was to meet with King Amapane. He immediately set off. The sky was clear, and the city gleamed in the bright sunshine. The air was scented with the smell of tlaxcalli disks baking in myriad kitchens and beans cooking in clay pots.

As he walked toward the palatial compound, Brand wondered what the king could want of him. He recalled all the people he had met since landing on the shores of this land. Some had been cruel and betrayed him. But others, like King Amapane, had been a surprising support. As he walked, Brand prayed to God in gratitude for those who had helped him—and he left the others to the mercy of heaven.

The king was sitting on a veranda outside his palace home. The shady spot was filled with flowering plants and trees of all kinds: a collage of green, yellow, pink, and red.

King Amapane greeted Brand warmly. He gestured for Brand to sit in a small wooden chair next to him. A kitchen servant offered Brand a frothy cup of the rich cacao drink. As Brand sipped the bitter brew, the king began to speak. His tone was serious.

"There is something I must tell you, Father Brand."

Brand felt his body shift to attention.

"The great canoe, the one that brought you to our land . . ."

The king looked directly at Brand, as he knew what he was about to say would cause a reaction.

"It is not gone."

There was a pause.

"What do you mean, *not gone?*" asked Brand.

"When you washed to our shores, the soldiers of Tollan found you and ransacked your vessel. After they led you away, my people found it. I had them float and drag it to another hidden cove. We pulled it out of the water, and it has been waiting for you all this time."

Brand still could not take it all in.

"Not gone? Waiting? But why have you not told me before?"

"I needed time to determine if revealing such information to you would be helpful to my people. Everything I do and everything I decide must be to their betterment."

Amapane gestured to a slave, who placed a large basket before him.

"I am confident in telling you this now because we know you are a messenger of the god Quetzalcoatl. We found his image inside the vessel."

A quizzical look flashed across Brand's face. He could not imagine what the king was talking about.

The king reached inside the basket. Brand watched in astonishment as Amapane pulled a wooden object from it and held it aloft. Brand looked at the carving and slowly moved his trembling hand to touch it.

It was Arn's dragon, the removable prow Kathleen's father had insisted upon so long ago when the *Sea Goat* was crafted in Dublin. With its dragon face and added ruff, it looked not unlike the face of the plumed serpent carved in stone in so many places in Tollan, Teotihuacan, and Cholollan. Brand remembered now that the prow had been hidden in a bit of kindling wood on the ship. In their haste, the soldiers from Tollan had not seen it during their ransacking.

"King Amapane, I must see the ship!" said Brand, hardly able to contain his excitement.

"Yes," said the king, smiling. "And so you shall."

The next day, with a small group of Cholollans leading, Brand and Tonauac began their walk to the place near the shore where the ship had been hidden. The trek took several days, even at a steady pace. Brand smelled the scent of sea salt in the air before they could see through the dense jungle. Finally, they emerged from the tangle of the trees and plants to the expanse of sandy shore.

When Brand saw the vessel, his heart beat faster. The *Sea Goat*! It was true—the *Sea Goat* still existed!

Tonauac and many of the Cholollans had never seen such a vessel before. They were filled with curiosity.

For that matter, Tonauac had never seen the ocean before. Seeing the vast blue horizon was quite enough to completely thrill and overwhelm him. And seeing the great canoe that had brought Brand and Kathleen from so far away excited his imagination. He abruptly sat down on the sand to take it all in.

The ship looked a bit worn and tired and somewhat broken in places, but she still appeared intact. Brand noted there was no rigging. The Cholollans explained they had removed the sail and ropes from the vessel. They had carefully wrapped and kept them dry in a stone storage room, most in large pottery vessels to keep rodents and insects from gnawing at the skin and fibers.

Slowly, carefully, Brand began to inspect the vessel. He walked around her many times, walked every inch of the interior and moved the styrbord back and forth. He poked the wool and tar stuffed between the oak strakes of her hull.

When he was done, he came to an astonishing conclusion. He wanted to get back to Cholollan as quickly as possible. He needed to speak again with King Amapane.

Upon his return, Brand approached King Amapane with some uncertainly, for he was unsure how the king would respond to what he had to say. As always, King Amapane was dignified, even when relaxed.

"King Amapane," Brand began, "I believe the *Sea Goat* can be restored. And that she can sail again."

Brand expected the king to object, so he had carefully rehearsed all the reasons why the king should agree with him and provide support for the repairs. He need not have worried.

"I was wondering how long it would take before you would come to me," said the king with a bemused look. "I know what you want, and the answer is yes."

When Brand shared the news with Kathleen, she insisted on seeing the ship and being part of the renovation. Within days, Brand and Tonauac, Kathleen and the babies, Nenetl, and Izel and Tlazohtlaloni all began the walk from Cholollan to the sea.

With the king's consent and generous support, the repairs began. Workers were dispatched and assigned to help. A temporary construction village was set up for the former Toltecs and the Cholollan workers.

Brand oversaw the renovation, but Kathleen made valuable contributions as well. She remembered how the master shipbuilders had pieced the vessel together in Dublin. Brand often asked her advice on some detail of the restoration

The Cholollans brought oak wood to the site, using their bodies to drag it from the highlands. They worked it as well as they could with their obsidian axes. Not as fine as the wood in Dublin, but acceptable. They had no iron, but fortunately, most of the *Sea Goat's* ironwork was intact.

Some repairs were needed to fill gaps and small broken places. Brand summoned the best of the Toltecan craftsmen from their new home in Cholollan. They studied the ship very carefully and added ingenious wood repairs.

Workers were sent to the nearest bitumen seeps, two days' walk away. They came back with large heavy baskets of the black goo on their backs. Then other workers processed the material with minerals and animal fats, making it sticky enough to adhere to the ship but not melt in the hot sun.

There was no wool for stuffing in between the oak strakes. Workers removed the old material, now stiffened and cracking, and stuffed the crevices with cotton mixed with the bitumen.

Henequen ropes replaced the leather ropes. The plant material was an improvement, as it resisted salt spray and weather better than the walrus ropes of the north. Workers retrieved the wool sail and restored its pliability with plant oils.

Each day produced new hope for a seaworthy vessel. In truth, it was not only a ship being restored; it was Brand as well.

CHAPTER FORTY-SEVEN

WHILE THE REPAIRS WERE BEING made, Brand simultaneously started lessons on sailing. A small group of Toltecs and Cholollans were interested in learning, and they showed aptitude. Of this group, none was more eager than Tonauac. He asked endless questions about currents and the sun and stars. He made diagrams for himself. He often sat near the styrboard, moving it in response to imaginary wind and waves.

Finally, the day came when Brand said, "I think the *Sea Goat* is ready."

First, they had to get the ship into the water. They placed logs in a pathway, so that the *Sea Goat* could roll over them to the sea. Ropes were carefully attached to the hull. Then the workers began to pull and ease her forward.

Slowly, slowly, the ship creaked toward the water; too quickly, and the stress might destroy all the repairs they had just made. Brand was grateful for the vessel's Norse design. A ship with a deep keel would be nearly impossible to get in or out of the water. But the lack of a deep keel meant the *Sea Goat* had a relatively simple transition from land to sea.

Once she entered the waves, the workers shifted positions but continued to push and pull until the magical moment when the water lifted her. She was free from the land at last!

A spontaneous cheer went up from everyone. Brand grabbed Kathleen in an exuberant hug, and she hugged him in return.

Everyone watched how the ship fared during the next few days. It was a great relief when it appeared that the bitumen and cotton were keeping the ship relatively water-free.

Next, rigging ropes and the sail were added. The *Sea Goat* was starting to look like her old self again.

Brand waited until conditions were just right, with light wind. The newly trained mariners took their placed on the ship. With a collective groan, the sail was hauled up. When the wind caught it, everyone felt as if a miracle had taken place.

After this, they spent all day, every day, navigating around the cove and the surrounding area. Brand himself was impressed with how quickly the men learned to maneuver the sail. And Tonauac was fascinated with the styrbord.

Once the crew had mastered the small area of the sea outside the cove, Brand decided they were ready for a real sail.

While Izel watched over the twins, Kathleen and Nenetl joined the crew on board. Brand stood next to Tonauac, coaching him at the styrbord.

With the sail in full expanse, the ship moved through the water faster and faster. Kathleen's long hair flowed in the wind, and Nenetl's little braids soared behind her back. They laughed and giggled as the ship glided through the waves.

They sailed but a little way down the coast, to the exact spot where the *Sea Goat* had originally gone aground. They made anchor, then Brand, Kathleen, and Nenetl went ashore. The three of them had something important to do.

They looked and looked and finally stopped at a spot where they thought Arn's bones lay, so hastily buried in an unmarked grave in time gone before. Nenetl brought lilies to remember her mother, though no one really knew where the raging waters had carried her. All of them knelt and prayed for the souls of their loved ones and for the grace through which their own lives had been spared.

CHAPTER FORTY-EIGHT

B RAND LEANED OVER AND STARED into the still water of a small tide pool. The angle of sunlight was just right, allowing him to study his reflection. He had long since lost his tonsure. His hair, lightened and dried by sun and salt, swirled around his head in disarray. He stroked his temples and noted that gray appeared there, as it did in his beard.

Yes, he thought to himself, *I am closer to the end than to the beginning of my life on earth.* Had he been a vain man, he would have sighed.

Since the initial restoration of the *Sea Goat*, he and many others—including Kathleen and their close circle—had remained near the shore. With a freshwater source close by and trade with nearby villages, their temporary-construction housing had evolved into something more permanent, with many small shelters of thatched palm.

Over the course of several months, the mariners sailed farther up and down the coast in short test voyages of two or three days, astonishing all who saw the great canoe in full sail. Each time they put down anchor and met with the people of the shore land, they learned more of the currents and weather patterns in that area. Once or twice, they encountered unexpected foul weather. Brand was pleased how they maintained control of the vessel despite the wind and waves.

A small idea, a possibility, began churning in Brand's mind. The more it worked in his brain, the more feasible it became. It would be a new voyage, long and dangerous. A voyage north.

A voyage home.

He hardly dared imagine it. But once he did, an even more audacious idea took on life: to not only voyage to the north but then to return again to this hot and humid land—and to his sheep, the people who had knit themselves into his soul.

Brand prayed and meditated but dared not share his idea—yet. In his private prayers, he asked God to open doors, if it was his will.

Once again, Brand decided to return to Cholollan with a proposal for King Amapane. He walked to the city with determination, but he was far from certain about what the king's reaction would be. The king might not allow such a plan. The voyage would be perilous, and it was possible the ship would be lost or destroyed. The king was shrewd and might be loath to lose his investment. To persuade him, Brand thought of the merits of such a venture: they could establish new trade routes and learn of other tribes as allies or rivals.

"And moreover," he explained to the king, "there are many people there, to the north, who know about the symbols drawn on matted plant fiber or the thin skins of animals and bound together. They know how to look at the symbols and understand what they mean, and they can show the symbols to others so they might have the knowledge as well."

He had gone through all his best arguments. Now he waited for the king's response. He silently prayed.

Again, Brand need not have worried, for the king had already thought the issue through.

"If there is a larger world beyond the horizon, it is better that we meet it now, rather than wait in isolation until it comes to us. If you, Father Brand, came here on the wind and waves, others will undoubtedly do so as well someday."

This man, thought Brand, *is one of the wisest men I have ever known.* The king's response confirmed to Brand that this decision was part of God's plan.

As he trekked back to the sea, Brand recalled the long-ago dream of his friend, Ibn Beshir, when they both had been captured and imprisoned by pirates. Ibn Beshir had shared a dream about Brand:

"You were sailing in a ship," Ibn Beshir had said. "But it was not a ship of the Christian pilgrims. Nor was it a trading ship of my people. The other people on the ship were not of your kind nor of mine. But they saw you as their leader."

After so many years, the strange dream of the follower of Mohamet was coming true.

CHAPTER FORTY-NINE

RAND'S FEET FAIRLY FLEW AS he returned to the shore. There was one person he had to speak to, one person with whom he had to share his news without delay.

Kathleen was sitting in filtered shade outside her palm shelter, preparing some beans for soaking, as the other women had taught. Brand glanced around and saw that Nenetl and Izel were not there. The twins—"Wolfie," as Ulf was commonly called, and Signy—had been fed. They were contently sleeping back to back in a little hammock.

"Kathleen," he said, trying to hide the anticipation in his voice. "I have something to ask you."

She barely looked up from the beans she was sorting. "Yes, of course. What is it?"

"What if we were to sail, in reverse, the way we came here, and return home?"

Kathleen stopped what she was doing and stared at him, unable to respond.

Brand began to pace with excitement. "What if we were to sail the *Sea Goat* back? Back to Vinland, then back to Brattahlid. Maybe even to Trondheim and Bergen?"

As if emerging from a fog, she asked, "Do you really think it is possible?"

"Yes, I do. Tonauac is showing real skill, and others are becoming sailors as well. I do not have Helgi's instruments, but we could overcome that. We would sail north, staying close by the coast. And when we got to

Vinland, there may be others there who could help us safely sail the northern seas back to Brattahlid."

"But why do you want to do this?"

"I have thought and prayed about it. The people back home need to know of this place. And the people here need to hear the message of God's love for them and how they are to love one another. I am alone. I cannot accomplish all that needs to be done to serve these people. Other priests and teachers could come here to help."

Kathleen nodded in understanding. She—of all people—knew Brand put his priestly vow to be a servant for God above all else.

"How can I explain it?" he said, holding his hands up to the heavens. "It must be the will of God that the ship was saved and restored. It must be for some greater purpose."

He waited for her reply, which was another question.

"Do you not have doubts?"

"Yes, of course. It has been many years since we—you and I—have had any news of home. Vinland may be a prosperous new settlement by now. Or it may have been abandoned. Who knows who now sits on the throne in Trondheim? And maybe the followers of Mohamet will have fulfilled their quest and conquered all the lands of the north. All I know is that God will be with us, no matter what the circumstances."

Kathleen sat awhile, taking in everything this astonishing proposal would mean. Despite Brand's favorable outlook, she knew what terrors such a journey could entail. Even now, she sometimes recalled in nightmares the deadly attack on the *Sea Goat*'s crew and the death of her father and the others.

She had given up any chance of ever returning home. But what if she could see Bergen again and all the people and places of her childhood?

And then there was Father Brand and all they had been through together. How could she live a day without him?

She had never forgotten what he had said to her when they stood close together by the river in Tollan at dusk. She remembered how he briefly held her in his arms and said, "I love you." But she also remembered how he had then quickly turned away.

She had never really stopped loving him, but the overlay of time and the struggles they had encountered since that night had changed the feelings between them. Their love had transformed into a different kind of bond, tempered and muted but still strong.

Brand decided to go ahead with his question.

"If I sail back to Vinland, will you go with me?"

It seemed to him that she took forever to reply. As Kathleen looked over at the sleeping twins, she realized there were many things she must consider.

"Father Brand, I cannot think only of myself, I must think of my children," she said, gesturing to them. "They are too young to sail anywhere."

"Yes, I know. But very young Norse children often spend many hours in a fishing boat with their fathers. We would wait until you believe the children are old enough. A year or two, perhaps." Then he added, "You do not have to decide now. It is just that—"

"I must think about this, Father Brand," she interrupted, and he pressed the matter no more.

Over the next few days, Kathleen could not stop thinking of the possibility of sailing back home. Was it too dangerous? How would people there react to her children? How could she leave the people she had come to know and with whom she had shared such joys and sorrows?

Yet how wonderful it would be to sing and converse in the language of her birth. And to worship with many others in churches built to honor the Triune God.

There was also danger if she stayed. Had not Tizoc, her own husband, been suddenly and mysteriously killed? No one had been able to adequately explain to her why. And even though they now lived under some protection from King Amapane, who knew how long that would last, or what might happen if a new king rose to power? She was torn.

Izel noticed her distraction.

"You are here, yet not here, Kathleen," said the intelligent and keen observer.

"It is nothing, Izel," she answered, not yet ready to share her thoughts.

At last, Kathleen asked to speak with Father Brand—privately. He knew she had made her decision. He prepared himself to accept it, whatever it may be.

She spoke to him in Norse.

"Yes, Father Brand. As soon as my children are old enough, I will go with you."

And his heart soared.

CHAPTER FIFTY

A S SOON AS KATHLEEN MADE her decision, she and Brand began to think about how to share the news. Kathleen was particularly concerned that Nenetl not hear of it from others.

Within the hour, Kathleen sat with Nenetl, patiently plaiting her hair.

"Nenetl," she said quietly, "I have something to tell you. In a year or two, Father Brand will sail the *Sea Goat* to a faraway place—the place where he and I come from." She paused. "And he will sail from that place back here."

The child seemed surprised at this idea but not astonished. In her young life, so many unimaginable things had already happened.

"The twins and I will go with Father Brand."

It took a moment for the girl to receive this revelation. Then a very dark shadow passed across her face.

"And me?" asked the child, not quite daring to look directly at Kathleen.

"Father Brand and I have discussed whether you should come with us on the voyage . . ."

Nenetl held her breath.

"We have decided you should join us on the journey."

The girl turned around, her face wide with a smile.

Kathleen put her arms around the child in a warm embrace. "You are old enough now—nearly eight years, we think. And you have shown many times that you are brave. You can help with the twins, and we will have each other."

Nenetl pressed her heart to Kathleen's heart. Kathleen placed her hand over the child's head. As she did, she heard the child whisper, "We are family. We are family," over and over.

Kathleen next shared the news with Izel. There was no question, however, about Izel's decision. She would stay. She would never leave Tlazohtlaloni, and it was not safe for him on the ship. As happy as she was for Brand and Kathleen, Izel already dreaded that day when the ship would sail away. But at least she had time to prepare while the twins grew and matured.

The news of the planned voyage spread like a sudden breeze throughout the settlement. It was met with open mouths and eyes made large with surprise, but also with great interest. A hum of activity energized everyone.

Many volunteered to be part of the crew. Brand carefully considered each man and his skills and temperament. The decisions were challenging. In the end, he was satisfied his chosen crew would hold together in adversity. He and Tonauac would lead the crew as navigators.

Brand also began to think of what lay in the future, things he so longed for: holding the Gospels in his hands, the sound of men's voices in chant, celebrating Eucharist with bread and wine, confessing and receiving absolution, learning from other monks and priests.

One night, he had a dream of Ælfheah, his bishop in Winchester. The bishop appeared to have been captured and then imprisoned—by Viking raiders. The prisoner cried out, "No, not one penny for my ransom!" Then in drunken frustration, his captors beat him to a gory death with sticks and ox bones.

Brand was unsure if this event had already happened or was yet to come. But he knew this was a prophetic dream. It had or would happen. He prayed to God he might see his teacher and mentor one more time.

Not long after the crew was decided, Tonauac asked Brand to walk with him on the shore. By now, Brand knew well enough that this meant Tonauac wanted to discuss something serious.

Tonauac got straight to the point. "Father Brand, I want to have the prima signatio ceremony."

"How do you know about that?" Brand replied in surprise.

"Kathleen told me about it. I was talking with her, and she observed that everyone in the crew is a baptized person. Except me."

Brand had not realized it, but it was true.

"I told her I wanted to be connected to everyone else on the ship. But I am not ready to be baptized."

"Yes, Tonauac, I know. It is my responsibility to tell you of the faith. I cannot force belief on you."

"Kathleen said that in her land—your land—there is a way to have a ceremony that is not baptism. She told me it is what her father had done."

"That is true, Tonauac."

Brand recalled Arn—his square jaw and impetuous nature. As brave and obstinate a man as Brand had ever known. Brand never knew if, with his dying breath, Arn had accepted Jesu or not.

"Tell me, Father Brand, what happens in this ceremony?"

"It is a first benediction. There is no water. It is not a christening, and you do not receive a Christian name. Rather, with this ceremony, you make a commitment to receive instruction in the faith. I say prayers and make the sign of the cross over you."

Tonauac chuckled. "Since the day I first met you, I have been receiving instruction! I have been learning the symbols and listening when you teach the others."

"Yes," Brand agreed, "you have always been learning. But this ceremony will show the others you are taking a step toward baptism."

Tonauac did not reflect long.

"I want to have this ceremony."

"Are you sure?"

"Yes."

It was announced that there would be a special ceremony for Tonauac. The next morning, the entire crew of the ship and many others who had been baptized surrounded Brand and Tonauac on the beach.

"Tonauac," said Brand, "you must declare your intention to God and to all those assembled here." Brand gestured to the people encircling them. Then he turned again to Tonauac. "Kneel down, Tonauac."

The Toltec knelt.

"Do you want to receive the prima signatio?"

"Yes."

"And do you promise to learn all you can to be a follower of the Triune God, who loves people and wants them to believe in his promises?"

"I do."

"Tonauac, may you find peace—the peace that passes all understanding—in the promises."

Brand smiled as he invoked the Father, Son, and Holy Spirit and made the sign of the cross over Tonauac—the man who had been at his side through so many trials, who had counseled him, and who had protected him as much or more than any brother in the faith.

CHAPTER FIFTY-ONE

KATHLEEN BEGAN TO DAYDREAM ABOUT the things she would show her children and the new things they would experience: falling asleep in warm furs, the thrilling majesty of the northern lights, playing on slippery ice, and building snow houses. And the foods they would taste: crisp apples, butter and goat cheese on chewy bread, lamb stew flavored with dried birch leaves, the tart and sweet taste of cloudberries swimming in cream and honey.

Then one morning she awoke early, unable to sleep. It seemed as if something were about to happen, but she did not know what. She said her morning prayers as Brand had taught her, yet she was still unable to dispel the feeling.

The day was already hot and humid despite the breeze from the sea. The twins were fussy. In her sweet voice, Kathleen sang them songs she had learned from her mother.

"Yaaah . . . yaaaah . . . yaaaah . . ." she intoned as she patted the squirming infants, just as her mother had comforted her.

As she did every morning, Izel stopped by to check on Kathleen and the babies and to help with their care. She suggested pouring water over their heads and bodies to cool them a little. Izel held Signy while Kathleen supported Wolfie in a turtle-shell basin filled with water.

Signy was teething. Drool dripped from her mouth onto her little chest.

"I know what might help you," Kathleen said to her daughter.

She searched in a red and blue cotton bag hung on a wall and pulled out an object. She gave it to the infant, who grabbed it with her

426

little fist, then placed it in her mouth. Signy began to chew intently on the perfectly smooth surface of the wheeled wooden deer carved so lovingly by Helgi and Kathleen when the *Sea Goat* had sailed the northern seas.

Kathleen loved watching how the twins changed and grew, almost overnight. They could hold their heads up now. Their thick hair, dark and soft as eiderdown, had grown quickly.

Wolfie began to fuss. She picked him up from the water basin and began to dry him off. Kathleen especially liked to caress her babies from the top of their heads to the nape of their necks, which seemed to soothe them.

She was stroking Wolfie's head and neck when suddenly her hand stopped. She ceased her wordless lullaby and stared hard for several moments—first at Wolfie, then at Signy. On each child, the hair spilled down from their napes to their tiny shoulders in a perfect little curve.

They had wavy hair. *Wavy hair.* There was only one other in all the land who had wavy hair.

These children are Tizoc's. I know it. I KNOW it. Tizoc still lives in them.

"What is it?" asked Izel, seeing the sudden change in Kathleen's demeanor.

"I must talk with Father Brand," she answered.

With no more explanation, she quickly grabbed both babies and ran, one child in each arm.

"Look. Look! Look at my children!" she cried out when she found Brand.

"What is it? What should I see?" asked Brand, somewhat confused with her excitement.

"Look at their hair! Their hair!" she repeated breathlessly.

Brand looked again at the infants but did not see what she saw.

"Only Tizoc had such hair. They are Tizoc's children!" she exclaimed.

Brand reached out a hand and stroked Signy's hair. Then he saw what Kathleen saw. She was right. He swallowed hard and stepped back, overcome with the emotion of the moment.

Something, she did not know what, moved from Kathleen's heart to her mind. She paused, not knowing how to say the next words.

"I cannot leave this place."

She waited for his response.

"What?" he at last said. "What are you saying, Kathleen?"

She struggled to answer him. After Brand had been shown to be innocent of violating her, she knew the father of the babies was Toltecan. But now that she knew the father was indeed Tizoc, everything seemed to have changed.

"Part of my children's blood is in this place. I am sorry Father Brand. I cannot leave."

Brand's mind raced with thoughts of all kinds. He could hardly imagine leaving Kathleen. He loved her, had loved her even before he had met her. Had loved her in his dreams. He loved her more than anything or anyone, except God.

"Are you sure you want to do this?" he asked.

She shifted the babies in her arms. Even as she spoke, tears spilled from her eyes.

"Yes, I am sure."

And with that, both of them knew there was nothing more to be said.

CHAPTER FIFTY-TWO

WITH NO NEED TO WAIT until the twins were older, serious preparations for the voyage began. There were decisions to be made as to all manner of provisions: water containers; food containers; the type and amount of dried grains and meat; and stores of salt, chilies, and other seasonings. There were considerations as to items for repairs, extra clothing, tent material, cloth to protect the mariners from the sun and rain, items for trade, fishing and hunting gear, some weaponry, and medicinal plants.

Finally, the date of the departure had nearly arrived.

King Amapane earnestly desired to see the travelers off, but he could not leave Cholollan. He was sick with a strange fever that lingered. In his stead, he sent workers ahead to bring more supplies and to prepare a great feast for the mariners. A retinue of the court and several priests of Quetzalcoatl also traveled to the coast.

Among the Cholollans was a medicine man, a healer. It was Patli. He knew the area where the ship was anchored. It was not far from where he and Tizoc had lived as small children. This trip would give him a chance to see his mother again.

More importantly, it was a chance to see Tizoc's son and daughter. He had heard the revelation through messages sent to the court. He knew it would be difficult to be near the place where he and Tizoc had first met Brand and Kathleen, but he was hopeful the painful memories would be replaced by joyful ones.

The day before the *Sea Goat*'s departure, there was much feasting, dancing, and drumming. A platform had been erected for the king's emissaries. Their extravagant feather costumes moved in the wind with glorious splendor, as brilliantly colored as the most unforgettable of birds.

Drummers beat out staccato rhythms at two speeds—fast and faster—to equal the excitement and exuberance of the people gathered. The dancers matched the drummers until, exhausted, they fell to the sand.

Then the servants moved through the gathering, offering plates of fruits and seafood of all kinds and gourds of sweet water to revive them all. After a period of rest, it all began again.

Finally, the day turned to dusk, and torches were lit along the shore. A full moon cast shimmering light on the water. The stars emerged into view and twinkled in the blackness of the sky.

The drummers had ceased. Now the air was filled only with the sound of a lone flute playing a beautiful yet melancholy tune.

Brand sought out Kathleen.

"Come walk with me," he said.

The two walked along the sand to a place apart from the others. Torches flickered in the distance. The moonlight was strong now, illuminating their faces.

"Kathleen, I am sorry to leave you. You cannot know how hard it is to leave you."

"I think I know, Father Brand," she said, lightly touching his cheek with her hand. "But someone must remain here to tell the people of God's grace and remind them you will return. And I will not be alone—I will have my children and Nenetl and Izel. And Tizoc's memory."

They stood facing each other, knowing it could be the last night they would ever see each other. He placed his hand on her cheek as well.

"This is true, Kathleen. You are not alone. We are not alone. No one ever is alone who feels the love of God."

She looked at him, her eyes soft and moist with emotion.

He trembled. Suddenly, he took her into his arms with a kind of love stronger than the most passionate embrace.

"Think of the wind," he said. "You cannot see the wind, yet you can feel it. That is how the love of the Holy Spirit is. It is always with you, even if you cannot see it."

He looked at her earnestly, intently.

"And that is how my love for you is, now and for always. Like the wind, I am with you. My love is with you. When you think of the wind, remember me."

CHAPTER FIFTY-THREE

T HE NEXT MORNING DAWNED CLEAR and bright. Venus, the morning star, was still visible in the sky. On the shore, Brand's band of loyal disciples had assembled for a blessing and final farewell. The royal delegates sat on the platform for the best view. Curious onlookers stood shoulder to shoulder, straining to see and hear all that was about to happen.

The priests of Quetzalcoatl made burnt offerings and chanted for good luck for the mariners. Copal scented the air as it billowed from censers placed in the sand. They murmured to one another how much they admired Arn's dragon-head prow—for them, the image of Quetzalcoatl.

Tonauac and the rest of the crew had already boarded the knarr and were waiting there for Brand to say his farewell to the people. The ship was anchored close to shore. The surf was very gentle so early in the day, so the crew could hear Brand's words.

The crew's hearts beat with excitement and trepidation, not knowing what the voyage would bring. The only certainty was belief in themselves and in their leaders—Brand and Tonauac. They were about to begin their journey in reality, though it had already begun, as all journeys do, in the imagination.

At the appointed hour, the royal delegates motioned for Brand to ascend the platform. Brand had asked for an opportunity to speak to the crowd, and it had been granted. He addressed the group with a loud and clear voice. The people listened closely, intent on hearing every word.

"I do not know why my journey brought me here, to this shore, along with Kathleen. I do not know why we were attacked and why many, including her father, were killed on our journey to you. I do not know why we survived. I do not know why Tizoc had to die. I do not know why many of our friends had to die. I do not know where this next journey will lead. All I know is, I must trust. I must trust that whatever happens, out of this evil will come good that somehow, someday, will be revealed."

Brand turned in nearly a full circle, looking intently at all the faces in the crowd surrounding him. He took them all in, as a thirsty man drains the last few precious drops of water from a cup. He raised his hand in blessing.

"I will miss you all. May God bless you now and always."

All the followers had stood, silent, on the shore. Now some of them began to weep.

Brand moved down off the platform, through the crowd, and toward the shore and waiting canoes. As he passed through the people, he murmured a blessing to them all. As he walked close to Patli, the two men nodded in acknowledgement. It was all that passed between them, but it was enough.

At length, Brand reached the edge of the water and prepared to say good-bye to those closest to him.

"Good-bye, Nenetl," Brand said as he bent down and gave the girl a warm embrace and a kiss on top of her head.

"Good-bye, Izel." He embraced the tall woman, who had been such a tower of strength. "You have protected us all. May God protect you."

"And may God protect you as well, Father Brand," she said, using the back of her hand to wipe an uncharacteristic tear away from her face.

"Good-bye, Tlazohtlaloni." The boy smiled as Brand placed his hand on his shoulder.

"Good-bye, Father Brand," the boy said, reaching up and patting Brand's hand with his own.

Brand turned last to Kathleen. He took her face into his hands and kissed her cheek.

Before he could speak, she looked up at Venus, still in the sky, then began her farewell.

"Father Brand, you are my morning star. You are the wind that speaks to me in the sunlight, in the moonlight. Father Brand, may God be with you."

She shifted the babies in her arms and glanced down on them.

"We will wait for you," she said, fighting tears. "We will never forget you."

Though he stood perfectly still, Brand's heart was pounding within him. He knew that if he did not leave now, he would not be able to control himself and that he would never leave her.

Brand kissed Wolfie and Signy, then raised his hand in final blessing to all those assembled.

"*Ma xipatinemi*. May you be well. Farewell."

Then he stepped into the waiting canoe and joined Tonauac and the others already aboard the knarr. When he was aboard, the crew fell wordlessly to their knees for a final blessing for the ship and all who were to sail on her.

Brand repeated the blessing Bishop Grimkell had said that long-ago day when he sailed away from Trondheim.

"Jesu, master most pure, we beseech you, shield our journey. And may the Lord of heaven bless us and stretch forth his hand in protection upon us."

Tonauac was ready at the styrbord. Brand stood resolutely at the prow of the bobbing ship. As the sail was raised, the wind suddenly caught it. The ship began to move with speed.

"I will return to you!" Brand shouted to the people on the shore, his voice still strong in the wind.

CHAPTER FIFTY-FOUR

THERE WAS MORE THAN ONE memory of what happened that morning on the shore. Some of the followers left on the sand said that they watched and watched the small craft until it sailed beyond the horizon. Others said they saw the wooden ship go up in flame, then saw a bird flying toward the morning star.

Whether Brand had sailed to a royal place of writing, or whether he had floated out to sea on a raft of serpents, or whether his body had been burned and his soul had flown up to Venus, the teachers and wise men were not in agreement.

Whatever happened, Father Brand was gone. The young child from Uppsala and Hedeby was gone. The priest who studied in England and negotiated between warring kings was gone. The kidnapped and ransomed ship slave was gone. The impetuous man who defended Kathleen and Arn from the fearsome berserker was gone. The man who would not break a vow was gone. The man who loved a woman he never could have was gone.

Generations passed. The various memories of Brand and the legends of Quetzalcoatl merged into one. Father Brand *became* Quetzalcoatl— their priest, their leader, their teacher, their god. He became the morning star, the Dawn Light Lord.

Quetzalcoatl was gone, but in faith, the people remembered his promise.

"He will return," they said. "Quetzalcoatl will return." On this point, there was unanimity.

They believed that when he was ready, when the year One Reed had cycled once again in their calendar, he would return. Once more he would come from the east, surrounded by light-skinned followers. Once again, he would teach the people and bring peace.

Out of the clouds, out of the mists, he will return to us, they always believed.

EPILOGUE

Some five hundred years passed. The city of Tollan had long since declined and been burned and abandoned. The Toltecan people had scattered. The Aztec civilization and its emperor, Moctezuma, now reigned supreme. The Tlaxcalans still resisted anyone who tried to conquer them. Human sacrifice continued on a grander scale than ever before. But the people never forgot Quetzalcoatl, god of the morning star and god of the wind, and his promise to return to them.

The calendar once again cycled to the year One Reed, which was the year 1519 in the European calendar. Strange men, light skinned and bearded, arrived in a "great canoe" and approached the Aztec capital from the east. Some of the people said, "It is our god, Quetzalcoatl, who has returned to us." They treated the strangers and their leader with the respect and honor a god required.

But they were wrong. The strangers were not gods but human conquerors from Spain. They brought with them much that was life-giving but also much that was destructive.

As they explored the Aztec lands, the Spaniards encountered a large capital city, a complex civilization, and many items of gold. Some things, such as sheaves of paper with symbols painted on it, they eventually destroyed.

Among the astonishing art and artifacts the Spaniards came upon, there was one most curious. In that land without wagons or carts, they found a small wooden deer with carved wheels where the hooves would have been.

ACKNOWLEDGMENTS

Writing is a solitary pursuit, more so when you are working on a historical novel set in multiple locations with multiple cultures. I have worked hard to make this a novel of integrity and interest. Its faults are mine. But I must acknowledge and give credit to many people who helped, encouraged, guided, or inspired me along the way.

I am grateful for the instructors and students at the Madeline Island School of the Arts and the Loft Literary Center in Minneapolis for their ideas and encouragement.

I salute my beta readers, Janey K. Christensen, Jim McGowan, and Susan Townsend. Their feedback and suggestions were invaluable and came at a time when I needed to know I had a story worth telling.

I thank Janet Hanson and Kaye Thibault for their loyal friendship and support, and I acknowledge Ann Jarvis for her many years of advice and counsel.

I have been inspired by the people of Tlaxcala, Mexico, where I lived many decades ago, and by the people of Central America, especially El Salvador. And early in my research about the Norse, I realized that many of my friends and neighbors growing up in central Minnesota—even my classmates—had names a Viking would be sure to recognize.

I have been helped by so many at Beaver's Pond Press, most especially my editor, Angela Wiechmann. The editing process was a saga in itself, and Angie's brilliant editing helped make my manuscript so much better.

Soli Deo gloria.